THE GLOBALIZATION OF GOD

Also by Dara Molloy (Dara Ó Maoildhia)

LEGENDS IN THE LANDSCAPE
Pocket guide to Árainn, Inis Mór, Aran Islands

Published by Aisling Publications

THE GLOBALIZATION OF GOD

CELTIC CHRISTIANITY'S NEMESIS

Dara Molloy

With 12 Poems by Tess Harper

The Globalization of God
Celtic Christianity's Nemesis

iUniverse books may be ordered through booksellers or by contacting:

iUniverse
1663 Liberty Drive
Bloomington, IN 47403
www.iuniverse.com
1-800-Authors (1-800-288-4677)

ISBN: 978-1-4917-6042-0 (sc)
ISBN: 978-1-4917-6043-7 (e)

Print information available on the last page.

iUniverse rev. date: 11/06/2015

I dedicate this book to the memory of
Ivan Illich and John Seymour*

* See Appendix I

CONTENTS

INTRODUCTION

It could be said that the seed of globalisation was sown when Moses declared to the Hebrew people that there was one commandment to be obeyed above all others. That commandment, the first of ten, was: 'I am Yahweh your God ...You shall have no gods except me'[1].

This was the beginning of monotheism as we know it today. Monotheism created the necessary container, or myth, that has facilitated the development of globalisation. The god of Moses, who ended up living in the heavens, has a global vision of the earth. From this perspective, the earth is seen as one unit. In economic terms, the earth is one market.

Monotheism is like a cuckoo's egg in the nest of another bird. If there is only one god, then belief in all other gods must be rejected. The existence of other gods cannot be tolerated. They must be thrown out of the nest. If there is only one god, then the correct way of seeing things is this god's way. All other ways of seeing things are anathema.

The relationship of this god to the earth is that of creator-created. According to the Genesis story[2], the earth was created and everything on it in six days. On the seventh day 'God'[3] rested. The implicit presumption in this story is that, after the creation, this god's work was done. He retired to the heavens and left the earth to fend for itself. While distant, he would be available if called upon.

Monotheism sets this god in the heavens as the ideal towards which we should all strive. We are invited to take a journey to the heavens, to be with 'God'. The journey it calls us to make is one that disconnects us from the earth.

Society has established this journey for us. The paths are already there for us to traverse. Many people have travelled this journey before

---

1   *Genesis 20:2*. All Biblical quotations in this book are from *The Jerusalem Bible*, standard edition, Darton, Longman and Todd, 1966.

2   *Genesis1:1-2:4*

3   In this book, the god of monotheism is referred to as 'God', in parentheses and with a capital 'G'. All other references to a god use the lower case 'g'.

us, including probably our parents. If we follow the path that society has laid out for us, consciously or unconsciously, we will journey towards disconnectedness.

We start this journey by removing ourselves from the local and the particular. We leave the land that we are familiar with, that we identify with. We deliberately leave behind the sense of belonging, of local community, of communal identity. We become individuals, disconnected from our roots, floating, as it were, above the surface of the earth.

As we continue this journey, we begin to see ourselves as separate from nature. We live in cities where we are removed from nature. We are on the earth but not of it. Nature then becomes an object, something other than us, a resource that we can use. We lose all sense of the sacred in nature. The old ways of seeing mountains as holy, lakes as the lairs of demons, trees as carrying special meaning, animals as spirit carriers, birds as mediators of the divine, wells as entrances into the womb of mother earth, are all gone. According to this monotheistic myth, the gods, the spirits, the divine energies, have removed themselves from the earth and now live in the heavens as one entity, leaving behind a spiritless land of products, resources and waste.

On completion of this journey towards 'God', we believe we will achieve the ultimate perspective – a detached view of the world from heaven or outer space. There we will become like this god[4]. We will lose our material dependence on this earth. We will lose any remaining connection with this earth. We will become one with 'God'.

Modern Economic Globalisation

Globalisation, as we know it today, is a movement towards oneness. All humankind is moving towards the hegemony of one point of view, of one way of doing things, of one style of living on this planet. The diverse ways in which humans have lived on this earth in the past are being discarded and now 'one size fits all'.

In the Western world, it is easy to see that most people no longer have a connection with the land. Garaged in cities and towns, they have lost the sense of community and local belonging that living on the land

---

4   Cf. *Col.3:1-4; 1Thess.4:13-18*

engendered. Their lives are deeply immersed in products and services. Like the god they believe in, they are creators. Their connection is not to the earth but to products of their own making.

The developed parts of the world have arrived at this state of total immersion in production and consumption. But in the less developed parts of the world, we can still witness the process of dynamic transformation that has to take place for people to reach this point. In these countries, people are being uprooted from their indigenous and subsistence ways of living. They are migrating to the cities, where they look for paid work. Their lands are being transformed into large-scale industrial food-producing units. Their markets are opening up to the multinational corporations.

In this process, people leave behind their deep-rooted connection to nature, to place and to community. Their loneliness at the loss of this connectedness is artificially eased by an attachment to products – an attachment that is encouraged by the global market and especially by advertising.

Products and Services

Products are materials of all descriptions that have been taken out of their natural setting and processed in order to be made useful to people who do not live in that setting. People in the developed world do not hunt for their food, nor do they grow it in their own gardens and farms. They buy their food in shops and supermarkets. All of their food comes in the form of products. As globalisation increases, these food products are becoming homogenised and available globally.

Today we live in a world of products and services. Our food, our entertainment, our means of transport, our education, our health care – all are now products or services, human creations, that we pay for and consume. It is hard to imagine living in a world without them. This is because it has been made impossible to live in any other way. Yet this world of production and consumption is only a recent phenomenon. Less than one hundred years ago, the people of the island of Inis Mór, where I now live, had virtually no modern products or services. They lived off the land and the sea and they cared for each other as best they could.

The word 'globalisation' has entered our vocabulary at this time because the availability of products and services has reached a critical mass worldwide. As this book illustrates, the journey towards globalisation began with the creation of the monotheistic myth. The first global products and services were created by corporate Christianity. Only in more recent times have multinational corporations become the main drivers of this process.

Progress, Development and Globalisation

It has taken from the time of Moses to today for changes to take place in the world to the point where it is now possible for nations to negotiate the opening up of their markets so that products and services from anywhere in the world can be sold there. From this steady progression we have coined the word 'progress'.

Progress means the achievement of steps in the direction of globalisation. Development is a word used to describe the creation of the necessary conditions for that progress to take place. Progress and development are key words that make sense only in the context of globalisation[5].

Globalisation is a snowball that has been rolling down the snowy slopes of the centuries and has now reached so massive a size that it is unstoppable. We can point to Moses as being the one who took the first handful of snow, squeezed it into a ball and set it rolling. It has been kept rolling by powerful people within the human family who furthered the potential of global power, global influence and global dominance throughout the centuries.

At this point in time, globalisation is no longer controlled by any one group of people or by any one nation. It is a world movement which has reached a massive scale because enough people across the globe subscribe to its vision and invest in its achievements. While the snowball continues to roll and gather further weight and volume, these people will be happy. However, they are not looking at the bottom of the mountain, towards which the snowball is hurtling.

---

5   Cf. Wolfgang Sachs, 'On The Archaeology of the Development Idea'. Published in 6 parts in *The AISLING Magazine*, Issues 1 - 6. Aisling Publications, 1991-92.

Global Infrastructure

Globalisation is not just the trading of global products and services. It is also the transformation of the earth's surface so that it has the necessary infrastructure to facilitate this trading. A land without proper roads, bridges, harbours, airports, electrical and communication networks, fuel supplies, factories, shops, banks and so on, cannot accommodate globalisation. The traditional lands of indigenous, polytheistic peoples do not have this infrastructure.

Globalisation, above all, is the harnessing of human energy worldwide into a lifestyle of production and consumption. The modern human relates to the earth as that of creator to created. All material things are either human products, resources for human creativity, or waste. Humans no longer live at one with nature but relate to nature as creators, planners and managers.

In summary, globalisation transforms the physical landscape and the lives of all humans living on that landscape. Ultimately, everything living on this planet is affected.

As humankind today reaches the penultimate stages of this journey towards globalisation, it is significant that the photograph of the earth from outer space has become an icon of our time. This photograph is a declaration that humanity has arrived at a place where it can view the earth from outer space. Humanity now has the perspective of 'God'. The monotheistic vision is almost fulfilled. Humankind is in the final stages of becoming one with 'God'.

This Book

This book takes a binocular look at the influence of monotheism and particularly Roman Christianity[6] on the spread of globalisation as we know it today. The phenomenon is looked at from two perspectives, which give the book two distinct halves.

The first half of the book looks at the macro picture – the roots of globalisation in monotheism and Christianity and the development of

---

6   During the course of this book, I refer more to Roman Christianity than to Roman Catholicism. This is because, in the modern mind, Roman Catholicism is distinct from Protestantism and from Orthodox Christianity. Most of this book deals with a period before these distinctions came about.

Roman Christianity as a global corporation. The second half of the book looks at the micro picture – the effect that an ambitious global, corporate version of Christianity had on a small, independent and indigenous Irish Christianity. It is hoped that the effect of combining the two perspectives in this binocular way will allow for a three-dimensional picture.

This book attributes the origin of monotheism to Moses. Monotheism emerged out of a milieu that was almost entirely polytheistic. Judaism became the first example of a sustainable society based on the idea of monotheism. However, it was not until Christianity began to develop its own institutional structure, having inherited the Judaic version of monotheism and adapted it to its own agenda, that the full possibilities of globalisation began to be imagined.

From the 4th century CE[7] onwards, mainstream Christianity committed itself to building an institutional framework, to creating a worldwide infrastructure and to developing its sacraments and services in order to achieve worldwide dominance. It became the first global corporation. Chapters 6 to 8 chart Roman Christianity's gradual achievement of these goals.

In the second half of the book, the issue of ecclesiastical globalisation is looked at from a different angle. The perspective here is from the other side – that of the recipient of globalisation. Celtic society, in Ireland and in northern and western Britain, was one of those societies on the edge of the known world that had absorbed the Christian story and made it its own. As the Roman church developed at the centre of Europe into an authoritarian institution with a so-called 'orthodox' creed, the version of Christianity being practised by the Celtic people became intolerable to it.

This book pieces together the story of the gradual erosion of Celtic Christianity from Britain, from mainland Europe and eventually from Ireland. The first confrontation between Celtic Christianity and Roman Christianity took place when the Celtic monk Pelagius challenged the teachings of Augustine of Hippo in the late 4th century. Despite the defeat of Pelagius in this confrontation, Celtic Christianity did not go away. It remained an irritant to Roman Christianity for a further seven hundred years and was, at one time, even a threat to its dominance. The matter was

---

7   In this book, I use BCE and CE (Before Common Era and Common Era) instead of BC and AD. The dates are otherwise the same.

eventually settled when the Roman church, accompanied by the Norman military, overran Ireland ecclesiastically and politically in the 12th century.

This book spans four millennia. It tries to weave together the strands of history in a new way. The view taken is that of someone standing at the edge of Ireland, in the Atlantic ocean, looking east across Ireland, Europe and the world. This view facilitates the recognition of a solid connection between what commercial global corporations are doing today and what organised Christianity, with a global mission, was doing over a thousand years ago. The results have been and are the same: the destruction of diversity, the disconnection of human society from nature, from the feminine and from place and the imposition of a hegemony, or 'one size fits all' for all people.

Each chapter is written with the intention of being complete in itself. This has led, in some instances, to a certain amount of repetition. For example, the collapse of the Roman empire in the 5th century had repercussions not just throughout Europe but in Britain and in Ireland. In separate chapters, where I deal with these places and this event, I must of necessity repeat the essential aspects of this moment in history in order to set the context for what is to follow.

Overall, I hope that the reader finds that the book has a cohesiveness to it. It is attempting to question our certainties, our hidden agendas and our unconscious attitudes. The thesis of the book is that we live in a bubble, a bubble that is four thousand years old. That bubble is defined by monotheism. Within it, the globalisation projects of religion and commerce find their home.

This book took many years to write. It is the result of a process of reflection over a lifetime. Much work has been required to clarify my thoughts and write them down in a linear and coherent fashion, for the purpose of producing this book. This has been the most difficult project I have ever undertaken. I owe deep gratitude to my wife, Tess Harper, for the love, patience and wholehearted support she has given me in so many ways throughout the project.

1

POLYTHEISM
A WORLD OF DIVERSITY

Polytheism and monotheism are two radically different perspectives on the world. The gods and goddesses of polytheism are to be found in the immediate natural environment; the god of monotheism is to be found in heaven. Polytheism of its nature embraces diversity; monotheism is essentially dogmatic. In this chapter, the polytheism of ancient Ireland is used to illustrate these differences.

Many people today experience a sense of the divine when they are out in nature. They take a walk in the forest or go down to the seashore or sit at the edge of a river. There they can feel a certain presence or energy or mystery. In ancient times in Ireland, the spiritual presence or energy or mystery to be experienced in these places of nature had the name of a specific god or goddess. One did not go there to talk to some abstract, general concept of god but to engage with a particular god or goddess associated with that place or object.

Polytheism, wherever one finds it in the world, is nature-based. Many of the gods and goddesses of polytheistic cultures are personifications of aspects of nature. To be more specific, they are personifications of the humanly experienced spiritual essence of a particular place or element of nature. These essences that are experienced are archetypical energies – that is, they are a common experience among humans everywhere. Diverse forms of polytheism found throughout the world are uncannily alike.[1]

---

1   Claude Lévi-Strauss. *Structural Anthropology*. Trans. Claire Jacobson. New York: Basic Books, 1963, p.208: 'On the one hand it would seem that in the course of a myth anything is likely to happen. [...] But on the other hand, this apparent arbitrariness is belied by the astounding similarity between myths collected in widely different regions.

Nature-Based Worship

It is incorrect to say that Celtic people worshipped trees and rivers, or the sun and the moon. But in a world where mystery was everywhere, each of these elements of nature triggered in these people a specific experience of magic and wonder. Take, for example, the oak tree. Why was it that the druids performed their rituals in oak groves? Were they worshipping the oak trees?

The answer to this question may lie in a fact of which we moderns, with our pathological disconnectedness from nature, are unlikely to be aware. When a forest, filled with a variety of tree species, is struck by lightning, the likelihood is that the lightning will strike the oak tree rather than any of the others.

We now know scientifically why this is the case. Lightning strikes oak trees rather than any others because the oaks are more conductive of electricity than other species.[2] Lightning will always take the easiest route into the earth and in a forest of trees the oak tree is the easiest route.

But the early Celtic people of Ireland did not have this scientific explanation. What they saw was, to them, an amazing phenomenon – that the oak tree was almost always the one singled out by lightning. This was wondrous and mysterious and it challenged the human imagination to come up with an explanation. Out of this search for meaning came a mythological story which explained the phenomenon.

The explanation came in the context of a belief in a god called Taranis who lived in the sky (as distinct from heaven). This god manifested himself through thunder and lightning and other such occurrences above one's head. When this god chose to communicate with the earth, he sent a burst of lightning down from the sky and often picked out an oak tree for its transmission. Therefore, if humans wished to communicate with this god, it made sense to gather at the base of an oak tree to do so.

This explanation of a phenomenon gave the Celtic people a particular relationship with the oak tree, which put the oak on a higher level than all other trees. The oak tree's spiritual properties were further defined by its

---

Therefore the problem: If the content of myth is contingent [i.e. arbitrary], how are we to explain the fact that myths throughout the world are so similar?'

2   Jacqueline Memory Paterson, *Tree Wisdom: The Definitive Guidebook to the Myth, Folklore and Healing Power of Trees*. Thorson, HarperCollins, 1996. p. 177.

relationship with another god, Esus. The energy, power and strength of this god Esus were believed to be contained in the oak.

Each species of tree had its own specific properties and these properties created their own associations with divine beings in the imaginations of the Celts. So Celtic people did not worship the oak tree or any other tree, but they used the oak tree to make a tangible connection with deities associated with the properties of that tree.

Similarly, Celtic people did not worship the sun but they did worship the god Lugh, who personified the essence of the positive human experience of the sun, that of its light and warmth and the help that the sun gave for the growing of the crops and the ripening of the harvest. The god Lugh was celebrated in rituals at the Lughnasa festival[3] which took place at the beginning of the harvest in early August.

A god named Balor personified the negative experience of the sun that one had when the weather got too hot or too cold, when crops withered from lack of rain, or died from frost, when spontaneous fires broke out, when there was a shortage of water, or when snow on the ground meant the animals had no grass. While this god was hated and feared, his presence had to be acknowledged and a way had to be found to keep him pacified. This was done by making sacrificial offerings to him. Mythologically, these sacrificial offerings were described as a heavy burden of tax placed on the people by Balor.

In Irish mythology, Balor and Lugh, the two sun gods, were in opposition to each other. As the new agricultural year began with the coming of spring, Balor and Lugh entered into deadly combat. Throughout spring and summer the battle between them raged. The people fought with Lugh but Balor had his army of Formorians. With the first signs of a harvest and the survival of the crop or of the new generation of animals, the victory of Lugh was declared and the Lughnasa festival began. The following year, the cycle would start again.

Echoes of the Lughnasa festival are still to be found throughout Ireland. At Croagh Patrick, a holy mountain in County Mayo, the festival is celebrated by the climbing of the mountain. In Killorglin, County Kerry,

---

3   cf. Seán Ó Duinn OSB, *Where Three Streams Meet: Celtic Spirituality.* Columba Press, 2000. Chapter 20, p. 302

the festival is celebrated by elevating a wild puck goat on a high platform in the middle of the village.

This experience both of the good and bad effects of the sun was an experience common to everyone. All were dependent on the weather and on the success of crops and of animal reproduction for their survival, as we still are to this day. The stories of Lugh and Balor created a container for and gave a broad context and meaning to, the annual struggle for survival and the production of adequate food for the coming year.

In this way, the Celts were able to explain to themselves and to their children why it was that each year they had to go through this struggle with their crops and animals before harvest time. To them, divine forces of good and evil were at work. Humans took part in the battle, but the battle was greater than them.

Nature-based polytheism meant that the divine presence of a particular god or goddess was encountered in a particular place on the landscape. One went to a certain mountain to honour a particular god and to a certain river to honour a particular goddess. In Ireland the goddess Bóinn was associated with the river Boyne *(An Bhóinn)* and the river was called after her. The mountain *Cruachán Aigle*, now Croagh Patrick, was associated with the god Lugh, the god of light. These places were sacred and were used for sacred worship. They could not therefore be desecrated by any form of inappropriate human behaviour.

A Rich Spiritual Vocabulary

The polytheistic gods personify the sense of the divine that people experience in relating to different aspects of nature. The experiences are available to anyone, without the mediation of priest or druid. Polytheism identifies the typical ways in which an ordinary person can experience the divine while going about his or her daily tasks. It projects a personality, face and name of a god or goddess onto this experience. This gives a language and a vocabulary to a wide diversity of spiritual experience and allows that language to be commonplace among the people.

Monotheism does not have this richness of language and vocabulary for everyday spiritual experiences. Because the god of monotheism lives in heaven and not on this earth, the language of monotheism did not develop to facilitate spiritual experiences associated with nature or with daily tasks. The language of monotheism focuses more on the inner transformational experiences associated with threshold moments in one's life – experiences such as birth, coming of age, marriage, illness and so on. In the Christian tradition, Francis of Assisi was a remarkable exception to this, as were the Celtic monks in general. Celtic Christian spirituality is also exceptional in that, quite specifically, the daily tasks of kindling the fire, making the bread, milking the cow, lighting the lamp and so on, are all imbued with spiritual content and meaning.[4]

Monotheism Is Dogmatic

Monotheism is dogmatic of its very nature. It requires one to believe in a particular all-powerful, all-encompassing god and forbids a belief in any others. Both Moses and Muhammad, the founders of Judaism and Islam, were adamant that their people must reject all other gods and believe only in their chosen, solitary god. This was their first commandment. It was a commandment that was impressed upon the people over and over again, until it became a mantra for them, as it still is among the followers of Judaism and Islam today.

Once this fundamental requirement of monotheism was established among its adherents, other dogmatic theological requirements were also elaborated. A creed of orthodox teachings emerged. Orthodox in this context means the teaching that has the stamp of approval of the main authorities. These teachings are controlled by a central authority structure and those who wish to belong are required to subscribe to these teachings. In the process, unacceptable tenets of faith are condemned and those who hold them are ostracised.

What has emerged within monotheism therefore is a strictly defined creed and a strictly interpreted mythological story that has no anomalies or contradictions in it. This creates exclusivity. Membership is available only to those who subscribe to this carefully defined set of beliefs.

Monotheism is radically different from polytheism in all its forms.

---

4   Cf. Alexander Carmichael, *The Celtic Gift of Nature: Selections from the Carmina Gadelica in Gaelic and English.* Floris Books. 2004. Also: Diarmuid Ó Laoghaire, *Ár bPaidreacha Dúchais: Cnuasach de Phaidreacha agus de Bheannachtaí ár Sinsear.* Foilseacháin Ábhair Spioradálta. 1990. First published 1975.

Within monotheism, the emphasis from the beginning has been on controlling what people believe. In polytheism, this type of authoritarian control of beliefs does not exist.

Polytheism Is Non-Dogmatic

Polytheism in Celtic society and wherever else it was found was not dogmatic. Unlike monotheism, where the emphasis was on subscribing to a particular belief, Celtic polytheism put the emphasis on relating to a particular divine energy as humanly experienced. There were no creeds in pre-Christian Celtic society, only mythological stories.

The mythological stories of polytheistic cultures are carried in oral traditions that allow for many different versions of the same story and many different stories about the same subject. There is no requirement to believe one version as opposed to the other. Each version of the story can be used as a way of looking at the mysterious elements of life. Similarly, there is no definitive list of gods and goddesses. People choose to engage with the gods and goddesses that are of most relevance to them in their particular situation. Polytheism, unlike monotheism, allows for diversity, overlap, paradox and contradictions in its stories.

To illustrate this, let us look at a collection of Celtic mythological stories about the land. For all polytheistic cultures, the land was sacred. In Celtic culture the land of Ireland was the body of a goddess. Her most ancient name was Anú, but she had many other names. One could see the outline of her body in the landscape. Two mountains in County Kerry represented her breasts and are known to this day as *The Paps of Anú*. The rivers were her veins. The wells were an entrance into her fertile womb. Through her, the land was a living fertile feminine being, producing new offspring among the animals and new harvests from the land every year.[5]

The goddess of the land of Ireland was a triple goddess who could appear in three different forms. In spring, she appeared in the land as a maiden. In the summer she appeared in the land as a mother. In the winter, she appeared in the land as an old woman or hag.

This triple goddess story takes another form in the story of the Celts

---

5   Cf. Michael Dames, *Mythic Ireland*. Thames and Hudson, London. 1992.

invading Ireland.[6] The Celts, or Milesians as they were then known, landed their boats near Kenmare in County Kerry and marched north-east towards the hill of Tara. As they marched, they encountered the goddess of the land of Ireland three times. Each time they encountered her she took a different form and had a different name. Her three names were Banba, Foghla and Eriú. At each encounter, her request was the same – she required the invaders to name the land after her.

From this story, we get the name Ireland, named after Eriú. Irish poets, over the centuries, have also used her other names, Banba and Foghla, to write patriotic poems about the land of Ireland.

This sense of the sacredness of all of the land and of certain locations on it, gave a direction to and marked a boundary around, the behaviour of the people within this environment. Their attitude everywhere had to be one of respect and reverence.

In a mythological sense, these people were married to the land. This myth was ritualised on the day their king was crowned. A ritual was performed which married this new king to the goddess of the land. The ceremony was known as *bainis rí* (the king's wedding). The partnership this created required that the king would rule his people justly and in return, the goddess of the land would make the earth fertile and the people would prosper.

These various stories about the goddess of the land represent different strands and influences within the cultural tradition. The tradition was oral; nothing was written down. The stories were passed on through the generations without any centralised control.

This is the essential difference between polytheism and monotheism. Polytheism embraces diversity and allows all forms and versions of stories to exist side by side. Those who practise it are not upset by contradictions or anomalies. Monotheism, on the other hand, cannot tolerate diversity of belief and has a need to exercise control from the top down.

A Rich Collection of Mythological Stories

The number and diversity of gods and goddesses within Celtic polytheism

---

6   Cf. Marie Heaney, *Over Nine Waves: A Book of Irish Legends.* Faber and Faber, London. 1994.

facilitated the development of a rich collection of mythological stories. These stories touched on the core issues of life, tackling human dilemmas, throwing light on aspects of human behaviour and giving explanations for natural phenomena.

In the Celtic tradition, Mananán was the god of the sea. He lived on islands off the coast and is most associated with an island seen dimly off the east coast of Ireland. This island, the Isle of Man, is called after him and was his throne.

Most of the phenomena connected with the sea – storms, mist, coastal erosion – were attributed to Mananán. He could make land appear and disappear. He was a master of tricks and illusions. His horse, Aonbarr, could ride both sea and land and could be seen from time to time on the waves. His boat, *Ocean Sweeper*, obeyed the thoughts of those who travelled on it and had neither sail nor oar. He had a sword Freagrach that no armour could resist.

Mananán wore a great cloak that could take on any colour, just like the sea. He was responsible for leading people who had died beyond the sea to *Tír na n-Óg*, the Land of Youth. He was also the defender of the land of Ireland and his roar could be heard from the sea whenever Ireland was attacked.

As Ireland was a small country surrounded by the sea, the stories of Mananán, god of the sea and of his father Lir, abounded. These stories captured the human experience of mystery and wonder associated with the sea and personified the forces that were at work in connection with it. However, while Mananán was the god of the sea, he was not the sea itself and he actually lived on land – on an island.

Polytheistic Mythology Acts as a Mirror

In traditional polytheistic societies of the past, the world of the gods reflected the world of the humans in an archetypical way. The gods were anthropomorphic archetypes, reflecting back to human society types of character, personality and human behaviour that were already in their midst. Gods were male and female; they married and had children. Polytheistic mythology acted as a mirror to society, as well as being a crucible in which society was formed.[7]

The lives of the gods and goddesses of polytheism were similar to those of humans. The tensions and difficulties between particular gods and goddesses were generally illustrative of archetypal patterns to be found among humans. The stories offered insight and often wisdom with regard to the problems of human living.

Modern psychology based on Sigmund Freud and Carl Jung has been able to use Greek and other mythologies to good effect in analysing and explaining the psychological mechanisms of human behaviour. Freud, for example, developed the notion of the Oedipus complex, based on the Greek legend where King Oedipus was destined to kill his father and marry his mother.[8] Freud used this story to explain the period in a male child's development, his oedipal stage, where the child is jealous of his father and wants to take his place as the mother's partner.[9]

What early polytheistic mythologies presented in story form, modern scientific disciplines of psychoanalysis, psychology and the social sciences present in a more scientific form. Science has taken over as a way of explaining life and mythology has been dismissed as an anachronism. The great argument for science over mythology is that science, being empirical, deals with objective reality. What is becoming clear today, however, is that even the scientific form is wrapped in the mythology of those who practise it and is not as objective as was once believed.[10]

---

7   Joseph Campbell, *The Hero With A Thousand Faces*. Princeton University Press.1968. First published 1949. Page 31 describes the four functions of myth.

8   The legend tells the story of how these unlikely events happened. Oedipus, not knowing who his true parents were, having been separated from them at infancy, unwittingly kills his father and then marries his mother. Freud saw the connection between this story and a developmental stage in the life of a child. This is the stage when the mother becomes the love object of the child. At this stage, the child sees the father as a threat to that love. Freud called this the Oedipus complex. He then showed that, when psychological damage is caused to the child during this stage, the symptoms of wanting to marry the mother and kill the father can manifest again in adult life.

9   A full version of Freud's theory is hard to find in any one piece of his writing, as he developed the theory over time. However, see L. Appignanesi & J. Forrester, *Freud's Women*, London: Weidenfeld and Nicholson, 1992, for a good summary.

10   Amit Goswami, *The Physicists' View of Nature: The Quantum Revolution*. Springer, 2002.

Polytheism Reflects the Complexity of Life

Stories of gods and goddesses reflect the complexity of human life. Deities were often presented in conflict with each other, illustrating that there were no easy answers to some of life's thorny issues. Cúchulainn was a legendary Irish hero who was married to Emer. However, he fell in love with Fand, the wife of Mananán and went to live with her for a while. While Cúchulainn lived in the world of humans, Fand and Mananán were divinities of the Otherworld. Cúchulainn could only come back to Emer when Mananán shook his cloak between the two lovers, so that Cúchulainn forgot about Fand.

This story is a way of describing a regular phenomenon among humans today. Most of us have come across a situation where a married man falls in love with another woman, the result of which is an estrangement between himself and his wife. He has, as it were, come under the spell of someone else. For many men this happens unintentionally and therefore unconsciously. It is as if the Otherworld has taken over. If the man wishes to resolve the dilemma and return to his wife, he will probably have to receive some form of therapy (a magical ritual) which would break the spell. If he attended a Jungian therapist, for example, he might learn that he had projected an archetype onto this other woman and fallen in love with this archetype rather than the woman herself. Having realised this, he might then decide to return to his wife and attempt to heal the damage in their relationship. The Cúchulainn story illustrates this dilemma in mythological form.

Another legend in the Irish tradition that illustrates this point is the story of Diarmuid and Gráinne. This story encapsulates the difficulties that arise between different generations.

Gráinne, the daughter of the Irish high king, Cormac Mac Airt, promised herself in marriage to Fionn Mac Cumhaill, the legendary Irish warrior. However, when she got up close to him on the day of their betrothal, she realised he was old enough to be her father and not quite as handsome as she had at first thought. So she ran away with a young warrior named Diarmuid Ó Duibhne. Diarmuid was a reluctant elopee. He wished to remain loyal to his leader Fionn and he also feared punishment.

Diarmuid and Gráinne were chased across the length and breadth of Ireland by Fionn Mac Cumhaill and Cormac Mac Airt for a period of sixteen years. They were never caught, but had to be constantly on the move and constantly one step ahead of their pursuers. As their adviser, they had the god of youth and romance Aongus Óg, who counselled them on how to avoid capture. This element of the story illustrates that at least they had one god on their side.

In the course of their long period of elopement, the relationship of Diarmuid and Gráinne grew and was cemented. Eventually a truce with Fionn and Cormac was called and they were allowed to settle down and rear a family. It took a further twenty years or so before a reconciliation was attempted between themselves and the older generation.

This story encapsulates the perennial difficulties that arise between different generations, where the younger generation believes in something, or wants to do something, that does not have the approval of the elders. This situation is typified, even today, in a son or daughter wanting to marry someone who does not have the approval of his or her parents. In the legend, the story lets the young people win, but only after paying the huge price of being on the run for sixteen years.

Humans Dependent on Divine Relationships

Gods and goddesses of polytheistic societies lived in another world that ran alongside the human world. They interacted with each other, just as humans do. However, human life was completely dependent on them. When these gods interacted with each other, the lives of the humans were affected also.

Lugh and Baoi were two such divinities in the Celtic realm. Lugh being associated with the sun and Baoi with the earth, they were seen as being in a sexual relationship. That relationship was essential to the welfare of the human population. For this reason, not only were there mythological stories concerning this relationship, there were rituals performed by the humans to ensure that the benefits of this relationship were delivered to them.

One such ritual developed around wells. Country people in Ireland to this day continue the tradition of visiting the local holy well.[11] At this well,

---

11   Walter L. Jr. Brenneman and Mary G. Brenneman, *Crossing the Circle at the Holy Wells of Ireland*. University Press of Virginia, 1995.

people walk around the well seven times before approaching it directly, kneeling at it and blessing themselves with the water. Nowadays, this is regarded as a Christian tradition and the well is usually named after a Christian saint. However, the practice of regarding the well as holy and performing ritual rounds at it predates Christianity.

In Irish polytheistic society, the well signified an entrance into the womb of the goddess of the earth. As such, it was a focus of feminine fertility. One visited the well to get in touch with the divine energies that made the earth and every living thing on it fertile.

Early peoples saw that the sun had a role to play in this fertility. The sun gave the appearance of rotating around the earth. It rose in the east, travelled across the southern sky and set in the west, to rise again in the east the following morning. Based on appearances and not on scientific data, the sun did a round of the earth each day.

To these people, the sun was associated with the male god Lugh, while the earth was associated with the female goddess Baoi. The relationship of Lugh and Baoi was expressed in this daily cosmic round. During the day they danced together as the sun traversed the sky. At sunset, they went to bed together. It was this relationship that gave fertility to the earth and brought forth the annual harvest.

The people saw themselves as being totally dependent on this relationship between the two divinities. Without this relationship, there would be no fertility or harvest on the earth. The important thing for humans was to be in harmony with the relationship of Baoi and Lugh and to imitate that relationship in their own lives. When ancient peoples visited the wells, therefore, they imitated the sun and walked around the well in a 'sunwise' direction. Having walked seven rounds, representing the seven known planets, they then approached the well for a blessing.

In doing this, they were aligning themselves with the energies of the cosmic cycle of sun and earth, balancing the reproductive energies of their own bodies with those of the cosmos and putting their fertility cycles in tune with those of the gods. As a result, many rituals associated with this myth were sexual.[12]

12　For example, sexual rituals were associated with Croagh Patrick in County Mayo up to the middle of the 19th century. Women climbed the mountain at the Lughnasa festival in order to witness the birth of the mother goddess. They climbed the mountain during

The Purpose of Myth

Mythology is the way in which the deepest meanings of life are conveyed for a particular culture. In the modern world, the stories of these ancient mythologies are often dismissed as not being historically true or accurate. The word 'myth' is used as a derogatory term. This is to miss the point. Mythology is created within a culture not to convey historical facts but to convey the deepest meaning and purpose of life within that particular culture. Myths may not convey accurate historical facts but they do convey depth of meaning and value.

Mythological stories contain nourishment for the soul. For this reason, like good classical music, they can be remembered and recounted again and again. They feed the human spirit at the deepest level. Stories such as these convey truths that are beyond history. The mythological story committed to memory acts like a slowly dissolving sweet in the mouth, gradually releasing the sugar of insight and meaning into the human mind and heart.

Humankind cannot live without myth. While modern Western society dismisses the mythologies of ancient civilisations, the truth is that modern Western society also has its myths. The most obvious modern myth is the myth of monotheism but from this myth are derived many others, such as the myths of 'progress' and 'development', the myths of 'materialism' and 'consumerism' and the myth that 'there is no alternative' to capitalism (known as TINA).

The challenge to us today is to consciously acknowledge our myths. This means naming them and recognising their existence. They are our unquestioned certainties. We see the world through them, like spectacles sitting on our noses, but are oblivious to the effect they are having on our vision. To become conscious is to become aware that our present day 'certainties' may not be the 'certainties' of the future. It is to acknowledge that the more we know, the more we know we don't know. It is to replace the arrogance of the West with a humility that connects us with the 'humus'

---

the night, sleeping at the summit in the 'bed' of the goddess. According to Rev. James Page in *Ireland: Its Evils Traced to their Source*, 1836, 'None but those that are barren go there and the abominable practices that are committed there ought to make human nature in its most degraded state blush.' (p.33). Cf. Michael Dames, *Mythic Ireland*. Thames and Hudson, London. 1992. p.167.

and that earths us. If we can live consciously within our mythologies, we will not be entrapped or confined or blinded by them.

The Otherworld

Those who lived in the Celtic world of polytheism were surrounded by the gods. They lived in a dual world – the material world which they could touch and feel, see and hear and the spiritual world peopled by gods and spirits who were active all around them and manifested themselves to them in many different ways. There was 'this world' and there was the 'Otherworld'.

In this world, the consciousness of the divine was a constant in daily life. The culture had created an association between each everyday item or event in a human's life and a particular spiritual energy. In the cosmos, for example, the sun and moon and all the planets represented divine figures. The days of the week were named after them, so that each got its day to be honoured. Even now, in the English language, Sunday and Monday are named after the Sun and Moon and Saturday is named after Saturn. We also have Thursday named after the god Thor and Tuesday, in some European languages, named after Mars. In the Irish language, the word for day and god are the same, *Dé*.

Within the natural environment in which these people lived, their deities were projected onto the rivers, the mountains, the lakes and the sea, as well as into the cosmos. Aspects and stories of these deities were associated with particular animals, birds and plants and were often specifically located in various areas of their landscape.

In Irish society, the raven was associated with the Morrigan, the goddess of death and the battlefield. The mistletoe berries were the semen of the god Esus whose spirit dwelt in the oak tree. Mistletoe was used to represent sexual fertility, love and marriage. Through shape-changing, the spirit of a human being could be manifested in an animal, so one was never too sure what or who one was encountering when an animal appeared. One could not go out into nature without being conscious of some god or spirit being close by.

The spirit world was also associated with certain dates in the Celtic calendar year. The Celtic festivals that divide the year into four seasons, *Imbolc, Bealtaine, Lughnasa* and *Samhain*, marked moments of transition in the cycle of nature and in the lives of the people. At these transition times it was believed that the veil between this world and the spirit world wore very thin. The spirit world opened up to the people and there was a heightened spiritual consciousness among them.

At these festivals, various ritual celebrations were performed. At *Imbolc*, the first day of spring, children went from door to door carrying a straw doll and invited people to welcome Brigid, the goddess of spring, into their homes. For each of these festivals, particular communal rituals brought into relief the presence and contribution of the gods in human affairs.

Some of these gods were nasty, ill-tempered, or downright evil. For example, Morrigan, the goddess of war, was violent and ruthless; Crom Dubh, the god of the harvest, was mean and Mananán, the god of the sea, was a trickster. It was the presence of these gods that explained the evil, the struggle and the pain in the world. The mythological stories explained in archetypal terms how things got to be the way they were. The humans, for their part, developed rituals to protect themselves and ward off this evil and pain.

Ritual and Worship

In these polytheistic societies, ritual was a daily part of life. While communities had their dedicated priests, druids or shamans to conduct the more important rituals, everyone practised ritual on a daily basis at a more mundane level. As the gods and spirits were a constant daily presence, rituals had to be performed regularly throughout the day to honour them, appease them or protect oneself from them. This could take the form of candles or oil-lamps being lit, incense being burned, food being offered, shrines being visited, as well as bodily postures, actions and formulae of words.

People's homes were full of reminders of the sacred – an altar, symbols, offerings and ritual items – and people used sacred water, as well as candles, oil and incense.

This spiritual awareness also found its way into people's language. Where language developed alongside a particular polytheistic mythology, the language itself became inseparable from this mythology. Greetings and farewells became a prayer of blessing with the mention of a particular god or goddess. Expressions during human conversation called in the aid of a particular deity or prayed protection against another. These theistic expressions are still present in the Irish language in phrases such as: *Bail ó Dhia ort, Go ngnóthaigh Dia dhuit, Beannacht Dé ort, Bail ó Dhia ar an obair.*

In this way, the mundane everyday events of human life were stitched into the great, overarching lives of the deities. As a result, life took on a deep meaning, purpose and value.

No Need For Religious Buildings

Because these gods and goddesses in polytheistic society were so omnipresent, so close by and so enmeshed in the natural environment of the people, there was no need for churches and religious buildings as we have them today. Some polytheistic cultures did create religious buildings, particularly where these cultures became great civilisations, as in Egypt, Greece and Rome, but on the whole one finds these deities worshipped in the home and outdoors in the landscape.

There were no religious buildings in pre-Christian Celtic society. For formal ceremonies, the druids gathered in sacred groves of oak trees. Their other sacred places were often marked by standing stones or stone circles or were simply hilltops, wells or cliff edges.

Divine and Human Intertwine

In this polytheistic world, where mythological mysteries were inseparably blended with the daily tasks and events of life, there was no escaping the consciousness or experience of the divine. The divine world and the human world were so closely intertwined that it was possible for someone to be born to a human mother and a divine father, or the other way round. Cúchulainn, the legendary hero, had a human mother, Dectera and a divine father, Lugh. In Irish legends, many gods appear in human form and interact with humans as if they themselves were humans. These ideas were later to manifest themselves in Christianity, where Jesus is a god who appears in human form and has a human mother and a divine father.

The Proximity of Gods and Goddesses

While we today live in a monotheistic world where the only god who exists lives far away in heaven, the gods of the polytheistic world were always close by. Some of them resided in the natural features of the landscape, such as mountains and rivers, others could be encountered by approaching various plants, animals or birds. Even those that were free of environmental anchors were imagined as living in the sky directly above.

There were certain gods whom one had to travel a long distance to encounter, but even these journeys, called *imram*, were imagined as taking place within the parameters of this earth.[13] While requiring heroism, they were humanly possible.

Polytheism – An Inculturated Tradition

Polytheism, wherever one finds it, is an inculturated, environmentally integrated and indigenous expression of spirituality. As such, it is part of the cultural tradition of a people, alongside their other cultural traditions. Ireland has had its own indigenous spiritual tradition that goes back millennia. This spiritual tradition stands alongside its music and dance traditions and its traditions in arts and crafts. Until interfered with by outside agencies, indigenous cultures were an integrated whole. Spirituality was interwoven with and inseparable from every other aspect of life.

Today, Western society lives with institutionalised religion. This means that spiritual practices are no longer the creation of a local, dynamic, indigenous culture but are generally set and controlled by an authoritarian system far removed from anything local or indigenous. In polytheistic societies, the religious beliefs and practices of the people emerged, for the most part unconsciously, through the community and were not encoded or enforced from the top down. Direction came from within a dynamic, creative and imaginative community rather than from an institutional framework.

Within these communities, the spiritual leaders who were priests, druids or shamans did hold some power. However, their power was limited by the extent of their ability to have an influence on the deities or to read their intentions. These deities were beyond their control and were often believed to be fickle, rash, or simply inattentive.

---

13   For example, imram Bran. Cf. Daragh Smyth, *A Guide to Irish Mythology*. Guernsey Press. 1988. p.75ff.

Some Indigenous Spiritual Practices Remain

Some of these ancient, indigenous Celtic practices remain with us, outside the control of institutionalised religion. Hallowe'en, as practised on the Aran Islands, is an example of just such a practice. The festival's more correct title is *Samhain*, meaning the transition time between the old and new year, which takes place in the Celtic calendar on the night of 31 October. According to the *Samhain* myth, this is a night caught between two years, a night when the veil between this world and the Otherworld is lifted. On this night, the human world and the spirit world come together more closely than at any other time of the year.

Traditionally, on the Aran Islands, this night is celebrated by adults dressing up in Otherworld clothes and going out into the night. Houses, pubs and public places are visited by these dressed up Otherworld creatures who are silent, mysterious and unpredictable. For the observer, the night is an eerie experience of the familiar blending with the completely 'other'.

This is an example of an indigenous spiritual practice that has survived in Ireland from pre-Christian times despite the presence of institutionalised religion. No committee organises this event and no authority controls it. It has never been institutionalised, yet it has remained true to an ancient mythology that was supposedly driven out of Ireland by St Patrick in the 5th century!

Divine Authority in Polytheism

Hierarchical power structures that were rooted in the divine authority of a god or of gods did not develop in polytheistic societies. Because these societies had so many gods and goddesses, divine authority was diffused. There were, of course, dominant gods and less relevant gods. Humans needed to be on good terms with the dominant gods and goddesses and so offered sacrifices to them, or honoured them in some way. But being on good terms with one god did not guarantee being on good terms with them all. Indeed, it is clear from the legends handed down from these cultures that these gods and goddesses were often at odds with each other.

In the Greek myths, there are many illustrations of this point: Zeus fights against the Titans and creates jealousy and enmity because of his sexual affairs; Gaia has Uranus castrated; Cronus swallows each of his children as they are born, fearing that one of them will take over his throne (this happens anyway).

In Celtic myths it is the same: Dagda has a secret affair with Nechtan's wife Bóinn and produces Aongus Óg; Macha fights and defeats her cousins, Díthorba and Cimbáeth, because they will not allow a woman take the throne as high king of Ireland; Balor throws the infant Lugh into the sea, believing that he will drown, but he is rescued by Mananán. Later in the story Balor and Lugh confront each other in battle and fight to the death.

In polytheistic societies, the influence of different gods and goddesses pulled people in different directions, often in conflicting directions. There was little chance of a cohesive vision coming from the myriad deities. Individual people could be looked after and guided by a particular god or goddess, generally for a specific task, but this is not the case for a whole society. Polytheism reflected diversity rather than oneness.

Polytheism Cannot Offer a Universal Vision

For this reason, polytheism did not offer a universal vision for society. While it served to reflect society to itself and also to contain that society within certain parameters, it did not offer that society as a whole a clear focussed direction. Polytheism of itself was not capable of producing concepts like progress or development.

While nowadays we understand time in a linear fashion and have a sense of evolution and of history, polytheistic societies understood time in a more cyclic fashion, based on the yearly round. Everything that they experienced was expected to come around again and again. Continuous linear change, which is so much a part of our own lives today, was not a part of their lives and was not how they saw the world.

Polytheism Cannot Be Fundamentalist

The rich mythology of polytheistic societies prevented the emergence of fundamentalism or even dogmatism. The answers to life's questions were contained in colourful stories of gods and goddesses. These answers were not dogmatic and one could make what one liked of them. There was room for choice and for interpretation.

Fundamentalism is the tendency to believe that one has the definitive answers to some of life's deepest questions. Modern monotheism, in all its forms, facilitates this tendency because it has, from the beginning, promoted the concept of dogma. Dogma is the institutionalised insistence that the institution's teaching is correct and all other beliefs are wrong. Those who make such dogmatic and fundamentalist pronouncements claim that their authority and their source of truth is in one god and that this god is the supreme being.

There were not the same possibilities for fundamentalist beliefs within polytheistic societies, particularly where nothing was written down. Hinduism today remains a good example of this. By and large, Hinduism is very tolerant of diversity in belief and doctrine. The belief systems of polytheistic societies did not allow individuals to claim exclusive access to divine authority, as monotheism was to do. It is clear from Greek polytheism, Celtic polytheism and many other polytheistic societies, that hierarchical social control mechanisms, which had divine beings at their head, were not present, except where political leaders themselves claimed to be gods.

Egyptian and Roman Society

In Egyptian and later in Roman society, a mechanism did develop whereby the pharaoh and the Roman emperor claimed divinity on their enthronement. In these situations, the Pharaoh and the Roman emperor were gods among other gods. Therefore they did not have ultimate control. Nonetheless, their status as gods among the people did confer upon them an absolute power. It gave them the status they required to exercise central control and served to help quell any rebellion against them.

Moses grew up in Egypt during the period of the Pharaohs. According to the story in the Bible, he was raised in the courts of the Pharaoh. He therefore saw how divine authority, channelled through a human, could be used to control and direct a whole society. Perhaps it was this experience which planted a seed, even subconsciously, in his mind. Later he was to take this idea a stage further through the introduction of monotheism.

Mist and Magic

There is a mist tonight,
So I ventured out.

Good god in sacrament!
I stilled to hold a dog-daisy
Covered in dew-dust.
I stilled, worshipping,
And saw my hand in the light of the mist,
Then jumped my gaze to imagine my whole person wrapped,
In that mesh of delicate, elusive vapour.

Caught up in its whispers,
My soul heard tales of what has been on this soil,
And how I am ever in its grasp,
Trapped by its passion.

The donkey cautiously watching from the stone wall,
Didn't frighten as I came up close.
We both stood, bound in the mystery for seconds,
In seconds fleeing to eternity and back.

On the road again I waited for the others,
All to head home together.
And hid the scene in a pocket of my mind,
To bathe in once more,
remembering mist and magic.

Tess Harper

2

MONOTHEISM
THE MOTHER OF GLOBALISATION

The change to monotheism, promoted under Moses, was a paradigm shift that separated Judaism from the prevailing polytheistic cultures of the time. What was new was not only a belief in a single god but a dogmatism that was not present in polytheism. This dogmatic approach facilitated the development of a hierarchical system of authority within Judaism which was different from surrounding cultures. In this system, 'God' was at the head. The result was a detailed system of laws, all of which were believed to come from this god. Israel became the first theocratic state. The success of Judaic monotheism opened up the possibility that one day all people on this earth would be connected to this one god, obeying the same laws and living the same lifestyle. Monotheism is the mother of globalisation.

When Moses came down from Mount Horeb in the Sinai Desert he brought with him the *Ten Commandments,* carved in stone. The first of these commandments stated that there was to be one god and one god only.[1] Monotheism is now the dominant form of belief in the world today. When one tries to find its source, one inevitably is led back to Moses.

One can argue that various forms of monotheism appeared in the world before the time of Moses. For example, the Egyptian pharaoh Akhnaton promoted worship of a single god Aton around 1350 BCE, approximately one hundred years before Moses. However, the monotheism that is present in today's world has its roots in Moses.

Moses introduced us to the idea that there is one god who created this universe and rules this world we live in. This god of Moses has become the god of three of the world's major religions – Judaism, Christianity

---

[1]   *Exodus 20:1 - 3.*

and Islam. The Sikhs, the Sufis and adherents of the Bahai also trace their god to Moses. These religions make up more than half of the world's population.[2]

The concept of the divine as one god who is male and lives in the heavens dominates the Western world. It is a myth in the true sense of that word – a fundamental belief that acts as a container of meaning for human living. Within the parameters of that myth, humans find a meaning for their lives and justification for their actions.

When the Hebrews came out of slavery in Egypt they developed a new theology which rejected the Egyptian pantheon of gods and all feminine images of divinity. It is clear from the Bible story that the primary task of Moses was to convert his people to a belief in this one god and to have them reject all others.

At the time of the exodus of the Hebrews from Egypt, around 1250 BCE, the Egyptian and all the surrounding cultures were polytheistic. These other cultures included the Canaanites and the Mesopotamians. Further afield were the Hindu, Minoan and Celtic cultures – all of whom were polytheistic.

The Egyptians, under whom the Hebrews suffered slavery, believed in dozens of gods and goddesses. These deities cared for all aspects of life, death and the next world. For a period, Egyptians also believed that their own kings or pharaohs were gods.

When the Hebrews escaped from Egypt under the leadership of Moses, they encountered the Canaanites in the desert. The most powerful deity of the Canaanites was Baal, the god of rain, storms and war. Baal's wife, Asherah, was a goddess of love. The Hebrews regularly fought against the Canaanites and eventually conquered them and took their land.

The Hebrews also encountered the Mesopotamians. These people lived in what now corresponds roughly to modern Iraq. Their beliefs involved many deities. Every village was under the protection of a deity who lived in a huge temple tower called a ziggurat.

In the middle of this polytheistic world, Moses introduced a new idea – one god and one god only. It is clear from the Bible story that Moses had

---

[2]   http://www.religioustolerance.org/worldrel.htm

difficulties converting his people to this belief.[3] It would not have come naturally to the people of that time. But for Moses, this belief was to be the bedrock of his new community of freed slaves. He had to be dogmatic about it if he was to establish it.

Having come out of an Egyptian polytheistic society, the Hebrew people were taught by Moses to believe in Yahweh and Yahweh alone. Moses presented Yahweh as someone with whom he had had a personal encounter and therefore knew existed as a living being. It was Yahweh who had made it possible for the Hebrews to escape from slavery in Egypt. Moses presented himself as being in continuous contact with this Yahweh, receiving regular instruction and guidance for the whole community.

The Establishment of Monotheistic Belief

The Hebrew people were forever slipping back into old polytheistic ways. Moses had to exercise strong, charismatic and authoritarian leadership in order to bring his people into line with this belief. He even threatened them with this god's anger.

It is accepted by scholars that the story of Moses was written long after the death of Moses. It did not take its final shape, according to the majority of scholars, under after the exile. If we take it that the exodus took place around 1250 BCE and the return from exile around 538 BCE, this means that the story of Moses took at least seven hundred years to gestate.

Similarly, while the Bible presents monotheism as originating with Moses, scientific studies suggest that monotheism was not fully embraced by the people of Israel until after the exile, that is, around the same time as the final draft of the early books of the Bible. During this seven-hundred-year interim period, the people of Israel were developing their concept of Yahweh, who became more and more central, while at the same time worshipping other gods such as Baal and goddesses such as Asherah.[4]

One can be fairly certain, therefore, that the Bible story, presenting Moses in the desert with his people, is not written as an accurate historical

---

[3]   In this chapter, I take the Bible story of Moses at face value. This is not to acknowledge any historical accuracy. It is clear from biblical research that the story evolved over hundreds of years. The point here is that the story as presented in its final version in the Bible has remained the prevailing myth of monotheism to the present day.

[4]   Karen Armstrong, *The Great Transformation: The World in the Time of Buddha, Socrates, Confucius and Jeremiah*. Atlantic Books, London. 2006. Chapters 1 and 2.

record, but as a mythological and legendary tale which weaves the events of history into a story that carries meaning, value, identity and direction for those who own it – the Judaic people from the 6th century BCE onwards.

The Judaic people needed a strong cultural identity to protect themselves from the alien cultures that surrounded them. They were in constant danger of being swallowed up. A belief in one sole god that belonged to them and them alone gave them that identity. Just as in the Bible story it took the strong authoritarian leadership of Moses to establish that belief in one god, it took an authoritarian form of leadership to separate the Judaic people completely from their surrounding cultures.

Monotheism facilitated this type of leadership because it recognised implicitly a hierarchy of authority that began with 'God' at the top. The Judaic leaders of the 6th century BCE claimed Yahweh as their supreme authority and Moses as their patriarch. The people were Yahweh's chosen ones and were in a special relationship with him. He would guide them and be in authority over them. All authority came to the 'chosen people' from Yahweh through Moses and his successors, the Judaic leadership.

A Shift in Human Consciousness

The biblical story of the Hebrew people's journey of transformation symbolises and embodies the radical shift in human consciousness that had to take place. It is a foundation story, not just for the Jewish people, but for all people who believe in one god. All of us who now find ourselves living in a monotheistic world can trace our roots back to a polytheistic society somewhere in the world. At some point in history, our ancestors made the shift from polytheism to monotheism. In the journey of transformation from polytheism to monotheism, humankind has learned to think of itself and of its world in a new way. It is a paradigm shift.

The Hebrews had escaped from a life of slavery and went on a journey towards freedom. That life had been sedentary – the Hebrews had lived as slaves in Egypt for six hundred years. Now they were on the move. While living in Egypt, they were surrounded by the presence of Egyptian gods and goddesses who lived in the landscape and were connected with the cosmic objects of the universe. Now, they had only one god and this god travelled with them, unconnected to any object of the earth or universe.

As they travelled, the Hebrews were becoming a new people, doing a new thing and being led by a new god. They were free. They had created a new reality for themselves, where the divine presence travelled with them on a journey towards the 'promised land'.

Space and Time

The radically new theology of monotheism led to a transformation of the human relationship with space and time. Space and time are the parameters in which we live. We are confined to one space and to one moment in time. However, if we can change how we understand space and time, we can change how we relate to our world. Changing our perception is a way of altering our lives. Polytheism had given the human imagination the scope to associate a divine personality with each of the dominant phenomena of the universe. Mountains and rivers, the sea and the land, the sun and the moon, the planets and the stars – all were places or objects associated with the divine. One's place on this earth and in the universe was imbued with the immanent presence of countless male and female deities.

Monotheism removed these deities from the visible universe and banished them into oblivion. In their place, the lone father-god was situated vaguely in the heavens without being associated with any one cosmic object. Humanity's relationship with place and space had all spiritual content removed from it. The earth became spiritless matter.

Similarly, with regard to the human relationship with time, there was a changed perspective. Polytheism had presented time as cyclic. Everything in nature repeated itself. Life was experienced as a continuous cycle of recapitulation. Feminine and masculine deities, often in sexual partnership, offered a divine connection with moon cycles, with the seasons, with the fertility of the land and one's own fertility and with the cycle of birth, death and rebirth. Humans saw themselves as part of a cosmic, cyclic rhythm.

Monotheism changed the human consciousness of time from cyclic to linear. Within monotheism, humans developed a sense of evolution through time, of purposeful journey year after year. Disconnected from the earth and its annual cycles, humans began to see themselves as constantly on the move. The one god became a voice calling them forward, a light in the sky showing them the way across new frontiers. Each year, progress towards certain goals or horizons could be measured. One could look back and see what one had achieved.

Monotheism created a sense of history. History looks at time in a linear fashion. The cyclic recurrence of annual events belonged to polytheism. The gods controlled the cyclic rhythm of birth, death and rebirth. Monotheism removed the deity from involvement with the yearly cycle of time. The father-god of monotheism lived in the heavens and was not tied to seasons or to the annual cycles of nature. He had a perspective which was detached from the earth. Humans too began to take this detached perspective, to disconnect themselves from cosmic cycles and to see time as linear.

One of the ways in which they did this was through the development of agriculture. Agriculture freed people from the need for daily hunting and gathering. Society could now more efficiently dedicate certain people to the tasks of agriculture while others could take on other tasks. A greater number of people were able to detach themselves from the process of producing their own food.

Another means of disconnection was the development of writing. Without writing, all communication was direct – human to human, human to animal, human to nature. Humans had a direct connection with their world. They were part of it and it was part of them. With the development of writing, that direct connection was broken. The written word came between humans and their world. That written word, such as the Judaic law or *Torah*, rather than anything in nature, became the touchstone of society.[5]

The One God Project

With the advent of monotheism, an identifiable project began among humans which I will call here the One God Project. From the time of Moses, monotheistic humans began to look forward to gradually making progress towards the realisation of long-term goals. They also began to look back at progress made and were able to chart their achievements.

---

[5]   Cf. David Abram, 'On The Ecological Consequences of Alphabetic Literacy'. Article in *The AISLING Magazine*, Issue 32. Aisling Publications, 2005. Also: Leonard Shlain, *The Alphabet Versus The Goddess: The Conflict Between Word and Image*. Penguin Compass. 1998.

Change became incremental, each new change building on the previous one. Each generation of young people grew up in a world that had changed from that of their parents.

Writing helped to chart this process. The first history book was what we now call the Bible. This book of books charts the story of the Hebrew people over a period of almost one-and-a-half thousand years. It sets the Jewish people into a context where they can see where they came from and where they are going. The concept of history is a fruit of the monotheistic viewpoint.

The journey to the 'promised land' took forty years, according to the Bible story. But in another sense that journey still goes on. We are still on that journey. The 'promised land' is always over the horizon. It is this promise that keeps us going. Initially the journey involved just a small Jewish tribe that travelled together, but with the growth and spread of Christianity and Islam, they were joined by large sections of the world's population. Nowadays, through economic globalisation, it has become a journey on which the majority of the people of the world are travelling.

From the time of Moses onwards people had a time-line on which they could place important events and personages, giving them a context of a 'before' and 'after'. Today it is the same. Our children are being born into a world that has changed significantly from the one into which we were born, just as we were born into a world that had changed significantly from that of our parents. The timeline is a story that spans over three thousand years. It had a beginning and it will therefore have an end. The contours of the story are defined by monotheism.

In today's world, we can quite clearly see that the changes that are taking place are being driven by the forces of globalisation. What this book seeks to establish is that the roots of globalisation can be traced back to the emergence of monotheism. Globalisation began with Moses and the One God Project. From the time of Moses onwards, we have been living in the bubble of monotheism. The story will end when the bubble of monotheism is burst. We will then have either ceased to exist as a species or we will have moved on and developed a new spiritual paradigm.

History as we know it began with Moses and the emergence of monotheism. That history is the story of the unfolding potential of the monotheistic viewpoint – the ecclesiastical, political and economic opportunities afforded by a global theological framework. Monotheism and globalisation are intrinsically linked. Globalisation is the modern road to the 'promised land'. Monotheism is the legitimating container for that journey.

A Global Theological Framework

The global theological framework afforded by monotheism allowed for the possibility of global ambitions. Judaism did not manifest these ambitions in any clear way but Christianity from its very beginning had them to the forefront of its agenda. In the four canonical gospels, there is no doubt that Jesus wanted his message to go out to the whole world. By the 4th century CE, Roman Christianity was organising itself to control the spread of this message worldwide. Later in history, the same global ambitions were expressed by the Christian political powers of Europe through colonialism. Today they are present in almost all sectors of society and constitute what has now become the phenomenon of globalisation.

The Promise of Salvation

An authority structure built around divine communication is an essential feature of that global theological framework. This structure gave the possibility of a divine stamp of approval to the opinions and actions of people in power. In the course of the development of global Christianity, these opinions became dogmatic pronouncements. All those who wished to achieve eternal salvation, however this was put, had an obligation to espouse these opinions. Not to do so was to earn eternal damnation in the fires of hell.

The divine communications mediated by Moses and later by Jesus and Muhammad, created a solid foundation on which to build an edifice of dogmatic opinion. Divine authority could now be used to legitimise and justify a certain way of thinking, a certain way of doing and ultimately a certain way of living, at the expense of all others.

In the Judaic phase of the monotheistic project, one was promised salvation through obedience to the law of Moses. In the Christian phase, one was promised salvation through belief in the Nicene creed. In our non-spiritual, materialistic modern phase, one is promised salvation through the embracing of a producer-consumer way of life.

Dogma

With the emergence of monotheism came the discovery of a new political tool by which people could be managed. That tool was what we now call dogma. Dogma is the exaltation of an opinion or hypothesis into a belief to which others must subscribe. Acceptance of that dogma becomes a *sine qua non* for membership of a particular community.

Dogma began among the Hebrews when it was taught to them that there is only one god and that people must accept this teaching or be lost. Once this primary dogma was established in the minds of the people, other dogmas could follow.

Dogma works, even today, when people are convinced that there is only one god and that that god has communicated his message through a specially chosen person. In the various traditions, the communications are written down and become established as the 'sacred scriptures'. The contents are seen as the 'word of God'. The interpretation of this 'word of God' by established religious authorities then becomes a secure platform for dogmatic pronouncements. Such pronouncements cannot be questioned, because to do so is to question the 'word of God'. All of the major monotheistic religions of the world operate in this way and are therefore fundamentally dogmatic.

Monotheism – Something Completely New

The creation of monotheism was something completely new in relation to divine communication. Monotheism funnelled all the many possibilities of divine communication into one source. The divine voices, which polytheistic people were accustomed to hearing from diverse places and in diverse ways and which were heard by anybody and everybody, were now reduced to one voice with one source. This allowed far greater possibilities for the harnessing of that voice and for the directing of that voice to certain ends.

In the story of the Hebrews, Moses establishes himself as the person in direct communication with this one god, Yahweh. Yahweh reveals himself to Moses, gives him guidance, works miracles through him when required and communicates to him his will for the people. The people are afraid and prefer to let Moses do all the talking with Yahweh. This gives Moses the supreme authority and the almost limitless power that was important for the instruction and leading of his people. While Moses is answerable to this god directly, the people are answerable to Moses. Moses dictates to the people the commands of 'God'. He eventually becomes established in a position where to disobey him is to disobey 'God'.

Moses is the one with the vision and the leadership abilities. But his people are fickle, weak and always complaining. As soon as Moses went up the mountain to speak with Yahweh, the people created a golden calf and began to worship it and offer it sacrifices. Moses descended the mountain in a rage. He ground the calf into dust and scattered it on the water.[6] Without strong, authoritarian leadership, the Hebrews would not have accepted monotheism.

Over time, the commands of 'God' communicated by Moses to the people became written laws. These laws began with the *Ten Commandments*, but by the time they were written down, there were 613 of them. Together they became known as the 'Law'. The *Ten Commandments* form the kernel of this 'Law'.

A Theocratic Society

The entry of the Hebrew people into the land to be called Israel began the creation of a new theocratic society. In this society, the supreme authority for the people was Yahweh, their solitary god. The laws of the land emanated ultimately from him.

Central to this process of transformation from Hebrew to Jew, from slave to free man and woman, from desert wanderer to settled town dweller, was this new centralised authoritarian form of leadership that traced all authority through a hierarchy of humans to a god who was the sole god of the whole universe.

Underpinning the One God Project is this hierarchical infrastructure. The one god is the supreme being at the top of the hierarchical pyramid. This god reveals his message to his people through one chosen person. In the case of Judaism the chosen person was Moses, in the case of Christianity it was Jesus and in the case of Islam it was Muhammad. The chosen person communicates this message from the god and it is written down.

---

[6]   *Exodus 32:1 - 35*

Certain people within the community then emerge as the bearers, the transmitters, the interpreters and the celebrants of this message. These are the people who, in the Moses story, later became the priests, rabbis, Pharisees and scribes within Judaism. Each of the monotheistic religions developed their equivalents.

A Theocratic Society Provides Effective Control

The development of Judaism as a law-based theocratic society that, at the time of Jesus, controlled people's lives in the most minute detail, illustrates how effective a belief in just one god can be in bringing about a hierarchically controlled society. The exercise of this control did not require heavy external policing. Once the people were educated into knowing and accepting the theistic interpretation of their history and the details of the 'Law', which had the stamp of divine authority, they policed themselves. Because the Jews believed, each of them had an inner authoritative voice that said: 'Worship Yahweh and live according to his Law'. This made the role of the rabbis and the Pharisees a lot easier.

The key point here is that, when people come to believe that a certain presentation and interpretation of events in their history is true and when this is mythologised into a story in which a divine person is the central figure, these people can then be led very effectively by strong authority figures. Their daily activities can be controlled down to the smallest detail. The story of Moses was the first illustration of how this could be done and the religious leaders of Judaism were the first to give it concrete expression within a settled people.

At the time of Jesus, the Jews had been settled in Palestine – with the exception of their period of exile in Babylon – for about 1200 years. The Judaic religion was well established, focussed on the Temple in Jerusalem and controlled by the priests and Pharisees. Over that period of 1200 years, the history of these people had been passed on orally and then written down in various books. Central to that story was the presence and influence of Yahweh in their lives. Everything that happened in Jewish history was interpreted in the light of the Jewish belief in Yahweh their god.

The Judaic 'Law' had been built up and developed so that every aspect of a Jew's life was controlled by the 'Law'. Detailed Judaic laws applied to ritual purifications of oneself and of objects, abstinence from work on the Sabbath, paying tithes, avoiding what was 'unclean', offerings in the Temple, the celebration of festival ceremonies and so on. Punishments were severe, the most serious offences being punishable by death by stoning. The people believed that they were Yahweh's chosen people and that their salvation was guaranteed if they were obedient to the 'Law'.

The Roman Empire had control over the Jewish province of Judea at this time. Nonetheless, within Judaic society itself, the structure was theocratic. That is to say, Yahweh was believed to be the law-giver and society was structured accordingly.

Tensions Within The System

During the course of these centuries, there was, of course, tension. Various prophets emerged within the culture who claimed to have received communications from Yahweh. Prophets such as Samuel, Isaiah, Jeremiah and Ezekiel confronted the Jewish leadership and sought to correct the direction their society was taking. Although the words and actions of these prophets were recorded and kept in various books, their message was largely ignored. As Jesus was to say: 'Jerusalem, Jerusalem, you that kill the prophets and stone those who are sent to you!'[7]

John the Baptist, one of the greatest of these prophets, was so angry with the direction his society was taking that he absented himself from it, choosing to live in the desert, eat wild food and wear animal skins. His message challenged the people to distance themselves from this society and to be converted to a new way of thinking.

Jesus took over where John the Baptist left off. As we know, Jesus railed against many of the Jewish laws and often deliberately broke them in a provocative way, saying that they were 'only human regulations'[8]. Jesus frequently made the point that while these often petty laws were being insisted upon, the weightier matters of justice, mercy, honesty and compassion were being ignored. In this, he echoed the message of previous prophets.

This tension was caused by two conflicting human impulses. On the

---

[7]   Mt.23:37
[8]   Mt.15:9

one hand, the prophets, including Jesus, represented the desire to direct human behaviour towards the highest human values and goals. On the other hand, the religious leaders were using the opportunities presented by the Jewish religion to achieve more political goals – that is, to maintain their own leadership and control over the people.

The tension has continued within monotheistic religions up to the present time. In order to achieve political power (in the sense of managing people), religious leaderships must emphasise the belief elements and the legal elements of the religion. The adherence of the people to dogmatic beliefs and their obedience to the church laws that emanate from these beliefs gives these leaders the political power they seek. Those who are more prophetic and less interested in political power see in spiritual traditions the potential to achieve higher human goals. They do not put the emphasis on dogmatic beliefs but on values, principles and the quality of human behaviour.

This latter approach is most clearly seen in the teachings of Jesus. His emphasis was always on the quality of human behaviour – loving your neighbour, forgiveness, mercy, compassion. Jesus was dismissive of theological issues. This was most clearly illustrated in his attitude to the Samaritans, a Jewish sect that had been ostracised by mainstream Judaism because of its theological beliefs.

The story of the Good Samaritan, told by Jesus, illustrates this point.[9] A Jew, attacked on the road and left for dead, is ignored by the passing priest and the Levite – both Jewish religious figures – but is helped by the Samaritan. The Samaritans were people with whom the Jews would not associate precisely because of their so-called heretical beliefs. But this Samaritan breaks the taboo on this association and goes to help the injured man. Jesus praises the action of the Samaritan and calls him a true neighbour to the injured Jew. Using this story, Jesus teaches that, in the final analysis, it is the quality of one's behaviour towards other humans that counts and not the tenets of one's religion.

This is a theme running through the teaching and example of Jesus. He condemns Jewish behaviour and praises Samaritan and Roman

---

[9] *Lk.10:29-37*

behaviour.[10] He dismisses the claims of people who believe they will reach heaven because they cry 'Lord, Lord'[11], clearly implying that belief will not be the criterion of entry. He shocks his Jewish listeners by saying that some Gentiles (non-Jewish) will get into heaven before them – because of the way they live their lives irrespective of their beliefs.[12]

For the Jewish prophets, including Jesus, spirituality needed to free itself from the shackles of religion in order to become a means of liberation for the human spirit. For religious leaders, religion needed to contain and control the expression of spirituality among the people so that it could be used to gain and maintain political power. This is an ongoing struggle within monotheistic religions, even to this day.

Separation of Religion and State

Western governments have today taken over the role of religion in encouraging a certain quality of human behaviour. Prohibitions which were initially in the *Ten Commandments*, such as 'Thou shalt not kill', 'Thou shalt not steal', are now on the statute books. The emphasis in many of the laws of Western governments today follows the themes of the Judaic prophets – justice, equality, inclusivity, non-violence and so on. Some political parties in the West now call themselves Christian. These parties are not connected to particular Christian churches, but claim to hold and promote Christian values. In today's world, the separation of religion and state has removed the regulation of human behaviour from the churches and vested it in the state.

In mature Western democracies, monotheistic religions and churches have been left with a paired-down version of their original roles. No longer the regulators of human behaviour, their influence is now confined to an emphasis on particular beliefs, traditional practices and the building of a community identity based on religion. This process has exposed their dogmatism, exclusivity and divisiveness in the public perception and has led to their decline.

---

[10]   *Lk10:29-37; Lk7:1-10; Lk13:22-30*
[11]   *Mt.7:21-27*
[12]   *Mt.8:5-13*

Monotheism – the Mythical Container

While Western states have to a large extent separated themselves from religion and while many of these religions of Western society are in decline, monotheism remains dominant and uncontested as the mythical container of the Western world. Western society continues to live within a bubble, the contours of which are defined by the myth of monotheism. We all live within it, regardless of our personal beliefs.

One cannot take a view without having a standpoint. One's theology and one's philosophy are what define the standpoint one takes when looking at life and the world in general. One's philosophy and theology are the coordinates, so to speak, of one's position and they define one's perspective. The standpoint of Western society has always been monotheistic. While Western society has become largely secular, its standpoint has remained monotheistic.

Illustrating this is the fact that the god of monotheism is mentioned unquestioningly in many national constitutions, national anthems and even on national coinage. The Irish constitution recognises this god of monotheism as the supreme authority. It begins: 'In the Name of the Most Holy Trinity, from Whom is all authority and to Whom, as our final end, all actions both of men and States must be referred...' The British national anthem is: 'God save our gracious Queen!' In the United States 'In God we trust' is written on every dollar note and coin. 'God' is part of everyday speech and everyday language in most Western countries. The president of the United States of America makes regular public references to 'God' and even the president of Russia is now seen in public making the sign of the cross.

It is this backdrop of a belief in the one god that has remained the constant of Western society. Through this one belief, Western society is united at its roots, despite religious differences on the surface. It has a unified perspective on the world: belief in a god who is male, lives in the heavens and is the creator of this earth and this universe. While Western society has become secular, it has not become agnostic, atheistic or polytheistic. It remains securely monotheistic.

Goddess

Old men, and not so old,
sat
in libraries,
dressed in black.
Marble corridors led
to a chapel called
The Gun.
Books dried and dusty
on Christ,
Christology,
ologies,
dry-shite-ologies.
About a God and Son.
A faith
one faith.
The One and Only Faith.
The One and Only God.

That I be worthy.
That I do enough.
That I succeed
and understand all their ologies and get a degree.
A career under your belt — daughter — that's what you want!

Is it?
Father.

I want that everything I do be valuable.
To watch the moon phases,
tides,
seasons,

sleep, rest,
darkness, light.
To not strive
and still be rich
with knowing.
Deep inside my body.
Inside knowing,
Deep inside.

To not compete
and know that I am worthy
because I simply am.
To follow desires, appetites
and not have to answer
to the 'informed conscience' that culls my nature.

That is what I want,
Mother.
Goddess.

'Everything you do is worthy child,
Worthy child.
God the Father
is out to tea,
Come in and play
a while.

He talks a lot of monks and penance,
God the Father and Holy Ghost.
But his heart is big
for all the talking
and his love is great for —
Goddess silence

in the moon phases,
seasons,
tides flowing,
Sleeping and resting,
In the darkness and light.

And everything you do is worthy child,
worthy child.
Everything you do is worthy child.'

Tess Harper

3

JUDAISM
A JOURNEY TOWARDS
DISCONNECTEDNESS

Judaism was the first religion to disconnect people spiritually from earth-based gods and goddesses. It did so by connecting them to a detached male god in the heavens. This was a changed perspective on the world – a paradigm shift. Societies who adopted this perspective in later periods developed a more global vision than other societies around them. The possibilities within this new perspective only gradually emerged. That potential is still being exploited today through the process of globalisation.

Economic Globalisation

Economic globalisation, as we know it today and in its pure form, does not recognise, nor show any respect for, a spiritual presence within nature. It does not see the earth, or any part of it, as sacred. Nothing in nature, apart from humans, has either soul or spirit. Nothing has any value in itself – its sole value is in its usefulness to humanity. Words such as 'resources' and 'exploitation' belong to this way of thinking.

Economic globalisation today requires that the earth and all material things on the earth be available for exploitation as resources for the market economy. This perspective represents a materialist way of thinking. It is not the only way of thinking. However, it is such a dominant way of thinking in the Western world that one might think there is no alternative.

Traditional polytheistic communities did not think in this way. To them, spiritual presences were everywhere in nature. In many of these societies, the spirit of an animal had to be appeased before the animal could be killed for eating. In Celtic society, the druids had to give permission before certain trees could be cut down for firewood. A polytheistic community saw its connection to the land as spiritual, not material. The divine, for these people, was manifested in and through the material world.

Economic globalisation, as we know it today, could not succeed if the spiritual connection of native peoples to their land was not cut. Throughout the world, over the course of history, one can see that this process of disconnection from the land has been largely successful. Native peoples have been either wiped out, removed from the land to which they had a sacred connection or they have been converted to monotheism.

The influx of Western peoples into native lands has in many cases wiped out the native peoples through war and the spread of disease. The destruction of the native American tribes during the European colonisation of America is a clear example of this. The spread of Christianity and Islam in Africa and elsewhere has replaced native polytheistic cultures with monotheism. In Central and South America, Australia and New Zealand and many other parts of Asia, the story is the same.

There continues in the world today a massive dislocation of people. Subsistence living on a small plot of land has given way to industrial farming. People are migrating from the land into cities and people are migrating from their native countries into other parts of the world. All of this creates disconnection and alienation from the land, a process that serves the agenda of economic globalisation.

Pockets of Resistance

Within Western societies one can still find small isolated pockets of resistance to this process. These surviving echoes of another way of thinking stand out in sharp contrast to the prevailing ethos and illustrate the shift that has taken place.

A good example of this is the holy mountain called Croagh Patrick on the west coast of Ireland. It is a place that people continue to visit on pilgrimage in a tradition that goes back to polytheistic times. In the late 1980s a mining company proposed to mine this mountain for gold. The company argued that it would work on the back of the mountain, out of sight and well away from the traditional pilgrim route to the top. Nonetheless, there was outrage and uproar. The government was forced to revoke the mining licence. No mining took place on the mountain.

That mining company has many other locations where its work can go ahead unimpeded by local objections. So it is not out of business. But what if local people everywhere regarded every bit of their local landscape as sacred? What if local people had a spiritual relationship with the trees, the animals, the rivers and streams, the hills and valleys, the very ground on which they walked? This was the case in traditional polytheistic societies.

Of course, many individuals who live in the countryside today do indeed have this type of relationship with their local landscape. They love to walk among the trees, sit by the river or climb to the top of the hill or mountain. They often describe their experience in these places as an encounter with the divine. These experiences nourish their souls. But when a 'development' is proposed for their area, these people are usually not strong enough or numerous enough to resist. The inroads of the dominant culture represented by words such as 'progress' and 'development' are too strong.

The Central Contribution of Monotheism

The central contribution of monotheism towards creating the potential for economic globalisation has been the detachment of people from a sacred connection to the earth. For many centuries, Christian missionaries, including many Irish, have been working very effectively to convert people from a polytheistic to a monotheistic viewpoint. In doing so they have been, perhaps unwittingly, preparing the ground for the economic globalisation of the remotest and most primitive of regions. For most indigenous cultures with whom they have worked, the inevitable outcome has already been, or will be at some future date, the complete loss of this particular people's connection to their particular place and, subsequent to that, the loss of all of the spiritual and cultural riches that went with a way of life that is now no longer possible.

In This World But Not Of It

What happened to the gods inevitably also happened to humans. All of the diverse ways of human living on this earth have been bundled into one way of living. Aspiring to see the world as this solitary god would, we have chosen to move our perspective into outer space, where we view the earth as if we were disconnected aliens. We no longer belong. To use the mantra of the Christian church: 'We are in this world, but not of it.'

Judaism provided a half-way house on this road to complete detachment from the land. For the Jews, the land of Israel was sacred, not because any god lived there, but because their one god had designated this land as 'the promised land', a land promised to them. This gave the Jews a continued connection with the land and a sense that the land was sacred, while at the same time removing from that land a sense of divine presence. To this day, it is still called the Holy Land. Perhaps it is to Jews, Christians and Muslims what a little bit of garden is to urban dwellers, who have forsaken the rural subsistence and farming lifestyle.

A Creator God Versus an Indwelling God

For monotheistic believers, the land is the creation of one god who lives elsewhere. This god does not dwell in the land nor is he even part of the cosmos. The creator god relates to the earth the way humans relate to something they have made. He looks on from outside the universe. The earth is a spiritless material creation. The only connection between this god and the earth is through human beings. Humans are the only creations of this god that have a soul. They connect to this god through their soul.

The action of humans in manipulating the materials of the earth in order to create other things is legitimised by this god, who operates in a similar way. Humans are co-creators with this god.

Belief in 'creation' is part of the monotheistic myth. The words 'creation' and 'creatures' are part of everyday Western language. These words appear unconsciously even in the speech and writing of those who claim that they do not believe in 'God'.

In polytheistic Celtic society, the relationship of the gods to the natural environment was not that of creator-created. The natural environment provided a medium through which the divine was manifested. One could experience the expression of a particular god or goddess in aspects of the natural environment. These gods and goddesses used various elements of nature to manifest their presence to humans.

For these Celtic people, relating to an aspect of nature was not simply a matter of relating to a material thing. One also had to relate to the spirit that was manifested through that material thing. Many artists today, who work with elements of nature such as stone or wood, understand this way of working. They seek to let the spirit of the object speak to them before they begin their work. This spirit guides their work. The finished work of art is often understood by the artist to be the spirit of the piece of matter giving expression to itself.

Monotheistic belief does not allow for a sense of the spirit being present in elements of nature. Consequently, there is no sacred attachment to the land. Attachment is switched to one male divine authority that resides outside the earth. The sense of the sacred is now in something other than the earth. This disconnection had deep implications for how people related to the earth. It also had deep implications for the way divine authority could be used to control people.

Changes in How People Relate to the Earth

In indigenous polytheistic societies, the people are connected to the piece of earth on which they live, primarily through their mythology. These people project their mythology onto the surrounding landscape, so that, in everything they see or encounter, an element of their own beliefs is reflected back to them. Their landscape speaks to them and provides the spiritual container for their lives.

Within this spiritual container, which takes the landscape as its material form, all of the needs of the people are met. This environment, which is both material and spiritual, provides them with shelter, food, clothing, protection, tools, weapons and sources of healing but even more so, through the mythological stories projected onto it, it provides them with the spiritual context for their lives. Within this context, they have an identity and their lives have a deep meaning and purpose.

Changes in How Divine Authority is Used

The lives of indigenous people with polytheistic beliefs are woven completely into the fabric of the landscape and the pattern of the yearly seasonal calendar. They are an integral part of space and time. They cannot be removed from this landscape without utterly destroying their lifestyle and belief system. In most cases across the globe, where this removal of indigenous people has taken place, the culture of the people has died, or it has survived only in an unsatisfactory or unsustainable form, as in the case of the Australian aboriginals and the Native Americans.

In polytheistic societies, people's lives are immersed in the divine. The divine speaks from every sunrise, every tree and every situation. Each person is in direct communication with divine energies and voices, which are to be found in the surrounding nature and in the events of each day.

But in monotheistic societies that connection has been broken. In monotheistic societies, a person must wait for a communication to be made through orthodox channels. One must go to the synagogue, the temple, the church or the mosque, to find and encounter 'God'. There, the message of 'God' will be communicated through the scriptures and through the orthodox teaching of the rabbis, priests, mullahs and imams.

Moses Created the Template

Three thousand years ago, Moses brought about a transformation of the Hebrew people. In doing so, he set the pattern for a process that has continued to this day worldwide. There were three steps to the transformation of the Hebrew people, which have become the template for what we now call globalisation.

The three steps that Moses took were:
- **Conversion** – converting his people from polytheism to monotheism
- **Dislocation** – removing his people from a particular land and lifestyle
- **Rehabilitation** – settling his people into a new land, a new lifestyle and a new belief system.

Since the time of Moses, that pattern has been repeated again and again throughout the world. We will look at each of these steps in turn.

Conversion

With over half of today's world population now believing in monotheism, it is clear that a worldwide process of conversion has taken place. While of course there are different monotheistic religions, virtually all of them trace their origins back to the god of Moses. What is of relevance to the forces of contemporary economic globalisation is that the key common element of all of these monotheistic religions is the belief that their god does not dwell on this earth. This belief is a prerequisite for economic globalisation. Because the earth is not the home of any god, one can view it as a material resource. The transformation of the earth by Western culture to accommodate economic globalisation can therefore proceed with at least the implicit support of these religions.

The conversion of peoples to monotheism took place through conquest, colonisation and missionary work. Christianity spread through all these three methods, whilst Islam spread mostly through conquest. Judaism, on the other hand, failed to spread to the same degree, mainly, it could be said, because it maintained a cultural and historical connection with the land of Israel. In this sense, Judaism failed to disconnect itself totally from the land and therefore is not as globalised as Christianity or Islam.

In the case of Christianity, preaching and missionary work played a significant role in its spread. In some instances, Christian missionaries were among the first Western people to settle among the indigenous peoples of the world, for example in the South Sea islands of the Pacific. Their work prepared the ground for further Westernisation of these people through colonisation. In other instances, the Christian missionaries travelled alongside the colonising forces, or came in their wake, as in the case of South America and Africa. In general, Christian missionaries today continue to collaborate with the economic globalisation project and have their own ecclesiastical globalising agenda.

The Christian missionary's basic message has always been the promise of salvation. The messenger must begin by convincing the people that they are sinners and therefore lost. They need to be saved, or at their death they will be condemned to the fires of hell. The only thing that can save them is conversion to Christ and Christianity.

A Christian missionary's role in entering an indigenous community was to convince the people there and especially the leaders, that a) salvation is necessary and b) that their own spirituality will not bring them that salvation. In the course of the spread of Christianity among indigenous peoples, native spiritual traditions were condemned and images expressing those spiritualities were destroyed. In smashing the icons of the native people's so-called 'false gods', the Christian missionaries were following the example of Moses who smashed the golden calf. Like Moses, they preached that only one god could save them.

The missionaries planted fear in the hearts of the native peoples. The new monotheistic religion built itself on the stirred-up fears of the people. In response to that fear, the people were taught to cling to the dogmatic teachings of the preacher.

Fear is at the root of all fundamentalism. In today's world, fundamentalism has come to mean a tenacious and blind faith in key doctrines of one's religion. It is often expressed as a belief in a literal interpretation of key passages of sacred scripture. Fundamentalism is expressed through dogmatic beliefs. One becomes dogmatic when one is afraid of the consequences of not believing.

Once indigenous people accepted the need for salvation, as preached by the missionaries, they were caught into a relationship of dependence on the preacher and his church. Only that church could provide salvation and it came through the services of the preacher. The mantra of the Christian church has always been: 'Outside of the Church, there is no salvation'. To be saved, a person needed church services and especially the sacrament of baptism. For many native peoples, baptism was the first step away from independence within a local community and towards global dependency. Baptism was their first taste of a global service.

Nowadays it is becoming clear that neither political colonisation nor missionary work, in the traditional sense, are necessary to prepare people for economic globalisation. Those people who have not yet been converted through political or ecclesiastical colonisation can still be converted through advertising.

Advertising is the modern form of preaching and missionary work. Its purpose is not to convert people to monotheism, as such, but to convert people to the mindset represented and promoted by monotheism. The characteristics of this mindset are:

- a global vision
- a belief in the need for global products and services

- a relationship to the material world and to material things that has been sanitised of all sacred connotations.

This latter form of conversion is most noticeable in India today. Contemporary Indian politics has fully embraced the globalisation model of society. The Indian nation is rapidly converting itself into a modern industrial and technological society, despite retaining Hinduism as its dominant religion. The globalisation process, however, requires that the people detach their beliefs from the land, which must be made available for development.

While Hinduism has not been wiped out, its influence in Indian politics has been minimised. The British colonisation of India, combined with the work of Christian missionaries there, have been critical in changing the mindset of the people sufficiently to make room for the transforming forces of globalisation, despite the best efforts of Mahatma Gandhi and others like him. Gandhi saw these forces of transformation coming, but he was not able to stop them.[1]

Dislocation

Globalisation cannot work among people who do not believe that they have needs. 'Needs' is a word that belongs to the vocabulary of globalisation. It is not a word that you will find among indigenous, subsistence-living people. The Native American peoples did not have needs.

Needs are those human requirements that cannot be provided directly from within a local environment and local culture. The provision of needs is facilitated by a market economy. Indigenous peoples who still live in their native habitats do not have needs, because their world is a virtually closed natural ecology within which there is a balance of giving and taking and all life is sustained.[2]

---

1   Cf. Ivan Illich, 'The Message of Gandhi's Hut'. Article in *The AISLING Magazine*, Issue 5. 1992. Also Ulrich Duchrow, 'Overcoming the Violence of Religion, Empire and Economy in the Inter-religious Spirituality of Gandhi'. *People's Reporter-A Forum for Current Affairs*, Vol 20, Issue 9, Mumbai/India, May 10-25, 2007, p. 3, under the title: 'Truth can never be achieved as goal'

2   Cf. Ivan Illich, *Toward a History of Needs*. Pantheon, Bantam, 1978 and Wolfgang Sachs (Ed.), The Development Dictionary: A Guide to Knowledge as Power. Article by Ivan Illich 'Needs'. Zed Books, 1992.

Today we use words such as 'self-sufficient', 'sustainable lifestyle', 'ecosystem' and 'symbiotic relationship' to describe how indigenous peoples have lived and continue to live in their native habitats. In these habitats, these people's housing, food, means of transport and other requirements for living are all provided for from within this natural, localised world, of which they themselves are an integral part. They are born into that world and that world is still there when they depart from it.

Needs come into play when the basic life-supports of indigenous peoples are removed. These life-supports are both material and spiritual. When Christianity began to replace the spiritualities of indigenous peoples, those peoples began to develop needs.

For example, through the preaching of the missionaries, an indigenous community developed a need for baptism and later for Christian education. They did not have these needs before the arrival of Christianity. They became aware of their spiritual needs through the preaching of Christian missionaries. The satisfaction of these needs required them to reach outside their indigenous culture and tradition and to make themselves dependent on a global church.

A similar change took place when the native people's material life supports were removed. This in some instances happened through colonisation. These people had lived in a holistic way as an integral element of a particular place, where food and drink, shelter and clothing were available within their immediate world. With the removal of direct access to food, shelter and their own place, they developed needs that had to be met by a market economy and without which they would not have survived.

Indigenous peoples throughout the world have been forced to leave their lands and change their lifestyles. The majority have had to move to the cities to find work and a way of surviving. Those who remain on the land often end up working that land for large corporations, or for the government, producing cash crops and using industrial, earth-polluting, methods. Not alone have these people been dislocated, the places from which they came are no longer there. Their natural habitats have been destroyed by development. There is no turning back.

Rehabilitation

Today, throughout the Western world, there is an unprecedented movement of peoples. The number of migrants worldwide has almost doubled in the last fifty years, from 75 million in 1965 to 120 million in the year 2000. Of 152 countries, 67 are now major receivers of immigrants.[3]

Ireland is one of the most recent countries to be hit by in-migration. In 1988-89, 70,600 native-born Irish people left Ireland to live and work abroad. By 1999, the tide had been reversed and Ireland received 80,400 foreign workers into its workforce that year. Until 2007, that rate of intake was maintained, while the numbers emigrating continued to decline.[4]

When Moses and his Hebrew people moved from slavery in Egypt to freedom in the land of Israel, they went through a process of transformation and rehabilitation that was essential for their survival. According to the Bible story, forty years were spent living in the desert before they finally settled in the 'promised land'. That forty years represents a generation of people. It indicates that the majority of those who finally settled in Israel were people who had not been born in Egypt. It took a new generation to make the major adaptations necessary for the new way of living in Israel.

Nowadays, most of the people migrating are people who come from cultures that are in the process of being economically globalised. These people, for the most part, already hold monotheistic beliefs and their countries operate open-market economies. This makes their adaptation to the culture of another country easier. However, where the people displaced have come from indigenous polytheistic cultures, the challenge of integration and rehabilitation has not been so easy.

There are clear examples of this latter situation in the problems associated with the Native American peoples in the United States and Canada and with the Aboriginal people of Australia. The colonisation and development of their lands have prevented these people from continuing to live in a traditional way. Yet they try to hold on to their identities and their traditions. This is extremely difficult for them because their identities

---

3   Peter Stalker, *Workers without Frontiers: The Impact of Globalisation on International Migration*, International Labour Office (ILO), Geneva and Lynne Rienner Publishers, 2000.

4   Statistics made available by the Central Statistics Office, Dublin. To be found in: *Administration Yearbook and Diary*, 2006, published by the Institute of Public Administration, Dublin.

and their traditions had a connection to the land in which they lived and to their traditional way of life which is no longer possible. Their removal and rehabilitation has left them like fish out of water. Their position is impossible – if they allow themselves to be totally absorbed into the Western culture, they will lose their identity and their traditions. But they cannot go back to the way they once lived. They are caught in the middle, in no-man's land.

The agendas of ecclesiastical and of economic globalisation are such that cultural identities and traditional ways of living may have to be and usually are, sacrificed. Identity, in terms of global Christianity, is reduced to a question of whether one is baptised or unbaptised. Being a man or woman, a slave or free, a Greek or a Jew, is of no concern.[5] Within the parameters of economic globalisation, identity is defined in terms of one's potential as a producer and consumer. In either system, whether one is male or female, black-skinned or white-skinned, or a native speaker of Russian, English or Chinese, is of no consequence

The objective of an economically globalised society is to remove all barriers to production and consumption on a global scale. This implies the removal of all barriers to trade, a process that is very much gaining momentum at the moment through the World Trade Organisation (WTO). Ultimately, however, this process will also lead to the removal of all barriers to the movement of people for the purpose of work. The expansion of the European Union and the new movements of people resulting from it, is a clear example of this. As people from different cultures and ethnic backgrounds mix and blend with each other, the distinctiveness of these individual cultures will be diluted and all cultures worldwide will be drawn closer to a more uniform way of living.

From this perspective, the integration of migrants into their new surroundings is an important aspect of globalisation. Western governments make great efforts to facilitate the adaptation of these migrants to the producer-consumer lifestyle of their economies. Their laws forbid any form of discrimination or racism against these migrants. The integration of migrants into the production process is made as smooth as possible. As potential producers and consumers, they are equal to everyone else,

---

5   cf. *St Paul's letter to the Galatians 3:28.*

regardless of their cultural or ethnic background. Of course, this is a good thing in the circumstances. However, it may be the right thing for the wrong reasons.

The rehabilitation of humans is a central part of the process of transformation necessary to move everyone into a belief system and a lifestyle that is congenial to the producer-consumer model of globalisation. All barriers to trade must be removed, including the barriers of religious belief, cultural identity and language. Only when people worldwide are fully disconnected from the earth, from beliefs that value the sacred in the earth and from subsistence ways of living that do not require a global market, will globalisation have achieved its ultimate victory.

The Dream Becomes A Nightmare

The biblical story of Moses is presented as a journey from slavery to freedom. Because of this, it has a universal appeal. It is a journey we all have to make. Encouraging people to participate in the global market is also presented in this way. Many people in the so-called under-developed world have already embraced the dream. Even the phrase 'under-developed' implies the dream. The world as a globalised market is the 'promised land'. The dream encourages us all to work towards the realisation of this dream and not to hold back from participating fully in it.

However, a closer look at the Moses story shows that it did not take long for the Hebrew people, who were in the desert, to regret their escape from Egypt and to long for the comforts of the life there that they now missed, despite the slavery. They remembered that in Egypt they had had cauldrons of meat and could eat as much bread as they wanted. In the desert with Moses, they were both hungry and thirsty.[6]

The majority of dislocated people in the world today have not reached the 'promised land'. While the promise of development and progress is held out to them, they remain stuck in a place where they can neither return to their native subsistence ways of living nor enter fully into the prosperity of the West. Barely surviving in the slums of overpopulated cities, they are in an arid wasteland, where they can go neither forward nor backward. The dream has not been realised and they have been left

---

6   *Exodus 16:3*

worse off than before. The changes brought about by globalisation have destroyed their traditional ways of living, dried up their sources of food and even of water and left them to starve or barely survive. The dream has become a nightmare.

Awe

We four figures,
With heads bent towards the sky,
Stood enthralled
As the heavens performed its drama.
Each heart jumping
As new wonders caught the eye,
And spirits whirled in the movement
Of every shooting star.
In lightning flash
We four figures stood,
Children of a cosmic jewel.

Tess Harper

4

JESUS
AND ORGANISED RELIGION

Among his fellow Jews, Jesus was an anarchist and a subversive. To the Pharisees, the Sadducees, the priests and the scribes of the time, he was provocative, challenging and, in the end, irreconcilably and fatally opposed. The consistency of the four canonical gospels in recounting Jesus's condemnation of the Jewish religious leaders of the time begs the question: would Jesus not be just as condemnatory of the religious leaders of today's Christian churches?

Jesus, it seems, is universally liked. His life and his teachings transcend his Judaism, his homeland and his historical time and continue to affect people of every generation throughout the world. No matter what people believe regarding his divinity, his miracles or his resurrection, his life and teachings still come across today as extraordinarily inspirational and relevant.

Were Jesus to come back today, what would he make of the Christianity now being practised in his name?

To make this judgement, all we have to go on are the written accounts of Jesus's life and teachings and primarily the four canonical gospels. These are not in the main first-hand accounts of eye-witnesses but compilations of stories gathered and edited for particular audiences between thirty and seventy years after Jesus's death. It is unavoidable that these accounts contain editorial bias, inaccuracies, misunderstandings, omissions and what we might call poetic licence. They also contain the beginnings of Christian theology – the thoughts of the early Christian community regarding who Jesus was and his relationship to the Judaic god. This new theology is clearest in John's gospel, the last of the four canonical gospels to be written.

Having four canonical gospel accounts instead of one, however, has helped to iron out some of these difficulties by providing comparisons. Scholars from all sides are surprisingly united in their conclusions on these texts.

These texts, along with the other non-canonical texts from those early centuries, are as near as we are going to get to the historical Jesus. Two thousand years after the event, we are far removed from the historical context, the culture and the mindset of the time. Nonetheless, we have a vast amount of accumulated knowledge and sophisticated scholarship to help us understand. Apart from this, the four gospel accounts are the same today as they were for Christians living in the year 100 CE. They remain the fundamental source for inspiration, spiritual nourishment and guidance in living a Christian life.

Since the time the gospels were written, we have, of course, had two thousand years of Christianity, which has developed into institutional forms and spread throughout the world. Today it is hard to think of being a Christian without being influenced by one or other of these institutional forms. How does one practise Christianity if one is not a member of a church? If one is a member of a church, one is influenced not just by the life of Jesus, as recounted in the gospels, but by the ethos, theology and practices of that church and by its perspective on Jesus.

Many Christians in the Western world today, while continuing to find Jesus inspirational, are no longer happy with the particular church in which they grew up. Some remain within the church, attending worship regularly but feeling frustrated and spiritually undernourished. Others have walked away from organised religion but have not yet found anything satisfactory to replace it and so continue to hunger for a satisfying spiritual life.[1]

Historically, diverse Christian denominations have emerged out of particular interpretations of the gospels and / or a particular disagreement with another denomination. The perspective established by a particular

---

1   In the Republic of Ireland, church attendance has declined from over 90% to well below 60% from the early 70s to the present. There has also been a decline in Northern Ireland in both Protestant and Catholic denominations. cf. *Conflict and Consensus: A Study of Values and Attitudes in the Republic of Ireland and Northern Ireland* by Tony Fahey, Bernadette C. Hayes, Richard Sinnott. Published 2005, Institute of Public Administration.

church, through its founding event, has, in general, been institutionalised so as to preserve and propagate it. When people attend this church for the first time, they encounter an established theological position, an established code of practice and a system of management and control. Institutionalised religion is, by its nature, conservative. The institution is there to conserve not just the core values and beliefs but also the system of control.

Church Ministry

For an institutional church to provide spiritual nourishment and facilitate spiritual growth in the way that Jesus did, one would expect that its leaders would imitate Jesus and that its structures would reflect the values that Jesus had. This is a tall order. In most denominations, the priest, pastor or minister is in a position of institutional power and has an elevated status among his congregation. Jesus, on the other hand, had no official position within Judaism and the only power or status he had came from his own inner authority and charism and not from any official role he took on.

Ministry in churches today is often a career choice with the hope of advancement along a career path. It is clear that Jesus did not choose any career path, but chose a way to serve that was unstructured and that left him vulnerable. He did not inherit a congregation but reached out to those who were spiritually hungry or lost or powerless like himself. How can appointed ministers act as Jesus did when the structures in which they are placed prevent them from doing so and give them a different agenda?

It is even more difficult for an institutional church to reflect in its structures the values that Jesus had. So much of Christian history has been to do with power struggles, control issues, political influence and self-propagation. From the 4th century, mainstream Christianity took on the structure of the Roman empire, a dictatorship, where the central concern, one could say, was that of power and control. It could not be argued by any stretch of the imagination that this structure reflected the values espoused by Jesus.

Jesus was not a dictator, nor did he seek to have power of any sort other than the power of his own personality and the power of truth and love. It is clear that Jesus, far from seeking power over people, encouraged them to claim their own power and to use that inner empowerment to liberate themselves from whatever oppressed and controlled them. The only power in which Jesus was interested was the power that lay dormant within people, a power that was to be released by the activity of an inner spirit.

The Anger of Jesus towards Organised Religion

Christian churches today come in many different shapes and sizes and many have introduced democratic processes and equality among the sexes. Nonetheless, the anger of Jesus towards the organised religion of his day was so intense that we have to ask the question – would he not feel the same anger today towards any other organised religion, especially one operating in his name?

Jesus was born and reared as a Jew. He was circumcised shortly after his birth and grew up in a devout family. He attended the synagogue in his home town and learned to read the sacred texts from his local rabbi. He and his family occasionally visited Jerusalem during festival time. We can glean all this information from the gospel stories. While these stories are not necessarily historically accurate, scholars agree that this was likely to be the pattern of the time with most Jewish families.[2]

Jesus lived in Nazareth, in the province of Galilee, almost a hundred miles from Jerusalem, the centre of power. Jerusalem was situated in Judea, from which Judaism got its name. The next province north was Samaria, from which the Samaritans, a breakaway group from Judaism, got their name. The Samaritans were hated by the Jews. The province of Galilee was further north again, where Jesus grew up. It probably got its name from the Celts who once lived or traded there[3].

To those who lived close to the centre of power in Jerusalem, Galilee was a backwater. They had a phrase, which summed up their attitude: 'Prophets do not come out of Galilee'.[4] When Jesus, later in his life, visited

---

2   Cf. John Dominic Crossan, *The Historical Jesus: The Life of a Mediterranean Jewish Peasant.* Harper San Francisco. 1991.
3   The word Galilee has the same root as other words that denote Celtic places or languages such as Galatia, Galicia, Gall, Gaul, Gallic and Gaelic. This root may be connected with the Latin word for a cockerel, 'gallus', which was a symbol for the Celts and is still the symbol of France. It raises the question – was Jesus a Celt?
4   *Jn.7:52*

Jerusalem as an adult, his Galilean accent and that of his friends marked him out as someone not worthy of respect.[5]

So, although Jesus was a Jew he was far removed from the centre of power. Jesus never occupied a position of power within Judaism – neither as an elder or rabbi in his local village, nor as a Levite, Pharisee, priest or scribe in the wider Judaic church. In modern terms, he was a lay person. However, on occasions he exercised the role of a rabbi and of a priest, without authority to do so.[6] He also regularly confronted the Pharisees and scribes on their behaviour and on their interpretation of the 'Law'. His lack of official authority to act in this way and to speak on these issues enraged these people.

Within Judaism, however, there was a role which did exist for Jesus and which the Judaic authorities were never able to control. This was the role of prophet. This was not an institutional role created by Judaism, but a societal recognition of a tradition that certain people rose up among them from time to time who would challenge and inspire them. Jesus fitted into this role very well. Like many of the prophets before him he denounced the authorities, said and did unpopular things and got himself into trouble for it.

It is interesting here to look at the relationship Jesus had with the two groups that held power in his society in Palestine. One group consisted of the Roman occupiers – the Roman governor, his bureaucrats, his army and his tax collectors. The other group consisted of the Judaic authorities.

In the course of his ministry, Jesus recruited a tax collector, healed a Roman centurion's servant and expressed a view about the Roman tax that was not anti-Roman.[7] In his last days, Jesus encountered the Roman governor, Pontius Pilate.[8] It is clear from this encounter and from all the other incidents with Romans recounted that Jesus did not see the Romans as the primary target for his opposition or his anger. This was despite the fact that they were a foreign occupying force in his country.

Jesus reserved the full force of his anger and his eloquence for the religious leaders of the time. Of this there is no doubt. His attacks on

---

5   Jn.7:40-52
6   Mt.21:23-27
7   Lk.5:27-28; Mt.8:5-10; Mt.22:15-22
8   Jn.18:28-19:11

them were vitriolic. Even by today's standards, his language towards them was very strong. He called them: 'hypocrites', 'blind guides', 'fools', 'whitewashed tombs', 'serpents' and 'a brood of vipers'. He criticised them for their hypocrisy, for leading people astray, for money grabbing, for loading burdens on people whilst not carrying them themselves, for seeking out the places of honour, for parading their so-called virtues and holy practices in public, for not practising what they preached.

Below are some of his more shocking remarks:

'Alas for you, scribes and Pharisees, you hypocrites! You who are like whitewashed tombs that look handsome on the outside, but inside are full of dead men's bones and every kind of corruption. In the same way you appear to people from the outside like good honest men, but inside you are full of hypocrisy and lawlessness.'[9]

'If your virtue goes no deeper than the scribes and Pharisees, you will never get into the kingdom of heaven.'[10]

'Be on your guard against the yeast of the Pharisees and Sadducees.'[11]

'Alas for you lawyers who have taken away the key of knowledge! You have not gone in yourselves and have prevented others going in who wanted to.'[12]

Jesus's anger at the religious authorities was so much a part of his ministry that Matthew dedicated what is now a whole chapter of his gospel, Chapter 23, to illustrating this side of Jesus.

---

9   *Mt.23:27-28*
10   *Mt.5:20*
11   *Mt.16:6*
12   *Lk.11:52*

Jesus Uses Parables to Invert the Values of the Time

In other ways too, Jesus taught that we should not look to the example of religious leaders for how to live our lives. In the parable of the Good Samaritan[13], Jesus illustrated that the exemplary behaviour came from someone whom Jews despised – a Samaritan. A man had been attacked on the road by bandits and left for dead. The priest and the Levite had passed him by.

In the parable of the Pharisee and the tax collector[14], Jesus illustrated how the religious leader, who thought himself righteous and pleasing to 'God', was the one who was less at rights with 'God' than the sinner who was humble and repentant.

Jesus's Anger at Institutionalised Roles

All through the four canonical gospel accounts, Jesus relentlessly undermined the authority of the religious leaders of the time and discouraged his followers from giving them any unearned respect. He was not prepared to give respect to anyone whose religious role within society gave him an exalted position. If his attacks had been on specific individuals, one could argue that Jesus was not attacking the position as such but the corruption of the person in it. However, Jesus's attacks did not make this distinction. His attacks were on the groups as a whole – the priests, the Pharisees, the lawyers, the scribes, the Sadducees.

One can only deduce from this that Jesus was opposed to the role of institutionalised religious leaders, as such, because it exalted them among the people and because it inevitably led to abuse, bad example, oppressive teaching, distortion of the truth, false impressions and a failure to be of assistance to people on their spiritual paths.

Jesus's Faithfulness to the Judaic Tradition

Despite his criticism of the religious authorities, Jesus remained steeped in Judaic tradition. He attended the synagogue in his home town, went to Jerusalem for the festivals, visited the Temple there and regularly quoted from the sacred scriptures of the time.

However, Jesus took a creative and imaginative approach to this tradition.

---

13   Lk.10:29-37
14   Lk.18:9-14

When he read from the book of Isaiah in the synagogue one sabbath day, he gave a novel interpretation to the passage he was reading and then rankled some of his listeners with interpretations of some other passages which reflected badly on them. The result was a riot and he was lucky to escape with his life.[15]

In his disputes with the Pharisees, Jesus questioned their laws – the law, for example, that a woman caught committing adultery should be stoned to death.[16] He also questioned their interpretations of the 'Law' – for example, the law concerning work on the sabbath.[17]

In relation to the law on the sabbath, Jesus made the remarkable statement that: 'The sabbath is made for man and not man for the sabbath; so the Son of Man is master even of the sabbath.'[18] It is clear here that he is claiming authority even over the sacred laws and institutions, an authority that Judaism certainly did not give him.

Even the *Ten Commandments* were not so sacred to Jesus as to be untouchable. In his *Sermon on the Mount*, Jesus took a number of these commandments and added to them. So, for example, he said: 'You have learnt how it was said: "You must not commit adultery". But I say to you: if a man looks at a woman lustfully, he has already committed adultery with her in his heart.'[19]

In perhaps his most creative and imaginative act, Jesus adapted to his immediate circumstances the ritual of the Passover feast. This was an annual festival commemorating the Hebrew people's escape from Egypt. It was celebrated by every Jewish family in their own home. Strict guidelines for the ritual meal were laid down in the *Deuteronomic Code*[20] and in the *Torah*. Each family was expected to follow these guidelines.

Jesus was not intimidated by these external controls placed on the ceremony. He clearly felt free to use the unleavened bread and the wine of the meal to add his own layer of meaning to the feast.[21] He also introduced a completely

---

15   *Lk.4:16-30*
16   *J n.8:1-11*
17   *Lk.14:1-6*
18   *Mk.3:1-6*
19   *Mt.5:27-28*
20   *Dt.16:1-8*
21   *Mk.14; Mt.26; Lk.22*

new ritual to the occasion, the washing of feet.[22] Not only were these acts in contravention of the customs of the time, but he told his disciples to continue to do these things this way in memory of him. It must have been shocking for Jews to see Jesus tamper with such a sacred liturgy in this way.

Jesus Was an Anarchist

In relation to the Judaism of the time, Jesus was an anarchist, in the true sense of that word. He was against all forms of institutionalised hierarchical authority that tried to rule over or control people's spiritual lives. His clear teaching was that people were to be humble, were not to exalt themselves and were to spend their lives loving and serving each other. He announced a society based on equality, where the exalted would be humbled and the humble exalted, where nobody would be excluded and all would be equal. In this teaching, he left no room for domination or control of others of any kind. 'The greatest among you must behave as if he were the least, the leader as if he were the one who serves.'[23]

In practically all the Christian denominations extant today there are positions for ministers, hierarchies of power and dogmas, rules and rituals that must be adhered to. It is hard to see how Jesus would have wanted this situation or could condone it among people acting in his name. These churches and their officials must ask themselves the question: how do they see themselves avoiding the type of disapprobation Jesus meted out to similar structures and institutions in his own time?

In my view, the evidence in the four canonical gospel accounts is clear that while Jesus participated in, supported and approved of a spiritual tradition that was rooted in the Judaic people's story, he was fiercely opposed to the institutionalisation, politicisation and centralised control of this tradition by elites. The only power and authority he recognised in relation to Judaic spirituality was the power and authority of the spirit that lay within each individual. A central focus of his ministry was the release of that spirit within individuals, the encouragement of people to live according to that spirit and the condemnation of all institutional structures that tried to hijack, compromise or suppress it.

---

22   *Jn.13*
23   *Lk.22:24-27*

Stillness

I emerged from the passage of stone walls,
My steps rapid, my breath intense,
To face a huge sea swelling and crashing,
Sending tremors through the cliffs beneath me.
With thoughts too tight, I sat,
Stilled myself
And slowly began to let go
One by one, the clinging webs of doubt.

The water, single unity, curved three times
Before it smashed many feet high and breathed upon me its spray,
Leaving me refreshed and grinning.
The light, a hidden orb peeping from the cloud,
Announced its departure.
It was a smooth farewell that stirred
Some murmured promise.

When I walked away, there rested upon the horizon
A fading pink blush, that silhouetted the stone walls.
My step was easy and integral
To the surrounding sounds.
There appeared a single star in the sharp blue sky,
A woman had come to milk her cow.
I came home knowing I had heard, seen and touched
Truth.

Tess Harper

5

CHRISTIANITY
EVOLVING FROM JUDAISM

Christianity emerged out of Judaism but mutated from it. While remaining monotheistic, it was different from Judaism in that it replaced Moses with Jesus and disconnected itself from the Judaic 'Law'. Its disconnection from the 'Law' and consequently from a strong central authority structure, led to its diversification. Christianity, both geographically and intellectually, spread in all directions at once.

Christianity has its roots in Judaic monotheism. Jesus was a Jew, all his work was among the Jewish people and all his immediate disciples were Jews. While Jesus sought radical reform within Judaism, he never questioned its monotheism. To Jesus, the fundamental tenet of Judaism – that there was one god in heaven and that this god had spoken through Moses – was acceptable. As Christianity developed, the monotheism of Judaism was taken as a given.

After the death of Jesus, the followers of Jesus remained Jewish and were located mostly in Jerusalem. However, they suffered increasing persecution from the Jewish authorities, because their teachings were regarded as blasphemous. In the year 70 CE the Romans sacked Jerusalem. The followers of Jesus, as well as the Jews themselves, were scattered. They regrouped in Antioch, among other places and from then on began to see themselves as Christians rather than as Jews.

Christianity now began to spread through the Roman empire and even further afield. In the early stages of this expansion, it continued to focus on the conversion of Jews and thought of itself as a Jewish sect. However, the apostle Paul was instrumental in broadening its horizons to include non-Jewish people. It is clear from Paul's writings that these non-Jewish converts to Christianity were not required to take on Jewish practices such as circumcision and abstinence from the eating of pork. This widened further the gap between Christianity and Judaism.

While early Christianity inherited, without question, the monotheism of Judaism, it differed from Judaism in that it saw Jesus as the promised Messiah. Judaism had heard the voice of 'God' through Moses, but Christianity claimed to hear the renewed and ultimate voice of 'God' through Jesus.

As Christianity separated itself from Judaism, it lost the unifying force of the Judaic Law. That 'Law' had facilitated a centralised authority structure that controlled the beliefs, practices and behaviour of all Jews. Without it, Christianity spread in many different directions. There were no control mechanisms over its growing diversity. With the passing of the first few centuries after the death of Jesus, that diversity increased exponentially.

Although from the beginning Christianity did have in place the essential foundation on which to build a hierarchical structure of authority – namely, a supreme god in heaven, who had spoken through his chosen messenger, Jesus – that message was only gradually written down and no mechanisms were initially in place to control its content or interpretation.

From the end of the 1st century onwards, many different so-called 'gospels' appeared,[1] reflecting the diversity of Christian beliefs and practices in the early decades and centuries. Christianity is today familiar with only four gospels, those of Matthew, Mark, Luke and John. But in the early church there were many other accounts that we know of, such as the Gospel of Thomas, the Gospel of Peter and the Gospel of Matthias.

The early church of the 2nd and 3rd centuries was made up of small, scattered communities, mostly in cities. These communities were what one would call today 'house churches', that is, they met in each others' homes or in the sizeable homes of rich patrons. A community's size probably averaged no more than thirty people.[2]

---

1 Cf. http://www.ntcanon.org/table.shtml for a complete list.
2 Cf. Robert Banks, *Paul's Idea of Community, The Early House Churches in their Historical Setting.* Exeter, Pater Noster Press, 1980.

The majority of Christians lived in the major cities that lay along the Mediterranean fringe. Rome, Nicea, Antioch, Jerusalem, Alexandria and Carthage all had substantial Christian communities. Each of them had a bishop as leader. But there were no church buildings or ways of coming together as a large community.

One can identify at least four different approaches to Christianity at this time, influenced by four key patriarchal figures: Peter, Paul, James and John. Each of these represented a strand of Christianity. Various communities within the Christian diaspora identified themselves with one or other of these:

- The Petrine strand, representing St Peter, emphasised authority, orthodoxy and the importance of an institutional church. The Roman Christians stood for this position.
- The Pauline strand, representing St Paul, emphasised community and the use of all the diverse gifts (charisms) within that community. Various communities founded by Paul throughout Greece stood for this position.
- The strand represented by James emphasised the continuity of Christianity with Judaism and sought to conserve as much as possible of that link. The Jerusalem Christians stood for this position.
- The Johannine strand, following St John the evangelist, emphasised freedom, the Holy Spirit and a mystical, feminine and creative approach to the Christian story. The Christian community of Ephesus stood for this position.

Diversity within Christianity from the 2nd to the 4th century was also clearly evident from the wide variety of theological opinions that were in existence among these various communities. Christianity was still a marginal religion, with only a small number of adherents relative to the overall population, but it seems that every group of Christians had its own opinions and was ready to voice them. We only know of the opinions that caused controversy, because the conflicts that arose led to copious writings, some of which have survived to the present time.[3]

---

3   J.N.D. Kelly, *Early Christian Doctrines*. Continuum International, 2000.

The known conflicts in belief that occurred during this period included: Sabellianism, Docetism, Monophysitism, Adoptionism, Apollinarianism, Arianism, Socianism, Donatism, Gnosticism and Pelagianism. The early Christian world was a ferment of debate and argument and every group held on to its own opinions.

One could argue that this diversity of opinion was a good thing. Diversity in nature is a good thing, so it should be a good thing among humans. Nature, when not interfered with by humans, creates diversity all the time. It is humans alone who have wanted to restrict diversity and impose the dominance of one opinion, one political system or one economic system over all others.

Had this diversification been allowed to continue, the Christian story would doubtless have found its way into many different cultures and societies and taken on a particular expression in each. It might well have spread throughout the world, as Jesus had requested.[4] However, it would have taken on diverse forms. Each culture would have inculturated the story for its own use. The Christian story would have travelled the route of many other myths and legends that crossed boundaries into other cultures and found a new and different expression within each.

However, this was not to happen. The diversification of Christianity took place more or less within the confines of the Roman empire. Throughout the empire, theological controversies raged among Christian factions. Each faction fought to have its own particular opinion achieve a dominant position among Christians. These controversies disturbed the *Pax Romanum* and occasionally led to violence in the cities and towns. In the year 325 BCE the emperor intervened. Something very new began to happen.

---

4 *Mark 16:15*

Questioning God

I may be stupid, but I want to ask you a few questions which puzzle me.
Go ahead.

You say you are a father?
Yes, I am the father of all creation.

And is there a mother of all creation too?
No.

How can there be a father and not a mother?
When you are god you can do anything.

Didn't you have a son?
Yes. His name is Jesus.

And didn't he have a mother?
Yes. That was Mary. But she was a human.

You had sex with a human to have this child?
No. Certainly not. The child was placed in her womb.

You mean she was a surrogate mother?
You could say that.

Do you mind me asking – have you had sex with anybody?
Please don't ask me that. I find the topic offensive.

Sorry. But isn't there somebody that you live with – the Holy Ghost
or something?
Yes. The Holy Spirit.

Is this a man or a woman?
Neither.

Bisexual?
No. I am getting angry now. What is all this obsession about sex?

Sorry. I am just trying to get my head around it. You are a single father, no sign of your partner or wife, have one son but didn't perform sex to have him, and you are living with someone who is neither male nor female nor bisexual!

One final question: as you are god, and the only god around, does this mean that people who believe in you should be following your example?

Dara Molloy

6

ROMAN CHRISTIANITY
THE FIRST GLOBAL CORPORATION

This chapter traces the development of the Roman model of Christianity as a corporate structure. The process began in the 4th century and has continued through to the present time. The papacy, once established, was always at the centre of this development. Key moments within the process were: the reign of Emperor Constantine, the collapse of the Roman empire, the great schism, the Gregorian reform and the Reformation.

Today, the world is filled with global corporations. These are multinational bodies that make modern products and services available throughout the world. Their primary objective is financial profit. For a significant number of them, their annual budget is larger than the gross national product of many countries.

These corporations are normally owned by shareholders who leave the running of the company to a chief executive and his or her professional staff. While these corporations have to respect the laws of any country in which they operate, often their power is so great, in terms of the amount of money they can pour into a country and the number of jobs they can create, that in reality they can operate with impunity. Today there are so many of them that together they constitute a dominant political force in the world – one which is non-democratic, unaccountable and non-transparent.

One can trace the origins of global corporations back to the 4th century. At the time of Jesus, global corporations did not exist. The only institutional structures Jesus encountered were those associated with Judaism on the one hand and the Roman empire on the other. Neither of these were global corporations as we know them today, even though the Roman empire had global ambitions at the time.

We now know that, in order for a corporation to be successful globally, it must be able to develop and distribute a product or a service and convince people to purchase it. These ideas and this language are familiar to people today. But in the time of Jesus and the early Christians, they did not exist.

The early Christians produced texts, or gospels, which claimed to record the words and actions of Jesus. In each of these gospels is found, repeated in a number of different ways, a clear indication from Jesus that he wanted his message to spread throughout the world. So, one can take it that, from the beginning, Christianity had global ambitions. The challenge for these early Christians was how they could make this happen.

In the first few centuries after the death of Jesus, Christianity did indeed spread, in small pockets, out through the Roman empire and even further afield. However, as it spread it changed. People responded to it in different ways. Egyptians took one view of it, Romans took another. Jews who had converted to Christianity tended to hold on to their Jewish practices, while the non-Jewish had other ideas. Everybody had their own interpretation of the Jesus story. There were constant disputes among his followers as to who he was and what was his message. Knowledge of Jesus and his message was spreading throughout the world but it was not the same Jesus, nor the same message, in every place.

The development of an institutional form of Christianity with its headquarters in Rome was one response to this challenge.

The Emperor Constantine

In the year 313 CE, Constantine became the new Roman Emperor. Although he did not accept baptism until close to his death, he was favourably disposed towards Christianity from the beginning. On his instalment as emperor, he declared an end to all persecution of Christians. He began to promote the Christian faith, building churches and granting privileges to priests and bishops.

Constantine was troubled by the constant disputes and controversies among Christians. In some cases, these disputes were causing social unrest and even violence in parts of his empire. In 325 CE, he called together some of the leaders of the Christian churches to meet at Nicea. At this council he focussed the church leaders' attention on finding a formula of beliefs to which they could all subscribe. This formula became known as the Nicene Creed, a statement of beliefs which, since then, has been the established orthodoxy (literally 'right teaching') among Christians.

Here, for the first time among Christians, was a package of beliefs that was centrally established as the body of belief to which every Christian should subscribe. The locus of authority had shifted from the individual and the local Christian community to the whole community of Christians within the empire. For the moment, that authority rested ultimately with the Roman emperor, but in the future it would shift to the Roman papacy.

Christianity now began developing in a different way to Judaism. Judaism had developed the 'Law' as the central controlling mechanism of its religion. The 'Law' controlled people's external behaviour. Christianity began the process of establishing belief as the central controlling mechanism. Controlling what people were to believe meant controlling people's minds and hearts, even their souls. It was a step further than controlling their external behaviour.

Christians who, in the 2nd and 3rd centuries, had been persecuted for their beliefs, were now about to persecute others who did not subscribe to the beliefs contained in the Nicene Creed. A revolution had occurred. The movement towards uniformity and centralisation, so necessary for any corporate body, had begun.

Centralised Leadership

Christianity now began to grow exponentially throughout the empire. Over the course of the 4th century, it became the dominant religion, pushing out polytheism wherever it was found. In the year 380 CE, the emperor Theodosius declared Christianity to be the official religion of the empire and the bishop of Rome was given the title 'Pontifex Maximus' (head priest). Until that time, the emperor himself had been the Pontifex Maximus. As of the year 380 CE, all citizens of the empire were expected to convert to Christianity.

The promotion of Christianity to an exalted position within the Roman empire presented irresistible opportunities to the leadership within Christianity. The bishop of Rome became equal in status to the emperor. Christian leaders were gifted with fine churches, tax exemptions and positions of honour. The possibilities for Christianity seemed endless.

As Christianity adapted to these new opportunities, its administration took on the political structure of the Roman empire. The bishop of Rome began to see himself as the head of a spiritual empire. He claimed primacy in the church over other Christian bishops.

Prior to the 4th century, the bishop of Rome's claim to primacy had not been readily granted by the other bishops within Christendom. Each major Christian community carefully guarded its own sovereignty. Jerusalem, Alexandria, Antioch and other cities of the Roman empire were centres of Christian authority in their own right and were unwilling to let all this authority go to Rome. After the foundation of Constantinople (now Istanbul) as the new headquarters of the emperor in 330, the Christians of Constantinople also laid claim to primacy. This claim was to cause much greater problems in centuries to come, when it led to the break between the eastern Christian church and Rome.

The bishop of Rome argued that both Peter and Paul had died in Rome. The bishop of Rome was the successor of Peter and Paul. Therefore, the argument went, primacy had shifted from Jerusalem to Rome during the lifetime of the apostles.

By the end of the 4th century, Rome's claim to primacy could no longer be resisted with any conviction. The majority of Christian communities accepted that Christianity would benefit from some central coordination. They reluctantly accepted Rome as that centre.

Supported by the emperor, Christian leaders now worked to create an infrastructure that would make the primacy of the bishop of Rome effective. This was modelled on the political structure of the Roman empire so that an ecclesiastical empire developed alongside the secular empire.

As the *Pontifex Maximus* of the ecclesiastical empire, the bishop of Rome took on the trappings of an emperor. He dressed in gold and silk, wore satin shoes, was carried in public in an uplifted throne shaded by a canopy and fanned by ostrich feathers. He was addressed as 'Most Holy Father'. People prostrated themselves at his feet and kissed the ring on his hand. To this day, a person writing to the pope is advised to begin the letter with the words 'Prostrate at the feet of Your Holiness, I have the honour to profess myself, with the most profound respect, Your Holiness's most humble servant.'[1]

Bishops became known as 'princes of the church'. This title gave them parity of status with the secular princes of the time. The regal dress code of these secular princes became a bishop's formal liturgical dress. Bishops began to live in 'palaces', took the title 'Lord' and wore rings that their subjects were expected to kiss. The word 'diocese', nowadays exclusively associated with areas of church jurisdiction, originally referred to a division of a prefecture, or a political sub-division, of the Roman empire.

From the late 4th century onwards, the two empires, ecclesiastical and secular, worked in parallel. For centuries to come, kings and emperors would try to influence the appointment of popes and bishops; popes and bishops would try to influence the appointment of kings and emperors. The political structure and the ecclesiastical structure imitated and fed off each other.

Historically it can be seen that this new structure gave the papacy an advantage even over the emperor. The pope, although equal in status to the emperor, was in a position to appeal to an authority higher than both of them – the divine authority of 'God', transmitted through Jesus and through the scriptures. The emperor would have to defer to the pope in these matters. The papacy had put itself into a position where it could, in the future, literally rule the world.

The Collapse of the Roman Empire

When the Roman empire collapsed in the 5th century, the newly institutionalised Roman Christianity was hit hard and struggled for survival. Its corporate structure, so identified with the empire, now had to find a way of surviving independently. This took a while. Things were going to get worse before they got better.

In the 5th century, Rome was sacked by the Goths. The Roman pope was replaced by a Gothic pope. The Goths were Arians: that is to say, they believed that Jesus was a lesser being than 'God' and they rejected the Trinity. Arianism also had a great tolerance for diversity in beliefs. Had

---

1   Cf. www.newadvent.org>Catholic Encyclopedia>Addresses

the papacy remained in the hands of the Goths, the corporate structure of the church would have unravelled.

However, the papacy was quickly won back by the Roman Christians. Not only that – by the end of the 6th century, the Goths, who had spread throughout Spain, southern France and north-west Africa, had accepted the version of Christianity proclaimed by Rome and turned away from Arianism.

In this period of political turmoil, Roman Christianity learned an important lesson about itself. While it had political power – that is, power to manage and control people – that political power was different and separate from that of an emperor or king. The political power of the latter was exercised within the boundaries of a geographical empire. The political power of a pope did not have this geographical limitation. The pope ruled over an ecclesiastical territory and that territory could potentially extend into any political jurisdiction. The pope could use to his advantage an alliance with a political power but his own political power was substantial. That power rested in his ability to manage and control Christianity as practised by the majority of Christians, no matter in what political jurisdiction these Christians lived.

Roman Christianity now became a political power in its own right. In Italy and in Rome in particular, the papacy acquired large amounts of property. By the 6th century, the pope was effectively the ruler of Rome. By the beginning of the 8th century, the papal states around Rome were formally established in a treaty with the Lombards.

The emergence of Christianity as a corporate entity independent of the state after the collapse of the Roman empire was an entirely new social phenomenon. Here was a corporate entity that had political power and social influence but did not have a limited geographical jurisdiction. Its essence was religious belief. It could infiltrate other political structures without collapsing them and live symbiotically within them.

As early as the first half of the 5th century, corporate Christianity, with its headquarters in Rome, was actively evangelising different parts of Europe. It sent missionaries both to Britain and Ireland, for example, during this period. However, with the gradual collapse of the Roman empire during the 5th century, the struggle for its own survival became paramount and during the latter half of the century missionary activity ceased. By the end of the 6th century, Roman Christianity had regrouped and we see missionary efforts beginning again. In 597, for example, a new mission was sent to Britain.

During this period, the Roman papacy learned the importance of building political alliances. In areas where it wished to evangelise, it developed relationships with the local political leaders, then moved in with its evangelists. The gradual success of these efforts throughout Europe increased the power of the papacy. By the end of the 8th century, the pope's ecclesiastical jurisdiction was far greater than any one political jurisdiction. The pope was claiming the power to select, crown and even depose emperors.

In the year 800, Pope St Leo III crowned Charlemagne as emperor of what was later to become known as the Holy Roman empire and also the first Reich. This was a loose confederation of German and Italian territories. By doing so, the pope fulfilled papal ambitions to be on a par with or even superior to a powerful emperor. In the process, he immensely increased papal wealth and papal political power.[2]

The Great Schism

In 1054, the ambitions of the papacy to unify Christianity throughout the known world received a cataclysmic setback. In this year, the great schism between eastern and western Christianity formally began. This schism had been brewing since the time when the emperor Constantine, in the 4th century, had moved his residence from Rome to Constantinople. Constantine's move led to the development of the eastern Byzantine empire and its parallel Christian church with its own 'patriarch' or supreme leader. This half of the empire survived the collapse of its western counterpart. Because of this, eastern Christianity remained strong while western Europe went through its dark ages.

At the time of the split in 1054, the differences between eastern and western Christianity were numerous. These differences did not, however,

---

2   This first Germanic-Italian empire lasted, in various forms, from the year 800 to the year 1806. The second Germanic empire lasted from 1871 to 1918. Adolf Hitler used the concept of the Third Reich (1934-1945) to link his ambitions for building a Germanic empire to these first and second Germanic empires.

include matters of faith. Orthodoxy had been established during the ecumenical councils of earlier centuries, with only a minority of dissenters. But the eastern churches had their own ways of performing their rites. Their dominant language was Greek and not Latin. They did not impose celibacy upon all of their clergy. Most significantly, they acknowledged the pope as having an honorary title only and did not accept that he had any power to make decisions.

For the papacy, it was not tolerable that parts of Christianity should remain outside its control. The Roman papacy was intent upon imposing its rules, its calendar, its language and its rituals in a uniform way throughout Christendom. Roman Christianity's vision of itself as a centralised corporate entity could not tolerate independent churches or loose federations. When the papacy began to enforce changes on the eastern churches, the formal split came. The two sides became permanently divided over the issue. Pope Leo IX and subsequent popes claimed superiority over the four eastern church patriarchs, while the patriarchs themselves claimed that the Fourth Ecumenical Council, the Council of Chalcedon in 451, had established equality between the bishop of Constantinople and the bishop of Rome.

The Gregorian Reform

In the 11th century, the Roman corporate church took another great leap forward in enhancing its own power and securing its future. Although named the Gregorian reform, after Pope Gregory VII, this reform movement began with Pope Leo IX in 1049, about thirty years before Pope Gregory VII. It did not reach completion until the fourth Lateran Council of 1215 called by Pope Innocent III. It therefore spanned almost two hundred years.

Pope Gregory VII was the main engine of this reform. He enunciated and enforced a vision of the church and Christianity that enhanced his power and authority over both secular leaders and over his own bishops and clergy. His vision was the following:

- The Christian church based in Rome was founded by 'God' and entrusted with the task of embracing all humankind in a single society.

- In this society, the only legitimate law was the divine will.
- The Christian church, in its capacity as a divine institution, is supreme over all human structures, especially the secular state.
- The pope, in his role as head of this church, is the vice-regent of 'God' on earth, so that disobedience to him implies disobedience to 'God'.

Had he fully realised this vision he would have become irrefutably the supreme leader of the whole world.

The reform set about, among other things, disentangling the Christian church from political meddling. The pope wished to remove church ownership and control, both actual and symbolic, from the lay lords. On the other side, he wished to disentangle the clergy from all involvement in politics and property. Putting it simply, the pope wished to separate church and state. The papacy regarded the lay lords of the time as having too much power and influence over church matters and it regarded the clergy as being too involved in worldly affairs.

With regard to the involvement of laity in church matters, two particular issues had to be dealt with. One was the practice of simony – the purchasing of church positions. The other was lay investiture. In the investiture controversy, kings were involved in the appointment of bishops and in the ritual of their investiture. At this ritual, the king bestowed upon the newly appointed bishop his ring and staff. However, the papacy contended that these were symbols of spiritual authority and that it was not appropriate for kings to bestow them. The papacy fought to take this role from the kings and give it to its own clergy. A great victory was won by the papacy in this regard, even though the controversy lingered on in various forms up to and even after, the 17th century.

Removing the clergy from involvement in worldly affairs meant that drastic measures had to be taken. Worldly affairs included having wives and children. Although this papacy was not the first to try to impose clerical celibacy, it was more ruthless in its imposition of it than any before. The children of priests were declared illegitimate. The papacy did not want church property being inherited by a priest's family, so a law was passed to prevent this.

During this time, wives and children were brutally removed from priests. In many cases, they became serfs and slaves of the church because they had nowhere else to go. Priests were forced to live in common residencies, sleeping in dormitories and eating in refectories. Married clergy had their revenues removed. Lay people were given permission to disobey their bishop if he did not impose celibacy on his clergy. Later they were even encouraged to physically remove married clergy from church property.

This disconnection of the clergy from their wives and from feminine influence was a further step on the journey towards disconnectedness written about in Chapter 3. The monotheistic god is a male god with no female partner. He does not perform sexual acts. He lives alone, disconnected from the earth and from everything feminine. Like all myths, this myth sets an archetypical pattern or template. It invites humans to live according to that pattern. The monotheistic myth is at the root of human prejudice and discrimination against women. It is not surprising, therefore, that it gets its most extreme expression within monotheistic religions.

Gregory set up the Roman Curia as a central bureaucracy to administer the newly-reformed church. He gathered all of the laws of the church into a legal code entitled Canon Law and added laws that enhanced his own authority. The overall result of this reform was:

- The increased power of the papacy.
- The increased power of the clergy, who now effectively constituted the church.
- The marginalisation of the laity, particularly women and children.

In corporate terms, the church corporation consisted of the pope, who was chief executive and his clergy, who were staff. The laity were those to whom services and products were provided for their consumption.

The ruthlessness and self-righteousness with which this reform was enacted throughout Christendom led inevitably to the Inquisition. The Inquisition was an organised way of dealing with heretics, through prosecution and tribunals. From around 1184, the combined papal and royal forces began to enforce orthodox doctrine vigorously. Opposition was dealt with by force of arms and thousands were slaughtered. Horrific massacres took place in which no distinction was made between the innocent and the guilty. The laity were subdued, forbidden to preach and allowed only restricted access to the Bible. Clerical power was supreme, reinforced by the threat of violence.

Hans Kung[3] has isolated the five central features of this Gregorian reform:

- **Centralisation** – around the absolute power of the papacy.
- **Legislation** – rooted in the new science of Canon Law.
- **Politicisation** – the primacy of ecclesiastical power over state power.
- **Militarisation** – the imposition of military solutions to society's problems using combined papal and royal forces. This continued in the crusading movement.
- **Clericalisation** – the almost total identification of clergy and church and the intense concentration of clerical effort on the control of church and society through the administration of law and sacrament.

During the course of this 'reform', the corporate Roman church, with the pope as chief executive, had greatly enhanced its position as a male, hierarchical, dictatorial and clerical institution. It had become very far removed from the vision, teaching and life example of its founder, Jesus, but was now well on its way towards becoming a truly global institution.

The Reformation Onwards

The Reformation in the 16th century opposed these Gregorian so-called reforms and tried to reverse them. All of the reformers of this time – Martin Luther, John Calvin, Huldreich Zwingli and John Wesley – rejected the papacy outright, both its spiritual and temporal power. They also, to various degrees, tried to restore the role and status of the laity. Within the

---

3   Cf. Hans Küng, *The Catholic Church: A Short History.* Modern Library, 2003.

Protestant churches, progress was made in the reinstatement of the male laity in leadership roles, but the inclusion of women was to come much more slowly.

Ironically, the Reformation strengthened the claim of the papacy to primacy within the Roman church. The Gregorian reforms in the 12th century had met with great resistance from both laity and clergy. There had been turbulence all over Europe. Bishops did not want to cede their powers to the pope. Although the papacy had largely won these battles, there remained a continuing undercurrent of resistance and discontent. When Protestantism finally split from Rome, it took with it all these dissenters. The Roman church was left with those who were compliant. For those who did not side with the reformers, the papacy became more important than ever.

After the Reformation, the papacy had an opportunity to further increase its powers. In 1870, a decree of the Fifth Lateran Council declared that the pope had primacy of jurisdiction over all bishops and that the pope's teaching was infallible in matters of doctrine.

From 1870 to the present time, the power and status of the papacy has been maintained. At present, it exercises power over more members of the Roman church than ever before and enjoys a prestige and influence worldwide far beyond its own jurisdiction.

Over a period of seventeen hundred years, the power of the papacy gradually established itself, so that it became supremely powerful both ecclesiastically and politically and put into place as it did so the mechanisms for its own survival. In the course of that history, it exercised a central and dominant influence over the development of Europe after the collapse of the Roman empire and later over the development of the new world, in the colonial countries and elsewhere.

While Judaism introduced the world to monotheism and was the first to develop a societal structure based on it, it was not until the expansion of Christianity took place, throughout the Roman empire, that the idea of a feasible global project began to emerge. Based ultimately on beliefs and not on geography, this project was not limited by the boundaries of political empires. The church achieved its ambitions by encouraging people to subscribe to its package of beliefs and then to avail of its services. With this formula, its influence could reach the farthest ends of the earth, just as that of multinational corporations does today.

It is ironic that Western secular society today embodies in its political structures more of the human values promoted by Jesus than does the largest denominational church that operates in his name. While the development of Western society has led to a greater emphasis on democracy, equal rights, gender balance, transparency, justice and due process, the Christian church of Rome has remained dictatorial, hierarchical, male dominated, misogynist, homophobic and secretive.

The reason Roman Catholicism continues to practise a non-democratic, single-person, corporate leadership as its preferred structure of governance is clearly due to the effectiveness of that structure in achieving its global goals. It is the structure of a global corporation. Today, Roman Catholicism remains the largest of the Christian denominations. It has a solid presence in practically every country in the world. As a global corporation, its achievements remain unequalled and unrivalled by any other corporation.

A central thesis of this book is that Roman Christianity has provided the template for contemporary commercial global corporations. As Roman Christianity developed over the centuries, it learned by trial and error how it could, on the one hand, spread its influence globally and, on the other, maintain centralised control. It did this through, what we might now call, the provision of global products and services and the promotion of a system of global marketing and distribution, while at the same time maintaining and developing a strong centralised and hierarchical corporate structure.

While Roman Christianity was never historically focussed on making financial profits above all else and never developed the modern concept of shareholding, both of which are intrinsic to modern global corporations, nonetheless, in terms of its corporate structure and its mode of operation, it became a template for success for modern global corporations. To this day, there are strong parallels between the Roman Christian corporation that bases its activities on religion and the global corporations that base their activities on economics.

The following three chapters trace the development of the Roman church in its three intrinsic dimensions: as an efficient centralised authority, as a provider of religious products and services and as a promoter and distributor of these products and services worldwide. In today's world, all successful global commercial corporations have had to develop similar structures and systems.

Silenced Son

I see you there,
Deformed, in form of pride.
They did it to you —
A mind moulded and distorted
Into their shape.
Submitting to the sentence,
You paid this price.
What was the truth you voiced
Before they cut out your soul-tongue,
As sacrifice to the Mother cruel?
A screaming soul,
Dumb now.
Do you ever embrace
The truth in the darkness,
And weep
For the light they've destroyed,
The song that's ceased?

Tess Harper

7

CORPORATE CHRISTIANITY
DEVELOPING PRODUCTS AND SERVICES

The challenge facing the developing corporate Roman church of the 4th century was to fulfil its mandate to 'spread the good news throughout the world' without losing control of that 'good news'. To do this, it had to treat the 'good news' as a commercial company today would treat its product. Over the course of the following centuries, it developed the mechanisms to do that. It created uniformity throughout its jurisdiction and put structures in place to maintain that uniformity. Each particular element became standardised, packaged and controlled. In this respect, its operations were no different than any modern commercial company with global ambitions.

Let us imagine that a particular indigenous tribe of people were discovered to have, as part of their diet, a flat cake of minced meat. A Western male entrepreneur discovers this and sees in it an opportunity to create a worldwide business. He takes the recipe for the flat cake of meat from the tribe and in his kitchen he experiments with making it in different ways and with variations in ingredients, until he comes up with a formula he is happy with. He then sets up a commercial corporation and opens his first restaurant. He calls the new invention he has patented a 'burger'.

His burger is a success and soon he has restaurants called after him all over the country. The burger replaces other forms of meat that people used to eat. Parents begin to send their children out to buy these burgers instead of cooking meals at home. Now the successful entrepreneur decides to go international. His restaurants begin to appear in cities all over the world. While minor adaptations are made to accommodate local culture and tastes, the basic recipe for the burger remains the same. The patented burger replaces the traditional foods of people in many different parts of the world. The burger becomes a standard worldwide food product, a fast food, unattached to any particular culture or region of the world. The global burger has the effect of replacing diverse local eating habits, practices and diets with a single culturally-disconnected product.

In order to achieve global dominance for a particular product or service, an entrepreneur or corporation may begin by extracting a relevant element from a particular culture. This element, in its raw form, is generally not suitable for mass distribution. It must be processed in some way so that it becomes standardised and universally applicable. Finally, it must be inserted into other cultures.

When the product or service of a multinational corporation is inserted into a new market, the objective is to 'corner the market'. If the campaign is successful, locally based enterprises or traditions will have been displaced and the lifestyle of the local people will have been drawn that little bit more into the global monoculture.

Commodification

The process of creating this uniform product is what we now call commodification. Something that is particular to a place or a people is extracted from that context and made into a universal product. Where it came from, or who was involved in its production, becomes irrelevant.

Most of what is available in shops today falls into the category of commodities. The item for sale is mass produced and distributed worldwide. It has lost its indigenous context, its local flavour and its cultural uniqueness. Most people today do not know or care where the sugar for Coca Cola comes from or the meat for the McDonald's burger. They do not know or care who the person was who harvested the beet that made the sugar, or tended the animal that produced the beef. This is the result of commodification. Before commodification, people generally knew where their food came from and who the people were who produced it. Commodification began, however, not with food, but with religious practice.

Before there were global products and services, there had to be global beliefs. The single, most important global belief necessary for the spread of global products and services was that one god created this earth and that that god lived outside the earth somewhere in the heavens.

The spread of this uniform belief through different cultures removed the diversity of gods and goddesses from the landscape and the human environment and cleared the way for the spread of a global way of life that would encompass everybody and everything.

There Is No Alternative

The causes of the death of diversity have their roots in mythology. Mythology underpins all human behaviour. It is the explanations we give ourselves as to the more mysterious aspects of life: what purpose it all has, what great power lies behind it, how we all came to be. Mythologies are culturally created ways of understanding these mysteries.

When the world was a less unified, less globalised place, many diverse cultures existed, each with their own mythologies, or ways of understanding the world. But with the spread of monotheism, followed by the spread of economic globalisation, one mythology has been made universal and the richness of diverse cultures have been weakened as people are drawn into a more globalised way of living. If there is only one god and that god is in heaven, then everything can be unified under him. Once 'God' is in heaven, there is only one way of seeing things and that is his way. When translated into our lives, that means that there is only one way to live life as humans on this planet. There is no alternative (TINA).

Monotheism provides a justification for the dominant viewpoint prevalent in today's world that Western culture has all the answers. From this viewpoint, Western democracy, Western capitalism, Western education, Western health systems and Western consumerism are the answers for everybody, everywhere. It is a fundamentalist viewpoint. Many people today and in some cases their governments, hold this view with religious fervour. They do not see any salvation, any future, for humankind outside of it. They are intent on creating a global monoculture and are ready even to impose this on others who do not want it, out of concern for the people's good.

The Cuckoo's Egg

A cuckoo is a bird that does not make a nest of its own. It lays its eggs in another bird's nest, usually one egg per nest. The unsuspecting dunnock or warbler sits on this egg with all her other eggs and hatches it out. The hatched cuckoo is genetically programmed to push the other eggs or hatched nestlings out of the nest and to take all the food that the foster-mother delivers for itself. It grows big and fat at a rapid rate, until it is much bigger than the foster-mother, much bigger than the nest and is ready to leave. A baby cuckoo is, in biological terms, a parasite.

Globalisation operates like the parasitic cuckoo. A global product or service, once it establishes itself in the nest of a particular culture or place, pushes out the work of more local enterprises and takes all the resources for itself. Today, we see this process happening quite clearly all over the world. But in centuries past, Christian missions operated in exactly the same way. Christian missions offered global products and services of a religious nature, such as baptism and communion, but the effect was the same. The local spiritual practices and the people who were involved in their performance, were pushed aside. Diverse local mythologies in many different parts of the world were replaced by a uniform global mythology.

In the past there were Christian church missions, today there are McDonald's food outlets. Whether it is a baptism or a burger that is being offered, the effect is the same. The church mission will try to sideline all the other local deities; McDonald's restaurant will try to sideline all the other local food operators.

As the parasitic cuckoo process continues, more global products are inserted into a particular culture or place. The end result is that everything local, everything about that culture and place that is particular to it and an expression of it, is eradicated, or put under threat of extinction, or morphed into a global product in its own right. Once the introduction of global products or services to a particular culture and place begins, local people's beliefs, lifestyles and language begin to change and adjust in a predictable progression, all moving in the one direction towards globalised and uniform monocultural living.

An End to Diversity

The hierarchical and centralised structure of authority emerging in the 4th century in the Roman Christian church created the possibility of bringing uniformity to that church. Christianity had developed in the first few centuries in diverse ways. There were diverse styles of leadership, diversity in the way ceremonies were performed, diverse languages in use, diverse beliefs and diverse interpretations of the life and message and even identity, of Jesus.

Nature has a built-in tendency to create diversity. Over millions of years, the evolutionary process has led to an ever broadening and multiplying array of life-forms. Because of this natural tendency to diversify, we have inherited a wonderful diversity of living organisms in the world. Within humanity, we have inherited a rich diversity of cultures, including languages and lifestyles.

Language Diversity

In the biblical story of the Tower of Babel[1], the whole world was made up of one people who spoke a common language. These people decided to create a city and a tower 'with its top reaching heaven'. Their god Yahweh came to have a look at the work and was alarmed. He said: 'They are one people and they have one language. If they carry this through, nothing they decide to do from now on will be impossible.' He stopped the project. The men were scattered across the face of the earth and their language was 'confused', so that they could no longer communicate with each other.

In this story, an explanation for the diversity of languages in the world is presented. It is seen as a deliberate act of 'God' to prevent humankind from 'reaching heaven'. Being united as one people speaking one language gave humankind that possibility, so 'God' scattered them and confused their language.

Although this story is as old as history itself, it remains relevant to our world today. While an evolutionary view of the earth would explain the diversity of languages as something positive that better ensures the survival of the human species, this biblical view sees language diversity as an obstacle placed in the way of humankind's global ambitions. This is indeed the case. The agenda of economic globalisation in today's world requires that more and more people across the earth speak the one language or at least are able to communicate with one another.

Language is an expression of a people living a certain way of life in a certain place. Languages have developed and survived because

---

particular natural boundaries have contained a people within a particular geographical area, an area large enough for them to survive. Within this area, they have developed, over many centuries, not just their own language but their own culture and their own way of life. When the language of a people dies, it is a clear indication that the culture and way of life of that people are also dead or dying. The death of a language is the tip of the iceberg. Beneath its death is the death of a culture and way of life of a people associated with a particular place. When languages die, we lose not only diversity of languages, but all the knowledge, skills and wisdom associated with particular ways of living.

Since the beginning of humankind's existence on this earth, language has developed and changed and diversified. Many languages have come and gone. Language extinction has been a natural occurrence throughout humankind's existence. In ancient times, certain languages achieved dominance within expanding empires, only to dissipate again when these empires collapsed. However, with the rise of political ambitions for global dominance in late medieval times, the diversity of languages and the cultures that they represented, came under serious threat. The expansion of European empires into the New World during this period destroyed many languages and cultures and achieved the dominance of languages such as English, Spanish, Portuguese and French across whole continents far from Europe, a dominance that still exists today.

The loss of cultural diversity today is alarming. About half of the estimated 6,000 languages spoken on earth are now spoken only by adults who no longer teach them to their children. 50 per cent of the earth's spoken languages are about to die. An additional 40 per cent may soon be threatened because the number of children learning them is declining measurably. In other words, 90 per cent of existing languages today are likely to die or become critically weak within the next century. That leaves 600 or so languages, 10 per cent of the world's total, that remain relatively secure – for now. In the 21st century, up to 5,000 of the 6,000 languages spoken today could be lost.

Latin – The Universal Language of the Roman Church

Long before the colonial expansion of Europe, the corporate Christian church was already making serious attempts to achieve its global ambitions and these ambitions included the promotion of a single language – Latin.

Latin had been the language of the Roman empire. With the integration of Christianity into the Roman empire in the 4th century, Latin also became the dominant language of Christianity, taking over from Greek. The barbarian invasions, in the 5th century, led to the collapse of the Roman empire and during the Dark Ages Latin lost its dominant position throughout Europe. It died as a language among the common people and in its place gradually emerged the diversity of languages that we find throughout Europe today.

Latin would have died altogether had Roman Christianity not kept it alive. In the interests of its global agenda, the Roman church found the language to be an essential tool. From the time of the Dark Ages onwards, Latin was maintained as the official language of that church. It used Latin as its official means of communication and for its laws, documents, ceremonies and rites. Its bishops, priests and monks were trained in the use of Latin from this time on.

To this day, Latin remains the official language of the Roman church. Popes continue to publish their encyclicals and other major writings in Latin. The Second Vatican Council, a gathering of all the bishops of the Roman church in the 1960s, was conducted in Latin and its official documents were published in Latin. Until the 1960s, the Mass was celebrated in Latin throughout the world and students for the priesthood conducted their theological studies through the medium of Latin. Latin was a subject taught in most schools in the Western world until the final decades of the 20th century.

From the time that Christianity initiated its global project in the 4th century through to the Vatican Council of the 1960s, the Latin language was an essential tool of the Roman church in bringing about and maintaining conformity and uniformity throughout its international organisation. Latin was established as the language of what became known as 'the Universal Church'.

In the same way today, the English language has become a tool for the business community throughout the world to conduct its global business. Both Roman Christianity and modern-day global corporations concur with the biblical view that diversity in languages is a barrier to humankind's global ambitions. In this, they work against the evolutionary principle that diversity is good and necessary for survival.

Developing Global Products and Services

Globalisation is a process whereby humans through their corporations consciously focus on inserting a uniform product or service into diverse regions and cultures of the world. These insertions replace local diversity and create uniformity at the expense of that diversity.

From the 4th century onwards, we can trace a clear line of development of global products within the Christian corporation. It began with an attempt to unify the diversity of belief among Christians at that time.

In 325, at the Council of Nicea, the first official creed of the Roman church was promulgated. The Nicene creed, as a written series of statements of belief, became a universal teaching promoted by the Roman church. This creed listed what Christians were required to believe in order to achieve salvation. Not to believe in this creed was to court damnation for eternity in the fires of hell. Even to this day, this creed is recited in churches throughout the world. As a text, it is a well-established global ecclesiastical product.

Also during the 4th century, the canon of Christian scriptures was established.[2] This canon excluded many versions of the 'gospels' that were in circulation at that time. It reduced the number of acceptable gospels to four – those of Matthew, Mark, Luke and John. Other documents, such as the letters of St Paul and the *Acts of the Apostles*, were also chosen for inclusion in this canon. Together, the creation of the Nicene creed and the canon of scriptures put a tight control on what Christians should or should not believe. 'Orthodoxy' became a word for the practice of Christianity within these tight controls.

Following the successful establishment of orthodoxy, the Roman church then began to develop, over the coming centuries, what one might now call religious products and services. These included the seven sacraments (Eucharist, Baptism, Confirmation, Marriage, Ordination,

---

2   Cf. http://www.ntcanon.org/

Blessing of the Sick and Confession), the *Roman Ritual*, the Roman calendar and the Benedictine rule. As these developed, what distinguished them from traditional Christian practices in particular geographical areas was their universality and uniformity. There was centralised control behind their usage.

For the Roman church, the process of establishing uniformity and universality took a long time. Nowadays, corporations can invent a product and have it marketed globally within a number of years. However, the Roman church was pioneering something completely new. Not only had the standardised formulations of ceremonies to be tried and tested but the church had to build an international infrastructure of communication and command, as well as of property and its clergy had to develop the equivalent of marketing skills. It took centuries before the Roman church began to succeed in its global ambitions.

In the first centuries after the death of Jesus, two common practices had established themselves practically everywhere among Christians. These were the practices of baptism and the breaking of bread. Other practices too were common, such as anointing with oil and laying on of hands. These latter practices were used in a variety of situations such as: tending to the sick, praying with a person or appointing a person to a position of authority within the community. As Christianity spread throughout the empire, these practices took on diverse expressions. Their form and content varied from place to place. Vernacular languages were used and the conduct of the ceremonies was often influenced by local spiritual traditions and practices. There was no uniformity.

The challenge to the Christian authorities based in Rome was to regularise and control the practice of each of these rituals. Even as early as the middle of the first century, we see St Paul struggling with this diversity in his letters. For example, in his first letter to the Corinthians[3] he tries to correct the way the people celebrate the breaking of bread together. He also has to battle against people who want to maintain Jewish practices such as circumcision.[4]

---

3   *1 Cor.11*
4   *Acts 15:1-35; Phil.3:2-6*

Religious Traditions as against Global Products

Religious traditions, if left to themselves, have their own dynamic. They live and grow and change within various cultures, in various places and through different times, adapting and developing and finding new expressions according to the local dynamic. Religious traditions are similar to musical or artistic traditions in the way they survive and are passed on to future generations.

Ideas and practices have always travelled across political and cultural boundaries. Generally these ideas and practices are adapted to the local culture and given a new expression within the new situation. The ideas and practices become inculturated and localised. One can find many examples of this today. The first day of May, for example, is a date celebrated in many parts of Europe. The celebration often involves a May Pole and games between teenage girls and boys. However, there is great diversity in the way the day is celebrated and this diversity is at local, as well as national, level. Hallowe'en, which is celebrated differently in different parts of the world, is another example.

Creating a Global Product or Service

Traditional cultural celebrations normally take place without centralised control. The local people themselves decide what is appropriate and generally they are faithful to the traditions of their own area. In so far as these practices are not regularised or controlled by some central authority, they remain part of a dynamic and living cultural tradition, connected to a certain people, a certain place and a certain time.

In the early centuries of Christianity, Christian practices were developing in a similar diversified and inculturated way. From the 4th century onwards, Roman Christianity began to interfere in this process in order to regulate these practices. Over the coming centuries, wherever it could, the Roman church removed local control and local influence from Christian celebrations. It replaced diversity with uniformity. A standard form and content of ceremonial was created that was intended for uniform practice everywhere.

The process of creating uniformity was a gradual one. After the collapse of the Roman empire, Europe entered the Dark Ages. Christianity came under threat from the spread of Islam and the general chaos of the time. It was only as Europe began to regroup and pull itself out of this dark period, that efforts were again made to gain centralised control over Christian life. Most of the work of creating uniformity within Roman Christianity took place in the period from the end of the 6th century to the middle of the 12th century,

Celtic Christianity

Among the biggest challenges to the Christian authorities of Rome at the beginning of this period were the flourishing Celtic monasteries of the western isles. Ireland, in particular, was a place where Christianity was hugely successful but the Christianity being practised there had its own inculturated expression.

During this period Ireland was not just a place that was physically cut off from mainland Europe. It was also a place that had never been part of the Roman empire. The Roman infrastructure that was so important for the establishment of Christianity in Europe had not been created in Ireland. Christianity in Europe had developed in cities. Bishops resided in these cities as leaders of urban Christian communities. There were no cities or towns in Ireland, only rural countryside divided into small kingdoms. In Ireland, Christianity developed in monasteries and the abbots and abbesses of those monasteries, not bishops, were the church leaders.

The expression of Christianity on the Celtic fringe of Europe was therefore very different from that of mainland Europe. As the Roman church authorities moved to centralise control of Christianity throughout Europe, Irish Christianity posed a huge challenge. The differences between the Roman church and Celtic Christianity were in every sphere – in beliefs, in authority structures, in the conduct of ceremonies, in the role of bishops and priests, in the way monasteries were run, in the way monks dressed and behaved and in calendar dates for festivals.

Roman Versus Celtic

The Roman church could not proceed with the creation of a global church until it had brought the Celtic monks and Irish Christianity into line. Future chapters of this book will go into detail as to how this was achieved. Suffice it to say here that this epic struggle began in the early part of the 5th century, when a Celtic monk travelled to Rome to oppose single-handedly the authoritarian, patriarchal and sin-laden model of church being developed by Augustine, Jerome and others of that time. That monk was Pelagius. The struggle ended with the defeat of Celtic Christianity in the 12th century, during the course of the Norman invasion of Ireland. It took eight hundred years to bring the Irish into line with Rome. In the process, Roman Christianity forged and refined many of its instruments for bringing about that uniformity.

The Roman Calendar

The Roman calendar was one of the products developed by Rome as a tool for promoting uniformity. The Roman calendar marked out the year, setting the dates for Easter, Christmas and other feast-days, festivals and seasons.

The date for Easter was the cause of particular difficulties with Celtic Christianity. From the time that Christianity began in Ireland, Celtic monks were using an old method for calculating the date of Easter but Rome had developed a new method. In 664, at the Synod of Whitby in north-east Britain, this question was decided upon and the Celtic church had to fall in line.

In modern times, the date for Easter Sunday is calculated as the first Sunday after the first full moon after the spring equinox (northern hemisphere). This places Easter Sunday in the middle of the planting season, when new life is coming into the landscape. Celebrating death and resurrection at this time makes sense, because death has been seen in nature throughout the winter and resurrection is clearly evident at this time of year.

However, it only works this way for those living north of the equator. In the southern hemisphere, this time of year is mid-autumn, when leaves are falling off the trees and winter is approaching. It makes no environmental sense to celebrate Easter at this time of year in the southern hemisphere, yet this is what Christians do. They do it because the Roman calendar is a global product, which means it is disconnected from nature and its cosmic rhythms.

The Roman calendar also includes the feast-days of saints. Only saints recognised by Rome are included. Most of the local saints celebrated in particular places are excluded. For example, although there are hundreds of known Celtic saints celebrated in Ireland[5], only four of them have been canonised by Rome and included in the calendar. These four are – St Malachy, St Laurence O'Toole, St Fergal of Salzburg and St Oliver Plunkett. They owe their canonisation as much to their loyalty to Rome in difficult times as to their life of holiness and good works.

This uniformity in liturgical practice was something completely new in the history of humankind. Roman Christianity developed a universally applicable way to control the celebration of human rituals – rituals that were at the heart of human existence and meaning. The imposition of uniform liturgical control was achieved through the creation of the Roman calendar and also of the *Roman Ritual*.

The Roman Ritual

The *Roman Ritual* is a complete compendium of instructions on the performance of Christian ceremonies. It lays down the sequence of words to be used and the actions to be performed in each ceremony and in every situation. The *Roman Ritual* represents the culmination of centuries of effort to bring uniformity into the celebration of Christian ceremonies.

From the 5th century onwards, efforts were made to make uniform the prayers and actions used during the Mass. Instructions were written down in books that were called Sacramentaries. However, no one sacramentary was ever established as the definitive one to be used by everybody. In the early 9th century, Charlemagne wished to unify the liturgy in his Frankish realm and used the sacramentary known as *Gregorianum-Hadrianum*, which he is said to have got from Pope Hadrian I, to do so. This was perhaps the closest the Roman church came to establishing uniformity in this area until after the Reformation. It is clear from the many sacramentaries that have been preserved from these centuries that there remained wide diversity in the celebration of the Mass up to late medieval times.

From the 7th century onwards, high ranking bishops began to produce what were called 'pontificals'. These were written instructions for bishops under their authority, indicating how ceremonies were to be performed. These pontificals were another attempt at creating uniformity. However,

---

5   Cf. Mary Ryan D'Arcy, *The Saints of Ireland.* Irish American Cultural Institute, 1974, 1985.

as with the sacramentaries, the wide variety of pontificals preserved from different places and different periods testify to continued diversity throughout Christianity for many centuries.

It was not until the year 1614 that an attempt was made to gather all the instructions for priests into one authoritative book. This book was produced by Pope Paul V and was called the *Roman Ritual*. Since then, various revisions of this book have been made and it now forms part of a collection of books issued by Rome as a guide to the conduct of ceremonies. These books are: the *Pontifical*, the *Ceremonial of Bishops*, the *Roman Ritual*, the *Missal* and the *Breviary*. The essential content of ceremonies within Roman Christianity is now centrally controlled.

The Benedictine Rule

The *Benedictine Rule* was a monastic rule written by Benedict, an Italian monk, in the 6th century. After Benedict's death it became a useful tool in the hands of the papacy to confront the spread of Celtic monasticism and to promote monastic uniformity and conformity.

By the end of the 6th century, Celtic monasticism had gained a strong foothold in the northern half of Britain and was also present in Wales. From this time also, through to the 10th century, many Celtic monasteries were founded throughout Europe. They had a huge influence on local populations and even on political leaders and the names of their founders are remembered in many parts of Europe to this day.

Celtic monasteries operated according to the style and inspiration of their Irish founders and were independent of each other. While sharing a common monastic culture and often federated, they did not follow a common written rule. Each monastic community was autonomous under its abbot or abbess.

Celtic monasteries in Europe were a thorn in the side of the Roman church authorities and particularly of the local bishops in whose jurisdictions they were established. This was because the Celtic monks had their own inculturated beliefs and practices and were intent on remaining independent from the influences of Rome. They did not show much regard for the authority of the local bishop. He was often a member of the urban aristocracy, living a sumptuous lifestyle, while they had a frugal lifestyle and worked with the rural people.

At the end of the 6th century, pope Gregory the Great was the first to see the potential of the *Benedictine Rule*. He used the monks of a Benedictine monastery in Rome to seed the spread of Benedictine monasticism in Britain. This acted as a counter-force to the influence of the Celtic monasteries there.[6] His successors, popes Gregory II and III, continued with this policy and instructed Boniface, who himself was a Benedictine monk from Britain, to convert the Celtic monasteries of northern Europe to the Benedictine rule. Boniface did this with great success in the 7th century.[7] In the 8th century, the Roman authorities imposed a universal church regulation that all monasteries were to live according to the rule of St Benedict. This imposition ended the diversity and independence of the Irish monastic communities and brought them much more under the control of Rome.

One could say, therefore, that the *Benedictine Rule* became a global product in the hands of the papacy, who used it as a means of imposing uniformity on monastic life.

Religious Orders

The progression towards uniformity and centralised control within monasticism across Europe led, in the 12th century, to the creation of religious orders. In 1115, St Bernard founded the Cistercians who practised a reformed version of Benedictine monasticism. This version differed from Benedictine monasticism in that it had a 'Superior General' in charge of the order and a 'General Chapter' that met regularly and regulated the order. Where Benedictine monasteries had a common rule but were otherwise autonomous, the Cistercians not only had a common rule but were regulated by a centralised body.

A religious order is an organisation of men or women who live in community according to the principles and guidelines of a written constitution. This constitution is based on the Benedictine Rule but will also have its own aims and objectives. All religious constitutions must have the approval of the Roman church authorities. Members of religious orders need not necessarily be monks or live in seclusion.

---

6   Cf. Chapter 11 for greater detail on this.
7   Cf. Chapter 12 for greater detail on this.

What distinguished religious orders from Benedictine monasticism was a structure of centralised control. Religious communities that belonged to religious orders were not independent. They were subject to a 'Superior General' and to the rulings of a 'General Chapter'.

During the 12th century, there was an explosion of religious communities throughout Europe. Along with the Cistercians, two religious orders founded at this time were the Franciscans and the Dominicans. It was not long before these and other religious orders established houses in Ireland under the umbrella of the Norman invasion. Their arrival marked the end of Celtic monasticism.

The Concept of Franchise

In today's world, the concept of a franchise as a way of promoting a business model is commonly known and used. When an entrepreneur finally establishes the correct formula for operating a business in a particular place, he or she can then franchise out that business to others. Whoever buys the franchise acquires permission to recreate the same business in another location. The franchise agreement requires the buyer to operate the business according to certain guidelines which maintain the formula of success that has been established. At the same time, the new owner is free to make a profit if the business is successful.

In Ireland today one can obtain, for example, a franchise for a 'Supermac's' restaurant. This allows one to set up a new restaurant and to call it 'Supermac's', provided one fulfils the terms of the franchise agreement.

The idea at the heart of the franchise system is the same one as that contained in the Roman church's development of the *Benedictine Rule* as a universal rule for all religious orders and monasteries. Establishing monasteries under the rule of Benedict was similar to establishing commercial businesses under a franchise today. In this sense, pope Gregory I was the inventor of the idea of franchise, although he did not coin the word. The franchise agreement is similar to the rule of St Benedict. It details all the essential elements of the operation.

Franchising is a key element in modern day strategies for economic globalisation. As with many other key elements of economic globalisation, franchising finds its roots in the globalisation strategies of Roman

Christianity. Pope Gregory I made it possible to, as it were, obtain a franchise for a Benedictine monastery. Franchise was the idea of a pope and its first manifestation was in Britain in the late 6th century.

Christianity – the Pioneer of Globalisation

Today, the uniform products and services of Roman Christianity can be found throughout the world. With its church buildings and its ceremonies, its priests and its festivals, it has as distinct a presence in a city as a McDonald's restaurant or a Coca Cola outlet. The products and services of Roman Christianity are available worldwide to those who seek to avail of them.

Stale Bread and Sore Knees

When I was little and asked my Ma
Why the man up there was wearing a dress
in front of the women with dangling beads,
She said not to ask questions in Church
or it'll hurt your head,
And she clattered me one to prove her point.

The man in the dress came down to us after
and we all stood and stuck out our tongues
trying not to chew the little white breads.

I wanted to ask why the bread was stale
but decided against it and rubbed my sore knees.

Tess Harper

8

THE GLOBAL AMBITIONS OF CORPORATE CHRISTIANITY

Every significant business today has its mission statement and an ambition to conquer the world. But before corporations had mission statements, the Christian church of Rome had missions and missionaries. Centuries prior to multinational corporations spreading their global products and services worldwide, there were Christian missionaries bringing their 'good news' to all nations. The methods that Roman Christianity developed to spread its message remain the template for global corporations today.

Today, mission statements are displayed in the public lobbies of all major institutions, from banks to schools to hospitals. It is well understood these days that without a clear agreed vision of where the corporation is intending to go, it will never get there. Small businesses are encouraged to develop an ambitious mission statement and to go out and conquer the world.

However, only a few generations ago, mission was a word used solely in connection with Christianity. A priest went on the missions. Mission stations were set up in the poorest parts of Africa. Money was collected for the missions. People who went abroad to work with the poor on behalf of Christianity were missionaries.

Christianity had a mission long before there was ever talk of a mission statement. That mission, according to Jesus, was to spread the gospel throughout the world: 'Go out to the whole world and proclaim the good news to all creation'[1]. He also indicated how to go about it: 'Jesus summoned the Twelve and began to send them out two by two'[2].

---

1   *Mark 16:15*
2   *Mark 6:7*

Making Disciples of All the Nations

While Jesus clearly wanted his message to go worldwide, he himself concentrated his work on the Jewish people. Limiting his travel to within Palestine, he stated that his own personal mission did not include anybody outside Judaism: 'I was sent only to the lost sheep of the House of Israel'.[3] Nevertheless, when he instructed his disciples, he encouraged them to take on the whole world: 'Go, therefore, make disciples of all the nations...'[4]

Political Empires

It is probably fair to say that all political empires of the ancient past had global ambitions. Over the course of time, they expanded their borders as far as they could. Within these borders, certain elements of what we now call globalisation were present: one language was promoted as the official language, one religion or set of religious beliefs took precedence over all others, one political structure was imposed throughout and one centrally administered army was visibly in control everywhere. These were the essential elements of infrastructure for holding the whole enterprise together.

The imposition of a uniform infrastructure on an empire reduced cultural diversity within that empire. Where the empire survived through generations, this diversity was further reduced as all the peoples of the empire blended into one great culture.

However, no political empire of the past ever achieved world dominance. In all cases, there were people and peoples beyond the borders of an empire. These borders expanded or receded according to the fortunes of the time and in the end, all these empires collapsed and diversity found its feet again.

The Spread of Christianity through the Roman Empire

At the time of Jesus, the Jewish people were subjects of the Roman empire. The Jewish state of Judea, where Jesus did most of his preaching, was a province of the Roman empire. Political power in Judea was in the hands of the Roman governor. Jesus's preaching upset the Jewish

---

3   *Matthew 15:24*
4   *Matthew 28:19*

authorities but it was the Roman governor who decided to put Jesus to death.

After the death of Jesus, the existence of the Roman empire was an opportunity for the first Christians. Jewish communities were scattered throughout the empire, even in Rome itself and Jews could travel freely throughout the empire. St Paul in particular seized this opportunity. While under arrest, he claimed Roman citizenship and used it as an opportunity to go to Rome and gain a hearing there.[5] From that time onwards he travelled extensively throughout the empire, creating and maintaining new Christian communities.

Christianity also spread as a result of persecution. From the martyrdom of Stephen onwards, there were sporadic persecutions of Christians. These persecutions led to the dispersal of Christians. Further dispersal took place when the Romans sacked Jerusalem in 70 CE in order to quell a Jewish uprising.

It is clear therefore that early Christians took the opportunities presented to them to spread Christianity throughout the Roman empire. Over the first three centuries, there were communities of Christians established in practically all the major cities of the empire.

It is less clear whether Christianity spread elsewhere during these first three centuries. However, there are convincing claims made that Christianity did spread to both India and Ethiopia during this early period.[6] As the method used from the beginning was that of 'evangelisation' or 'spreading the good news', it was done by word of mouth. Wherever trade routes were open between territories, there were opportunities for the spread of Christianity.

This method of 'evangelisation' has been unique to Christianity. Judaism never actively engaged in proselytising and the spread of Islam happened mainly through military campaigns. Generally speaking, world religions do not proselytise. Christianity alone has sent out evangelists or missionaries.

For the first few centuries of Christianity, as has been discussed in the previous two chapters, there was no cohesion in the message that

---

5   *Acts of the Apostles 25:21*
6   Heinrich Ernst Guericke et al., (1857). *A Manual of Church History: Ancient Church History Comprising the First Six Centuries.* New York: Wiley and Halsted.

Christians were preaching. Every Christian preacher seemed to have his own opinions.

Preaching Within A Corporate Body

In the world of computers, there are pieces of software that are described as 'Freeware'. Freeware is downloadable software that one can use without ever having to pay for it. The inventors of Freeware are generous souls who are happy to share their inventions with others without asking for anything in return. The preaching of the Christian message began in this way. One could accept the message of a preacher without having to sign up, without any strings attached and one could reject the message without any negative consequences.

However, once a central authority emerged within the empire that attempted to control Christianity, this was no longer the case. From the time the Nicene Creed was established, if one accepted the 'orthodox' message of Christianity contained in it, there were strings attached. One became a member of a corporate organisation. One was expected to accept the teachings of authority figures within that organisation and one was obliged to regularly receive the 'sacraments' from that organisation in order to be assured of 'salvation'. If one rejected the message of this organisation, the consequences were, at the least, that one would be condemned and under threat of eternal damnation. In the case of many during this early period, their rejection of the orthodox message meant that they were ostracised, persecuted or put into exile.

In the 4th and 5th centuries, much of the energy of this newly emerging corporate church of Rome was put into opposing 'heretical' teachings and imposing orthodoxy. In the early 5th century, Germanus was sent to Britain and Palladius was sent to Ireland, to confront the Pelagian 'heresy' prevalent in these places. While there is little evidence of missionaries being sent out during this period to convert unbelievers (Patrick's mission to Ireland may have been an exception), there is plenty of evidence of efforts being made to confront 'heresies'.

Had Christian preaching remained totally generous, as it was at the beginning, the teachings and stories of Jesus would have been absorbed into local communities in an organic way, without any outside strings attached. These communities would have continued to operate from the inside out, influenced by the Christian spiritual tradition but not controlled by any larger corporate body.

Organic Christianity in Ireland

An example of this unattached, organic and inculturated Christianity was to be found in Ireland in the early centuries, prior to the arrival of the missionary St Patrick. Patrick arrived in Ireland as a missionary in the year 432 CE. Christianity was already present in parts of Ireland at this time. Through a process of osmosis and without the presence of foreign preachers, Irish people had absorbed the Christian story and had made it their own. They did this, it would seem, by coming in touch with the Christian tradition through their own travels and by bringing home the aspects of that tradition which inspired them.

The Christianity which Palladius and Patrick found in Ireland was a Pelagian form of Christianity[7] which did not have the strings of a corporate church attached to it. It was an independent, inculturated Christianity that the Irish had made their own. An element of Patrick's task was, clearly, to attach these strings.

Patrick, as part of his mission, was required to bring Irish Christianity into line with the corporate church of Rome. He did not succeed in his own lifetime and he may not have been very committed to doing so. He himself had had difficulties with the corporate church of Rome.[8] However, he did begin the process. How the corporate church eventually succeeded in attaching those strings to Irish Christianity is a story that spans eight centuries. The independent Irish church did not fully come into line with Rome until the 12th century. This story will be told in detail in future chapters of this book.

Christian Preaching

Evangelisation is the preaching of the Christian message to strangers. St Paul travelled from town to town and engaged with people on the streets and in the town squares. He came with a theological interpretation of the story of the historical Jesus and tried to convince people that his

---

7   Cf. Chapter 10 for details on Pelagian Christianity.
8   Cf. Patrick's *Confession*, verses 26-32. Can be found on http://www.ccel.org/ccel/patrick/confession.html

message was true. If people accepted what he said and began to believe it, as many did, their lives were changed. Belief in the message gave them a new perspective on life – a new mythology or theology within which their lives could operate.

But Paul's message was free. He did not require anything in return. Those who accepted his message generally joined a community of believers in the locality and met with them on a regular basis. Paul moved on to the next town. The community of believers was left to fend for itself. Paul probably remained its mentor, but it had little or no other reference point apart from the occasional visit of other Christians and hand-copied documents or 'gospels' circulating. Apart from Paul, there was nobody from outside the community telling it what to believe or what to do.

When Paul preached to people in towns and villages in the 1st century, he had one objective – to convert people to belief in Jesus, the son of 'God'. Later, from the 4th century onwards, preachers who represented orthodox Christianity had two objectives. Their first objective remained the same – to convert people to belief in Jesus – but their second objective was to make those they converted members of the Roman church. One became a member of that church by accepting its authority. The spread of the gospel and the spread of the Roman church became twin goals that were often construed as one and the same. Through the preaching of evangelists within the Roman church, the allegiance of people was won not just to the 'gospel' but also to an international corporate body.

Christian evangelisation was the beginning of advertising as we know it today. Modern-day advertising is not just information being made available to the public. It is the concerted effort of corporations to draw people into a relationship with them, so that people will, in the first instance, be attracted to buying a product or service from them but then will continue in relationship with them through further purchasing. Corporations selling products and services like to get a hold on their customers, to attract their loyalty and to have them return again and again for further purchases. This was a practice first developed by the Roman corporate Christian church.

Roman Empire as Mother of Roman Christianity

Corporate Christianity developed with the support, the protection and the encouragement of the Roman empire. The Roman empire was its mother. Within the womb of the empire, this new ecclesiastical body was formed. It developed and grew in influence under its matronage. This formative experience left an indelible mark on the corporate church. To this day, there are distinctive characteristics of the Roman church that identify the empire as its mother.[9]

The experience of being nurtured within the womb of the empire taught the Roman church how it could operate within a friendly political structure. This was an important lesson which it applied in subsequent coalitions and alliances with many other political powers. It could exist and operate within a political system without being swallowed up by that system.

When the Roman empire collapsed in the 5th century, Roman Christianity was born into the world as an independent entity. Like most births, it was a traumatic event and for a while it was not clear if it would survive at all. But survive it did. It quickly learned that its survival and spread were not necessarily dependent on any one political structure or boundary. It could survive that structure's death and outlive it. Roman Christianity was to do this again and again in future centuries.

Through the collapse of the Roman empire, Roman Christianity was birthed to become an independent political entity in its own right, one without geographical boundaries. Although it was the progeny of the Roman empire and similar to it in structure and form, there were significant differences between them. For example, the Roman church discovered that, unlike a political empire, it could spread its influence without the use of military force. While the military power of its allies could and often did, assist its establishment and growth, Roman Christianity did not need its own army to spread the faith, because it had instead its preachers and its missionaries. The power of the word was mightier than the sword.[10]

---

9   See Chapter 6 p.98-99.
10 This is not to say that the pope did not have his own army. From the time of the forma-
    tion of the papal states in the 7th century through to the present time, the pope has had
    an army. Nowadays, it is only a symbolic army, represented by the Swiss guards, but in
    earlier times it was a fighting band, sometimes numbering tens of thousands of soldiers.
    The primary purpose of this army has been to protect the pope and the papal states.

Modern commercial corporations operate in a similar way. They benefit from the support of national governments but often survive without them. Their entry into a new region is announced through the advertising of a particular product or service. They do not need military might to impose their will because they can rely on the power of the word and image, communicated through advertising, to win people over.

The Dark Ages

After the collapse of the Roman empire, during the period known as the Dark Ages, corporate Christianity struggled to stay alive as Europe was realigned and as the religion of Islam made its presence felt. Christian communities were scattered, weak and unsupported. The arrival from Ireland of communities of Celtic monks, who wandered throughout Europe and established monastic settlements, greatly aided the rebuilding of the Christian faith among the rural people. However, these Celtic monks had no attachment to Roman corporate Christianity and did not show much respect for its representatives, the bishops.

Roman Christianity needed to reassert itself. As it got to its feet, it began to send out missionaries, not so much to convert people to Christianity, as to confront heresies and to bring Christian communities that were acting independently under the control of Rome. The defeat of Arianism (a Christian 'heresy' among the Goths) in western Europe, the work of Augustine of Canterbury in England and the work of Boniface throughout northern Europe epitomise this period.

The work of Roman Christianity during the Dark Ages in reasserting itself, confronting heresies and building alliances was similar to what any modern-day corporation would do today to secure its position in the markets, protect its patents and defeat its competitors.

Maintenance and Mission

Roman Christianity inherited from its mother, the Roman empire, a strong, authoritarian and hierarchical infrastructure. This infrastructure of authority was to work well in the future. The pope as head of the church had his archbishops and bishops throughout Christendom. Church territory was divided into regions and dioceses. Within each diocese, a bishop had his team of priests who were assigned to parishes. This infrastructure created a line of command which facilitated communication and control from the top of the hierarchical ladder to the bottom and from the centre to the periphery.

However, while this structure facilitated the maintenance of an established position, something else was needed when these positions were weak, or when new positions were required to be established. One of the most effective instruments for the re-establishment of Roman Christianity throughout Europe and later its consolidation, was Benedictine monasticism. Celtic monasticism did not offer this option, because it was too independent and could not be controlled centrally. In contrast, the rule of Benedict was a standardised regulatory instrument that could be applied everywhere. It gave the Roman church the facility to control monasticism throughout its jurisdiction. Prior to the imposition of the Benedictine rule on all monasteries, monasteries were once-off foundations that did not necessarily serve the needs of the corporate church.

Had it not been for Pope Gregory I, Benedictine monasticism would most likely not have come into existence. It was he who began to establish monasteries using the rule of Benedict as a template. He began in Britain. Subsequent popes brought the idea back into Europe, imposing the rule of Benedict on existing monasteries, while at the same time promoting the establishment of new Benedictine monasteries throughout the rest of Europe. Over the course of time, monasticism became streamlined and manageable under the rule of Benedict.

Religious Orders

Between the 7th and the 11th century, Benedictine monasticism swept mainland Europe, replacing Irish monasticism wherever it had manifested itself. It was the dominant expression of religious community to be found throughout Europe during this period.

From the 12th century onward, religious orders took over where monasticism left off. The religious houses of the Cistercians, Franciscans and Dominicans appeared all over mainland Europe. At this time, there also developed communities of secular priests called 'canons', which were formed to maintain celibacy among the clergy.

The creation of religious orders for both men and women added another layer of sophistication to the effectiveness of the Roman church globally. The constitutions for these religious orders had to be ratified by Rome. Mechanisms were now in place that, on the one hand, could facilitate the replication of particular projects, such as parish development and, later, schools or hospitals, anywhere in the world (as with the franchise idea), while on the other hand, the whole complex set of operations could be controlled by a centralised, hierarchical system of command that reached back to the pope himself.

A key feature of religious orders in fulfilling the global agenda of Roman Christianity was their ability to establish a new community anywhere. Whether the membership of that community was native or imported, its rule of life remained the same. Communities of a particular religious order are often scattered throughout the world, yet they remain connected to each other through a central coordination. The residence of the Superior General is usually based in Rome.

From the 12th century onwards, religious orders became one of the Roman church's most powerful instruments in the promotion of its global ambitions. Men and women who joined these orders renounced their families and their cultural ties and dedicated themselves totally to the spread of the church and the gospel. Today, the presence of these religious orders in countries throughout the world is another example of the success of globalisation within the Christian corporate church.

Modern Corporations

Nowadays, some commercial companies choose to spread their operations using the franchise method. This gives a franchise operator a certain autonomy within the parameters of the franchise agreement. But other commercial companies like a bit more centralised control. These companies do not offer franchises, but instead replicate their operations throughout the world using a template, while at the same time having a system of centralised, hierarchical management that allows for flexibility from one operation to the next.

Before commercial organisations ever had these structures, they were to be found in the structures of the Roman church. The central role of the Superior General of the religious order is balanced by the rules of the order and by the meetings of the general chapter. In the case of the global corporation, the central role of the chief executive is balanced by the board of directors and by the annual meeting of the shareholders. Once the right structure is in place, then as now, it is possible to plant cells of that corporation virtually anywhere in the world.

Post-Columbus Colonial Expansion

Taking a broader view of history afforded to us by today's perspective, one can see that it was not until the discovery of the New World by Columbus, in the 15th century, that the real explosion of the Roman church's missionary activity took place. From this time on, various European countries vied with each other to expand their empires throughout the Americas, Africa and Asia. The Roman church and other Christian churches, generally speaking, came into these areas on the coat-tails of the colonisers.

The Roman church had its religious orders, some of whom were specifically founded to participate in these colonial projects. The Jesuits had missions to China and Mexico in the 17th century[11], while, during the new wave of colonialism in the 19th century, many new missionary religious orders were founded, including, for example, The Society of African Missions (SMA), founded in France in 1856. These were highly organised and totally dedicated groups of men and women who were ready to leave home, never to return and give up their lives for the sake of the spread of Christianity to foreign parts. The Roman church was therefore in a very good position to take advantage of the new opportunities afforded by the new colonies. In truth, the real undeclared winners of this period of colonial expansion were the corporate Christian churches.

While each political power had to be satisfied with its own conquests and could not take a share of anyone else's, the churches benefited from participating in all the political conquests. While England, France, Belgium, Spain, Portugal and other countries expanded their separate empires into these continents, corporate Christianity's expansion happened throughout all of them. Christian missionaries, representing these ecclesiastical

---

11   Cf. Luke Clossey. *Salvation and Globalization in the Early Jesuit Missions*. Simon Fraser University, British Columbia. 2008.

corporations, travelled with each of the colonising forces and so found their way into every colonial country.

Corporate Christianity was not only the major victor in this expansion, but it was also the only ultimate victor. Its success was more sustained than that of its political allies. One can say this because, today, many of these colonial countries have achieved independence from their political colonisers, but not from the Christian corporate churches. Corporate Christianity has remained. Ecclesiastical colonisation has proven itself to be far more successful and sustainable than political colonisation.

In a repetition of the pattern that had been established in the early centuries, corporate Christianity expanded on the back of expanding empires but was not limited by the political borders created by those empires. It survived in those areas where it became established, despite the collapse or withdrawal of those empires.

The spread of economic globalisation has followed the same path as ecclesiastical globalisation. The possibilities for economic globalisation were greatly enhanced by the conquests and expansions of the European colonies. Since the withdrawal of colonial powers from many of the world's developing countries, it is clear that the economic infrastructure created by these powers has, for the most part, remained in place, thus accommodating further economic globalisation. Like ecclesiastical globalisation, economic globalisation benefits from the support of national governments but is not totally reliant on them.

Ecclesiastical Colonisation in its Own Right

In the last five hundred years, missionaries representing corporate Christianity have also gone to places where no European political coloniser had ever gone. Corporate Christian churches have been independent colonisers in their own right, opening missions in the most remote and primitive of places, for example, the south Pacific islands. Until modern times, their missionaries were people who left home without much likelihood of ever returning. They willingly put themselves at risk of fatal diseases and violent deaths and were prepared to take on great hardships in their daily lives. They had a commitment to the church corporate goal that is almost impossible to match in the business world. They were largely successful in their own terms but caused appalling cultural destruction.

Drawing People into a New World

When missionaries entered the world of an autonomous, indigenous tribe of people, they brought with them a message from the outside world. That message, if accepted, was full of promise; if rejected, it carried a dire warning. Once a tribe was caught on the hook of the preacher's words, its life was slowly drawn into a world that was defined and controlled by a corporate entity outside the ambit of the tribe.

This preaching described a world that was not anchored to a particular piece of earth, to a particular culture or to a particular political system. Once caught on this hook, the tribal members and eventually the tribe itself had their gods and goddesses removed from them and their traditional religious practices and customs curtailed. The process of disconnection, begun by the preachers, continued with the arrival of agents of economic globalisation. These agents could enter because the door had been opened to them by the corporate churches. Gradually, these global forces work to disconnect the tribe from local dependencies and local self-reliance. New dependencies and connections tie the local people irrevocably to global corporations, the global church and a global way of living.

In the world of indigenous peoples, preachers were unnecessary. Children grew up immersed in the spiritual traditions of their ancestors. Their spirituality was an integral part of their daily lives and of the natural environment in which they lived. In the world of a globally ambitious church, preachers were essential – as essential as advertising is today for global economies. Both preaching and advertising have performed the role of making the first inroads into an unconverted community. Once the work of conversion has been done, both preaching and advertising continue to play a vital role in keeping that community true to the new paradigm for living, whether that be church or global economics.

While Christian preaching was the main instrument used to introduce Christianity to a new community, other instruments, such as churches, schools and health services, quickly developed alongside to maintain it. Preaching became just one element of a much bigger picture.

Owning the New Product

Two thousand years ago, the news of Jesus of Nazareth's life, death and resurrection spread throughout the known world as precisely that – news. People heard the news and passed it on. It was freely available to anyone who wished to listen to it. But Roman Christianity managed to capture that news and, as it were, patent it. As a commercial corporation might do today, they guaranteed the quality of that news, that product, only if it had their logo on it.

The story of Jesus, in the hands of the Roman corporate church, became a product – a clearly defined and packaged 'message' – guaranteed to have come from 'God' and therefore unequivocally the 'truth'. In theological terms, this message was called 'the deposit of faith'. It contained a direct communication of 'God' through his 'son', Jesus. The role of the Roman corporate church was to guarantee the story's authenticity, supervise its application and organise its distribution throughout the world.

While the message of Jesus had been a message of personal liberation and empowerment, the Roman church taught that that liberation and empowerment could only come through its intermediacy. One had to enter through the doors of the Roman church and be baptised. Forever after that, one remained within the community of the Roman church, nourished by its sacraments and instructed by its clergy. Only then was one liberated, empowered and ultimately saved from the jaws of hell and from eternal damnation.

A key first step in the building of a global corporation is to claim ownership of the product. Global corporations today regularly go to court to claim ownership. They take out patents on what may be very natural substances – for example, a healing herb or the genetic make-up of a seed. If the patenting is successful, the substance is processed, packaged and marketed as a global product. What was initially freely available to the public in a certain place becomes a commodity one has to pay for that is available globally.

The Commodification of Christianity

Commodification is a global trend that privatises what has been commonly and freely available to the public of a certain place. Examples in recent times are the privatisation of water and of public spaces. This privatisation of the 'commons', as it is known, is happening at an accelerating rate worldwide. Private companies and global corporations are greedily taking over what were once publicly owned and freely available resources and services. It is a creeping but unstoppable tide.

What people may not see so clearly is that Christianity began this process way back in the 4th century. Until a corporate body claimed ownership of Christianity, the traditions and teachings associated with the legends of Jesus were freely available to the public. People could interpret them, practice them and celebrate them as they wished. By taking over control of the Christian tradition, the Christian corporation was able to transform this tradition into a selection of religious products and services, which were then marketed globally.

Missionary Zeal

The preserved stories of Jesus found in the four canonical gospels offered two contrasting ways of spreading the message globally. One way was preaching: 'Go out to the whole world and proclaim the good news to all creation'.[12] The other way was witnessing: 'You are the salt of the earth... You are the light of the world...Your light must shine in the sight of men, so that, seeing your good works, they may give the praise to your Father in heaven'.[13] Preaching meant leaving home and going to preach in foreign parts. Witnessing meant concentrating on one's own life and allowing the 'salt' and 'light' of that life to have an influence on others. In the lives of individual Christians, the two could be and often were, combined.

Historically, Christianity chose the method of preaching over the method of witnessing in its efforts to spread its influence. Missionary work came to mean being sent to preach in foreign parts and to establish or maintain the church in these places. When one speaks of missionaries today, one is clearly talking of people such as these preachers.

This form of mission identified the church as a corporate body with the spread of the Christian message. The two were one and the same. When one spread the message one was also spreading the church. A measure of the success achieved in spreading the message came to be the number of

---

12   *Mark 16:15*
13   *Matthew 5:13 -14*

baptisms performed, the number of mission stations established and the number of churches built. Another measure, at a later stage, would be the number of native priests being ordained.

The essential element found in Christian preaching, when that preaching comes through a corporate body, is the insertion of something into a local community from outside. That 'something' is like a bait on a hook at the end of a line. Those nibbling the bait may not see the line or appreciate the implications of consuming the bait. The long string attached pulls the individual out of his or her immersion in a local self-reliant community and creates an attachment to a corporation – in this case the Roman Christian church. That attachment is then built on with further attachments, until the individual has completely lost his or her self-reliance within a local community and has become globally dependent both ecclesiastically and economically.

Today, Christianity is present in many parts of the world where other forms of globalisation have yet to make a real impact. These places, for example, in parts of Africa, are categorised by Western thought as 'undeveloped'. In these places, Christianity has been the forerunner, opening the door to the concepts of development and progress that are so much part of the globalisation package today. A close look at many church projects on the ground in these places shows how aligned the Christian churches are to the globalisation project generally, introducing global-style education and health services and working to create the local physical infrastructure necessary for the arrival of economic globalisation.

While economic globalisation today is being blamed for the death of diversity in the world, the first serious threat to that diversity came from the expanding and globally ambitious Christian churches. Christianity created the mindset. That mindset designated people who did not belong to Christianity as pagans and savages.[14] They were lost souls who needed to be saved.[15]

---

14 For example, this quote from a school textbook: 'Untouched by the civilization or religion of Rome, they were thorough savages and pagans.' Page 27 of *Outlines of Mediæval and Modern History: A Text-book for High Schools* by Philip Van Ness Myers, 1901.
15 This was the case even in the 1950s and 60s when, in Ireland, Irish missionaries to Africa were understood to be working among 'pagans and savages' and when, in the U.S., cowboy movies were depicting the 'red Indians' of America in the same vein.

Christianity gave a motivation to missionaries and colonisers alike. They believed that they were saving people from damnation. They believed that they were bringing civilisation to a savage people. The terrible destruction of cultures, of languages, of spiritualities and of diverse ways of living was seen as a positive advance. A fundamentalist arrogance and self-righteous zeal dominated the minds of both coloniser and missionary alike. That arrogance and self-righteousness continues to exist today in the minds of many politicians, bureaucrats and business people who promote economic globalisation.

How Things Could Have Been Different

Looking back through history, it is hard to imagine how things could have been different. Recognising that a human hunger for power will always be present, how realistic is it to imagine that the Christian tradition could have spread throughout the world as a positive influence, without some human organisation attempting to get its hands on it and control it? And is it not the case that, within the gospels themselves, there are the seeds of the global corporation that Christianity was to become?

The answer to the first question – could Christianity have spread without a corporate takeover – lies in the example of Buddhism. Buddhism is a spiritual tradition older than Christianity. It is to be found in many parts of the world but it has spread without aggressive proselytising. It has its holy scriptures, its traditional rituals, its gurus and its teachers, but it does not have a global hierarchical corporate structure that tries to control everything. It has not converted its spiritual practices into global products and services and it is not a threat to global diversity. It does not have global ambitions and is tolerant and respectful of other traditions.

So the answer is yes. Christianity could have spread as a spiritual tradition without having to be controlled in a centralised way by a corporate body or church.

The answer to the second question – were the seeds of the corporation not there from the beginning – lies in the example of Irish Christianity that emerged fully fledged in the 6th century. Irish Christianity was a form of Christianity that did not have a corporate structure. It maintained and developed, rather than destroyed, the Irish spiritual and cultural tradition. It did not have colonial or imperial ambitions. Irish Christianity was an authentic expression of the message and teaching of Jesus that actively resisted the centralisation of power and the destruction of local autonomy.

A regular catchphrase of the Celtic monks in their dealings with European bishops and with the pope was that they wanted to be left alone without interference.[16] They valued their own unique expression of Christianity and could not understand why it would not be tolerated. This form of Christianity suffered continuous assault from the corporate church of Rome from the 4th century onwards. Rome was, for most of that time, the stronger combatant, yet it took until the 12th century to finally subdue Celtic Christianity. Even then, violent means had to be used.

The success of Celtic Christianity and its survival under constant pressure from Rome for eight hundred years shows that Christianity could have survived within a large society and across national and geographical boundaries, without a tight, hierarchical, corporate structure and without the necessity for every aspect of its rituals and ceremonies to be controlled, packaged and made uniform. But it would have been a very different form of Christianity than the one we are familiar with today.

---

16   Cf. Letters of Columbanus, Epistle 2,6 referenced in *The Irish Monks and the See of Peter*, by Joseph F.T.Kelly, in *Monastic Studies*, No.14,1983, Benedictine Priory of Montreal.

Shuddering Silence

I'll stay silent
if that is what is required.
Hold my breath
and the rage that bubbles
deep within.
Macha's rage
seething,
searching for voice
to curse
the man
who forced her to run
when her pleas for justice
fell to silence.

But I won't stay silent forever
or for long more.
Soon – very soon
I will pierce the compartments
they've constructed,
and with a single searing honesty
I will announce my word.

Tess Harper

9

CELTIC CHRISTIANITY

Celtic Christianity has its roots in a pagan indigenous spirituality that was panentheistic[1] and polytheistic. One could say that these pagan roots are its 'Old Testament'. It is a Christianity that is indigenous, organic, inculturated, non-dogmatic and anarchic. Celtic Christianity is not reconcilable with a global form of Christianity, no more than one can reconcile a McDonald's restaurant with one which serves local food and local recipes. It is non-transferable. Those who are inspired by Celtic Christianity, but not living in a Celtic region, can use that inspiration to root their spirituality in their own place, their own heritage and their own history.

When Christianity developed in Ireland, it spread in a natural, organic way. By this I mean that Christianity did not come to Ireland via an invading colonial army or large bands of foreign missionaries. Christianity came to Ireland, one could say, by a process of osmosis. Irish people absorbed from Europe the aspects of Christianity that were attractive to them and gave expression to these in an inculturated way.

While all Christianity spread in this way in the first few centuries, there are few, if any, other examples of Christianity surviving so independently for so many centuries anywhere else in the world. Throughout the Roman empire, Christianity became the established religion by decree of the emperor. Outside of that empire, most of the countries that are Christian today received that Christianity from invading colonial forces, from missionary activity or through migration from Europe. Irish Christianity was exceptional from the beginning.

---

1   Panentheism is a belief that the divine is to be found everywhere in nature but is distinct from it. Pantheism is a belief that elements of nature are actually divine.

The history of the spread of Christianity throughout the world is not a proud one. In its worst manifestations, the Christian churches colluded in the genocide of whole peoples, as on the north American continent. In other countries, the Christian churches were eager to come in on the back of invading colonial forces that used them as one arm of an oppressive regime. In places such as the South American continent, India and Africa, these Christian churches colluded with many forms of injustice in order to establish themselves.

Even in countries where the Christian missionaries arrived first, before any other significant outside political forces, as in, for example, the south Pacific islands, their work involved the condemnation of local spiritualities and spiritual traditions and the introduction of Western-European culture.

This history records the imposition, sometimes by force, sometimes by persuasion, of a European pre-packaged form of Christianity. Christian missionaries, usually with the assistance of other colonial forces, destroyed or marginalised indigenous spiritualities and showed little respect for indigenous cultures. Their purpose was the globalisation of Christianity.

Ireland was an exception. In its process of becoming Christian, Ireland was neither invaded by a colonial army nor converted by bands of missionaries. According to legend, which is reinforced by archaeological evidence, Christianity began to be practised in Ireland in the late 4th century as a result of Irish people returning home after visiting some of the earliest monasteries of Europe. What inspired these Irish people was not mainstream Christianity, which was to be found in the cities, but the beginnings of monasticism in places like Tours and the island of Lérins – a monasticism which had its roots in the Egyptian desert.

One can isolate three main sources of inspiration for Celtic Christianity: the hermits of Egypt, St John's Gospel and the story of Abraham.

The Hermits of Egypt

The Egyptian hermits were a particular inspiration to the Irish. The form they gave to their expression of Christianity attracted the Irish. These hermits, men and women, had left the cities for the desert of Egypt. They were either living alone or had gathered into communities under the leadership of one person. Some of them were, or had been, married. This early monastic movement in Egypt pre-dated Benedictine monasticism by approximately two hundred years.

The writings of John Cassian[2] in the late 4th and early 5th centuries had popularised the Egyptian hermit tradition in parts of Europe. A number of monastic foundations had developed under his influence in southern Gaul. It was these monasteries, particularly those of Martin in Tours, Honoratus on the island of Lérins and Germanus in Auxerre that drew the Irish.

The two great names of the Egyptian hermit tradition were Anthony the hermit and Paul of Thebes. Their fame travelled as far as Ireland. Subsequently images of them appeared in Irish art, such as on the great stone Celtic crosses.

It is not immediately obvious why Irish people found the lives of these desert monks so attractive. The backdrop to their choice of desert life was their rejection of city life. Irish people had no experience of city life, as there were no cities in Ireland at this time. Nor had the Irish any desert to go to! What appears to have inspired the Irish in the lives of these monks was not the physicalities of city or desert life but the heroism exemplified by these monks in their complete dedication to the Christian ideal. Heroism had always been a central feature of Irish mythology.

Young Irish men and women of that time grew up in the countryside in the midst of their extended families. They lived in rural communities that were banded together to constitute small kingdoms. When some of these chose to become monks (male and female) and founded a monastery, they normally did so within the confines of their own kingdom. Some Irish monks did choose to live in remote, inaccessible places, such as Skellig Michael off the Kerry coast. Yet, ironically, the most successful of the early Irish monasteries were those that were founded in places that were easily accessible. Clonard in County Meath, on a tributary of the Boyne, and Clonmacnoise, on the river Shannon, are examples of these. These monasteries were situated not just on rivers, which afforded easy

---

2   John Cassian was a Roman theologian and mystic who lived for a number of years in the early hermitages of Palestine and Egypt. He later founded a monastery near Marseille. His writings, contained in his books *Conferences* and *The Institutes*, were one of the main inspirations for western monasticism.

transport, but also on the main east-west road, the *Slighe Mhór,* following the Esker Riada[3] through the centre of the country.

The creation of monastic communities of hermits on Irish soil represented a paradigm shift in Irish thinking. Irish people saw for the first time the possibility of living in a community of people who came together not because of family connections but because of a shared common ideal. A community of monastic hermits offered the possibility of shaking off the confinement of family politics and creating something completely new.

For Irish women, the possibilities were even more exciting. A Celtic woman, while experiencing many freedoms that were not available to Roman women, was nonetheless required under Brehon law to be under the protection either of her father or of her husband. With the advent of Christianity, Celtic women saw the opportunity to free themselves from these ties. By becoming hermits and living in monastic communities, they saw themselves as marrying Christ. This freed them from the ties of father and husband. St Patrick, in his writings, remarks on how many women were becoming 'virgins for Christ', even against their families' wishes.[4]

When young Irish men and women chose to become hermits and to gather others around them in a monastic community, they were consciously imitating Christ and his twelve apostles. The Irish monastic ideal was to have a community of this number. But Christ began his public life by spending forty days in the desert alone. Only gradually did he gather the twelve who were to be his disciples. For this reason, Irish monks often began their monastic lives on their own as hermits, only gradually gathering numbers around them to form communities.

The life of Martin of Tours provided an inspiration for Irish monks. Martin had been a Roman soldier but, having converted to Christianity, he found it impossible to reconcile his military duties with his religious convictions. He left the army and became a conscientious objector. He

---

3   The Esker Riada is a ridge across the centre of Ireland made up of rocks and sand. It was deposited by the receding ice at the end of the Ice Age about ten thousand years ago. Elevated above the otherwise impassable bogs and forests of Ireland's midlands, it formed a naturally drained road. During medieval times it was used as a boundary between the northern and southern kingdoms of Ireland. Cf.Geissel, Hermann, *A Road on the Long Ridge, In Search of the Ancient Highway on the Esker Riada.* CRS Publications, 2006.

4   Cf. Patrick's *Confession,* par.42. Can be found on http://www.ccel.org/ccel/patrick/confession.html

grew to abhor violence. This was illustrated in an incident in his later life. Despite his disagreement with the teachings of a man called Priscillian, teachings that were declared heretical by the Roman church, he strongly protested against the man being put to death. Priscillian was put to death despite Martin's protests and became the first Christian to be put to death by Christians. This happened in 383 CE.

Irish society was a warring society. Boys grew up with the choice of being either warriors or druids. War and violence were honourable activities for the Irish and various clans and kingdoms were at constant war with each other. St Martin's opposition to war and violence and his teaching that it conflicted with Christian values gave inspiration to the Irish monks to create communities that were at peace with each other. As monasticism grew in Ireland and peace began to reign throughout the country, the peace dividend became very evident. Energies that had been put into making war, were now put into religious, artistic and creative work. With the advent of monasticism and peace, Ireland was about to enter its golden age.

The importance of the monastery of Martin of Tours as a model for Irish monasticism is emphasised by the fact that Martin's feast-day, 11 November, became an important festival in the Irish calendar. Until recent times, it was still being remembered and celebrated in rural Ireland. On this day, Irish people traditionally slaughtered surplus animals that were not required for the following year. Martin is still a common name among Irish men.

The Gospel of John

The second main inspiration for the Irish monks was the gospel of John. John's gospel was written much later than the three other canonical gospels. In it is contained a more mystical understanding of Jesus. It presents less of the historical person of Jesus and more of the poetic reflections of the writer. John presents Jesus as the 'Word of God' that was there from the beginning and that then became flesh.[5] He also emphasises the eucharistic presence of Jesus in the community. Jesus is present in the breaking of

---

5   Jn 1:1

bread.[6] Thirdly, John emphasises love.[7] John is the disciple whom Jesus loved.[8] Peter is asked three times does he love Jesus.[9]

The expression of Christianity that developed in Ireland reflected the emphases of John's gospel. It took a right-brained approach to Christianity. That is, its emphasis was on the creative, imaginative and poetic side of Christian spirituality. The Irish monks' reflections on the gospel writings led not to theological analysis and dogmatic pronouncements but to artistic illustrations on the pages of their manuscripts. Irish monks translated the gospels into art and poetry.

At the time when the mainstream Christian church in Europe had become hierarchical and dogmatic, Irish monks were being attracted to an alternative form of Christianity that was Johannine. This Johannine form of Christianity had originated in a community in Ephesus and was brought to southern Gaul by St Irenaeus, who had known St Polycarp the disciple of St John. From there, it influenced the new monastic foundations of Martin, Honoratus and Germanus.

In John's gospel, Jesus teaches that the 'Holy Spirit' is present as a guide in everyone.[10] The gospel emphasises brotherhood and community[11], implicitly rejecting the idea of a hierarchical authority structure. It also has a liberal attitude towards women and shows women in a very positive light. The stories of Mary and Martha, the Samaritan woman and, above all, Mary Magdalene, who is depicted in the gospel as the first person to know of the resurrection, give women a prominent place within the Christian community.[12] All of these emphases were to be found later in Celtic Christianity.

Celtic Christian spirituality today is the resurgence of a tradition which celebrates the Jesus story without an emphasis on dogma. It is a tradition that cannot legitimately be claimed by any one denomination of Christianity. Unlike many of these Christian denominations, who put an emphasis on issues of creed and dogma, Celtic Christianity puts the

---

6   Jn 6
7   Jn.13:34-35
8   Jn 21:20
9   Jn 21:15-17
10 Jn.14:15-17
11 Cf. Jn.13:14; 13:34.
12 Jn.11:1-44; 4:1-42; 20:1-18

emphasis rather on how one lives one's life. What one *does* in the world comes as a fruit of who and how one *is* in the world. Irish monks sought a perfect, sinless, heroic life. They wished to bring the expression of their love for Christ to heroic levels. This was their goal. Their work amongst others was the fruit of that. Their focus therefore was on 'being' rather than on 'doing', on quality of life rather than on levels of achievement.

The Story of Abraham

The third inspiration for Irish monks was Abraham. Abraham's story is the story of an heroic journey. Originally known as Abram, he left his homeland and his secure surroundings and headed off for 'a place that God will show him'.[13] His obedience to this call held the promise of great fruits. 'I will make you a great nation'.[14]

Prior to the arrival of Christianity, the Irish had many stories of heroic journeys. In the Irish tradition, an heroic journey was in a category of story that was called 'imram'. The journey of Bran is such a story, as is the later story of Brendan the Navigator. Bran is lured to an Otherworld island by the promise of beautiful women, endless amounts of food and an absence of suffering and death. The story of Brendan is a Christian version of this, where Brendan and his companions travel the seas in a small currach seeking out the Island of the Blessed or *Tír na nÓg*.

The inspiration of Abraham's journey led Irish monks to recognise the divine call within themselves to leave the security of home and to travel to where the spirit would lead them. In response to this inspiration, pilgrimage became a key aspect of Celtic spirituality. This pilgrimage was not a journey to a set destination but a type of wandering which the Irish called *peregrinatio pro Christo*, a wandering for Christ.

The Abraham story was the inspiration for young men and women to leave home and wander throughout Ireland searching for a place to settle. This place, when eventually found, they called their 'place of resurrection'. In the course of their wanderings, they visited monastic communities throughout the land, where they picked up skills, knowledge and a vision for their future life. Monasteries of that time were obliged to

---

13   *Genesis 12:1*
14   *Genesis 12:2*

offer hospitality to the stranger, so there was never any difficulty finding a place to stay.

The story of St Gobnait, a 6th-century nun, illustrates this practice. While on her *peregrinatio*, she travelled to Inis Oírr, one of the Aran Islands, to visit the monastery of St Caomhán. An angel came to her there and told her that she would find her place of resurrection when she saw a field with nine white deer grazing in it. She left Inis Oírr and continued her wandering until she arrived at Ballyvourney, in County Cork, where indeed she came upon nine white deer grazing in a field. Recognising the vision as the one the angel had described to her, she built her monastery there. She had found her 'place of resurrection'.

The Abraham story was also the inspiration for monks such as Columbanus to leave Ireland altogether and wander throughout Europe. A monk who left home and country left behind all the supports and comforts that were a protection to him, but that could also be a hindrance to him on his spiritual path. Entering into the vulnerability of the wilderness made room for the spirit to lead.

It is therefore a mistake to think of the Irish monks in Europe as missionaries, in the normal sense of that word. They were not part of the Rome-based centralised global mission. These monks were not in Europe primarily to spread the gospel, to evangelise local peoples or to baptise their children. They were there as a result of an Abrahamic call. Their focus was to live the gospel, to perfect their own lives and to show their love for Christ. The effect they had on local populations wherever they travelled was a fruit of their lives but not the object of their lives.

The Irish in Europe

While Irish monasticism did not have colonial or imperial ambitions, it did indeed expand into Western Europe in the early medieval period and made its presence felt there. Its motivations were entirely different from those that dominated the later expansion of Christianity throughout the New World.

Irish monks travelled to mainland Europe as a way of bringing their own lives closer to a state of perfection. According to the Irish spiritual tradition, as it had developed at this time, one perfected one's Christian life by living heroically. Heroism was the way in which one faced into danger and suffering, for the sake of a high ideal. The early Irish legends of Cúchulainn and Fionn MacCumhail exalted this heroism. For the Christian Irish, death by martyrdom was the ultimate act of heroism.

Martyrdom was very prevalent during the persecutions of the early Christians in southern Europe. The martyrs, along with the apostles, had become the first saints of the Christian church. The example of their deaths was kept in people's memory by the continuous recounting of their stories. Martyrdom became the highest ideal of all Christians and the ultimate guarantor of salvation.

However, from its beginnings, Christianity in Ireland had never suffered persecution. There were no martyrs in early Christian Ireland. St Patrick, as far as we know, died from old age, despite his claim that he was under threat of being put to death many times.[15] The resulting dilemma for Irish Christians, who could not achieve the martyrdom they desired, was resolved when they expanded the notion of martyrdom to include other forms of hardship that did not immediately lead to death at the hands of another. This broader concept of martyrdom was divided into three categories – red, green and white.

'Red martyrdom', for the Irish, was that most obvious form of martyrdom which one suffered as a direct result of one's life as a Christian. There were very few, if any, Christian martyrs of this kind in early medieval Ireland.

'Green martyrdom', for the Irish, was where one proved one's love and commitment to Christ by taking on a life of penitence and hardship. This form of martyrdom was expressed in the many extraordinary penances that Irish monks took on, the best example of which is monks eking out a life in atrociously hard conditions on a bare rock in the Atlantic ocean – Skellig Michael in County Kerry.

Of most relevance to our subject here is the third form of martyrdom practised by Irish monks, which was called 'white martyrdom'. This way of perfecting one's spiritual life required that one left the land of Ireland completely. The monk set out on a journey with little hope of ever returning. He (or sometimes she) left behind his beloved family and

---

15   Cf. Par. 52-59 of Patrick's *Confession*.

homeland, a comfortable, prosperous and peaceful Ireland where he had status and security.

This was not the forced economic migration that was to happen much later in Ireland under colonial rule. Ireland, especially during the 7th and 8th centuries, was a highly civilised, economically successful and peaceful society. The Europe on which most of these monks set their sights was immersed in the Dark Ages. It was in a state of turmoil with the collapse of the Roman empire and the invasion of the Goths, Huns, Vandals and others from the east and north. Ireland was a far better place to be than the rest of Europe at this time.

Responding to the challenge of white martyrdom, groups of Irish monks travelled all over western Europe from the 5th to the 10th centuries. There is evidence that they got as far south as Sicily and even into Egypt, as far east as the Ukraine and as far north as Iceland. There is even evidence that they made it to the North American continent[16] before it would have had that name. The marks of their presence are to be found all over Europe today in the preserved stories of their lives, in the remains of the monasteries and churches that they founded and in the influence that they had on local histories.

The iconic image of this Irish spiritual journey towards white martyrdom was that of a small Irish currach (a skin-covered boat) filled with twelve monks and an abbot, floating on the surface of the sea without sail, rudder or oar. It was an image that emphasised the community aspect of the journey, the vulnerability of those travelling and the complete reliance on the 'Holy Spirit' for direction. They were travelling as Jesus and the twelve apostles had travelled.

Irish monks who travelled across Europe in small groups during this period were responding to a gospel imperative to be 'the salt of the earth' and 'the light of the world'.[17] Putting their own lives in order and following the guidance of the 'Holy Spirit' was their chief goal. The priorities of these monks were very different from those of the corporate church of Rome. Yet the presence and work of these monks throughout Europe left a lasting legacy.

---

16   A petroglyph was found on the wall of a cave in West Virginia. It is in the ogham script, with Christian references and is dated in or around 7th century. Cf. Ida Jane Gallagher and Barry Fell, 'Irish In America Before Columbus'. *The AISLING Magazine*, Issue 17.

17   *Matthew 5:13 -14*

Irish monks are credited with saving European civilisation when it was in danger of being snuffed out altogether during the Dark Ages.[18] Without ever having the arrogance of an Augustine of Canterbury, the fundamentalist zeal of a Wilfrid or the intolerance of a Boniface, all of whom worked for the Roman church (cf. Chapters 11 and 12), they succeeded in exercising great influence among both the poor and the powerful and they effected enormous change for the good throughout Europe.

St Patrick

The history of Irish Christianity has been written from a Roman perspective. From this perspective, Patrick takes centre-stage in the spread of Christianity throughout Ireland. That is still the dominant perspective today in both academic and ecclesiastical circles.[19]

Christianity existed in Ireland before Patrick. The Irish calendar of saints has four pre-Patrician saints who are well remembered and celebrated in their local areas. These are St Ciarán of Saighir, St Ailbhe of Emly, St Ibar of Wexford and St Declan of Ardmore. Each of these was a monk and founder of a monastery. In the locations where these saints worked, legends about them remain alive in the folk memory today and marks on the landscape such as monastic remains provide a tangible connection to their lives.

These four saints who pre-dated St Patrick lived in the south of Ireland. It appears therefore that Christianity was well established in the south of Ireland before the advent of Patrick. It may be for this reason that Patrick began his mission in the north.

Patrick in his own writings claimed great success in his mission. He wrote of 'many thousands' of Irish people being converted and baptised, of the 'masses lately come to belief'. He claimed he had ordained clergy everywhere and that great numbers were becoming monks and virgins for Christ.[20]

---

18 Thomas Cahill, *How The Irish Saved Civilisation, The Untold Story of Ireland's Heroic Role from the Fall of Rome to the Rise of Medieval Europe.* London, Hodder and Staughton, 1995.
19 The Catholic Encyclopedia nonchalantly claims that Christianity began in Ireland with St Patrick, that Patrick established Armagh as the primatial see from the very beginning and that anything to the contrary was never a question for historians. Cf. http://www.newadvent.org/cathen/11554a.htm
20 St Patrick's *Confession*, paragraphs 38-41, 50.

There is no reason to disbelieve his claims. He was the only successful missionary Ireland ever had. Nonetheless, his story as it is presented today is a revisionist one, with a clear pro-Roman bias. The view of Patrick as the founder of Christianity in Ireland is the view of a victorious Roman church that did not establish itself fully in Ireland until the 12th century. If one takes a view from the 6th century, when Celtic Christianity was flourishing, one finds that St Colmcille (Columba) was the real hero of that century and that Patrick was practically forgotten.[21]

When tensions developed in Ireland during the 7th century between the Celtic model of Christianity and the Roman model, the Roman apologists claimed Patrick as their own. It became a battle between those who supported Patrick and those who supported Colmcille.

Patrick was not the ideal candidate to hold the flag for the Roman side, but he was the only one the Roman apologists had. To begin with, Patrick, although raised a Christian within the Roman empire, was a Celt. The Britons of Britain at that time were of Celtic origin. This may have made Patrick sympathetic to Celtic ways.

Secondly, his return to Ireland as a missionary, after he had been there in his youth as a slave, was the result of a personal calling. He came back to Ireland because of his own burning desire to do so. He needed and received ecclesiastical sanction for this but primarily this was a personal mission. In terms of the Irish spiritual tradition, he had found his 'place of resurrection' in Ireland. What drove him, while he was in Ireland, was his personal vocation, not any particular desire to please his masters or to promote the Roman church project. It is unlikely that Patrick ever visited Rome.

Thirdly, the Roman church authorities, based in Britain, had been reluctant to commission Patrick as a missionary in their name because of his lack of education (he had poor Latin) and because of a sin he had committed in his youth, which gave them doubts about his character.[22] They reluctantly commissioned him only as a result of his own insistence and determination.

A previous mission to Ireland, led by Palladius, had been a failure

---

21   Máire Herbert, *Iona, Kells and Derry: The History and Hagiography of the Monastic Familia of Columba*. Four Courts Press, Dublin. 1996.
22   St Patrick's *Confession*, paragraphs 26-32.

and, it would seem, the authorities had little hope that Patrick's would be successful. Rome's aim in sending the earlier mission to Ireland was to counteract a form of Christianity that was in Ireland already, known as Pelagianism. I will deal with this in greater detail in the next chapter. Patrick shows no evidence in his writings of having opposed this form of Christianity while in Ireland. This may be because he was sympathetic to it himself.

However, Patrick in his *Confession* does display what were to become typical attitudes of missionaries promoting the global project of Christianity. He describes Ireland as a place where: '(they) never had any knowledge of God but, always, until now, cherished idols and unclean things'.[23] This statement shows complete disdain for the spiritual practices and traditions of the Irish people prior to the advent of Christianity and ignores the sophisticated awareness of the divine that was present in Ireland from earliest times.

It is clear from the writings of native Irish monks a century or two later that this ignorant attitude of Patrick was not shared by all. Irish monasteries became the places where these earlier spiritual traditions were remembered and recorded for posterity. The rich reservoir of spirituality present in Ireland prior to Christianity has been made available to us today mainly through the writings of Celtic Christian monks. Without these writings, one could not understand Celtic spirituality, which in its fullness is a blend of the old and the new, Christian and pre-Christian.

While one could take Patrick's word for it that he was successful in preaching Christianity in the northern part of Ireland, one cannot say that he succeeded in establishing the Roman infrastructure of the corporate church on Irish soil. This is not surprising. The structure of Irish society did not facilitate the Roman infrastructure. The major centres of Roman Christianity were in the cities of Europe. This is where the powerful and influential bishops resided. The influence of the Roman church radiated out into the countryside from these cities. Structurally, the Roman papacy presided over an urban and episcopal church.

---

23   St Patrick's *Confession*, paragraph 41.

There were no cities or towns in Ireland at the time of Patrick. Irish Christianity, from its very beginnings, even before Patrick, was monastic. Despite Patrick's work at ordaining priests and bishops, the model of church that survived Patrick, after his death, was monastic and not episcopal. The significant Christians in Ireland in the centuries after Patrick's death were abbots and abbesses, not bishops.

There is little doubt that Patrick did ordain priests and bishops. However, these bishops and priests were absorbed into monasteries, either at the time of Patrick or some time later. They lived in monasteries, were subject to the abbot of that monastery and performed specific sacerdotal duties within the community. Patrick, in his writings, clearly announces himself as a bishop but never claims to be a monk or to have founded a monastery. For future generations of Irish monks, he could never therefore be a suitable role model. Later, the pro-Roman hagiographers of Patrick[24] claimed that he had founded the monastery of Armagh and that he had become its first abbot.

While Patrick, according to his own *Confession*, was successful in converting large numbers of Irish people to Christianity (and there is no reason to doubt this), the form of Christianity that they embraced was an indigenous Irish expression of monasticism that had been in existence in Ireland before Patrick's arrival. In this sense, Patrick's work strengthened the independence of Irish Christianity by increasing the number of adherents. His work did little to bring Irish Christianity into line with the rest of Europe.

After the death of Patrick, he was not replaced by any other bishop nominated from Europe.[25] There was no further contact with Rome. The authorities in Europe either did not see fit to follow up his work by appointing someone else to succeed him, or they were in such disarray after the collapse of the empire that they had more important things, such as their own survival, on their minds. Patrick's name disappeared almost into oblivion. Even the location of his grave is unknown, although it is claimed to be in Downpatrick.

---

24 Tírechán and Ó Muirchiú, two separate accounts of Patrick's life, written in the 7th century.
25 Legend has it that his disciple Benan, an Irish man, replaced him.

St Colmcille or Columba

Patrick died sometime between 461 and 493. His name and fame receded and, with the flourishing of Celtic monasticism in the following century, a new name appeared on the horizon. That person was Colmcille. Colmcille, or Columba, as he became known in Scotland, was the most significant person of early Irish monasticism.

Born in 521, Colmcille could not have ever met Patrick. He came into the world with an impeccable pedigree. His father was a grandson of Niall of the Nine Hostages, who had been high-king of Ireland in the 4th century, while his mother was a princess, who came from the Leinster family of kings. Three of his cousins became monarchs of Ireland. Colmcille grew up with natural and charismatic leadership abilities and his powerful physical presence drew people to him. Had he not been a monk, he would have been a king. In a way, he was a king. He became high-king of Irish Christianity.

Colmcille provided inspirational leadership for the growth of Irish Christianity. The achievements of his life gave him unrivalled status in Ireland and beyond. Where Patrick had never founded a monastery (although later it was claimed he did), Colmcille founded many monasteries throughout Ireland. To this day, one finds place-names and legends associated with Colmcille in almost every part of Ireland. When he moved to Iona, an island off Scotland, as a form of white martyrdom, he established a centre of Celtic Christianity there that was to transform the northern half of Britain. For many centuries after his death, Colmcille was the shining light of inspiration and leadership for every Irish monk.

Although Colmcille lived in the century after Patrick, his name and not Patrick's was the name that became associated with the foundation of Celtic Christianity in Ireland. At the Synod of Whitby in 664, those arguing in favour of the Irish date for Easter appealed to the authority of Colmcille and not to the authority of Patrick to bolster their case. Had the Celtic model of Christianity survived in Ireland, the big Irish festival today would be the 9th of June (St Colmcille's Day) and not the 17th of March (St Patrick's Day).

Abbots and Abbesses

An abbot or abbess of a Celtic monastery was called a 'co-arb' of the founder. This title implied that the new abbot or abbess took the place of the founder. Generally, a 'co-arb' was chosen from among suitable candidates within the family of the founder, in the same way that kings were chosen. This family, from which both kings and abbots came, had ownership of the monastic lands. The successive abbots of Iona were all chosen from the northern O'Neill royal family. As Celtic monasticism developed, various monasteries federated under the name of one founder. The federation of the Iona monastery of Colmcille included monasteries in many parts of Ireland.

This procedure created monastic family dynasties that lasted centuries. It also kept the monasteries under local control. There was no room for direct interference from an hierarchical church. In order to protect the lineage, these abbatial families had to procreate. While celibacy was an idea that had come in from the European church, for many of the monks and abbots and also for the priests and bishops it was not a practised reality. Even Colmcille was believed to have fathered a child.[26] The records in the annals clearly testify to this. The position of an abbot or bishop was often taken by the son of the former incumbent.[27]

---

26 Cf. Margaret Odrowaz-Sypniewska, *Saint Columba*. http://www.angelfire.com/mi4/pol-crt/StColumba.html

27 For example, the *Annals of the Four Masters* record that Conn na mBocht, who died in AD 1031, was head of the *Céile Dé* ('Partners with God'), a community of anchorites, in Clonmacnoise. (The *Céile Dé* was a reform movement within Irish monasticism). He was called 'na mBocht' ('of the poor') probably because the *Céile Dé* had an obligation to look after the poor. Conn was married and his son Maelfinden became the 'comharba Chiaráin', that is the next abbot of the monastery. Another son, Maelchiarain (comharba Chiaráin), also became abbot and died 1079. He was held in great esteem. It is most likely that one of the family held the position of head of the *Céile Dé* until the beginning of the 12th century when it passed on to the Ui Neachtain family.

Of Conn's family, the Ui Ceallaigh Breagh in Meath, Gorman had been 'comharba Mochta' in Louth and died 753. His son Torbach, scribe and abbot of Armagh, died 807. Aedhagan, Torbach's son, abbot of Louth, died 845. His son Luachan, father of Ecertach, 'airchinneach Eclais Bec', Clonmacnoise, died 893. His son, bishop of Clonmacnoise, died 953. His son was 'ferlegind' and anchorite of Clonmacnoise and died 1005. His son Joseph, 'anmchara' of Clonmacnoise, was father of Conn na mBocht and died 1059.

This information is taken from : Peter O'Dwyer O.Carm, *Céile Dé–Spiritual Reform in Ireland 750-900*. Carmelite Publications, Dublin. 1981. p.25-27.

Similarly, the *Annals of Ulster* record the coarbs of Moninna, 517 CE, foundress of a monastery at Killeevy, close to present-day Dundalk. It records that 'the thirteenth abbess was the daughter of Foidemnn, king of Conaille Muirthemne around Dundalk, in which Killeevy lay. Her sister and daughter were successively abbesses here. The eighth abbess was grand-daughter of the fifth, and the ninth and tenth were sisters, nieces of the eighth.' Cf. Catherine Thom, *Early Irish Monasticism*, T&T Clark, 2006, p.82.

Monks, Bishops and the Pope

By the 7th century, Celtic monasticism had established itself in every corner of Ireland. It had become an integral part of Irish society. Christianity in Ireland found its expression through the monasteries. Abbots and abbesses were the spiritual leaders of the people. Priests and bishops were members of monastic communities, subject to their abbot or abbess.

Brigid, the abbess of Kildare, had a monastery of men and women. Her community included a bishop, Conleth, who was subject to her authority. Brigid's jurisdiction covered an area as large as the province of Leinster. According to legend, she herself was a bishop.

When Irish monks and monastic communities began to go abroad and travel across Europe, they followed the practices they had had at home. According to this protocol, their first port of call on arriving somewhere was the local king. He was asked to allocate them some land on which they could establish their communities.

From various sources of historical evidence, it is clear that Irish monks in Europe had little respect for local bishops. The Irish tended either to ignore them or to condemn their extravagant lifestyles. When one sees the background from which they came, one can understand this. Bishops in Ireland had little status or power. They lived as monks themselves. Irish monks had no practice in acknowledging the high status of a bishop. This attitude resulted, however, in many a clash between Celtic monk and local European bishop and brought the Celtic-Roman tension into the heart of church politics in Europe.

St Columbanus

St Columbanus was the greatest of the Irish monks who travelled to Europe seeking 'white martyrdom'. In 585 CE he travelled with a group of monks and landed in what is now Normandy. Ignoring the local bishops, he approached the king, Gontram and sought permission to build a monastery in his kingdom. Within a period of twenty years, Columbanus had built three foundations in close proximity: Luxueil, Annegray and Fontaines. Despite this, he did not have enough room for all those who wanted to join him.

The local bishops were not happy with these developments. The practices at these monasteries were at variance with the mainstream tradition. They called a synod and summoned Columbanus. Columbanus failed to attend. Instead he wrote a letter in which he defended his freedom to live according to the traditions of his elders. In it he said: 'One thing alone I ask of you, holy Fathers, permit me to live in silence in these forests, near the bones of seventeen of my brethren now dead.' He also reprimanded the bishops for their lifestyle.[28]

As a result, there was no love lost between the bishops and Columbanus. In the end, the bishops conspired to get rid of him altogether. They did this by turning Queen Brunehault and the young king Thierry against him. Columbanus and his Irish monks were then driven out of that kingdom.

Columbanus did not, however, go home to Ireland. His boat was hit by a storm and he, with his Irish companions, were shipwrecked and thrown back on the shores of mainland Europe. His subsequent journey brought him through France, Germany, Switzerland and down into Italy. Along the way, he established many foundations and left marks of his presence that are still discoverable by us today. By the time of his death, in Bobbio, Italy, he and his disciples had founded more than one hundred monasteries[29].

Columbanus was a towering figure in Europe at this time. Well acquainted with kings and disliked by bishops, he was not afraid to challenge the pope on certain issues. Letters written by Columbanus to Pope Gregory I and later to Pope Boniface IV show him disagreeing with the popes on the Easter question. While Columbanus, in these letters, shows respect for the pope and his position, this does not prevent him from expressing disagreement and advising the pope as to certain actions he should take.[30]

Celtic Christianity and Rome

Despite these recorded tensions between Irish monks and the pope and his bishops, one cannot put Celtic Christianity into the category of Protestant, any more than one can put it into the category of Roman Catholic. Nor can

---

28 Columba Edmonds, 'St Columbanus' in *The Catholic Encyclopedia*, Volume IV. Published 1908. http://www.newadvent.org/cathen/04137a.htm.
29 Cf. Róisín Ní Mheara, *In Search of Irish Saints*. Dublin, Four Courts Press. 1994.
30 Joseph F.T.Kelly 'The Irish Monks And the See of Peter' in *Monastic Studies*, No. 14, Montreal. 1983.

one say that Celtic Christianity belongs to the Eastern Orthodox tradition. Celtic Christianity predates the Reformation by over one thousand years and predates the split between Rome and Constantinople by up to six hundred years. In all these tensions between Rome and the Irish, the basic position of the Irish was that they wished to be left alone and allowed to do it their way. The basic position of the Roman church was that it could not tolerate this independence.

It is important to clarify here the exact relationship between Celtic Christianity and Rome. This is best described as a clash between the global, uniforming project of Rome, which was intent on building a Holy Roman Empire and the interest of the Celtic tradition in keeping its expression of Christianity an integral part of its own culture and society. The tension that was felt in those centuries is a tension that is still in the world today between the forces of globalisation and indigenous cultures.

Celtic Christianity was never cut off from Rome. It simply wished to keep its distance from Rome and not allow Rome to interfere with its unique expression of Christianity. European influences, such as the use of Latin, were present in Celtic monasteries from the beginning and no Celtic monastery ever cut itself off from these influences. Celtic Christianity's uniqueness lay in the fact that these influences were absorbed and digested, becoming integrated and inculturated into a consistent Celtic expression. When Roman practices began to be imposed from outside without this process of integration, Celtic Christianity lost its integrity and uniqueness.

From Rome's perspective, Celtic Christianity was a loose cannon. Rome was not in control of it and it resisted attempts at control. From the 5th century through to the 12th century, Rome had virtually no way of directly influencing Celtic Christianity in Ireland. It had to wait for the Irish themselves to be persuaded that bringing their practices into line with Rome was the best way forward. From the 7th century onwards, an internal debate on this issue fermented within Celtic Christianity.

The Irish in Europe

By the 6th century, Irish monks were being welcomed far and wide throughout Europe by the secular authorities. Clovis, the Frankish king, was the great benefactor and protector of the Irish monks. He had invaded Gaul in the late 5th century and on his success had converted to Christianity. He showed a real determination to establish Christian principles within his Merovingian dynasty, which was to hold sway for 250 years. At a time when European clergy were thin on the ground, the Celtic monks were a godsend to him and his successors in achieving these aims.

Europe was in its Dark Ages at this time, still reeling from the collapse of the Roman empire and the chaos caused by the invasion of the Huns, Vandals, Goths and others, as they roamed across the landscape seeking to establish themselves on new territories. Europe was in the process of deep transformation. As these new peoples settled the lands, the language of Latin was lost as a vernacular and replaced by a wide variety of languages.

New borders were drawn and new political structures established. The Vandals were in north Africa and the Goths were in Spain. In the northern part of Europe, Germanic tribes were in the ascendant. The Angles and Saxons had invaded southern Britain, the Franks had expanded into Gaul,and other Germanic tribes were in control of northern Europe east of the Franks. Gradually, over hundreds of years, a new Europe was born – a Europe that is still with us to this day. The Irish monks played a leading role in the establishment of this new Europe.

Irish monks were welcome in Europe because they brought with them the civilisation and scholarship which had been lost in the chaos of a collapsed Roman society. They also brought with them a renewed and vibrant Christianity. They were welcomed by the civil authorities and the local people, to whom they became of real service.

However, these Celtic monks and their monasteries were a threat to the established Roman church. The Roman church had been compromised by its collusion with the Roman empire. It had suffered a severe shaking with the collapse of that empire. After that collapse it was weak and disorganised. For a while Celtic Christianity became a serious threat to that church. Europe was in danger of converting to a Celtic style of Christianity.

What worked against the Irish monks ever achieving this imperial goal was that that goal was never part of their ambition. Irish monks had not travelled to Europe primarily as missionaries or evangelists, even less so as colonisers or imperialists. They did not have a global vision.

Although Irish monasteries were founded all over western Europe during this period, their presence there was not part of some strategic plan to convert Europe to Celtic ways.

Irish monks were in Europe, one could say, for personal reasons. Their travel to Europe was a form of self-imposed exile for the purpose of perfecting their spiritual lives. However, continuous pressure from the episcopacy and from the Roman hierarchy gradually wore down their independence and resistance. A number of them, most notably Fergal of Salzburg, were themselves appointed to episcopal positions. Eventually, over a number of centuries, these monasteries were absorbed into the mainstream.

To this day, the presence of these Irish monks throughout Europe is remembered in towns, villages and rural areas. In France, Germany, Austria, Switzerland, Italy and other countries their names have been given to streets, parishes and hospitals, their graves and tombs have become places of pilgrimage and statues have been erected in their memory and honour.

Indigenous Christianity

The uniqueness of Celtic Christianity was that it produced an inculturated, indigenous form of Christianity that grew organically upon the fertile topsoil of an earlier Celtic spirituality. The pre-Christian spirituality of the Celts is the Old Testament of Celtic Christianity. Many of the pre-Christian beliefs and stories of the Irish foreshadowed aspects of the Christian story. To give some examples: the triple goddess of Ireland, with three names – Eriú, Foghla and Banba – pre-figures the Christian Trinity Father, Son and Holy Spirit; Dagda, the great Celtic father god, is a prefiguration of God the Father; Lúgh, the Celtic god of light, is a Christ figure who defeats the forces of darkness. That victory, like Easter, is celebrated annually in the Lúghnasa festival. Ireland even has the great tomb at Newgrange, which was designed to admit sunlight to its innermost cavern on the darkest days of the year.[31] One could argue that this prefigures the empty tomb of Jesus,

---

31   Newgrange is a 5,000 year old tomb which was used for the burial of bones of the dead. At sunrise on the day of the winter solstice, the sun shines through a strategically placed opening above the entrance and travels down a narrow corridor to light up the cavern where the bones are laid. The light in the tomb lasts only seventeen minutes. Newgrange predates Christ's death by 3,200 years.

proclaiming light in the darkness, life after death and the resurrection of nature after the severities of winter.

Celtic Christianity developed in Ireland at a time when the influence of European Christianity was weak. Ireland grew its own organic version of Christianity without interference. While it is true that the message and stories of Christ came from Europe to Ireland, the Irish transformed them, giving them a new form, a new emphasis and a new expression.

The other significant difference at the time was that Irish Christianity was monastic in a rural environment, whereas European Christianity was episcopal in an urban environment. Apart from a handful of monasteries, such as St Martin's at Tours and St Honoratus's on the island of Lérins, the monastic movement that flourished in Ireland from the 5th century onwards had no equivalent on mainland Europe. Although St Benedict had lived in the early 6th century, the monastic movement based on his rule did not begin in earnest until the 7th century. It was then used by Rome to counteract the influence of the Celtic monasteries.

Spreading the Jesus Story – a Different Way

Celtic Christianity is an example of how the Jesus story could have spread throughout the world without being institutionalised and commodified. Diverse peoples could have chosen to inculturate the inspiration of the life of Jesus into their own spiritual traditions, enhancing and enriching them rather than destroying them.

It is reasonable to take the position that Jesus was a universally inspirational figure, a person whose life could have relevance for anyone in the world. However, his story and his teachings could have been transmitted without being wrapped in the cultural trappings of an institutionalised Europe and without the condemnation and destruction of all other spiritual traditions and practices.

The Decline of Celtic Christianity

While Celtic Christianity was a unique example of how Christianity could have spread without being institutionalised and centrally controlled, it did not survive in this form into modern times. From the 7th century onwards, there were pressures coming from European Christianity which forced it to change and come into line with the rest of Europe. After the defeat of the Irish viewpoint at the Synod of Whitby in 664, Celtic Christianity was in retreat. From then on, it lost ground continuously to the influence of Rome.

By the 12th century, Celtic Christianity as a unique, inculturated expression of Christianity, had all but gone. During this century, Irish monasteries and monks were replaced in their central role by bishops and priests. Ireland took on the same ecclesiastical structure as the rest of Europe. The objective of Pope Gregory VII's, 'Gregorian' reform was achieved. The practice of Christianity throughout his realm was made uniform.

During this century Ireland was invaded by the Norman king, Henry II. Henry had been given permission and encouraged to invade Ireland by Pope Adrian IV, the only Englishman ever to sit on the papal throne. This led to the colonisation of Ireland by the Normans and subsequently by the English – a situation that was to last for 800 years. Both ecclesiastically and politically, the 12th century was a period of intense change in Ireland. Oppressive forces, intent on breaking the unique spirit of the people of Ireland and on harnessing them to the imperial drive for power and domination, had gained control. Central to the achievement of their aims was the uprooting and destroying of all that made these Irish people independent.

The 12th century marks the beginning of a period when Ireland's back was broken. It was a huge historic turning point – outside forces acquired a significant foothold on Irish soil which led over time to the fulfilment of their ambition to gain control of the land of Ireland, its people and its Christianity.

The military and political campaigns which took place at this time and the subsequent colonisation of Ireland, are well documented. Irish people today are well aware of it. However, there is little or no documentation available to the Irish public of the ecclesiastical colonisation that took place at the same time. As a result, there is little consciousness or awareness of it among the contemporary Irish. While Ireland has shaken off its political colonisers, it remains ecclesiastically colonised, with the centre of ecclesiastical power residing firmly in Rome.

The Bountiful Harvest of Celtic Monasticism

The uniqueness of the Celtic model of Christianity had brought Ireland to its finest hour, reaching its peak in the 7th and 8th centuries and termed the Golden Age. Ireland had never before and has never since reached those heights of scholarship, sanctity and artistic creativity. The whole country had become monastic. It was a country that was prosperous, at peace with itself and its neighbours and revelling in the celebration of its unique identity.

Bubbling over with enthusiasm for the Christian ideal, Irish monks had built their monastic cells on the tops of mountains, on small islands in lakes and rivers and on the most forbidding of rocks in the Atlantic ocean. Monks had set sail in small, vulnerable crafts made of sticks and leather hide, creating monastic communities in the Faroe Islands, in Iceland and all across western Europe. In monasteries back home, works of art were produced that have yet to be surpassed – works such as the *Book of Kells*, the Ardagh Chalice, the Tara Brooch and the stone cross at Monasterboice.

The bountiful harvest of Celtic monasticism in Ireland produced a large surplus of monks who chose voluntary exile on the continent of Europe. In doing so, they became key players in the rebuilding of Europe during the Dark Ages after the fall of the Roman empire. These Irish monks had achieved a level of sanctity and scholarship to which their European neighbours aspired. Their presence in Europe and the fame of Ireland abroad, led to many Europeans coming to Ireland to study in the monasteries, a phenomenon which earned Ireland the title 'Land of Saints and Scholars'.

The extraordinary success of Celtic monasticism in and beyond Ireland has given a lasting heritage to the world. In its most tangible form, that heritage is what is today termed Celtic spirituality. Celtic spirituality is unique in today's world in that, although Christian, it has its roots in indigenous, pagan spirituality. As a pagan spirituality, it is similar to other native spiritualities such as Native American. But unlike other pagan spiritualities, it has a Christian dimension. The unique mix of pagan and Christian gives this expression of Christianity a rootedness in nature and a connectedness to place and to people.

Many people today are drawn to Celtic spirituality, believing that they can integrate it into their church-going lives as mainstream Christians. This is to put Celtic spirituality in the same category as other Christian spiritualities such as that of St Thérèse of Lisieux or of the Marian apparitions of Medjugorje. In its superficial aspects, one can do this, but once one delves into Celtic spirituality more deeply, one is challenged to leave the institutional, global forms of Christianity aside and to return to a spirituality that emerged out of local community and the immediate natural environment of that community.

Irish monasticism in its purest form was anarchic, unregulated and untainted by a desire for power and control. In its less pure form, power struggles were present but their focus tended to be the struggle for supremacy between monasteries. I will deal with this issue in Chapter 13. Communities were deliberately small, ideally thirteen people, imitating Christ and the twelve apostles. Although each community had a clear-cut leader, the abbot or abbess, there were no higher levels of authority to which these leaders could aspire. The aspiration, on the contrary, was to live an heroic life in imitation of Jesus and in this way to become, in gospel terminology, the 'salt of the earth' and 'the light of the world'.

This model of a life's mission, that is focussed on changing and perfecting oneself rather than on changing others or changing the world, is a valuable antidote to the dominant Christian view that one must go out and preach the gospel. It is also an antidote to the globalisation project, which has now become secularised and which envisages the whole world becoming Western and capitalist.

A Paradigm for Personal and Social Transformation

Celtic Christianity offers an alternative paradigm for the organisation of human community. It shows how the essential elements of a radically spiritual community can be extracted from the Jesus story and the Jewish historical context and transferred successfully into another cultural context and another historical time.

This paradigm offers a template for how small groups of people can come together to live out a common vision. As in the Jesus story, these people leave aside the pattern of life that they have grown up with and create a new pattern, inspired by a spiritual vision and upheld by spiritual principles.

What the Celtic monastic paradigm establishes beyond doubt is that this form of spiritual community can achieve not only personal transformation but the transformation of human society. Personal and social transformation can take place without war or violence, without an imperialist or colonial agenda and without any top-down imposition of ideas. Celtic spirituality offers the possibility of avoiding dogmatism, fundamentalism and all other temptations to control or change the behaviour of others from the outside. It emphasises change in oneself and invites an heroic commitment to one's own transformation.

Celtic monasticism clearly shows that the best way to bring about change in human society, whether in civil society or in church structures, is to model that new society or new church in one's own life and in one's own community – to become that new society or new church in a small but visible way.

Present-Day Realities

The Christian church in Ireland at present is in decline. There is an ever-growing shortage of clergy and a steep fall-off in practice. This is leaving a vacuum. There is no sense of an alternative church or spirituality emerging. People who leave the Christian churches are not joining other churches or religions. Many Irish people who are disillusioned with the Christian church today continue to attend that church because they don't know what else to do. The communal memory of a form of Christianity without the shackles and uniformity of a multinational institution has been forgotten. The Irish imagination, which was fired so magnificently by the thought of political liberation, has yet to find the spark that will ignite it in relation to ecclesiastical or spiritual liberation.

In Ireland today there is a renewed interest in practising the disciplines of a healthy lifestyle – eating healthy foods, taking exercise and avoiding excessive indulgence. There is also a growing interest in meditation of various kinds, in the martial arts and in a wide variety of therapies and practices that calm the mind, reduce stress and heal the body in a natural way. In parallel with this is a revival of many of the artistic traditions of Ireland, such as music, dancing, local crafts and even the Irish language. All these are forms of spiritual expression.

In all these trends one can see a common direction. From the bottom up, from within the community itself, is emerging a new expression of spirituality that has virtually no connection with church or ecclesiastical institutions. Irish people are already reclaiming their musical and dance traditions, as well as other artistic traditions and integrating them into their modern-day lives. They are also engaged in the difficult process of reclaiming their language, through Irish-language schooling, an Irish-language television station and through new legislation. The final stage of this process of reclamation will be the reclaiming of their spiritual tradition, Celtic spirituality. The more the Irish people move in this direction, the more resistant they will be to the all-encompassing standardisation and hegemony of a globalised world.

The Wish of Manchán of Liath

I wish, O son of the Living God, ancient eternal King,
for a secret hut in the wilderness
that it may be my dwelling.

A very blue shallow well to be beside it,
a clear pool for washing away sins
through the grace of the Holy Ghost.

A beautiful wood close by around it on every side,
for the nurture of many-voiced birds, to shelter and hide it.

Facing the south for warmth,
a little stream across its enclosure,
a choice ground with abundant bounties
which would be good for every plant.

A few sage disciples, I will tell their number,
humble and obedient, to pray to the King.

Four threes, three fours, fit for every need,
two sixes in the church, both south and north.

Six couples in addition to me myself,
praying through the long ages to the King
who moves the sun.

A lovely church decked with linen,
a dwelling for God of Heaven;
then, bright candles over the holy white Scriptures.

One room to go to for the care of the body,
without wantonness, without voluptuousness,
without meditation of evil.

This is the house-keeping I would undertake,
I would choose it without concealing;
fragrant fresh leeks, hens, speckled salmon, bees.

My fill of clothing and of food
from the King of good fame,
and for me to be sitting for a while
praying to God in every place.

(Irish. Author Unknown. 10th century translation)

10

PELAGIUS AND AUGUSTINE

By the end of the 4th century CE, Christianity had become the religion of the Roman empire. Christian leaders were in a privileged position. The church's power was becoming centralised and its theology dogmatic. The dominant voices on behalf of Christianity during this period were those of Augustine and Jerome. Together they promoted a model of church that was authoritarian and misogynistic and a theology that was sin-laden. From the Celtic regions, a single voice rose to oppose them – Pelagius.

The crowning of Constantine as Roman emperor in 313 CE was a turning point in the history of Christianity. From this until the death of Constantine, Christianity was transformed from a minority religion, that had been subject to many persecutions, into being the official religion of the empire. Constantine was instrumental in not only giving Christianity this official status, but in encouraging the Christian leadership of the time to come together and establish a common platform. From this platform, a body of orthodox teaching began to emerge and the bishop of Rome gained recognition as the primary leader.

This transformation was itself a serious threat to the integrity of the gospel message, with state patronage almost guaranteed to use Christianity for its own ends. Christians who understood this felt more comfortable being persecuted than being privileged. But at the same time, the two great figures of Augustine and Jerome were championing a theology that justified the emergence of a corporate church with imperial powers and global ambitions of its own. For some, it was time to act to oppose these developments.

But first, what were Augustine and Jerome teaching? The central issue, around which everything else turned, was the concept of original sin.

According to Augustine, a child at conception inherited the sin of Adam and Eve. Every person born was corrupted by that sin to such an extent that they were not capable of living without sinning again. That person could achieve salvation, or heaven, only by the grace of 'God'. The grace of 'God' was mediated exclusively by the orthodox Christian church through the administration of the sacraments. Outside this corporate church there was no salvation. That was the position of Augustine and Jerome.

Augustine, on the one hand, believed that all people, including himself, were irredeemably corrupt and sinful. On the other hand, he believed that hope of redemption could come only through the established Christian church. A child could be saved from original sin only through baptism in the Christian church. All non-baptised children were lost to the fires of hell. One could only maintain one's hope of salvation by regular attendance at the church and regular reception of its sacraments. Even then, the grace of 'God' could not be earned. You were predestined either to be saved or damned.

Augustine taught that humanity was fundamentally doomed through the inherited sin of Adam. 'Every man therefore brings into the world a nature already in so ruined a condition that he is not only more inclined to evil than to good but he is not capable of anything else but sin'.[1] From the time of Adam, humans were born corrupt. The original sin of Adam and Eve was, according to Augustine, the sin of concupiscence. It was passed into each newly-conceived child through the concupiscence of its parents. This inherited corruption of the soul left an uncontrollable inclination to sin, even after the soul had been cleansed in baptism.

For Augustine, the only way to be saved was through Christ. Christ was the saviour from sin whose saving graces were exclusively mediated through the established church and its sacraments. In Augustine's view it was impossible to free oneself from the inclination to sin without the grace of 'God'. He believed that 'God' did not give that grace to everybody. Certain souls were predestined to be saved.

Augustine's theology attributed to the corporate church immense power over a Christian's life. If one could not find salvation outside

---

1   Gustav Friedrich Wiggers. *Versus einer pragmatischer Darstellung des Augustinismus und Pelagianismus.* Hamburg. 1833, page 100.

that church, that church and its ministers became the mediators of that salvation. With this theology in place, the corporate church was in a position to regulate the most intimate details of a Christian's private life.

Augustine in his own lifetime became a dominant figure within mainstream Christianity. He was a prolific writer, tireless in his opposition to all sorts of teachings he did not agree with and he had the political skills to build strong campaigns against his opponents. After his death, his theology, expressed through his copious writings, became the established position of Roman Christianity. Even today, practically all the major Christian denominations subscribe to his views.

In the Celtic areas on the fringe of Europe at this time, a very different type of Christianity was being lived. These Celtic Christians had a theology and a church structure that celebrated the freedom of the human person. Emphasis was on how one lived one's life rather than on what one believed. Unlike the teachings of Augustine, hierarchy, orthodoxy and sinfulness were not dominant themes.

When Pelagius appeared on the streets of Rome during the lifetime of Augustine, he represented this Celtic view from the margins. He had travelled by boat and on foot from the north-western edge of Europe, to almost single-handedly oppose the political and theological developments that were taking place within mainstream Christianity at this time. His crusade took him not just to Rome but to Jerusalem. He was not ultimately successful, but the power of his personal authority and his teachings put down a marker that the Celtic Christian people were not going to be easily subdued by the Roman and Augustinian church.

Who Was Pelagius?

Pelagius was a Celtic Christian monk who travelled to Rome probably from Ireland or Wales in or around 394 CE. Although a monk, Pelagius did not belong to a monastic community, nor was he a cleric. He wore a simple monk's garb and a Celtic tonsure (the hair shaven at the front of his head from ear to ear). He was a big man, heavy-set and slow-moving. On the streets and in the squares of Rome he spoke to anybody who would listen to him. He engaged as much with women as with men and he taught women the scriptures. His opponents used all these aspects of him to make him an object of derision. Jerome called him '…that ignorant traducer ... that stupid fool, labouring under his load of Irish porridge ... he barks like a mountain dog of immense bodily size who can tear better with his claws than with his teeth.'[2]

Although Pelagius had no institutional authority (he was neither a priest nor a bishop), he carried a personal authority that influenced his listeners. He never claimed to speak for anybody other than himself. He did not found a school, recruit supporters or claim ownership of a tradition. He spoke as an independent, free individual. Nonetheless, he was a highly learned and saintly person. He was fluent in Latin and Greek, knew the scriptures extremely well, was ascetic in his lifestyle and taught the spiritual life with wisdom and eloquence. All this made him a force to be reckoned with.

Pelagius challenged the authoritarian form of church that was developing at this time. He preached that every person, man or woman, had the freedom to go his or her own personal Christian way. His advice to people seeking a spiritual path was to look into their own soul or find a good 'soul friend' (anamchara). 'If you seek a rule for your lives,' he said, 'write down with your own hand on paper what God has written with his own hand on the human heart.'[3]

Pelagius vociferously disagreed with the position of Augustine on original sin. For Pelagius, there was a spark of the divine in every person. Through acts of the will, that spark could be nourished into a flame. He believed that a child was born innocent and free of sin. Pelagius rejected outright the concept of original sin as interpreted by Augustine. Sin, to Pelagius, was the result of an act of the will, choosing evil over good. He argued that it was at least theoretically possible to live a life completely without sin. 'All the good and all the bad ... is not born with us but is set in motion by our acts; because we are capable of either, we are not born full but we are procreated both without any virtue and similarly without any vice. Before the action of one's own will there exists in a human being only what God has established.'[4]

---

2   *St Jerome: Letters and Selected Works.* 1893, 499. Parker (Oxford) and Christian Literature (New York), and George de Plinval, *Essai sur le style et la langue de Pélage.* 1947, 55.
3   *The Letters of Pelagius,* 66
4   Quoted in Augustine, *De gratia Christi* ... II, c. XIII, p.180

For Pelagius, therefore, the road to salvation lay in acts of the will performed independently by each individual. One was saved by the way one lived one's life. He believed that this salvation was available to all, even to people who lived before the coming of Christ. However, Christ's presence among us, his teachings and the example of his life, revealed the way to us as never before. It was an extra grace available to us that pre-Christian people did not have.

In this theology, where the free will of the individual is paramount, the role of a church community is one of guidance, teaching and support. That church community is not the mediator of salvation. 'Man, created free, is with his whole sphere independent of God and the church, the living body of Christ – though Christ, church and sacraments mightily teach and help.'[5]

Pelagius, therefore, put great emphasis on how one lived one's life. He was a monk who preached asceticism and a disciplined life. Even Augustine was impressed by this aspect of Pelagius. When Pelagius arrived in Rome from the Celtic regions, he was shocked at the laxity of Christians living there. This laxity, he felt, was encouraged by the prevailing doctrine, promoted by Augustine and Jerome, which said that one could be saved only by grace and not by good works. Augustine's teaching put no great emphasis on how one lived one's life. This criticism of the laxity of the Roman church and especially of its bishops and clergy, was to be a recurrent theme among Celtic monks in the following centuries.

Augustine's emphasis was on doctrine, on right teaching or 'orthodoxy'. He spent a great part of his life fighting various heresies, such as the Manicheans, the Donatists and now the Pelagians. But for Pelagius, doctrine was not the central issue: 'You will realise that doctrines are the invention of the human mind, as it tries to penetrate the mystery of God. You will realise that scripture itself is the work of human minds, recording the example and teaching of Jesus. Thus it is not what you believe (in your head) that matters, it is how you respond with your heart and your actions. It is not believing in Christ that matters, but becoming like him.'[6]

5 Pelagius, *De Libero Arbitrio* (*On Free Will*)
6 Pelagius, *Letter to a New Christian*, 380 AD.

In contrast to this view, the Mediterranean church at the time had developed a fixed body of doctrine, a creed. It had standardised the orthodox creed at the Council of Nicea in 325 CE. This creed was a summary of 'correct' doctrine and all Christians were obliged to subscribe to it. Augustine claimed that the mainstream church had divine authority to enforce this 'orthodoxy' and to require obedience. This did not allow for independent thinking or for Christians to go their own way, as Pelagius taught.

It was inevitable that Pelagius would be opposed. The more responsibility his teaching allocated to the individual, the less control or authority it gave to the church institution. The institutional church's developing vision of being in control of the global spread of Christianity was undermined by the Pelagian message. Augustine led the opposition to Pelagius, strongly supported by Jerome. These two, one a theologian and a bishop, the other a priest and a scholar of scripture, were towering figures in the Christian church at the time and continue thus to this day.

Augustine used the developing centralised authority structure of the institutional church to bring Pelagius to heel. Numerous councils were called in various parts of the Christian world to confront Pelagius. Pelagius himself attended councils in Jerusalem and Diospolis in Palestine. Others were held in his absence. Pelagius was a formidable opponent and not every synod or council sided with Augustine.

Pelagius was condemned at a synod in Carthage, a city close to Augustine's home town of Hippo, in 412. But in 415, a council in Jerusalem exonerated him, after Pelagius had visited and spoken to its members. In December of the same year, a second eastern synod in Diospolis, at which new charges were brought against him, also acquitted him. However, Augustine worked to bring about a second synod in Carthage in 416 and here achieved again the unconditional condemnation of Pelagius.

Despite the arrival of Pelagius in Rome and Jerusalem as a complete outsider, his views found considerable support in many quarters. He had widespread support in southern Italy and Sicily. He was also supported by the Origenists throughout the east, by the Jerusalem Christians and by the Christians in Constantinople. Both John, the patriarch of Jerusalem and Nestorius, the patriarch of Constantinople, took his side.

As the eastern church had broken with Augustine on this issue, Augustine now appealed to Rome for a verdict. Innocent I was bishop of Rome at this time and was delighted with the invitation to intervene. He was keen to establish Rome and his bishopric, as the highest court of appeal in questions of doctrine and he was delighted that Augustine was now recognising this. Until this time, the bishop of Rome, despite being declared *Pontifex Maximus* by the emperor Theodosius in the year 380, was not universally acknowledged as pope and head of the established Christian church. There were a number of urban centres within Christianity struggling to maintain their own sovereignty and gain dominance: Carthage and Alexandria in North Africa, Constantinople and Jerusalem in the east and Rome in the west.

Innocent condemned Pelagius on the grounds suggested by Augustine. He used the situation to his advantage and wrote: '...that nothing in the whole world was to be decided without the cognisance of the See of Rome; in particular in questions of doctrine all bishops would have to turn to St Peter' [that is, the bishop of Rome, the pope].[7]

However, this was not the end of the matter. Innocent died two months after this judgement and was replaced by Zosimus. Pelagius and his friend Celestius appealed against the earlier decision and Zosimus called a fresh synod in Rome. This synod rehabilitated Pelagius. Augustine was enraged by this decision and a wave of indignation spread across North Africa. Yet another synod was called in Carthage, this time with a huge attendance and the condemnation of Pelagius was renewed.

Pope Zosimus was now put under enormous pressure. A Roman monk, Constantinus, staged a 'rising of the people' against Zosimus, condemning his support for Pelagius. Meanwhile, the supporters of Augustine won the favour of the emperor, Flavius Honorius, who was now living in Ravenna. He issued a decree condemning Pelagius and threatening to march on Rome with his army if Zosimus did not put an end to the matter.

In May 418, Zosimus succumbed. Pelagius and Celestius were banished into exile. Their writings were publicly burned. Pelagian bishops were removed from office or forced to change their position. Any

7   Augustine, *Letters*, 181-183.

Christian who held Pelagian views was persecuted. From then on, the Roman corporate church was determined that no trace of the teachings of Pelagius would be found anywhere among Christendom. Pelagianism was equated with arch-heresy.

Pope Celestine took over the papacy in 422 and focussed his attentions on ridding Britain and Ireland of the 'heresy' of Pelagianism. He sent Germanus of Auxerre[8] to Britain and Palladius to Ireland. These missions were, however, a failure.[9] Celtic Christianity remained predominantly Pelagian up to its final collapse in the 12th century. Pelagian writings survived, despite the burnings. They were copied and translated by Celtic monks, often under a pseudonym. Quotations by Pelagius are to be found in Irish monastic writings up to and including the 9th century.

In Europe, some of the works of Pelagius survived by being attributed to other authors. Works of his have been found attributed, ironically, to both Augustine and Jerome. One such document was found preserved in the Vatican library.[10] Modern day scholars have been able to identify his writings by its style and content. The rediscovery of the writings of Pelagius is ongoing and there is hope that many more of them will be revealed.

Pelagius was not an original thinker. His viewpoint was that of his tradition. This viewpoint and tradition were reflected in the lives of Irish monks both at home and abroad in later centuries. Irish monks sought the *inpeccantia* of Pelagius, the living of a sinless life. They went to heroic lengths to prove their love for Christ and to curb their inclination to sin. Those who travelled abroad did so, primarily, to perfect their lives through the process of 'white martyrdom'.[11] They avoided doctrinal controversies and concentrated instead on asceticism and good works. Like Pelagius,

---

8   This is the same Germanus whose monastery in Auxerre attracted the Irish, cf. Chapter 9. Clearly it was the monastic structure and lifestyle and not the theology, that the Irish found attractive.
9   When St Patrick came to Ireland in 432, he does not seem to have had this anti-Pelagian mission. His views, as expressed in his extant writings, reflect, if anything, the Pelagian viewpoint. For example, his writings do not mention the doctrine of original sin. He may not have been aware of it. As a Celt himself, his cultural background would have inclined him towards Pelagianism.
10   *Libellus Fidei*, believed to have been one of Augustine's sermons, until identified as authored by Pelagius. Found in the Vatican library.
11   Cf. Chapter 9.

they were appalled by the lax morals and luxurious lifestyles of Christians and especially of the bishops of the time.

The Teachings of Pelagius

Pelagian ideas have remained popular in Britain and Ireland, even to the present day. Pelagian theology, as expressed by Celtic Christianity in Britain and Ireland, gave that tradition certain attributes which distinguished it from the developing Mediterranean tradition of the established church. In summary these attributes were:

- a love of providence and a trust that it will direct one's life
- a denial of transmitted original sin and a belief that all children are born manifesting the glory of 'God'
- an awareness that the divine manifests itself in nature and that grace works through nature
- a belief that one has to live an ethical and ascetic life if one is to achieve salvation
- an heroic striving for *inpeccantia* (sinlessness) and a belief that this sinlessness is possible to achieve
- a support for the practice of peregrination for Christ – a wandering that could bring one far from home, being led by providence and seeking one's 'place of resurrection'.

These attributes remained part of Celtic Christianity throughout its existence up to the 12th century.

Pelagius was the original Celtic *peregrinatus* or wanderer for Christ. He was the prototype of the Celtic wandering monk, travelling the roads to distant lands. Many other Irish monks were to follow his example. We do not know what happened to Pelagius after his condemnation. It is probable that he returned to his homeland and died there. There is no record of where he is buried.

Augustine and Pelagius Today

Looking at the case of Pelagius from today's perspective, his opinions make a lot of sense to many people. In contrast, some of the teachings of Augustine appear highly suspect. Augustine taught, for example, that although a man was made in the image of 'God', a woman was not. He wrote: 'As regards the woman alone, she is not the image of God, but, as regards the man alone, he is the image of God as fully and completely as when the woman too is joined with him in one'.[12]

Augustine's teaching on original sin led to the practice of burying the bodies of unbaptised infants in unconsecrated graveyards without ceremony or the presence of a priest. These children, according to Augustine, were lost and would not find a place in heaven. While not assigned to Hell, they would remain forever in a place called 'Limbo'. Such graveyards, called 'cillín' or 'reilig na leanaí', are to be found all over Ireland.[13]

Augustine's image of the human was of an irredeemably damaged person. This person was helpless without the grace of 'God'. Augustine taught that that grace was not always forthcoming. 'God' was free to choose whosoever he wished to be saved and he did not choose everyone. One could do nothing to influence 'God' in this choice. People's lives were predestined.

This teaching left people feeling corrupted, ashamed and powerless. People who had been reared in this theology, learnt to think of themselves as helpless in the face of their own sinfulness. They learnt to feel permanently guilty. They were perpetual sinners, unable to pull themselves out of the mire of sin, as expressed in the words of the popular prayer : 'Poor banished children of Eve...sinful and sorrowful...mourning and weeping in this valley of tears.'[14]

This is a teaching which, when taken to heart, breaks the human spirit. It prevents a person from building up a confidence in one's ability to reform oneself and change for the better. One's only hope of salvation is in developing a dependence on the Roman church, its clergy and its sacraments.

The Augustinian doctrine on human sinfulness is a shocking corruption of a central message that is clearly present in all four canonical

---

12   Augustine, de Trinitate 7 7, 10
13   The practice in Ireland continued up to the 1940s. While the Roman church has softened its attitude towards these children and, instead of condemning them, now entrusts them to the mercy of 'God' and while the concept of Limbo itself has been discarded by the Roman church, these graveyards and their human remains, continue to exist in a limbo in relation to this church.
14   From the 'Hail Holy Queen', a traditional prayer recited at the end of the Rosary.

gospels. That message is that all people, even the lowliest, most ostracised and abandoned, are loved by 'God' and have a power within themselves to bring about their own healing and transformation. The gift of the 'Holy Spirit' is for everyone and that spirit becomes the voice of 'God' within oneself that can be used to direct one's life. Phrases such as: 'Your faith has made you well'[15], 'The truth will set you free'[16], 'Go and sin no more'[17], 'You shall move mountains'[18] are scattered throughout the four gospels and make it irrefutable that Jesus pointed to a power within all of us that could redeem us, heal us and give direction to our lives.

It is also clear from the four gospels that Jesus was adamantly opposed to religious structures that would oppress, disempower or restrict the spiritual lives of people.[19] The Pharisees, in particular, were attacked by Jesus for enforcing these structures. Yet here was a Christian church acting in the name of Jesus and creating the very structures that would oppress people and make them dependent on it. Is it any wonder that Pelagius was so vociferously opposed to this teaching? The real wonder is that so many others went along with it.

The concept of original sin does not appear in the gospels. An idea with some likenesses to it appears in St Paul's letters[20], where he compares Jesus to Adam. According to Paul, Adam was the first to bring sin into the world and since Adam sin has remained. Jesus is the new Adam, who banishes sin from the world and gives us the opportunity to return to the garden of paradise. Augustine created a theology of original sin around these passages and this theology has remained until the present day.

When the teachings of Augustine and the teachings of Pelagius are laid side by side and compared with the message contained in the four gospel accounts, it is clear that Pelagius is much closer to the original teachings of Jesus than Augustine. Augustine was a creative and original thinker. Many of his teachings are traceable more to his own life-history and perspective than to any teachings of Jesus. This is particularly true in relation to his teachings on sexuality and women.

---

15 *Mt.9:22; Mk.5:34; Lk.8:48.*
16 *Jn.8:32*
17 *Jn.8:11*
18 *Mt.17:20; Mk.11:22-23; Lk.17:6*
19 Cf. Chapter 4.
20 *Rom.5:12-21; 1 Cor. 15:21-22.*

The changes that took place within Christianity in the 4th and 5th centuries mark the beginnings of the serious corruption and hijacking of the Christian story. A story of empowerment and liberation, of being loved and being freed, of being healed and made whole, was first corrupted and then patented and packaged to become the source of political power for an authoritarian, male-dominated church. That corruption and hijacking might not have been long-lasting had it not been cemented and preserved in church institutions which are with us to this day.

During this critical stage of Christianity's development, Pelagius and others raised their voices in protest. Pelagius was heroic in spearheading this opposition. He fearlessly appeared on the streets in the centres of power, spoke at synods and councils, appealed to the highest authorities and wrote extensively. Unfortunately, his message did not prevail. The Celtic tradition from which he came continued to confront the mainstream church through its witness. However, to survive it had to remain independent. This independence was not tolerable to the Roman church and gradually the Celtic church was suffocated and died.

Night Prayer

Ah God come to our aid,
for the woman she's a heathen,
and she would do anything for her man —
before you God.

Ah God come to our aid,
such is half the race you betrayed,
such is half the desires you laid,
for I, the heathen woman.

O Lord make haste to help us,
for he prays ... and so do I.

Tess Harper

11

CELTIC CHRISTIANITY CONFRONTED IN BRITAIN

Pelagius travelled from the Celtic isles to Rome to confront the dogmatic theology and the authoritarian model of church that was emanating from Rome and north Africa. He was defeated in that confrontation. Then the tide turned. The Roman church began to send missions to the Celtic isles to stamp out the Pelagian and Celtic influence entirely. The first successful mission to Britain was that of Augustine of Canterbury at the end of the 6th century.

In the 5th century, Pelagius had brought the Celtic tradition to the attention of the Mediterranean church. His influence had spread throughout the Christian communities, so that, even after his condemnation in 418, he still had supporters in Jerusalem, Italy, parts of Africa and in Gaul, as well, of course, as in the Celtic isles.

Pope Celestine, who took over the papacy in 422, was vigorous in his attempts to stamp out the Pelagian influence. In 429 Celestine sent Palladius to Ireland and a Gallic synod sent bishops Lupus and Germanus to Britain. These expeditions were specifically anti-Pelagian but were not very successful. However, Patrick's mission to Ireland, which began three years later, does not seem to have had an anti-Pelagian theme[1].

Following this initial attempt to suppress the Pelagian viewpoint in Britain and Ireland, there was a period of non-interference, which lasted one hundred and sixty-eight years. The Roman church, during this period, was taken up with its own survival after the collapse of the Roman empire. In Roman Britain, Christianity was all but wiped out following the Roman

---

1   Cf. footnote 9 in previous chapter.

withdrawal. In mainland Europe west of Rome, Christianity had become sparse and isolated.

Celtic Christianity Expands and Strengthens

Meanwhile, in both northern England and Wales, Christianity as expressed through Celtic monasticism continued to survive, while in Ireland it flourished beyond all imagining. Towards the end of that period, in 563, one of the greatest of the Irish monastic founders, Colmcille, moved from Derry in Ireland to the small island of Iona in northern Britain and founded there a monastery whose light was to shine brighter than that of any other Irish monastery before or since. Through Iona, the influence of Celtic Christianity now began to consolidate and expand southwards through the northern half of Britain.

The expansion of Celtic Christianity in northern Britain was an event of which Rome had little knowledge and even less control. There was virtually no contact between the Irish monasteries and Rome at this time. The Irish monasteries had a strong sense of their own independence. No part of Ireland had ever been under the control of the Roman empire. The northern third of Britain, with Hadrian's Wall as its boundary, had also remained free. When the Roman empire collapsed, these places were relatively unaffected. While Christianity on the mainland of Europe was struggling to extract itself from the rubble of the collapsed empire, Celtic monasticism in Ireland and in the north of Britain was thriving.

Meanwhile, in southern Britain, the withdrawal of the Romans had left a vacuum which was filled by invading Angles and Saxons. They brought with them their own religion of gods and goddesses. The Christianity that had been in Britain, as part of the Christian Roman empire, was all but wiped out. Southern Britain reverted to paganism.

However, the Anglo-Saxons did not colonise the area we now call Wales. The people living there were of Celtic origin and had retained their own language. After the withdrawal of the Romans, this western part of Britain, which included Devon and Cornwall, kept its Christianity but gave it a Celtic expression, in line with what was happening in Ireland and northern Britain.

Pope Gregory The Great

When Gregory I, known as Gregory the Great, became pope at the end of the 6th century, he focussed some of his energies on the re-establishment of Christianity in southern Britain. This entailed sending a mission from Rome to bring about the conversion of the Angles and Saxons. In sending a mission there, he ignored the possibility that this work could have been done by Celtic monks, who were vigorously expanding their monastic settlements southwards from the north and who were also in a strong position in the western part of Britain. Later, his emissary was to seek the cooperation of the Celtic monks in the mission, but these discussions collapsed, as we shall see.

Pope Gregory and the Monks of Benedict's Monastery

In order to explain Pope Gregory's approach to the mission in Britain, it is necessary to recount his connections to monasticism. Pope Gregory the Great was the first monk to become a pope. The monastery he belonged to followed the rule of Benedict.

Benedict was an Italian monk who had died in 543. He had founded only one monastery, that of Monte Cassino in Italy. Thirty-three years after his death, that monastery was sacked by the Lombards. The monks fled to Rome. There they met Gregory, who was at the time a young man in his thirties and had yet to become pope.

Gregory was an aristocratic gentleman, whose family had lands in the centre of Rome. He made some of this land available to the homeless monks. A new monastery was built on Caelian Hill, near the Colosseum. Gregory then joined the monastery himself and later, four years before he became pope, became the abbot of that monastery. In the monastery, the monks followed the rule that Benedict had written for his community at Monte Cassino.

It is important to point out here that Benedict had had no thoughts of spreading this form of monasticism worldwide. His famous *Rule of St Benedict* was written for his monks at Monte Cassino and not for anybody else. These monks were unmarried laymen who wanted to live a dedicated Christian life. The rule was the result of lessons Benedict had learned during failed attempts at creating monastic communities earlier in his life.

In the hands of Pope Gregory I, the rule of Benedict became the key to the spreading of Benedictine monasticism throughout the Christian world. As an ambitious and skilful pope, he was able to use the spread of Benedictine monasticism as a pivotal strategy for the re-establishment of Christianity throughout Europe.

Comparing Benedictine and Celtic Monasticism

In comparing Benedictine monasticism to Celtic monasticism, one must first omit St Benedict's monastery at Monte Cassino from the equation. Benedict founded his monastery at Monte Cassino in exactly the same way that any Celtic founder would have founded his or her monastery in Ireland or elsewhere. That is, he founded it according to his own lights and inspirations. Benedict's monastery at Monte Cassino, like all Celtic monasteries, was a once-off. There was no plan to replicate it elsewhere.

Benedictine monasticism, on the other hand, was the replication of a particular model of monasticism throughout the Roman church's jurisdiction. Each monastic community lived in exactly the same way, according to the same rule. Benedictine monasticism was the cloning of a particular expression of monasticism. Celtic monasticism was never cloned. Each Celtic monastery took on the inspirations and emphases of its founder.

The monks of these Benedictine monasteries lived in a different way to Celtic monks. Where Celtic monasticism challenged its monks to live heroic lifestyles and to wander the earth in search of their places of resurrection, Benedictine monks were encouraged to be moderate in all things and to live sedate, contemplative and routine lives in one place. Benedict himself had never travelled and his rule did not encourage others to do so.

The Benedictine form of monasticism was attractive to the Roman church authorities because it was uniform, sedate, predictable and could be easily controlled. Each Celtic monastery, on the other hand, had its own separate style and expression established by its founder, was not linked to any central authority and practised a theology and a political outlook that was Pelagian.

Where all Celtic monasteries and Benedict's own monastery at Monte Cassino, had been founded from the bottom up by individual men and women who were giving expression to their own personal vision and vocation, Benedictine monasteries were generally founded, or encouraged to be founded, from the top down by dominant authorities in a centralised organisation.

In the hands of Pope Gregory, Benedictine monasticism became a powerful new tool for the spread of a uniform, centralised and authoritarian version of Christianity in Britain. Later, the promotion of Benedictine monasticism would become a key element of the strategy to eliminate Celtic monasticism from mainland Europe.

Augustine of Canterbury's Mission to Britain

In the year 597, the year of Colmcille's death, the first emissary of Pope Gregory the Great arrived in Britain on a mission to convert the Angles and Saxons. His name was Augustine (he became known as Augustine of Canterbury, to distinguish him from Augustine of Hippo). He came directly from Rome, where he and his entourage of forty others had been monks in the monastery built by Pope Gregory, which followed the rule of Benedict.

Augustine and his band of forty monks landed in Kent in southeast Britain. The door was opened to this mission by Bertha, wife of the Anglo-Saxon king Ethelbert who had invited the pope to send a mission to Britain. Bertha was a Christian, the daughter of Charibert, one of the Merovingian kings of the Franks. She had come from mainland Europe to marry Ethelbert.

Augustine's first task was to convert Ethelbert, Bertha's husband. He succeeded in doing this within the first year. This led to a legendary baptismal ceremony for 10,000 of the king's subjects at Christmas in 597. Augustine's mission had made an excellent start.

The mission strategy was to focus on the conversion of the political leaders of the time and to promote Benedictine monasticism. This strategy met with continuing success. Augustine built his cathedral at Canterbury, the capital of the Anglo-Saxon kingdom. Next to it he founded a Benedictine monastery. Canterbury was a strong focus for the Roman church in Britain up to the time of the Reformation. Augustine also founded the Benedictine monastery of St. Peter and St. Paul (later to be called St Augustine's) outside the walls of the city. Other Benedictine foundations in Britain were to follow.

It was inevitable that the mission of Augustine to Britain would occasion an engagement with the Celtic Christians to the west and north of the country. Pope Gregory claimed primacy over the whole of Christianity. He was intent on creating mechanisms throughout the Christian world that would promote uniformity and obedience. The independence of Celtic Christianity could not be tolerated.

Celtic Monasteries in Europe

Both in Britain and on the continent of Europe, Celtic Christianity was posing a challenge to the Roman authorities. By the early 7th century, Benedictine monasticism had yet to be established anywhere outside Rome, other than in Britain, whereas Celtic monasteries were being successfully founded throughout north-west Europe. These Celtic monasteries were acting independently of Rome, promoting a model of church that was non-authoritarian and non-dogmatic, preaching a Pelagian theology, practising rites and ceremonies according to their own customs and calculating the date of Easter differently to Rome. Precisely because it had no centralised authority structure, Celtic Christianity was difficult to confront.

Columbanus was the prime example of a Celtic monk from Ireland who had travelled throughout Europe and founded monasteries. Born in 543, the same year that Benedict died, he left Ireland in his early thirties with a band of twelve monks. He and his fellow monks founded monasteries everywhere they went. They left their marks throughout France, Germany, Switzerland and Italy. The city of San Gallen in Switzerland is called after one of his monks, St Gall. His final foundation was in Bobbio, northern Italy, where he died and is buried. Bobbio in its time was probably the most famous abbey in Europe. It flourished for twelve centuries until Napolean closed it in 1802. The feastday of St Columbanus on 23 November is celebrated throughout Italy.

The presence of Celtic monasteries as far south as Italy itself must have greatly focussed the mind of the papacy at this time. Columbanus, while respectful of Rome, did not share the papal viewpoint on many issues. When settled in Italy, he sided with the local bishops who were in schism with Rome over the so-called 'Three Chapters' controversy.[2] Nor was he shy of confronting the pope when he thought the latter was in error. During the period of Gregory I's papacy, Columbanus wrote to him disputing Rome's way of calculating Easter. He also wrote to subsequent popes. In these letters he defended the independence of the Irish monasteries and asked that they be left alone. These letters illustrate the tension that existed between Rome and Celtic Christianity during this period.[3]

It would take many centuries before Celtic Christianity was brought under Rome's control, but Gregory I's enthronement as pope and the arrival of Augustine of Canterbury in Britain marked a vital chapter in that long-drawn-out battle.

Celtic Christianity and Augustine of Canterbury

Bede, a pro-Roman Benedictine monk from Northumbria, who wrote in the early 8th century, records the first encounter between Augustine and some Celtic clerics from Wales. This was an arranged meeting between the two sides in 602 or 603 CE. Augustine, obviously taking the situation seriously, travelled a long distance through dangerous territory to meet the Celtic delegation. The place where they met became known as 'Augustine's Oak'. It is believed to have been somewhere close to the present Welsh border with England.

It was a frosty meeting, with Augustine, acting in an 'arrogant and ill-tempered'[4] fashion, insisting that the Celts use the Roman date for Easter, administer baptism according to the Roman method and agree to actively evangelise the Saxons. The Celts were unimpressed and refused to give a commitment. They asked for more time to consult with their brethren and to gather a more representative group of leaders for their next meeting.

The second meeting was no more successful than the first. Bede recounts[5] that the Celtic contingent, as they were about to set out for the conference, went first to a holy and prudent man, who lived as a hermit among them, to consult him as to whether they ought to forsake

2   Joseph F.T. Kelly, 'The Irish Monks and the See of Peter', in *Monastic Studies*, No. 14, 1983, Benedictine Priory of Montreal. ISBN 0-919815-03-0
3   ibid.
4   Bede II. 2. Cf. Bede (tr.Leo Sherley-Price). *History of the English Church and People.* Penguin, Baltimore, Md., 1955.
5   ibid.

their own traditions for the preaching of Augustine. He advised them to follow him 'if he is a man of God'. They asked, 'But how can we tell?' The hermit answered, 'The Lord said: "Take my yoke upon you and learn of me, for I am meek and lowly of heart." If this Augustine is meek and lowly of heart, we may well suppose that he bears the yoke of Christ himself and is offering it to you to bear; but if he is harsh and proud, it follows that he is not from God and we have no need to regard what he says.'

Once more they said, 'But how can we know even this?' He said, 'Make sure that he and his followers arrive first at the meeting place and, if he, on your approach, will rise to meet you, you will know that he is a servant of Christ and will listen to him obediently; but if he despises you and is not willing to rise in your presence, even though you are the larger party, you should despise him in return.'

Bede continues: 'They did as he had said. It happened that Augustine remained seated while they were coming in; when they saw this, they became angry, noting him as a proud man and they argued against everything he said. "Nay, if he will not so much as rise to us, how much the more, if we now begin to subject ourselves to him, will he hereafter deride us and set us at nought?"'

Further attempts were made by Augustine's successor Laurence to bring Celtic Christianity into 'full union with the universal Church'. However, these were not invitations to open dialogue but an insistence that Celtic Christianity take on the uniform practices of the Roman church and forfeit its own identity.

Wilfrid's Climb to Power

Wilfrid began his adult life as a Celtic monk in the monastery of Lindisfarne in Northumbria, Britain. After some initial training in that monastery, he travelled to Rome where he was blessed by the pope and was converted to the Roman ways. He then spent three years with the archbishop of Lyons, until the latter suffered martyrdom at the hands of the dukes of Burgundy. Wilfrid would also have been killed, but was released in recognition of his Saxon identity.

When Wilfrid returned to Britain, at the age of twenty-seven, the local king Alchfrith appointed him abbot of the Celtic monastery at Rippon in north Yorkshire. Wilfrid imposed the Benedictine observance and Roman practices on this monastery, despite his Celtic monastic background.

Wilfrid now began an all-out attack on the Celtic form of Christianity. His character had become harsh and inquisitorial. He had taken on the arrogance of Rome and he used his knowledge of the European church to intimidate the Celtic monks and to force them into submission.

The Celtic and Roman models of church in Britain were now moving towards direct confrontation. Benedictine monasticism had developed in the south; Celtic monasticism was flourishing in the north. The location of that confrontation was to be Northumbria, where the two streams met.

The Synod of Whitby

In the kingdom of Northumbria, Irish monks and their British brethren had established a Celtic model of Christianity. King Oswy, who ruled this kingdom, was a Celtic Christian. However, King Oswy had married Eanfled, a woman from southern Britain who had grown up with Roman Christianity. So in the one household, the king celebrated Easter on the date calculated by the Celts, while his wife followed the Roman date. The result was that in certain years the king would be celebrating the festival of Easter while the queen was still fasting through Lent! That situation was due to occur in the year 665.

In 664, King Oswy called a synod to resolve the issue. The two factions met at the Celtic double monastery[6] of Whitby, where Hilda was the abbess. Colman, the abbot of Lindisfarne, spoke on behalf of Celtic Christianity. On the Roman side was Wilfrid.

At Whitby, Wilfrid argued eloquently and convincingly that Rome had more authority than Iona and that St Peter had more authority than St Columba (Colmcille). Colman was no match for him. King Oswy was eventually left with the dilemma that if he did not side with St Peter, who held the 'keys to the kingdom of heaven', the gates of heaven might not be opened to him when he died.

---

6   Double monasteries were common at this time, where men and women lived as monks in separate areas of the one monastery. St Brigid's monastery, in Kildare, Ireland, was another such monastery. In these monasteries, a woman held the prime position, even though there may have been a bishop among the male monks, as was the case in Kildare.

As a result of the Roman victory at Whitby, Colman resigned as abbot of Lindisfarne and returned to Ireland with many of his monks. It was clear on this occasion that these Irish monks were not prepared to accept the decision of the synod on this matter. Wilfrid was appointed bishop of Northumbria. He refused to be consecrated by the Celtic bishops, whom he regarded as schismatics and instead went to France to be consecrated there. Within his diocese, he introduced the Roman rituals and Latin as the language of the church.

From this time onwards, Celtic Christianity lost some of its confidence and determination to remain independent. Many Celtic monasteries in Ireland, especially in the south, while not going so far as to take on the Benedictine rule, did take on Roman practices, thus earning themselves the title *Romani*. Others tried to withstand the Roman pressure to change and were known as *Hibernenses*.

By 678, Wilfrid had become so fanatical and unwilling to exercise any restraint that he was dismissed as bishop by Egfrid, Viceroy of York. However, after Egfrid's death he returned as bishop with Rome's blessing and remained there until he died shortly afterwards in 709.

Underlying the clash of cultures at the Synod of Whitby was Rome's irritation at the independence of Celtic Christianity. Not only had Celtic Christianity a different method for calculating Easter, it had many other singular ways of doing things. Celtic monks spoke the Gaelic language, looked and dressed differently and practised a version of Christianity that was at odds with Rome. One of the issues debated at Whitby was the Irish tonsure. An Irish monk shaved his head at the front, from ear to ear and left the back long. The Benedictine tonsure was a circle of shaven hair at the crown of the head. The fundamental problem for Rome was that it could not tolerate these differences.

The First Pontifical

Celtic Christianity also had its own way of performing the rite of baptism and the rite of consecration of a bishop. This difference was not particular to the Celts. Throughout the Christian world there was great diversity in these matters. From the Roman perspective, a means had to be found to impose uniformity. In these early days, there were no mechanisms to hand by which one could do this.

The earliest attempts to impose uniform practices within these ceremonies are to be found in writings that were called 'pontificals'. These pontificals were written descriptions of the way bishops were to perform ceremonies such as the consecration of a priest or confirmation. They sometimes included instructions for priests also. They were issued by a pope or archbishop for dissemination throughout his jurisdiction.

The *Pontifical of Egbert* is the earliest extant book to prescribe the way rites were to be performed in the Roman church. Egbert was the archbishop of York in Britain a generation after Wilfrid. His pontifical was an instruction for the bishops under his jurisdiction. Quite clearly, it was directed particularly at the behaviour of Celtic bishops in northeastern Britain.

The pontifical represents the earliest version of a mechanism used to impose uniformity in the Roman liturgy among bishops. It is no coincidence that the first known pontifical was created in response to the independent style of Celtic Christianity.

In its mission to Britain, the Roman church had begun to use two important tools as a means to achieving uniformity and control. These two tools were the Benedictine rule and written pontificals. Over the coming centuries it would expand that toolbox until in gained total control of the Irish church. Celtic monasteries would become a thing of the past.

The Survival of Celtic Christianity in Britain

Celtic Christianity remained present in Britain for a number of centuries after the Synod of Whitby, despite its defeat at that synod in the 7th century. The monasteries at Iona and Lindisfarne remained important centres of that Christianity until their destruction by Viking attacks in the 9th century. The Norman invasion of Britain in 1066, which brought with it an allegiance to the Roman church, ensured that any remaining traces of an independent Celtic church in Scotland or Wales were wiped out and replaced by a Roman church structure.

Vision Song

I go to a rock
On the top of the mountain
In the mist,
To remember the vision-song.

I often let it go, this music,
But it finds its own way home.
Wild and free
It sings at the top of its voice
Loud and raunchy –
The original vision song.
I know I will die each time I forget it.

The wind is wild on this rock
On the mountain, in the mist.
This music is ours to call upon.
Let go, it finds its own way home.

I'll sing by it, untiringly
And all else that is false
will fall away,
faded and pale.

Tess Harper

12

CELTIC CHRISTIANITY CONFRONTED IN EUROPE

In its Augustinian mission to Britain, Rome had found a successful strategy for its confrontation with Celtic Christianity and Pelagianism. It now needed to apply that strategy throughout Europe, where hundreds of independent Irish monasteries had established themselves – even in Italy itself. Boniface, a Benedictine monk from Britain, was the man appointed to lead the campaign.

The battle to curb the expansion of Celtic monasticism, initiated in Britain in 597 by the mission of Augustine of Canterbury, was now taken into mainland Europe. The papacy began to promote the spread of Benedictine monasticism throughout its jurisdiction. The Benedictine monastery of Monte Cassino in Italy was rebuilt. It was reopened at the beginning of the 8th century, one hundred and fifty years after it had been sacked. The rebuilding was commissioned by Pope Gregory II, Gregory I's successor.

With the Benedictine rule in one hand and the support of the political powers in the other, Rome began a campaign to convert all existing monasteries in Europe to the rule of Benedict. That campaign was led by Boniface, a British Benedictine.

Boniface the Benedictine

Boniface was born in Devon in 672. He became a Benedictine monk in his homeland before embarking on a mission to the Frisians on Europe's northern coastline at the invitation of the Frankish king.

Boniface's mission to the Frisians was a failure. He subsequently went to Rome and was commissioned by Pope Gregory II to work for the Roman church throughout the Germanic and Frisian regions. During this period he visited the Celtic monastery of Hesse, which had two Irish monks who were twins sharing the abbacy. Boniface convinced the abbots that they must convert to Roman practices. This led to the re-baptism of everyone in the area according to the Roman rites.[1] The success of this mission was reported to Rome as 'conversions of thousands of heathen.'[2]

On Boniface's second visit to Rome, he was ordained a missionary bishop. According to his biographer Willibald (one of his pupils): '[The pope] put into his hands the book in which the most sacred laws and canons of the Church and the decrees of episcopal synods have been inscribed or compiled, commanding him that henceforth this norm of Church conduct and belief should be kept inviolate and that the people under his jurisdiction should be taught on these lines.'[3]

In the oath of office taken by Boniface at the grave of St. Peter, he said: 'Should it come to my notice that some bishops deviate from the teachings of the Fathers, I will have no part or lot with them, but as far as in me lies I will correct them, or, if that is impossible, I will report the matter to the Holy See.'[4]

Following this, Boniface reportedly used violence to destroy a Celtic settlement in Büraburg at Fritzlar. In a letter to Bishop Daniel of Winchester he wrote of 'false priests and hypocrites' in Thuringia, complaining that many were sinfully married and that he had to fight them because they had a hold over the people.

Boniface is credited with the foundation of many Benedictine monasteries throughout Germany but in reality many of these monasteries were initially Celtic. What Boniface did achieve was the conversion of these monasteries to the Benedictine rule. In this process of forced conversion, Boniface called not only on the authority of Rome but on the authority of the state. The papacy at this time had built up a strong relationship with the ruler of the Franks, Charles Martel. Boniface was given letters of introduction to Charles Martel and regularly called on the assistance of his soldiers to help in the enforcement of Roman church practices.

---

1   Otto Wissig, *Iroschotten und Bonifatius in Deuthschland*. Gütersloh: Bertelsmann 1932
2   Johannes Heinrich August Ebrard . *Die iroschottische Mönchskirche*. Gütersloh. 1873
3   R. Buchner, 'Briefe des Bonifatius,' *Ausgewählte Quellen zur deutschen Geschichte des Mittelalters*, Vol. 4b. p.129. München. 1963
4   C.H.Talbot (ed.). *The Anglo-Saxon Missionaries in Germany*. London: Sheed & Ward and New York, 1954. pp 85ff.

In all the correspondence between Boniface and the pope there is no mention of Celtic Christianity or of Celtic monks or clerics. Instead, they are spoken of as pagans, heretics, heathens, hypocrites and 'people who live outside the rule of the Church'.

After the death of Pope Gregory II, Boniface made a third visit to Rome to acquaint himself with the new pope, Gregory III. He was then appointed papal legate. In all of his dealings with Rome, the key emphasis was on his allegiance to Rome and Roman practices and the promotion of the latter among the peoples to whom he was sent.

Boniface's power was now at its height. In 742 he requested the king, Charles Martel, to summon an all-German Council. Only pro-Roman delegates were invited to this council. The Bavarian bishops were not invited and others refused to attend in protest. At this council, Boniface declared that in future only bishops consecrated by him would be recognised. Celtic priests were to be removed from their positions. Celibacy was to be compulsory and Roman vestments were to be the only permitted vestments for ceremonies. In particular, the following decision was made against priests and bishops coming from Ireland: 'We have decided that in accordance with the warning given in the statutes of the Church we shall allow no priest or bishop coming from abroad, no matter from whence he comes, into the service of the Church without the approval of the synod.'[5]

After this council, 'a fierce conflict developed with the uncanonical elements in the native clergy'.[6] This conflict lasted for twenty years, continuing even after Boniface's death in 754 CE.

While Boniface is now venerated as the 'Apostle of Germany', there is little evidence that he did in fact convert many 'heathens'. The groundwork for the spread of Christianity throughout Germany had been done by Irish monks. In accounts of Boniface's work, it is clear that his main energies were directed at confronting the activities of the Celtic monasteries, driving out Celtic clergy and replacing them with clergy faithful to Rome. The main work of Boniface was the conversion of the Germanic peoples

5   R. Buchner, 'Briefe des Bonifatius,' *Ausgewählte Quellen zur deutschen Geschichte des Mittelalters*, Vol. 4b. p. 267.. München. 1963.
6   Theodor Schieffer.   *Winfried-Bonifatius und die christliche Grundlegung Europas.* Freiburg: Herder, 1954. p.152.

from Celtic Christianity to Roman Christianity. Celtic priests and bishops were removed from office and Celtic monasteries became Benedictine.

Salzburg and San Gallen

Boniface was resisted by the Irish monk and abbot Fergal (Virgilius) of Salzburg. As was the Irish custom, Fergal, as abbot, employed a bishop within his monastery to carry out the sacramental duties. At this time Fergal had not himself become a bishop. Fergal resisted the reforming zeal of Boniface, clashing with him over formulae for the administration of baptism and other matters. Boniface reported his alleged unorthodoxy to the pope. But the pope could not condemn one who was as popular as Fergal in his own locality.

After Boniface's death, Fergal became bishop of Salzburg. His life was a brilliant embodiment of the free and independent Irish school of thought. Fergal remained all his life in close contact with the monastery of Iona. Almost five hundred years after his death, he became, in 1233, the first of only four Irish saints ever to be canonised by Rome.

Nonetheless, other Irish monasteries, including the great Irish monastery of San Gallen in Switzerland, did accede to Boniface's power. In 747, the monastery of San Gallen was forced to introduce the Benedictine rule and dress. For some decades afterwards, however, the monks of San Gallen wore the white Irish habit underneath the brown Benedictine cowl.

Charlemagne and the Holy Roman Empire

At the beginning of the 9th century, the Merovingian empire was replaced by the Carolingian empire. On Christmas Day in the year 800, Pope Leo III crowned Charlemagne emperor of the Franks. This heralded a new era for Christianity. Roman Christianity had recovered from the collapse of the Roman empire and the invasions of the Germanic tribes throughout western Europe and was now intent on building its own Holy Roman empire.

For the next thousand years, the concept of the Holy Roman empire would be used to create an alignment between the territories and people of the Roman church and those of the state. The pope would regard the empire as the church's civil arm. Church and state would work together. The state would be required to support and protect the Roman church and the papal states.

Pope Leo continued the work of his predecessors in imposing the Roman rite for Christian liturgy upon all Gallic and Celtic churches and the Benedictine rule upon all monasteries. This had the effect of accelerating the decline of remaining indigenous forms of worship and diverse cultural expressions of Christianity.

Nonetheless, the Irish monks remained in Europe and continued to have a significant influence for many centuries to come. While their monasteries now practised the Benedictine rule, they maintained many Irish traditions and customs.

Charlemagne was particularly welcoming of the Irish monks, termed 'peregrinos' or 'wandering pilgrim', into his jurisdiction. He invited them to serve at his court. Those mentioned in his biography include Dungal who was asked to explain to Charlemagne the meaning of a solar eclipse and Dicuil, the first medieval geographer. Another Irish courtier was Sedulius Scotus. A number of manuscripts copied by him, with his own glosses penned in on the margin, are still in existence. It is clear from these that Sedulius was conversant in both Greek and Latin. At a time when literacy across Europe was almost non-existent and Charlemagne himself was unable to read or write, the presence of someone as literate as Sedulius Scotus was a marvel.

John Scotus Eriugena

The greatest of the Irish *peregrini* of this period was undoubtedly John Scotus Eriugena. While Scotus means 'Irish', Eriugena means 'born in Ireland' to distinguish him from Irish who may not have been born in Ireland. John Scotus Eriugena was born about 810 and travelled through Frankish Gall, where, in his thirties, he took a position at the Cathedral School of Laon, under the patronage of Charles the Bald, Charlemagne's successor.

Eriugena was the first truly Christian philosopher to emerge in Europe since Augustine, four hundred years earlier. He was fluent in Latin and Greek and his most famous book *The Division of Nature* is a presentation of Irish spirituality, one that is rooted in nature and presents a type of panentheism found also in Pelagius. He argues that reason is of a higher order than any authority: 'Now we have to follow reason, which traces the truth of things without allowing itself to be restricted by any authority...'[7] This teaching did not go down well in Rome.

Eriugena's writings are on a par in quality with Augustine and Thomas Aquinas. *On The Division of Nature* offers a non-dualistic philosophical synthesis that is cosmic, ecological and incarnational. For this reason, it has much relevance for the human search for meaning today. It is 'an astounding synthesis of theology, philosophy, cosmology and anthropology'[8] which constitutes the only philosophical alternative in the West to the Aristotelian scholasticism of Thomas Aquinas.

The spirituality of Eriugena was Johannine, which again put him at odds with Rome. He wrote that St John, as distinct from St Peter, invited a deeper penetration of the mysteries. In his *Homily on the Prologue to John's Gospel*, he argued that the Christianity of the future must build on a Johannine approach and not on a Petrine approach.[9] The Johannine approach, which was very much part of the Irish tradition, emphasised brotherhood and community over hierarchy and dogmatism. It recognised the presence of the spirit as a guide in everyone. Women and men are equal and must be treated equally. The Roman church at the time was and remained, decidedly Petrine.

Eriugena, it would appear, thought in Greek but wrote in Latin. His work of translation of the most important documents of Greek-Christian Platonism was crucial to the future development of Christian thought.

While Eriugena was strongly influenced by Platonic thought, he was not impressed by some of Augustine's teachings. On the subject of the Augustinian doctrine of double predestination – the doctrine that held that all human beings were predestined by 'God' to either salvation or damnation – his view was that it was 'a most cruel and stupid madness'.[10]

Eriugena's writings stirred up controversy. In 855 CE the Synod of Valence condemned his work. Echoing the condemnation of Pelagius by Jerome, the synod termed his work 'Pultes Scottorum', or 'Irish porridge'. Within the episcopacy of the Roman church at this time there was a

---

7   Ludwig Noack. *Johannes Scotus Erigena*. Philosophische Bibliothek. 1876. p.98.
8   Ibid. p10
9   Christopher Bamford (translator and editor), *John Scotus Eriugena, Homily on the Prologue to the Gospel of St. John*, *The Voice of the Eagle*, Lindisfarne Press, 1990.
10   Christopher Bamford (ed.), *The Voice of the Eagle*. p.8.

general dislike of the Irish. Hincmar, the archbishop of Rheims, was one such bishop, who hated all things Irish. When Hincmar died, Eriugena wrote:

Hic jacet Hincmarus, cleptes vehementer avarus,
Hoc solum gessit nobile: quod periit.

Here lies Hincmar, crook. But savage greed aside,
He did one truly noble thing: he died.

His famous wit, evident here, is also contained in the following interchange, where he plays with two similar Latin words 'sottum' and 'Scottum'. As he dined at table with the emperor Charles the Bald, Eriugena asked him:

Quid distat inter sottum et Scottum?
What separates a fool from an Irishman?
Tabula tantum.
Only the table.

Legend has it that his students stabbed him to death with their pens![11]
Eriugena's *Homily on the Prologue to the Gospel of St John* is regarded as 'one of the greatest homilies of medieval spiritual literature'.[12] Despite being neither a monk nor a priest, he wrote it to be used in the liturgy of the third Mass on Christmas Day. It was used extensively throughout the Middle Ages and many Benedictine and Cistercian manuscripts of it exist. However, it was rarely attributed to Eriugena.

In 1225, Pope Honorius III issued a papal bull condemning Eriugena's work and ordered that all of his writings be burned. Despite this, most of his writings have survived.

The Donation of Constantine
The 9th century was a time of great turbulence across the whole of Europe. The Vikings and Danes were attacking northern Europe. From the 830s,

---

11   Ibid. p14.
12   D. Moran, *The Philosophy of John Scottus Eriugena: A Study of Idealism in the Middle Ages*, Cambridge, 1989.

the Muslims were attacking Italy and the papal states from the south. The Carolingian empire was falling apart because of internal feuding and the Magyars were also making forays. It was a time of chaos and corruption.

In Rome, the papacy had become the plaything of several feuding Italian families. Popes were taking mistresses and having children, some of them in the hope that their papacy would become hereditary. Legend suggests that an English woman called Joan became pope during this period.

What is more certain is that documents were forged, documents which became the official basis for Roman ecclesiastical power. One of these documents was the *Donation of Constantine*, which purported to give the papacy dominion over the city of Rome, Italy and the western Roman empire. Included in this so-called gift of Constantine were 'the various islands'. In the 12th century, Pope Adrian IV was to use this as a pretext for claiming that Ireland was a papal fiefdom and for encouraging Henry II to invade the country on his behalf.

The Irish Schottenklöster

During the 9th century, the Irish presence continued within Europe, but now in a more Romanised form. Specific Irish monasteries continued to exist, although they now practised the Benedictine rule and were more integrated into both the Roman church and secular state.

Viking attacks in Ireland began in the 9th century and continued all through the 10th and into the 11th century. This caused a new wave of Irish monks, escaping the Viking depradations, to spread throughout Europe. As well as filling again the traditionally Irish monasteries on the continent, this wave founded new Irish monasteries.

One particularly fine example of a new foundation during this period was the monastery founded by Marianus Scotus. His Irish name was Muiredach MacRobartaigh. He had travelled to Europe with a band of companions from Donegal in about 1067. On arrival at Ratisbon (also known as Regensberg) in southern Germany, he was persuaded by the local abbess Emma to settle there. His sanctity and scholarship were so impressive that abbess Emma, with the consent of the emperor Henry IV, gave him the church of St Peter. A local citizen, Bezelin, built him a monastery adjoining it. This became the monastery of St Peter at Ratisbon.

After the death of Marianus, his monastery continued to be headed and occupied by Irish monks. A new monastery was built with funds from both Ireland and Germany and became known as the Abbey of St James. Over the coming decades, this monastery was to receive various privileges and protections from both emperors and popes. From here, twelve other foundations were created including Würzburg, Nürnberg, Erfurt, Constance and Vienna. The Vienna monastery had a foundation in Kiev, in the Ukraine, for a short time before the Mongol invasion. This was the most easterly foundation of the Scotti or Irish. Kiev marks the eastern boundary of the Irish monastic influence across Europe.

These *Schottenklöster*, as they became known, were particularly valued for their role in scholarship, teaching and learned advice. A papal bull established them as a separate congregation of the Benedictines and appointed the abbot of St James of Ratisbon the abbot-general. King Henry bestowed upon him the privilege of the Half-Eagle of the empire on his coat of arms, denoting that his congregation ranked among the states of the empire. These monasteries flourished most strongly during the 12th and 13th centuries.

This *Schottenklöster* however had a strange fate. With the collapse of the Irish monastic church after the Norman invasion of Ireland in the 12th century, links between these *Schottenklöster* and Ireland were broken. The flow of Irish monks to these monasteries ceased and the Irish funding dried up. The world at large and particularly Rome, forgot that the term Scot applied exclusively to the Irish. The new Scotland began to lay successful, if false, claims to the achievements of the ancient Scots (Irish) all over Europe. In particular, the Scots made a claim that the foundations of Marianus Scotus belonged to their nation.

In 1515, Pope Leo X issued a bull which 'restored' the foundations to their 'proper owners', the inhabitants of Scotland. The Irish were expelled from Ratisbon, Constance and Erfurt, after being charged, among other things, with having made a 'fraudulent' entry into the records that Ireland was *Scotia Major*. These monasteries continued in Scottish hands until their suppression in 1847.

Pope Instructs Normans to Invade Ireland

From the mid-point of the 11th century onwards, the Roman church in Europe entered into a period of cataclysmic struggle for greater control. This struggle became known as the Gregorian Reform, named after Pope Gregory VII.

Central to this reform was control of the clergy. The aim was to remove the clergy from all lay influence, including that of wives and children. As part of this reform, abbots were forced to become bishops and monks to become priests. Convents of nuns were assigned to the control of bishops or emptied altogether and replaced by men. Throughout Europe, a deep-seated institutional reform took place that was to change the face of Christianity up to the present day.[13] The pope proclaimed himself holy and infallible, claimed the power to depose emperors and required all princes to kiss his feet in subjection.[14] Pope Adrian IV displayed the use of this newly acquired power in his letter *Laudabiliter*, instructing the Norman king Henry II to invade Ireland, a place that the pope regarded as his fiefdom.

The Gregorian reform and the subsequent Norman colonisation of Ireland completed successfully the centuries-old effort of the Roman church to snuff out the Celtic flame throughout Europe. How it succeeded in killing Celtic Christianity in Ireland itself is the subject of the next chapter.

---

13   The Gregorian Reform is described in greater detail in Chapter 6.
14   Pope Gregory VII *Dictatus Papae*.

Sailing with Brendan

I am in the small frail boat of Brendan
with a few stalwart friends.
I have cut the rope
that tied me to the familiar land.
I have pulled the anchor
that held me back
and would not let me go.
We bob up and down on a vast ocean,
no land in sight.
We are led by intuition.
The old maps do not work.
The old language does not work.
What is real is the water beneath us,
the sky above us,
the wind that blows,
the rain that falls
and the sun that travels through the sky each day.
We have returned to the sources of life.
We have started again.
We have been born again.

Dara Molloy

13

ROMAN CHRISTIANITY
IN IRELAND

By the 7th century, Irish monasticism had established itself in every corner of Ireland. It had transformed Ireland into an island of scholarly monks. Irish Christianity was vigorously independent and Rome had no foothold on Irish soil. In order to create that foothold, the bones of Patrick the missionary were taken out of the cupboard, the founding of the monastery of Armagh was backdated to him and the flag of the Roman church was hoisted on Armagh hill.

Saint Patrick[1]

The collapse of the Roman empire took place during the lifetime of St Patrick. Alaric the Visigoth sacked Rome in 410. Patrick spent six years as a young slave in Ireland around this time. In 431, the city of Hippo on the northern coast of Africa was under siege, as St Augustine lay there dying. In 432, Patrick began his mission to Ireland.

Patrick had been reared a Christian in Britain. His father was a deacon. However, during the period of his upbringing, the Romans were withdrawing from Britain, leaving a vacuum that was to be filled by the Angles and Saxons. As a result of this, Roman Christianity was dying in Britain. In contrast, the beginnings of Celtic Christianity were fermenting in Ireland, northern Britain[2] and Wales.

When Patrick came to Ireland as a missionary, he came as a bishop appointed by the Roman church. There is no direct evidence that Patrick ever founded a monastery or became a monk. There is evidence, from his

---

1   St Patrick and St Colmcille have already been written about in Chapter 9. I begin this chapter by presenting this material from a slightly different perspective, in order to set the context for what is to follow.

2   What we now call Scotland was called Caledonia at this time.

own writings, that he visited and stayed for a period in monasteries in Gaul and that he sent many young converts into monasteries in Ireland. If he had become a monk or founded a monastery, it is likely that he would have written about it.[3]

Patrick's Name Disappears after His Death

After the death of Patrick in Ireland in the latter half of the 5th century, there is little evidence of his mission continuing through his successors. Nor is there any evidence of Rome having any further interest in this mission. Unlike Augustine of Canterbury's mission to southern Britain a century and a half later, Patrick's achievements were absorbed into the Celtic monastic form of Christianity and his name slipped into relative oblivion.

By the following century, the name on everyone's lips was not Patrick but Columba (Colmcille). By the time he died, in 597, Columba had become the icon of Celtic Christianity. There were no similar claims being made for Patrick at this time.

Christian monasteries in Ireland were in existence from the late 4th or early 5th centuries. Some were founded before Patrick. The pattern these monasteries followed did not change after his arrival. Each monastery came into existence based on the inspiration of its founder. The founder's vision remained the cornerstone of the monastic community's ethos throughout its existence.

In Chapter 11, I recorded how the 7th century marked the beginning of the clash between the Roman church represented by Augustine of Canterbury and the Irish monasteries in Britain. That dispute, which became focussed at the Synod of Whitby in 664 CE, was one that had its reverberations throughout Ireland. Irish monasteries became either pro-Roman (*Romani*) or pro-Columba (*Hibernenses*).

The Struggle for Primacy

Until the middle of the 7th century, there is little evidence of an hierarchical ecclesiastical structure within Ireland. All monasteries

---

3   For a discussion of this topic, see Alfred P. Smyth, 'Bishop Patrick and the Early Christian mission to Ireland' in Bradshaw, Brendan and Dáire Keogh (eds), *Christianity in Ireland, Revisiting the Story*, Dublin, Columba Press, 2002.

followed the inspiration of their own founders. A monastery's rule of life was controlled by its abbot or abbess. An abbot's successor was appointed from members of that abbot's extended family. Politically, a monastery belonged to and was protected by a kingdom. Monasteries and kingdoms were closely aligned and lived symbiotically in co-dependence. Apart from the occasional synodal gathering of religious and lay leaders, called together by a particular Irish king, there was no higher ecclesiastical authority in Ireland and no person on which to pin that authority.

Seventh-century Ireland was a conglomeration of small tribal kingdoms, with a strong spirit of competition, rivalry and even enmity existing between them. Often, smaller kingdoms allied themselves to more powerful ones and the powerful ones sought to have the high-kingship of the whole country. With the development of Irish monasticism, this competitive spirit transferred itself to the monasteries. Some monasteries had grown into large towns and had become both wealthy and powerful. Many monasteries began to federate together and a number of the more influential ones sought ultimately the primacy of the whole country.

The biggest of the Irish monastic federations in the early 7ᵗʰ century were centred in Iona, Armagh, Kildare, Clonmacnoise and Cashel. These were engaged in a struggle for ecclesiastical supremacy – a struggle that went hand-in-hand and was interwoven with the political struggle for the high-kingship of Ireland, which was going on at the same time.

Patrick and the Monastery of Armagh

In order to bolster its claim for ecclesiastical supremacy, the monastery of Armagh declared that St Patrick had been its founder and first abbot. This is unlikely to have been historically true. Historians point out that Patrick's headquarters were most likely to have been in Downpatrick, where he is believed to be buried, and that he was never a monk. However, this did not prevent propagandists, such as the bishop Tírechán and the priest Muirchú, from making such a claim in the late 7th century.

One can see clearly that the rise of Patrick's name to prominence, after two hundred years of oblivion, coincided with the rise in the influence of Rome on Irish Christianity. At the heart of this re-emergence of Patrick was the pressure coming from Rome to bring Celtic Christianity into line with Roman practices. Patrick was the only historical connection the propagandists could find between Ireland and Rome and he had to be used. The claim of the monastery of Armagh to primacy in the Irish church was based on its connection with Patrick and Patrick's connection with Rome.

Armagh Versus Iona

By the end of the 7th century, the struggle for primacy became a contest between Iona and Armagh, between Colmcille and Patrick. The claims of other monastic federations had receded. Armagh stood firmly on the side of Rome and wanted the Irish church to take on Roman practices. The Columban federation of Iona represented Colmcille's position of loyalty to the uniqueness of the Irish church and resisted the intrusions of Rome.

The influence of Rome was an incoming tide that was probably unstoppable. Nonetheless, the struggle for supremacy between these two monastic giants continued for a further three hundred years before it was finally resolved. In the course of those centuries, fate was to play a part in weakening the Columban position and strengthening the Roman one. The Viking attacks on both Scotland and Ireland played into the hands of the Roman agenda.

Attacks of the Vikings on Lindisfarne (793) and Iona (806) destroyed those monasteries. Further attacks throughout the 9th century gradually eradicated the presence of the Celtic church in Scotland. The headquarters of the Columban monastic federation moved back to Ireland from Scotland and the abbot of Kells became the new co-arb of Columba[4]. The Columban federation lost Iona, its iconic mother house.

On two occasions between 989 and 1007, the political turmoil of the time forced the Columban federation to unite with Armagh, under the one abbot, for its own survival. During these two brief periods, the abbot of Armagh was also the abbot of the Columban federation.[5]

---

4   The famous *Book of Kells* also moved from Iona to Kells at this time. Most of it had been written and illustrated in Iona.

5   Máire Herbert, *Iona, Kells and Derry: The History and Hagiography of the Monastic Familia of Columba.* Dublin, Four Courts Press. 1996. Chapter 6

Viking Christianity and Rome

Fate also played its part through the settling of the Vikings in Ireland. The Vikings, although defeated at the Battle of Clontarf in 1014, remained living in the cities they had founded and were at this point Christian. However, in line with their British counterparts, the Vikings in Ireland practised Roman Christianity and their church structure was the Roman episcopal model. A bishop was in charge of each of the Irish Viking cities – Dublin, Waterford and Limerick. Rome, through Canterbury, was in control of the appointment of these bishops. These bishops were to play a crucial role in promoting the Roman agenda in the coming century.

The Primacy of Armagh

From the beginning of the 11th century onwards, the primacy of Armagh within the Irish church was established. Brian Boru, high-king of Ireland, had underscored this with his support for Armagh during his reign and with the burial of his body at Downpatrick, after his death at the Battle of Clontarf, in 1014. It had taken four hundred years for the Irish people to make the transition from acknowledging Colmcille as the foundation stone of Irish Christianity to accepting Patrick in his place.

By the end of the 11th century, Ireland had reached an accommodation with the Roman church. The pro-Roman monastery of Armagh was unequivocally recognised as the primary monastery in Ireland. Its abbot was the accepted primate of the Irish church. Patrick had replaced Colmcille in the minds of Irish people as the founder of Irish Christianity and Irish monasteries had succumbed to a number of Roman practices, including how they calculated the date of Easter.

Despite this accommodation, the Irish church was still very unlike the rest of Europe. An abbot, rather than a bishop, remained the supreme leader of the Irish church. Irish monasteries kept their own rules and had not converted to the uniform Benedictine rule. The only place where Rome had direct control was in the appointment of bishops to the cities founded by the Vikings.

Rome needed and wanted more control than this. Many Irish people agreed that it should have it. By the beginning of the 12th century, steps were being taken to gain this control. The initial steps were taken by Irish people. But then the floodgates opened. Within a hundred years, Ireland would be changed utterly, both politically and ecclesiastically. How this was to happen is the subject of the next two chapters.

Reluctant Homecoming

The woodland in Sligo soothed a tired heart,
Sent healing waves on its lakes,
And bathed me in green grass and tree spirits.

Too weary was my spirit
And too harsh my homeland Aran seemed
In that cool fairy place.
Mists around the trees standing tall
On an island in the lake.

I came home to gales raging around
Bent and ugly wind-raped shapes.
Sad trees on a bare rock,
Inis Mór in wintertime.

But I came back,
Something deeper than my heart
Grew excited as we bumped down the runway
To land in a hailstorm.
And as I walked four miles,
Some connection, deep and elemental
was soothed and glad to be home
On a bare windswept island.

Today, as if all reward was due,
The calm after the storm.
Vivid beauty to the eye, the senses,
the gut most of all,
captivated
beyond words.
What magic binds us to this place.

Tess Harper

14

BETRAYAL
FROM WITHIN IRELAND

Both ecclesiastically and politically, the 12th century was a watershed in Irish history. The ecclesiastical transformation took place first, with a series of synods beginning in 1101. The presence of the Vikings in the major towns of Ireland and their influence as Christian converts, were pivotal in this process. But the key people in this transformation were the abbots and bishops of Armagh. Of these, Malachy of Armagh became the central figure. Years before the Norman military arrived in 1167, a shift of power was taking place in the Irish church as the leadership was transferred from the Celtic abbots and their monasteries to the Irish bishops and Rome.

As we saw in earlier chapters, the power of the papacy was at a new height in the 12th century. This power was both ecclesiastical and political and even included power over military armies. The Gregorian reform, as it became known, was effectively centralising and enhancing papal power beyond what it had ever attained before. During this century, the Norman empire expanded throughout western Europe, and Rome had its first Norman pope.

The intensity of the process of church institutionalisation on the continent of Europe in the 12th century was sufficient to send tidal waves towards Ireland that were to swamp it, despite its independence. Papal power allied to military power was at a high water mark and when they combined to focus their attention on Ireland, there could be no adequate resistance.

The transformation of the Irish church in the 12th century took place on two fronts. Firstly, the intensity of the Gregorian reform led to numerous synods throughout Ireland, where decisions were made which changed forever the nature of the Irish church. Secondly, the Norman invasion of Ireland, carried out on the papal pretext of bringing about church reform, supported this agenda and accelerated its completion.

The Synod of Cashel 1101

The century opened with the synod of Cashel in 1101, in the presence of the papal legate. The focus of this synod was ecclesiastical reform. The synod was under the influence of Anselm, the Italian archbishop of Canterbury (later canonised), who sought the Romanisation of the Irish church and the extension of his own territory throughout Ireland. Canterbury was the headquarters of the Roman church in Britain and had been so since the time of Augustine the missionary monk, who arrived there in 597.

The synod of Cashel dealt with ecclesiastical benefices, jurisdictional boundaries, clerical concubinage, the right of sanctuary, matrimony and the problems caused by the fact that the appointments of *comharba* (abbot or successor to the founder) and *airchinnech* (prior) in monasteries were not covered by canon law. This latter was particularly significant, as it showed clearly that Rome had no influence on these appointments within monasteries.

Since the 11th century, the towns founded by the Vikings in Ireland, having converted to Christianity, had looked to Canterbury for episcopal ordination. This had facilitated Anselm in placing pro-reform bishops in key positions. The appointment of the bishop of Dublin for example, was controlled by the Vikings who had settled there. They chose that their bishop be consecrated at Canterbury rather than by Irish bishops. Consequently, Dublin was regarded more as a part of the British church than of the Irish church.

Other Viking towns throughout Ireland also had similar practices. Anselm consecrated Máel Ísa Ua hAinmhire, or Malchus, who had been a Benedictine monk at Winchester, in Britain, as bishop of Waterford in 1096. Later, in 1106, he consecrated Gilla Espaic, or Gilbert, who had been a Benedictine monk with Anselm in Rouen, France, as bishop of Limerick and made him papal legate. These two bishops became key pro-Roman reformers in southern Ireland.

Another key to the success of the reform movement was that the high king of Cashel, Muirchertach Ua Briain, a descendant of Brian Boru, was also pro-Roman. Muirchertach was a claimant to the high-kingship of Ireland. Cashel was in the jurisdiction of the bishop of Waterford and so bishop and high king worked together under the direction of Anselm of Canterbury and in constant correspondence with him.

The Synod of Cashel in 1101 did not resolve all the issues around the Romanisation of the Irish church. Other synods were to be held throughout the century until the reform was complete.

Cellach of Armagh

The reform movement was now joined by Cellach Ua Sínaig, who had become abbot of Armagh in 1105. Armagh had been actively pro-Roman since the late 7th century, claiming Patrick as its founder. However, traditionally the abbot of Armagh was neither a priest nor a bishop. Often he was married. By the end of the Viking period, Armagh had degenerated and needed rebuilding and renewal. Cellach as abbot was the man to do it. He was a layman, but he was not to remain a layman for long.

In 1106, Cellach made a tour of Munster urging on the reform. While he was there, the bishop of Armagh died. The pro-Roman bishops of the south took this opportunity to ordain Cellach a bishop, declaring him to be bishop of Armagh, *comharba* (successor) of Patrick and primate of Ireland.

It is ironic that these pro-Roman bishops went against Roman canonical practice in consecrating Cellach in this way. According to Roman canonical practice, Canterbury should have been involved in his consecration. But these bishops were taking the ball on the hop and could not afford to miss the opportunity to promote their own Roman agenda. Canterbury was unlikely to complain too loudly.

The Synod of Rath Brasil 1111

After the synod of Cashel, Gilbert, the newly consecrated bishop of Limerick, came forward with a plan for diocesan and parochial organisation for Ireland and for a uniform Roman liturgy. This document was called *De Statu Ecclesiae*. It was presented at the synod of Rath Brasil in 1111.

The synod of Rath Brasil, near Cashel, was a national synod presided over by bishop Cellach as primate and Muirchertach as high king. This synod divided Ireland into twenty-four sees, replacing the old monastic organisation. It is worth noting that this synod was convened by Muirchertach the high-king and attended not just by clergy but by lay rulers.

Malachy

Before Cellach died in 1129, he named Malachy as his successor as bishop of Armagh. Cellach had groomed Malachy for this job since he first noticed him, at the age of twenty, at the time of his enrolment in the monastery of Armagh in 1115. By the age of twenty-five, Malachy had been ordained priest and sent by Cellach to Lismore near Waterford for instruction under the pro-Roman bishop Malchus.

Malachy came from a background steeped in Irish monasticism. His father was the chief lector at the monastery of Armagh. His mother's family held the lands and lay abbot succession of the famous monastery of Bangor. His mother's brother held this abbacy, but, since the monastery had been completely destroyed by the Vikings, there were no buildings or monks, only land revenues.

On Malachy's return from Lismore, he was instructed by Malchus to rebuild the monastery of Bangor. His uncle stood aside to allow Malachy to take over the abbacy. However, Malachy did not take over the revenues accruing from the land. These remained with others. This probably made it easier for Malachy to gain the abbacy.

In 1125, Cellach ordained Malachy bishop of Down and Connor. This area had been devastated by the Vikings and Malachy, who had successfully rebuilt the monastery of Bangor from the ruins, was now commissioned to rebuild a much wider area. Four years later, in 1129, Cellach sent his staff and a letter to Malachy from his deathbed designating him as his choice of successor, best fitted to administer the primacy.

This designation caused serious political problems. Cellach had combined the office of abbot of Armagh with that of bishop of Armagh. It was his intention that this would remain the case with his successor, so that Armagh could re-establish itself as a primatial ecclesiastical centre. However, the abbacy and see of Armagh had remained hereditary within Cellach's family for generations. Malachy was not a member of this family.

When Cellach died, the abbacy of Armagh was claimed by a kinsman of Cellach, Murtagh. Malachy was not the sort to fight the issue, so that is the way it stood. However, the power and influence of the reformers were building up and by 1132 a resolution came about. The abbacy and revenues would remain with Murtagh, but Malachy would take over the spiritual role of bishop and primate.

This compromise solution represented a very significant shift in Irish ecclesiastical politics. The primacy, which had been claimed by the monastery of Armagh since the 7th century, had always been in the hands of the abbot of Armagh. On this occasion, the primacy transferred from being held by the abbot, who was often an unordained layman, to being held by a bishop. This was the turning point where the balance of power shifted. The Irish monastic church gave way to the Roman episcopal church. A bishop replaced a monk as head of that church.

The separation of the abbacy of Armagh from the primacy continued throughout Murtagh's life. However, problems continued to exist for the pro-Roman reformers. One of these was that the abbacy was hereditary and therefore remained outside their control. When Murtagh died, he was replaced by another kinsman, Niall. The reforming church parties and the princes who supported them, now tried another push. This time they succeeded in breaking the hereditary chain.

In 1137, Niall relinquished the relics considered to be the very title deeds to Armagh – the *Book of Armagh* and the bell and staff of Patrick. As part of the deal now struck, Malachy resigned the primacy and Gilla Mac Liag, or Gelasius, was appointed abbot and primate. The primacy reverted to the abbot of Armagh, but that abbacy was no longer a hereditary position. The pro-Roman church authorities now had control over it.

Gelasius was a more acceptable candidate than Malachy for the job, because of his family connections and his high status previously as abbot of Derry. Gelasius was also pro-reform. He proved to be a good choice from the Roman perspective. As a result, Gelasius remained abbot and primate for a further thirty-eight years. Meanwhile, Malachy remained bishop of Armagh.

Malachy now concentrated on completing the reform. This entailed setting up the newly structured Irish church as an independent entity, separate from Canterbury but connected to Rome. To do this, Malachy had to negotiate with the pope. In the same year he relinquished the primacy, 1137, he set out for Rome with three pack horses and a number of companions. On his way, he visited the famous monastery of Clairvaux, founded by St Bernard.

The Benedictines of Clairvaux

Bernard and Malachy became instant friends. It is easy to see how they did. Both were from aristocratic families, both were zealous Christians and reforming monks and both had re-established monasteries that had fallen into dereliction. Where Bernard was busily reforming Benedictine monasticism, Malachy was busily reforming Irish monasticism. Unfortunately for Ireland, Malachy was so taken by the new order of Benedictines, now to be called Cistercians, that he abandoned any hope of reforming Celtic monasticism and instead decided that Irish monasteries from now on should be Cistercian. This was to have disastrous consequences for Celtic monasticism.

Monasticism based on the rule of St Benedict was already the norm in Europe. From the 8th century onwards, Irish monasteries throughout Europe had been adopting the Benedictine rule. By the 12th century, there were no monasteries based on Irish rules in mainland Europe. However, in Ireland the reverse was the case. All of the monasteries in Ireland at the turn of the 12th century continued to claim allegiance to the inspiration of their founders and Benedictine monasticism had made no inroads into Irish life. All this was now about to change and Malachy was the key to initiating this change.

Before leaving Clairvaux, Malachy invited Bernard to set up Cistercian monasteries in Ireland. He then proceeded to Rome where he sought from the pope two *pallia*[1], or titles to archbishoprics, in Armagh and Cashel. This was essentially a request to create a church in Ireland independent of Britain and Canterbury.

Although Malachy was well received by Pope Innocent II, his request for the *pallia* was refused. The pope required that such a request come from a full national gathering of the bishops, clergy and nobles of the

---

1   A *pallium* (plural: *pallia*) is a circular band about two inches wide worn about the neck, breast and shoulders, with two pendants, one hanging down in front and one behind. Its traceable history goes back as far as the 5th century. Normally it is given by a pope only to an archbishop who is taking up metropolitan duties. To receive it, the archbishop has to swear an oath of allegiance to the pope.

country. However, he did appoint Malachy as papal legate. On Malachy's way home, he again visited Clairvaux and also Arroaise in Flanders and left some of his monks in these places to learn the Cistercian and Arroasian rules[2], with a view to establishing houses under these rules in Ireland.

Within three years the Cistercians had arrived in Ireland. Their arrival in 1142 opened a door that was never to close. For the first time, a religious community that was not of Irish origin established itself in Ireland. Soon enough, establishments of this kind would totally replace the indigenous Irish monasteries. It was the beginning of the final chapter in the Romanisation of the Irish church.

Malachy had been working for the transformation of the Irish church on two fronts. On one front, he was intent on bringing the Norman Cistercians to Ireland. On the other, he was determined to complete the paradigm shift in Ireland from Celtic monastic to European episcopal. Dying in 1148, in the arms of St Bernard, on his second journey to Rome, he did not live to see all the fruits of his work, but before his death he had done enough on both fronts to make the changes that were coming irreversible.

The Central Role of Malachy

No history of this period of transformation in the Irish church can be written without Malachy being at the centre of it. In 1190, he became the first of only four Irish saints ever to be canonised by Rome. His achievement was that of Romanising the Irish church at the expense of its traditional indigenous monastic structure. Due to a movement in which he played a central role, the Irish monastic system was replaced by an episcopal diocesan system and the Irish monasteries themselves were replaced by European religious orders.

The Breaking of Traditions

When Malachy became bishop of Armagh, an Irish tradition was broken. That tradition required that the see of Armagh and the abbacy of Armagh remain within a certain family. Malachy was not a member of that family. From the time of his appointment as bishop onwards, it would not be the

---

2   These were variations of the Benedictine Rule acceptable to Rome.

family that decided who the next bishop was to be, but the other bishops of the country, in union with Rome.

A second Irish tradition was broken when Malachy for a brief period held the primacy – the leadership position in the Irish church. This primacy had always been claimed by the abbot of Armagh. Malachy was not the abbot of Armagh when he took the primacy. Later, the primacy did move permanently to the archbishop of Armagh.

Malachy then participated in breaking a third Irish tradition – that of hereditary abbatial succession – by cooperating in placing the abbot of Derry, Gelasius, in the position of abbot of Armagh and primate of Ireland. Gelasius did not belong to the family that had held this hereditary position for centuries. The system of appointment changed with Gelasius and Malachy played a big role in this transition.

All of this breaking with traditional practices wrested power from the hands of local families and kingdoms and put it in the hands of the Irish episcopacy and Rome.

Malachy's visit to Pope Innocent II, subjecting himself to him and seeking the *pallium* from him, was also a departure from tradition. No Irish monk had ever approached the pope in this way before. To receive the *pallium*, one had to make a vow of allegiance. The Irish monastic church had always acknowledged and respected the pope, but nonetheless made it clear that it wished to remain independent and free from papal interference. The Easter controversy and the letters of Columbanus to the popes attest to this position. Until this time, the Irish monastic church at home had no direct connection with the pope. It was for this reason that a later pope, Adrian IV, encouraged the Norman king Henry II to invade Ireland.

The changes that took place in Malachy's life mirrored the changes that took place in the Irish church. Malachy began his life as a monk in the Celtic tradition and went on to be an abbot. But then he became a bishop, a primate and later a papal legate in the Roman tradition. For whatever reason, Malachy had little loyalty to, or nostalgia for, the Irish tradition. His eyes were firmly on the continent of Europe and on Rome. His willingness to jettison the Irish tradition was embodied in his eagerness to become a Cistercian monk himself and join Bernard's monastery. When he was not allowed to do so by Pope Innocent II, he left some of his own party in Clairvaux and these subsequently came back to Ireland as part of the new Cistercian colonisation of Ireland.

Malachy was an Irishman who did not display the arrogance of Augustine of Canterbury, the fundamentalism of Wilfrid or the aggression of Boniface. Nonetheless, he did possess a steely doggedness and an ability to achieve what he envisioned. Within the period of his lifetime, the ecclesiastical structure in Ireland was transformed utterly. Malachy was the pivotal person in that transformation.

The Synod of Kells

Malachy, who died in 1148, had seen the arrival of the first Cistercians into Ireland. However, his death came before the Synod of Kells. At this synod in 1152, what Malachy had failed to achieve on his first visit to Rome was realised. The papal legate, Paparo, brought with him to this synod four *pallia*. With these he established the four archbishoprics that to this day form the basic infrastructure of the Irish church. These four archbishoprics were established in Armagh, Dublin, Cashel and Tuam, one for each of the four provinces of Ireland. Ireland now became a separate national church, directly subject to the pope and independent of the British church and Canterbury.

With this change, many of the Irish monastic territories became episcopal sees. Their abbots became bishops and their monks became Augustinian canons[3]. The establishment of the Augustinian canons in Ireland was a delayed victory for Augustine of Hippo, who had so opposed Pelagius and all that Celtic Christianity had stood for back in the 5th century. Communities with his name were now replacing Celtic monastic communities in Ireland. It took over seven hundred years for his point of view to gain dominance in Ireland, but this was now achieved.

---

3   Augustinian canons were communities of priests who lived with their bishop. Augustine of Hippo had created this model of community in the early 5th century, when he, as bishop, lived with a community of priests. The usefulness of the Augustinians in Ireland at this time was in facilitating the change over from monastic to episcopal community, as happened to the Columban monastery in Kells in 1152. There the abbot was made a bishop and his monks became Augustinian canons.

Conclusions

Irish monasticism had been part of an indigenous spiritual movement that was vibrant and self-renewing for over seven hundred years. It had proved itself over and over again as an agent of spiritual and social transformation. By far the majority of the Irish saints we know and celebrate today were monks from these monasteries. The movement produced some extraordinary people who left profound marks on history in Ireland and throughout Europe and whose impact is still felt today: Colmcille the patron saint of Scotland, Columbanus one of the founders of modern Europe, Brigid of Kildare who had churches named after her in many parts of western Europe, Brendan the Navigator whose story *Navigatio Brendani* became a European bestseller and who gives his name to the Brandenburg Gate in Berlin.

Both at home and abroad, Irish monasticism had made a profound and unprecedented impact. Why was it that Malachy and other native Irishmen were so intent on killing the goose that laid the golden egg? One cannot argue convincingly, as the invading Henry II tried to, that Ireland was 'rude and ignorant'. Nor can one argue that the Irish church was corrupt and decayed, as was the view of various popes[4]. The Irish church and Irish society in general, continued to renew itself from within and showed great evidence of that, even during this latter period.

During the first half of the 12th century, despite the fundamental changes happening in Ireland with regard to Romanisation, Irish monasticism was in the process of yet another profound renewal. To this day, one can see the evidence of this renewal in the vibrancy of the architecture, the exquisite artistry of the stonework and metalwork and the amount and quality of the written publications. The doorway of Clonfert cathedral in County Galway is a fine example of the architecture of the time. We have wonderful examples of that period's stonework in the Dysert O'Dea cross in County Clare and of its metalwork in the Cross of Cong. Manuscript writing, as in *The Book of Leinster* and poetry writing, as in *An Leabhar Breac*, was also flourishing. This period produced a plethora of written works in both Irish and Latin. The Irish monks of this

---

4   The Papal Bull *Laudabiliter*, in which Pope Adrian IV, the only British born subject ever to achieve the papacy, authorised Henry II to invade Ireland, states unequivocally that Ireland is 'ignorant and barbarous'.

time recorded for posterity the ancient legends of Ireland, including the wonderful story of *The Táin Bó Cuailgne*.

All we can say, by way of tentative hypothesis, is that Malachy and his allies had internalised the negative view of the Irish church that was clearly present at the time among the powerful political and church leaders on the continent and in Britain. From the latter half of the 7th century, the pressure for change had always been there, but was held in check by those who opposed it. In the early 12th century that pressure for change reached a critical mass. Within Ireland, two key figures emerged in favour of the change – Malachy on the ecclesiastical front and Muirchertach, the Cashel-based claimant to high kingship, on the secular front. There were no equivalently strong people on the opposite side at the time and so the old edifice gave way.

The Norman conquest of Ireland that occurred in the latter half of the 12th century ensured that the transformation of the Irish church went even further than Malachy might have either expected or wanted. We deal with this topic in the next chapter.

Church Meeting

Waiting in the whistling,
Tapping toes and lighting of cigarettes.
Waiting in the whistling,
For the go-ahead to talk to change the world.
Beginning with the church.

Stand up Mother Church –
You are now up for trial.

You have ignored woman,
You ignore her still – I sat in a room with two men priests
And felt myself sink into a swamp of non-entity.
They'll blame me for I did not speak –
but it was not of my language – woman.

You have ridiculed your men
by giving them an identity without a soul
by telling them they were whole when they were not –
far from it.

Women-less men
I weep to see their scars
that you lashed into them
for the crusading cause.

You have warped your children
for they,
by perverse birth in darkness, in ignorance
(such have you tabooed earth's special act)
cringe now at the light
and take flight like beasts to preserve their blindness.

See your family, Mother Church.
You shame earth's nature under your sterile gaze.
You have named it foul.
But nature will survive,
will free her own
and you shall fall –

Your fate – to wait, and watch your own decay.
Life-less monument
You have ruled too long!

Tess Harper

15

ECCLESIASTICAL CONQUEST IN IRELAND

The Norman conquest of Ireland took place on two fronts, ecclesiastical and political. The ecclesiastical front began its operations twenty five years before the political front. The Cistercian monks, who arrived in Ireland in 1142 to set up the monastery at Mellifont, were the first Normans to set foot in Ireland. When the military arrived in 1167, the two fronts worked side-by-side and hand-in-hand to complete the subjection of Ireland both politically and ecclesiastically.

While the ecclesiastical structure of the Irish church was being successfully transformed from monastic to episcopal, prior to the Norman invasion, this did not mean that all the Irish monasteries were closing down, nor that they were converting to a Benedictine rule. What it did mean was that power in the Irish church was transferring from abbots to bishops and that these bishops were no longer living as monks in monasteries.

Within these changing times, some Irish monasteries were continuing to hold their ground while others were succumbing to outside pressures. One Celtic monastery in particular that not only held its ground, but grew in status and power, was the monastery of Derry, which at this time had established itself as the primary monastery in the Columban federation.

The Columban Monastery of Derry

As a result of a synod held in 1158 in Brí Mac Thadhg in Meath, convened by the primate Gilla Mac Liag of Armagh, ex-abbot of Derry, abbot Ua Brolcháin of Derry secured his position as *comharba* of Colmcille. The position of *comharba* had moved from the Columban monastery of Iona to the Columban monastery of Kells during the Viking invasions. But after the Synod of Kells in 1152, the monastery of Kells had become an episcopal see and its monks had become Augustinian canons[1]. The synod of 1158 facilitated the successful transfer of the *comharba* from Kells to Derry. In the presence of the papal legate, the abbot of Derry was given the same status and authority as a bishop.

By this time, the high-kingship, such as it was, had moved from Munster to Ulster and was now claimed by Mac Lochlainn. Mac Lochlainn's base was in Derry and he therefore supported Ua Brolcháin and his monastery there. The rise of the Derry monastery could not have taken place without the support of this high king. It was Mac Lochlainn who assembled the next synod of clergy and nobles in 1161. At this synod, the Columban federation was given freedom from secular tribute. This meant that the tribute the Columban monasteries might have had to pay to a secular overlord was now paid to Derry. After this synod, both Mac Lochlainn and Ua Brolcháin began an expansive building programme in Derry.

The story of the rise of the Derry monastery in a period after the episcopal reorganisation of the Irish church and immediately prior to the Norman invasion shows that an accommodation was being reached between the forces for Roman reform and traditional Irish monasticism. The episcopal reorganisation had not, on its own, meant the death of Irish monasticism. One has to say, however, that this reform had greatly weakened the traditional structures. Those traditional structures were further weakened by the arrival and spread of Cistercian monasteries in Ireland.

The Cistercians

The Cistercians were the first of the new European religious orders to establish themselves in Ireland. Irish monasticism was unlike both Benedictine monasticism and religious orders. Irish monasteries were autonomous and followed the spirit of their individual founders. While written rules of some Irish founders did exist, there was not a great

---

1   Augustinian Canons are not monks. They are priests who live together in community with their bishop. They trace their roots back to St Augustine of Hippo who as a bishop lived with a group of his priests. The Gregorian reform promoted the spread of Augustinian canons as a way of ensuring clerical celibacy.

emphasis put on following a written rule, even where monasteries became federated.

The Cistercians came to Mellifont in 1142. Invited by Malachy, the Armagh monk and bishop, they represented the Norman empire in ecclesiastical form. This was the first time the Normans had set foot in Ireland. While invited and welcomed by the Irish, the Cistercians represented the ecclesial arm of a colonial power with a global vision. Their arrival in Ireland was the first step in a process that would transform Ireland utterly – for the worse.

The land for the monastery was given by the king of Airgialla in whose kingdom Mellifont was to be built. When the building was completed in 1157, it was consecrated in the presence of an assembly of bishops and kings. Many gifts were given to the monastery on this occasion. The high king Mac Lochlainn granted a hundred and sixty cows, sixty ounces of gold and a townland. Sixty ounces of gold was given by the king of Airgialla and another sixty ounces of gold was given by the wife of Tiernan O'Rourke, king of Breifne.

The abbot who was appointed to this monastery was an Irish monk who had trained in Clairvaux, but the rest of the monks were French Normans. They brought with them their French culture and their French language. When Irish monks joined this monastery and later such monasteries, they were expected to adapt to this new culture and become French-speaking.

The Cistercians spread rapidly in Ireland. By 1165, two years before the Norman soldiers set foot in Ireland and only eight years after the completion of Mellifont, there were twelve Irish Cistercian abbeys. The arrival of the Cistercians to Ireland had the strong support of both bishops and kings, although not necessarily of Irish abbots. It is also clear that the order had little problem recruiting in Ireland.

The spread of the Cistercians in Ireland, however, has to be seen in the context of the broader political and social picture. The Cistercians themselves were Normans. The papacy had seen that the best way to spread the influence of the Roman church throughout Europe was through the Norman conquests. Therefore the Roman church had allied itself with the Normans. The growth of the Cistercians was the most significant of the religious movements within the Roman church at that time. Pope Eugenius III, the pope who gave the *pallia* to Ireland, had himself been a Cistercian under St Bernard. The arrival of the Cistercians in Ireland was the frontline of the Norman invasion.

Dermot McMurrough and the Norman Military

Malachy of Armagh and Dermot McMurrough can be placed side by side as the two people who brought the Normans to Ireland. Malachy brought the Norman Cistercians: Dermot was to bring the Norman overlords.

Dermot was a defeated Irish king who left Ireland seeking help in reclaiming his lands in Leinster from his arch-enemy Tiernan O'Rourke. He found that help in Henry II and his Norman Welsh knights. With Strongbow at the helm of an invading force, Dermot returned to Ireland. Thus began the Norman military conquest in 1167. Malachy, twenty-five years earlier, had brought the ecclesiastical arm of this same colonial force to Ireland.

While supported by the Norman king Henry II, this was not a planned massive invasion of Ireland. It was a small Welsh force who came to give assistance to Dermot McMurrough. However, this small invasion opened a door, which allowed entry to a continuous flow of warriors and migrants to Ireland over the next three decades. The summation of these events resulted in the Anglo-Normans gaining control over much of Ireland.

The Normans were originally Vikings who had settled in the northern half of France in the 10th century. Gradually their power and territory increased. Under William the Conqueror they had invaded England in 1066. At the time of the invasion of Ireland, the Normans were in control of both France and England. Norman kings had a sizeable army always at the ready because of the feudal system in force in their kingdoms that subjected nobles as vassals to them.

Henry II, although king of England, had been born in France and was French in his language and culture. He had married Eleanor of Equitane, ex-wife of King Louis VII and through this had doubled his French holdings. In 1159, Pope Adrian IV, an Englishman, issued a bull *Laudabiliter* investing Henry with the governorship of Ireland. The pope laid claim to Ireland as his fiefdom, appealing to the *Donation of Constantine* (believed now to be a forgery), which gave all the islands of the world to the Roman church in the 4th century. The bull *Laudabiliter* made Ireland a feudal possession of the King of England under the nominal overlordship of the papacy.

The pope wanted Henry to take control of Ireland as, in his view, the Irish church had degenerated into barbarism and needed reform. When Henry eventually did set foot in Ireland in 1171, his proclaimed purpose was to 'enlarge the boundaries of the church' and 'to proclaim the rules of the Christian religion to a rude and ignorant people'.

The allegations of both pope and king of this period, the two most powerful people in Europe, were completely contrary to the facts. These facts must have been available to them, as there were communities of Irish monks throughout Europe, including in Rome, at this time. However, they obviously chose to ignore them for their own political ends.

In the 11th and 12th century, there had been a revival of scholarship and the arts in Ireland. The great monastic schools were producing many new manuscripts, some of them quite remarkable, in both Latin and Gaelic. These so-called 'rude and ignorant people', in that very period, had laid the basis for a prescriptive grammar of the Gaelic language, the first such grammar of a western European language. Decorative metalwork and the illumination of manuscripts had taken on new artistic forms and there was a boom in new building projects, introducing Romanesque and Gothic architecture for the first time into Ireland.

Henry II did not take up the invitation of the pope immediately, as he was busy with other campaigns. When Dermot McMurrough went looking for Henry, he found him in the deep south of France. Henry was too busy to come to Dermot's aid directly but he issued Dermot with a letter in which he invited his subjects to rally to Dermot's aid. Dermot found suitable allies among the landless Norman knights in Wales. Their leader, Strongbow, drove a tough bargain with him. Dermot had to promise him his eldest daughter Aoife in marriage and the right of succession to the kingdom of Leinster.

Norman Landings in Ireland

A small Norman invading force landed in the south-east of Ireland in 1167. This invasion was not particularly successful, but in 1169 a much larger force landed, capturing Wexford and Waterford and then marching on Dublin. Having captured Dublin, the Normans began to fan out across the country. They had more success in the south than in the north.

In 1171, Henry II landed in Ireland. His real reason for coming was to ensure that the gains of these landless adventurers would accrue to the crown. He had no real interest in Ireland, as it offered no real advantages to him.

By the year 1300, most of Ireland was in Norman control. The Irish church was also under its control. In church terms, control meant making sure that the positions of bishops and abbots were filled by Anglo-Normans, or at least Irishmen who were loyal to the crown. By 1254, roughly one third of the episcopal sees in Ireland were occupied by foreign bishops and this proportion increased in the second half of the thirteenth century.

The Norman invasion of Ireland was not a clear-cut, carefully planned campaign to conquer a nation. It succeeded mainly because the feudal system of the Normans had reached its capacity in western Europe. Landless feudal knights were looking for property to claim for themselves. Landless peasants were looking for land to till. The Norman Cistercians were searching for lands that were free of feudal responsibilities.

Migration into Ireland

At the time of the Norman invasion, the lands of western Europe were overpopulated. It did not take much encouragement for people to begin a migration towards Ireland, where the population was small and the land good. The Norman invasion opened the way for a flow of Norman migrants into Ireland. They settled in the lands conquered by the Norman knights. Their arrival was not part of a planned plantation or colonisation of Ireland and no attempt was made to control it. Fundamentally, it was an overflowing of western Europe into Ireland.

The military conquest and subsequent migration were so successful in southern Ireland that certain areas became almost an Anglo-Norman preserve, with French the dominant language and culture. By the reign of Edward I (1272–1307), a population of small free tenants of English, or occasionally Welsh, origin had been settled in the modern counties of Meath and Westmeath, in Tipperary and Limerick and in parts of Cork and Kerry. In some districts, these new settlers far outnumbered the native Irish.

With the Norman invasion of military and migrants, the social and political landscape of Ireland was changed utterly. Political power shifted away from Irish kings to Britain. Irish kingdoms collapsed and with them the support they gave to Irish monasteries. Many of the Irish monasteries also lost their land to the invaders and migrant settlers.

The Norman invasion brought Irish monasticism to an end. It did not die instantly, but die it did. Had the Normans not invaded, there were signs that an accommodation could have been reached between the old and the new order.

Comparing Dermot and Malachy

Dermot McMurrough could not have anticipated the disastrous consequences of his actions for the future history of Ireland. In this, his actions are on a par with the actions of Malachy on the ecclesiastical front. While what Malachy did was clearly an act of profound betrayal of the Irish monastic tradition, he may not have anticipated such a total annihilation of Irish monasticism as what actually came about. However, in comparing Malachy to Dermot McMurrough one would have to conclude that Malachy's actions were more focussed and more deliberate. Malachy was a visionary where Dermot was not. Malachy clearly foresaw many of the consequences of his actions. Therefore, one would have to hold him more responsible for those consequences.

It is clear from the evidence that the main thrust towards change in Ireland came from outside Ireland – the papal reform movement known as the Gregorian reform, the spread of French culture through the Norman conquests and the flourish of new European religious orders that began with the Cistercians and the Augustinians, but was to continue with many others. However, for those forces to make inroads into the politically and ecclesiastically independent island of Ireland, they needed Irish people to open the doors for them. Those people were Malachy on the ecclesiastical front and Dermot McMurrough on the political front.

The Cistercians in Ireland

Ireland's wealth of spiritual and cultural tradition had been concentrated in its Celtic monasteries. When these collapsed and were in the process of being replaced by Cistercian monasteries and Augustinian canons, a rearguard action took place to try to make these new foundations as Irish as possible. Many Cistercian monasteries became, indeed, very Irish and began to look like the Celtic monasteries they had replaced. On this battleground, the last war was fought between the *Romani* and the *Hibernenses*.

Initially, many of the Cistercian monasteries played an important part in continuing the Gaelic monastic tradition and in acting as centres of Gaelic culture. They provided a focal point for tribal loyalty and made buildings available for meeting and assembly. Wherever Irish territories continued to be ruled by Irish kings, or the Brehon laws prevailed, people continued to have a traditional attitude towards their monasteries, even if these monasteries were Cistercian. As a consequence, the royal family of Airgialla (whose territory equated with the modern counties of Louth and Monaghan) had special ties with Mellifont, the royal family of Meath with Bective, the king of Offaly with Monasterevin, the king of Ossory with Jerpoint and Kilenny and the king of Thomond with Maigue, Suir, Holy Cross, Kilcooly, Fermoy and Corcomroe.

However, from the perspective of the Cistercian general chapter based in Clairvaux, such an employment of the monasteries was a betrayal of the ideals of uniformity and universality of the order and amounted to a schismatic movement. As the Cistercians grew in strength and influence, supported by the Norman conquest and the inflow of Norman migrants, the influence of the Irish monastic tradition was ruthlessly removed.

The first hundred years of the Cistercians in Ireland tells a dramatic tale of the scale of the ecclesiastical and cultural destruction that took place at their behest. The Cistercians were a universalist order that made no concessions to culture or place. They were opposed to any process of adaptation to local customs. The Cistercian rule and lifestyle in Ireland was the same as that in France. There was an insistence on uniformity of observance and there could be no departure from Cistercian tradition. The style and architecture of the first Irish monastery at Mellifont were exactly like a Cistercian monastery in France. This building made the statement and set the scene.

In order to ensure that this policy of uniformity was followed, it was necessary for every Irish Cistercian monastery to have a contingent of

French monks and ideally a French abbot. Where this did not happen and the dominant group of monks was Irish, the practice of the monastery veered in the direction of Celtic monasticism. Hereditary rights began to be put in place and the monasteries became more Celtic than Cistercian.

By the end of the 12th century, Ireland had ten Anglo-Norman Cistercian monasteries with French speaking abbots in control and about twenty-nine other Cistercian monasteries with Irish speaking abbots in control. This produced some differences. However, the Cistercian leaders were Anglo-Normans who saw that political unification and stability under the Anglo-Norman king were in the best interests of religion in Ireland. It was clear, therefore, that Cistercian monasteries in Ireland had to be under the influence and authority of the Anglo-Normans.

In 1217, the king, Henry III, instructed his justiciar (the administrator of the crown) in Dublin to prevent any Irishman being elected or appointed bishop to any cathedral church in Ireland. This also became the policy among the Cistercians. Irish abbots in Cistercian monasteries were replaced by French speaking Anglo-Normans and the number of Anglo-Norman monks in communities ensured the dominance of French culture. The French culture was regarded as superior to Irish culture, which was thought to be barbaric. Therefore, the spoken language of the monasteries had to be French.

These policies led eventually to the complete removal of Irishmen from every position of importance in the Irish church, in those areas where the Anglo-Normans were in control. The positions of abbots, bishops and holders of other important benefices, were all eventually held by Anglo-Normans.

The Crisis at Mellifont

In the course of this process, the clash between the two cultures came to a head in the mother house of the Irish Cistercians at Mellifont. In the first half of the 13th century, the area north of Dublin, which included Mellifont, was still neither fully under the control of the Normans nor of the Irish. The monastery at Mellifont reflected this instability. It had remained Irish since its foundation: that is, with an Irish abbot. By the early 13th century, it had a large body of Irish monks and claimed considerable local allegiance and support.

Mellifont by this time had also attained a large filiation of other Irish-dominated Cistercian monasteries, with Irish abbots. From the point of view of Clairvaux, the mother house of the Cistercians in Europe, these houses were seriously irregular and out of control, because they were so much under the influence of the Irish tradition, language and culture. The general chapter of the Cistercians decided on drastic action, which involved replacing the Irish abbots with Anglo-Norman ones.

In 1216, official Cistercian visitors were sent to Ireland to enact this remedy. They were met at Mellifont by an angry crowd of Irish monks, led by their abbot, who shut the gates against them. The same opposition was shown at Jerpoint, Baltinglass, Kilenny, Kilbeggan and Bective. During this visitation, despite the opposition, the abbots of Mellifont and Jerpoint were deposed and replaced. In the other monasteries, the visitation was successfully resisted.

In 1220, the Cistercian general chapter resorted to even more extreme measures. They brought in the Norman military to enforce the changes that were required. This worked only in areas where the Normans had already established complete political control. The problem, therefore, remained unresolved in some of the monasteries.

Finally, in 1221, the Cistercian general chapter resolved to disperse some of the Irish monks to monasteries abroad. Their places were filled with Anglo-Norman monks. From 1222 to 1225 there was a relative calm, but then in 1226 trouble erupted with more ferocity than ever. This period of the trouble came to be known as 'the Mellifont Conspiracy' because it was alleged by the Cistercian general chapter that the resistance was being organised centrally throughout the Mellifont filiation of Irish monasteries.

This new bout of trouble was caused by yet another visitation from Clairvaux which attempted to sort out the remaining rebel monasteries. When this delegation arrived at Baltinglass, the newly-appointed abbot of Baltinglass and his minders were driven from the gates by the whole community of monks and lay brothers. He was thrown from his horse and his seal of authority was taken from him. Later he returned, to be instated, at the head of a large armed force.

Other violent events happened elsewhere. In the monastery of Owney in modern day County Limerick, the newly appointed abbot was greatly resented. Over the winter, he had his horses stolen, his cattle maimed and his servants killed.

The English Abbot Stephen

The final chapter of this story of trouble among the Irish Cistercians has Abbot Stephen from England in the leading role. Stephen entertained a particularly strong racial prejudice against the Irish. He combined this with what he believed to be a 'necessary' ruthlessness. The Irish were 'bestial' and their kings were 'living in little huts made of wattle of the type used by birds when they are moulting'. These Irish kings, according to him, possessed neither castles nor halls, nor even proper houses or harness for their horses.[2]

Stephen's remarks, directed particularly at the king of Thomond, were very far from the truth. The king of Thomond at the time was in complete control of a relatively large area, with Limerick as his seat of power. Contrary to Stephen's jaundiced view, he had a reputation as a builder of monasteries and churches and had also constructed other substantial buildings for secular and military purposes, including castles at Croom and Adare.

On Stephen's arrival in Ireland in 1228, armed with supreme powers to quell this 'conspiracy' by whatever means necessary, he encountered unprecedented violence and opposition. At Mellifont, sixty-eight out of a total of hundred and ten monks had taken to the hills to avoid him. They carried with them the monastic charter, chalices and books of the monastery as well as the processional cross.

Stephen used this flight of the monks to his advantage. Only twenty-eight of these monks were allowed back. The rest of the returned fugitives were sent to monasteries in England and France. Their places in Mellifont were filled by monks sent from Clairvaux. Jocelyn, a Frenchman, was placed in charge as abbot.

Abbot Stephen then sent an advance party to Dunbrody in Wexford to announce and prepare for his impending visit. This party was, however, ambushed and viciously assaulted by a group of monks, led by the prior.

---

2   Cf. Barry W. O'Dwyer, *The Conspiracy of Mellifont, 1216 – 1231*. Pamphlet published for the Dublin Historical Association, 1970.

A delegation of Irish monks, among them certain pro-Cistercian abbots, was then sent to make the prior see reason. However, this delegation was met by a band of armed monks drawn up in battle order, led by the prior, who had a sword in one hand, a lance in the other and a scabbard hung around his neck.

When Abbot Stephen arrived later, he got the same treatment and, but for the intervention of some nobles he had taken with him for protection, he might well have been murdered. The revolt in Dunbrody collapsed when Stephen was allowed to address the community as they stood drawn up in battle order.

At the monastery of Maigue in Limerick things were even worse. The Irish monks there had driven out the abbot and all the English and other monks who had been introduced there to promote reform. The Irish monks fortified and provisioned the abbey for a siege. The building was turned into a castle and the tower above the altar was fortified. When Stephen arrived, he excommunicated all of the rebellious monks and requested the bishop of Limerick to send in armed support. At the cost of some lives, the abbey was recaptured and the foreign monks who had been driven out were reinstalled.

One has to admit that abbot Stephen displayed a fearless courage in carrying out his duties. He travelled throughout Ireland in obvious danger of losing his life. Apart from armed confrontations at the gates of abbeys, he was also regularly waylaid, attacked and robbed on his journeys.

The reader might, at first, be shocked at the violence displayed by Irish monks of this time. Throughout Europe, it was a time of war and violence. One could argue, moreover, that the Irish monks were justified in their violent opposition. The Cistercian onslaught was robbing them of their monastic tradition and their cultural identity.

At any rate, the violence continued. At Monasterevin, Stephen had secured an Anglo-Norman abbot in position in 1228. Two years later this abbot had his eyes put out by the Irish monks. Putting eyes out was a tactic used by Irish and Anglo-Normans alike and was not restricted to monks. From it we get the very common Irish surname Sullivan (Súilleabháin, meaning 'one eye'). In 1230, the monks at the monastery of Fermoy succeeded in murdering their newly-appointed abbot.

The extreme measures employed by Abbot Stephen eventually defeated the Irish resistance. These measures included: the dispersion of the Mellifont filiation, with all rebellious monasteries now under the jurisdiction of foreign monasteries; the imposition of Anglo-Norman abbots; the re-composition of Irish monasteries by increasing the number of Anglo-Norman monks and by sending some of the Irish monks abroad; a prohibition on the election of Irish-born abbots; and severe restrictions placed on the acceptance of Irishmen as novices. To be accepted as novices, Irishmen now had to be 'educated', that is, first attend colleges in England or France.

The resistance of the Irish monks to the imposition of an alien language and culture and to the policy of prohibition of native monastic traditions and customs, must be seen from the wider perspective of the overall Norman conquest and migration. All the 'troublesome' monasteries were situated in areas where there had been a great influx of new peoples, who had come in numbers sufficient to swamp the existing population. For the Irish, everything of value was being taken from them, other than their lives. They were losing their land, their political power, their monastic tradition, their language and even their spiritual and cultural identity.

Other European Religious Orders
The arrival of the Cistercians in Ireland was quickly followed by that of other European religious orders. The Augustinian canons came at almost the same time as the Cistercians, encouraged by Malachy to do so.

It is instructional to note that the English-born pope Adrian IV, who issued the papal bull *Laudabiliter* in 1155 instructing Henry II to invade Ireland, was an Augustinian canon, while Eugenius III, who was pope from 1145 to 1153 and gave Ireland the four *pallia*, was a Cistercian monk and friend of Bernard of Clairvaux. Both the Augustinians and the Cistercians had reached dominant positions within the Roman church at this time and their presence was now being felt in Ireland.

The Cistercians and Augustinians were followed to Ireland by the Franciscans, the Dominicans and the Carmelites. The native spiritual tradition was pushed aside by these arrivals. Celtic monasteries were emptied of monks or were converted to European-style religious communities. The native spirituality of the Irish, represented within

Celtic monasteries, was replaced by European spiritualities, imported by the many European religious orders that arrived. Anglo-Norman families, loyal to the British crown, who had gained control of large swathes of the Irish landscape, invited these European religious orders to come and build their houses and monasteries on the land and to assist in the development of a new societal order. Throughout Ireland today, the remains of these 12th- and 13th-century religious buildings are to be found in the landscape.

Some Conclusions

It is well established in the consciousness of modern Irish people that Ireland was politically colonised from the 12th century onwards. What remains to be acknowledged among Irish people today is that Ireland was also ecclesiastically colonised in the same century. Irish people remain ignorant of the fact that the political colonisers and the ecclesiastical colonisers of Ireland were co-conspirators, colluding to bring about the suppression of everything Irish and to subject the Irish people to foreign control. Adrian IV, the only English pope ever and Henry II, a Norman who had become king of England, planned the conquest together. The monk turned bishop, Malachy of Armagh and the deposed king, Dermot McMurrough, were the two Irishmen who opened to doors to them.

From the 12th century onwards, Irish traditional spirituality found itself in a backwater, no longer expressed, encouraged or even recognised by the dominant church structures. The 12th century marks the tragic moment in Irish history when the graph that tracked the Irish people's celebration of their own freedom fell below zero. That graph was to remain below zero for 800 years, reaching terrible depths during the time of the Reformation and hitting an all-time low for the three years of the famine in the 1840s. For all the 800 years of pain and struggle, religion and politics were inextricably linked.

Only since 1921 has Ireland at last seen that graph rise again above zero and its people begin their recovery from centuries of oppression. With the dawn of the 21st century, that new freedom has led to an awakening of everything Irish. The Irish people again celebrate their unique identity through music, dance, art, poetry, drama, literature and their own language. The world is again gifted with the unique culture and spirit of the Irish.

The political emancipation of the 20th century released an explosive new energy in many areas of Irish life. Nonetheless, the Irish public has yet to come to terms with the fact that it was and remains, ecclesiastically colonised. While Irish people are acutely aware of the difference between political oppression and political freedom, there is as yet little consciousness of the equivalent in church terms. Political colonisation is a well-used phrase in relation to Irish history, but ecclesiastical colonisation is a phrase that has yet to emerge into regular usage.

The ecclesiastical emancipation of Ireland may have begun at the turn of the millennium with the widespread disillusionment felt towards the Roman church. But if it is to be fully achieved in the 21st century, it will require the exorcising of the demons of the global church. In its place, Irish people will return to their traditional spirituality and give it new expression.

Woman

If I stand up and say I survived
Will you look me in the eye
And know I speak the truth?
If I laugh as I do
Will you see that nothing,
no one
can bring me down?
I'll rise and shake the dust of their bad will
from me
and from mine.
Swat them away
like you'd swat flies
cluttered around some wholesome thing.
If my eyes sparkle
and I wiggle my hips
wearing my big black boots,
will you know that I've raised corpses from cupboards,
tamed dragons of rage,
and can still dream of beautiful things?
If I sing
will you hear
that in all the struggle
I still rejoice
in being woman?

Tess Harper

16

THE HISTORY OF GLOBALISATION

Globalisation is a modern word. Its usage is so recent that you will not find it explained in any but the most up-to-date dictionaries. This may give the mistaken impression that globalisation is a recent phenomenon. It is not. It has a history that goes back four thousand years. This chapter summarises the main thesis of this book.

Globalisation – the Offspring of Monotheism

Globalisation is the offspring of monotheism. Although monotheism initially manifested itself in one small Judaic nation and remained small and isolated for over a thousand years, it eventually began to flourish through the growth of Christianity and later Islam. Other monotheistic religions, based on the same originally Judaic god, also developed. Nowadays, monotheism is the belief of more than half of the world's population. It is also, by far, the wealthier half. It is this worldwide dominance of the monotheistic perspective that has created the mindset that enabled globalisation to occur.

In polytheistic societies, globalisation could not have occurred. Polytheism, in all its forms, declares that life is complex and that there are no straightforward answers. Polytheism celebrates diversity. There is a diversity of gods and therefore a diversity of ways of seeing and understanding things. Polytheism breeds tolerance.

In particular, there is no one divine source within polytheism in which all authority is vested. Without that one divine source, a hierarchy cannot be created among humans to connect to that source. There are too many deities and too much direct contact imagined between these deities and humans for any particular hierarchy to grow. Polytheism disperses divine authority among its many gods and goddesses. This dispersal makes it impossible for humans to gather that authority into one focussed point.

Where a culture is polytheistic, it has built into its way of thinking a tolerance and a celebration of diversity. It expects and can cope with contradictions in life. It can live with mystery and the lack of answers. The mythology of polytheism, with its pantheon of gods and its large collection of stories about them that are neither complementary nor synchronous, reflects the diversity and complexity of the human family. Fundamentalism as we know it today cannot survive within polytheistic societies.

Within monotheism, on the other hand, there is only one god and all authority emanates from this one source. From this one god, a hierarchical flow of command can be created. In all the monotheistic religions, a key person has been established who is the carrier and transmitter of the divine message – Moses in the case of Judaism, Jesus in the case of Christianity, Muhammad in the case of Islam. From these people and from the written words attributed to them, a human hierarchy of authority can be and has been, created.

Judaism

Judaism was the first to discover the potential of this system. With all authority resting in one god, Yahweh and with Moses established as the clear receiver and transmitter of his message, a hierarchy of authority was created among the Jewish people that centralised control of society at a soul level. The words of Yahweh transmitted by Moses and written down, became the 'Law'. One could not be saved without obeying the 'Law'. Israel became a theocratic, god-ruled, state.

Fundamentalism is intrinsic to this system. I use this word in the sense of a strictly-held belief that is not tolerant of other viewpoints. The cornerstone of the monotheistic system is the fundamentalist tenet that there is only one god. Once this belief is established among the people, many other fundamentalist positions can be established. The word of 'God' is the unquestionable truth. The truth becomes the 'Law'. Obeying the 'Law' brings eternal salvation.

This fundamentalist process suppresses dissent, discourages questioning and criticism and subdues people into compliance. How can one question 'God'? How can one say one disagrees with 'God'?

Judaism nonetheless historically remained small and isolated. To this day it has never lost its connection with the land of Israel. For this reason, perhaps, it never developed a global perspective, even though it had the potential to do so.

Christianity was a mutation of Judaism. It took much of what Judaism had to offer but it developed new features which gave it more global potential. In particular, Christianity released people from a connection with the land of Israel and sought to spread its message throughout the world. This radical shift opened up the possibility of turning local spiritual practices into global products.

Christianity's Global Vision

In the Christian canon of writings there are phrases such as: 'Go out to the whole world and proclaim the good news to all creation'[1], 'You will be my witnesses. . .even to the ends of the earth'[2] and 'the voice of those preaching resounded all over the earth and their voice was heard to the end of the world'[3].

These words signify a global perspective. While Jesus himself kept his focus on his own Jewish people and did not travel outside the perimeter of Palestine, it is clear that even the earliest Christians had a more global perspective. Peter and Paul, for example, travelled extensively and both died in Rome, a long way from home. For them, the Christian message was for the whole world.

However, the spread of the Christian story throughout the world does not in itself represent globalisation as we know it today. Many cultures, for example, possess the story of the great flood in their legends, but one could not say that this story is therefore a product that has been globalised. Globalisation today requires that a product's content be defined and controlled at source before it is distributed. It remains essentially the same, wherever it goes. The story of the flood did not have these controls as it spread through various cultures. Each culture that received the story absorbed and integrated it into its own repertoire, changing and adapting it as it did so. Christianity, in the time of Peter and Paul, was spreading

---

1   Mark16:15
2   Acts 1:8
3   Romans 10:18

in the same way. People who heard the stories of Jesus interpreted and adapted them as they pleased, producing many different versions of Christianity. While one could say that Christianity was spreading globally, one could not say that it was becoming globalised in the way that products are globalised today.

The Diversification of Christianity

As a result of this lack of centralised control, Christianity, as it spread, began to take on diverse forms and even diverse content. In the first few centuries, there were many written versions of the 'gospel', of which only four are now regarded as canonical. There were diverse styles of Christian leadership reflecting the styles of people like James, John, Peter and Paul. Christianity also found expression in different languages and cultures – Judaic culture, Roman culture, Greek culture – and as a result took on different cultural forms.

In the early centuries, there were also popular and widespread movements, such as Gnosticism and Arianism, which gave the Christian story interpretations and emphases very different from what became the mainstream. Ireland, being on the very edge of the known world of the time, developed a unique form of Christianity, which became known as Celtic Christianity.

This diversification of Christianity, as it spread, was a natural process that is to be found in all of nature. Had this diversification been allowed to continue, the Christian story might indeed have traversed the whole world but each culture that absorbed it would have given it its own unique expression within its own indigenous tradition.

Orthodoxy

From early times, there were significant Christian communities located in many of the cities of the Roman empire – Jerusalem, Antioch, Alexandria, Carthage and of course Rome itself. These communities and in particular the bishops who led these communities, did not always see eye to eye with each other. This was partly due to the fact that each community was independent and had its own set of beliefs and ways of doing things; and partly it was due to a power struggle between the bishops of these communities, as they vied with each other to be *primus inter pares*[4], or pope – a position which did not exist until the end of the 4th century.

In the 4th century, the controversies among Christians became so public across the Roman empire that the emperor Constantine called a council of bishops and insisted that these issues be resolved. It was only as these bishops began to pull together and exercise a form of communal leadership that the diversification of Christianity began to be halted. The version of Christianity put out by the bishops who attended this council became known as 'orthodox', literally 'right teaching' and all other teachings which were not orthodox became regarded as heretical.

In this way, the word 'catholic' came into common usage. It became a label for distinguishing those who practised 'orthodox' Christianity from those who did not.

Catholic – Another Word for Global

The version of Christianity that was deemed to be 'catholic' was a version that was widespread and mainstream. It was the version of Christianity that was to be found in the major cities of the empire, under the leadership of bishops who were of the same mind or who had come to an agreement. As Cyril of Jerusalem put it: 'Now it [the church] is called catholic because it is throughout the world, from one end of the earth to the other.'[5]

Being 'throughout the world' meant that people were to be found in all parts of the empire and even beyond, who practised what had now become the orthodox version of Christianity. The word 'catholic' used in this sense needed only a small 'c'. But it quickly acquired a capital 'C' as it came to designate a particular church organisation with a common faith. From being a catholic or universal set of beliefs and practices, it became the Catholic Church.

The word 'catholic' is therefore a control word in this context. It distinguishes from all others a set of 'orthodox' beliefs, or beliefs subscribed to by the 'catholic' organisation. If certain beliefs are 'catholic', then other beliefs are 'heresies'. The word 'heresy' became a pejorative

---

4   'First among equals'
5   *Catechetical Discourses*, Section 23.

word used to describe and dismiss the opinion of others with whom the 'catholic' organisation did not agree.

Organised and 'orthodox' Christianity became known as the Catholic Church in the late 4th century. Its hallmark was a set of 'catholic' beliefs that had been agreed at the Council of Nicea in 325 CE. Nowadays, Catholicism is most associated with Roman Catholicism but other churches, such as the Eastern Orthodox churches and the Anglican federation of churches, also call themselves Catholic, because they subscribe to the same set of beliefs.

This homogenisation of Christian belief and practice was an early example of the process of globalisation. People were now able to claim a Catholic identity for themselves, regardless of their geographical or cultural background, solely by subscribing to a fixed set of beliefs. The Nicene Creed became the first clear example of what one might call today a global product. Similar to a copyrighted book, song or poem today, it was available for global distribution with its content secure.

Roman Catholicism

For some people, the designation 'Roman Catholic' is a contradiction in terms. 'Roman' designates local, or particular, whereas 'Catholic' designates universal or general. However, in my view, the two together capture the essence of globalisation as we know it today.

Roman Catholicism signifies that a local brand of Christianity particular to Rome has been made universal. What was originally local and particular has been extracted from its immediate environment and made into a global product – a human creation, with a standard content and form, distributed everywhere.

As Christianity spread throughout the world over the centuries, many distinctly Roman aspects of that Christianity became globalised. So, for example, the Latin language, which was the language of Rome at the time of the Roman empire, became the language of the 'Universal Church'. The rule of Benedict, a Roman monk, became the universal rule for all monasteries in Western Christendom and the Roman calendar, which set the year of Christ's birth at '0', became the calendar for the whole world.

By identifying the first global products as being the fruits of Christianity and therefore of monotheism, one can see more clearly how it was that monotheism created the necessary container for globalisation or the movement towards homogeneity that has occurred. Monotheism is the mythological container for the globalised world we live in today. A monotheism that places its one god outside the earth has, at its core, a dynamic and irresistible magnetic attraction that draws the world towards homogeneity. As long as we remain living under the mantle of monotheism, we will be caught up in an irresistible flow of energy that draws us towards uniformity – one way of living, one economic system and the one set of global products and services available to everybody.

Attempts at Globalisation Before Christianity

Before the advent of Christianity, there were earlier attempts at globalisation. Every empire in history had ambitions for further expansion. Had any of them been able to, they would have continued to expand indefinitely. In general, there were no limits to the ambitions of empires. Their perspectives were global.

The empire with which we in the West are perhaps most familiar is the Roman empire. By looking at the expansion of this empire, it is easy to see how the early concepts of globalisation worked. It is also possible to see where the weaknesses in these concepts lay.

The Roman empire overran a number of different cultures and peoples. To maintain its power in these foreign lands, it had to place its own people in these places, people who would be answerable to Rome. So in Palestine, the land of the Jewish people at the time of Jesus, we find Jesus hauled before the Roman governor by Roman soldiers. Rome kept control in Palestine by placing there a Roman governor and a garrison of Roman soldiers.

The authority structure of the Roman empire was hierarchical. It was a pyramid of power with a sole emperor at the top and the ordinary people at the bottom. In between were those who were given authority over people below them but who were also answerable to people above them.

This pyramidal authority structure was a key instrument in the expansion of the empire and in its success. A direct line of command stretched from the emperor at the top and in Rome, to the lowliest soldier at the bottom and at the farthest reaches of the empire.

The proven success of this structure has led to its survival through the centuries. It became the structure of the corporate Christian Church from the 4th century onwards. It is the structure still used to this day by global corporations. The Roman emperor, the pope and the chief executive of today's multinational corporation are all of a kind.

The Romans built roads, bridges, aqueducts and many other physical structures throughout their empire. They did this in order to strengthen their power and to continue their expansion. While the local people in far-off regions of the empire may have benefited in certain ways from these 'developments', it was not for their benefit that they were built. Rome needed quick access for its armies to all parts of the empire. These armies needed food and water wherever they went. The structures were built for them.

This type of development is what we call today 'infrastructure'. Infrastructure, like development, is a key word in the vocabulary of globalisation. The building of infrastructure is essential for the globalisation project to work. The Roman empire needed its roads and bridges: the Roman Catholic corporation needed its churches and schools. Economic globalisation today requires a vast transformation of the landscape everywhere to provide transport, energy, communications, factories and trade outlets for global products and services.

While empires such as that of Rome would have continued their expansion indefinitely had they been able to, their power was always limited to within their borders. To expand their power, they had to expand their borders. The larger the empire became, the more difficult it was to do this. At a certain point of expansion, policing the borders of the Roman empire became impossible. There were not enough soldiers and not enough resources to maintain them.

Empires prior to Christianity may indeed have wanted to conquer the world but they all failed to do so. Nonetheless, they invented some of the tools necessary for this achievement. They were all hampered by the need to police and expand their borders. Their weakness was their focus on the military control of geographical territory.

The Power of Persuasion

It was within the Roman Christian corporation that humans realised for the first time that one could expand one's power globally without being limited by political and geographical borders. The Roman corporation found that it could use a political structure such as the Roman empire to expand its power across that empire but it could also pass beyond the boundaries of that empire into other lands and to other peoples. It was also within the Roman Christian corporation that humans realised for the first time that, to gain control or influence over people, one did not need necessarily to subdue them by force. One could convince them by persuasion.

The Judaic state of Israel had established a formula which unified, controlled and subdued its people through a theocratic system of beliefs and laws. In Judaic society, church and state were one and the same. Christianity took this formula a step further when it discovered, after the collapse of the Roman empire, that it could survive and have effective power and control even without the state. By the end of the 6th century, corporate Christianity had established that it could expand beyond the boundaries of the state and that it could also survive the collapse of the state.

The essential element in the new formula for the survival and expansion of one's organisation was the employment of the art of persuasion. If people could be persuaded that monotheistic Christianity promoted by the Roman church was more attractive than their traditional polytheistic beliefs and their locally-based spiritualities, the Roman church's power and influence could expand anywhere in the world. The Roman church gained control or influence as soon as a person professed a belief in a god whose 'message' was interpreted through an authority structure centred in Rome.

The art of persuasion, developed by the Roman church in the early centuries, was that of holding out a promise with one hand and a threat with the other. People were encouraged to subscribe to this belief by being promised salvation. At the same time, they were warned that the consequence of not believing or not obeying was the threat of eternal damnation.

Up to this time, political regimes had attempted to control people by controlling territory, using armies and systems of law. These legal and military mechanisms put limits on people's public behaviour. But what the leadership of the Roman corporate church realised, having gained from the Judaic experience, was that, if one controlled what went on in people's minds, people's public behaviour was also controlled – from within the people themselves. Armies of soldiers and bands of lawyers, who forced people to behave in a certain way or be punished, could be replaced by armies of priests and missionaries who used the force of persuasion to convert people and who could threaten eternal damnation if they refused.

Preaching and Advertising

The modern phenomenon of globalisation uses political structures to establish itself and to expand within particular nations but it is not totally limited by these structures. It has found its way into every society throughout the world, regardless of political boundaries. It has done this through persuasion – not the persuasion of priests and missionaries (although these may indeed have helped) but through the persuasion of advertising.

Preaching and advertising are both tools of globalisation. When people lived in a subsistence way within their own culture, their own spirituality and their own local landscape, 'needs' as we know them today did not exist. People who live a subsistence lifestyle in an indigenous culture do not need to go to the shops, make a telephone call, jump in the car or even go to Mass or confession. It is only when one removes the possibility of a natural and organic subsistence way of life from people that one creates a vacuum into which one can then introduce 'needs'.

For Christianity, the message preached was that people needed salvation; for the global economy, the message preached is that people need goods and services. Preaching and advertising are the way to convince people of these needs.

Roman Catholicism – Top Global Corporation

From the time of the collapse of the Roman empire to the present day, the Roman Christian corporate church created and held power for itself in Europe and later throughout the world. It regularly clashed with political powers and often claimed supremacy over them. To this day, it is a world power, not in the strictly political sense but in the sense that it can influence so many people worldwide. We have seen in recent times that the visit of a pope to a country almost anywhere in the world has drawn crowds that no politician and no rock concert will ever match. This is a measure of its influence.

The globalisation of Christianity and of Roman Catholicism in particular, has been extremely successful. One third of the world's population is Christian.[6] A half of these, or 1.1 billion, are Roman Catholic.[7] Before there was ever a bottle of Coca Cola distributed to any part of the world, there was a Roman Catholic Mass on offer to people in the most remote of places. Before there was ever a McDonald's restaurant established in any city worldwide, there was a Catholic church building containing standardised objects and offering standardised services.

Roman Christianity, the corporate church founded in the 4th century CE with its headquarters in Rome, was the first global corporation. It developed its global products and services and its global marketing strategies centuries before we ever heard of other corporations. Without the benefits of modern travel and communications infrastructure, it penetrated into the most primitive, most inaccessible and remotest corners of the earth and successfully established itself. No modern corporation has come close to matching its success.

The Development of the Colonial System

Colonialism represents a further development of the concept and practice of globalisation. Most of the colonisation that we talk about today occurred from the 16th to the 19th centuries. However, Ireland was one of the first modern countries of the world to be colonised. Its colonisation began in the 12th century, when it was invaded by the Normans.

The colonial system developed in Ireland over hundreds of years. The Normans achieved political control in Ireland by militarily defeating the local opposition. Once control was established, large numbers of immigrants swarmed in from the Norman mainland and took whatever land was available. In later centuries, the British coordinated more organised plantations, taking into Ireland people who were loyal to the king and spoke the king's language. The local indigenous Irish people were removed from this land and left homeless.

---

6   http://www.religioustolerance.org/worldrel.htm#wce
7   http://news.bbc.co.uk/1/hi/world/4243727.stm

In order to manage and farm these lands, the immigrant landowners in some cases offered work to the homeless Irish and allowed them build new homes on the land. Workers were paid a small sum for their work and usually had to pay a large proportion of that back in rent for their homes, leaving them just enough to keep them from starvation.

The currency for pay and for rent was the currency of the coloniser. This ensured that the money could only be used within the colonial system. In this way, Irish people who had not been killed or driven away by the invading armies were made completely dependent on the coloniser.

Once the colonial system had been established, Ireland was then used as a resource for the British economy. Ireland's trees were logged and Ireland became a big food producer for Britain. The collection of rent from the native Irish became a source of great wealth for landlords, some of whom remained living in Britain, leaving agents on their land in Ireland to collect the rent.

It was this situation in Ireland in the 19th century that gave rise to the Great Hunger. For three years in succession in the late 1840's the potato crop failed due to blight. As the native Irish people had been reduced to living almost totally on potatoes at that time, they starved or died from consequent diseases in their millions.

Although commonly called a famine, this was not a famine. There was no shortage of food. Enough food was being exported from Ireland at that time to feed everybody in Ireland and leave a surplus. The people were starved by a system of oppression that did not allow them access to the food that was available when their own supplies failed.

Lessons learned in the colonisation of Ireland were applied by Britain in other countries, as its empire expanded from the 16th century onwards.

The Expansion of Colonialism

Other methods of colonisation, some similar, were taken up by the Spanish, the Portuguese, the French, the Dutch and other European colonial countries. From the 16th to the 19th century, large portions of the world were colonised by European countries, including all North and South America, India and other countries in Asia and all Africa, Australia and New Zealand.

In these colonial countries, the language, norms and customs of the invaders were imposed. On the back of these invaders came the Christian missionaries. The material and labour resources of these countries were used to contribute to the growing wealth and power of the colonising countries. The colonised countries became quarries for production.

In terms of globalisation, the overall result of colonialism was a huge advance in the creation of a worldwide infrastructure that facilitated the imposition of European languages, European economics and European monotheism on native peoples. From the 18th century onwards, the expansion of colonialism coincided with the industrial revolution. This revolution set in motion the world of production and consumption of products and services as we know it today. The raw material for this revolution came largely from the colonies.

In this process, the broad expanse of the diversity of human activity and human ways of living in the world narrowed greatly. Many of the great cultures of the world were seriously undermined or destroyed. The Native American cultures, the great cultures of South America, the African peoples, the Australian Aboriginals, the Maoris – all of them came under great pressure to change to European ways or die. This was the ruthlessness of a one-dimensional vision. It was blind to the terrible destruction of valuable diversity and cultural treasures and blind to the longer-term consequences of its actions which we are now facing in terms of the survival of the planet.

Political Colonisation Unsustainable

Colonialism, as it came to be practised by European countries, was not sustainable in the long-term. The maintenance of foreign rule became increasingly expensive and the revolts of the native peoples became more persistent. The 20th century witnessed the withdrawal of the majority of colonial powers from foreign soil. Colonised countries, one after another, declared independence.

By this time, however, much of the groundwork had been done in these countries to facilitate a different type of global dominance. In the main, these ex-colonial countries were left with a European language, European Christianity and European economic structures in a strong or dominant position. Local, indigenous, polytheistic environments, structures and ways of life had been pushed to the margins, weakened or destroyed.

Despite the colonial withdrawal, enough change had happened in many of these countries for the construction of a global economy and consequent global way of living to proceed unhindered. Although there had been a political withdrawal, there was never an economic withdrawal. This was most clearly illustrated in the establishment of the British Commonwealth, a confederation of ex-British colonies who, among other things, promoted trade agreements with one another.

The Sustainability of Ecclesiastical Colonisation

When one talks today of the history of colonisation, one is usually referring to political colonisation. However, another form of colonisation took place alongside political colonisation, with at least equally damaging effects. Ecclesiastical colonisation was a process conducted by corporate Christian churches in countries where they wished to impose a centralised, global version of Christianity. In general, this process took place in tandem with the political colonisation of a country. The church and the colonising power, while operating as two separate entities, worked largely hand-in-hand. It was a symbiotic relationship, with both sides benefiting from the partnership. As a result, wherever the European colonial powers penetrated, the European Christian missionaries were there before them, came with them or followed in their wake.

The history of ecclesiastical colonisation in Ireland offers a particularly clear example of the difference between a native expression of Christianity and a global Christianity. From the time that the Celtic version of Christianity was first noticed in the 5th century, the corporate Christian church of Rome was unhappy with the independence of the Irish church. For centuries, Rome fought against Celtic Christianity using considerable powers of persuasion. The Celtic monks resisted but nonetheless their monasteries throughout Europe and Britain gradually succumbed to the pressure. In Ireland itself, Rome needed the military assistance of the Norman armies to put an end to the Celtic church on Irish soil. In order to crush the Celtic church in Ireland, Rome colluded in the military and political destruction of its people.

This military and political destruction of Ireland's native structures opened the way for Roman Christianity to replace *in toto* any vestiges of the Irish tradition. Waves of European religious orders such as the Cistercians, the Augustinian canons, the Dominicans, the Franciscans and many others over time, flooded Ireland and established themselves in every county. The natural landscape of Ireland today speaks as much of ecclesiastical colonisation as it does of political colonisation. Wherever one finds the remains of a Norman castle, one also finds the remains of a European religious house or monastery.

When the colonial political powers withdrew from Ireland in the early part of the 20th century, the ecclesiastical powers of the Roman church remained.

What happened in Ireland in the 12th century happened in many other countries of the world in the 16th – 19th centuries. In each of these countries, political and ecclesiastical colonisation went hand-in-hand. The two arms of the colonising process ruthlessly imposed global structures and global products, replacing local languages with the colonial language and local spiritualities with the colonial religion. Cultural and spiritual diversity were systematically destroyed, as they continue to be to this day.

While political colonialism has receded in today's world, ecclesiastical colonialism remains strong. Global versions of Christianity remain in the ex-colonial countries, as they do in Ireland. The global ambitions of corporate Christian churches remain focussed and their numbers and influence in many places continue to grow. Running alongside them at an ever-increasing pace is the process of globalisation in the world economy.

Neocolonialism

Globalisation as we know it today is a form of neocolonialism. It is a more efficient way to achieve some of the same objectives as colonialism. Weaker countries and economies lose out to the stronger ones. World trade agreements force weaker countries to admit transnational corporations, who then use the cheap labour and the rich resources of these countries for their own gain. In the process, the local economies are absorbed into the global economy and the local people are absorbed into a global way of life.

A globalised world economy will sit comfortably enough with any globalised monotheistic religion, particularly Christianity. This is so because both have similar global objectives and use similar methods. They are members of the same family. What a globalised world economy and a global Christian church cannot tolerate is the existence of indigenous subsistence cultures that are self-sufficient, have their own economies and live according to polytheistic and nature-based beliefs. These truly sustainable ways of living are intolerable because they do not acknowledge any 'needs' for the goods and services of a globalised economy and a globalised church.

The Unsustainability of Economic Globalisation

While sustainability has become a key word within the global economic debate, there are no clear signs yet that the global economy has any chance of becoming sustainable. On the contrary, there are many clear signs, especially on the environmental front, that the globalised world is heading towards almost inevitable disaster.

It is alarming, therefore, that all forms of human ways of living on this planet, other than a globalised, homogenised way of life, are being, or have already been, wiped out. These are the alternative ways of living that may keep alive the possibilities for continued human life on this planet.

This book was written to expose the historical roots of modern-day globalisation. These roots are to be found in corporate Christianity and in the global dogmatism of monotheism. Any attempt at opposing and any serious attempt at reversing the trend of globalisation in the world today must take into account these deep roots. Monotheism and corporate Christianity are an integral part of the globalisation of the world we live in.

THE TEN COMMANDMENTS
OF GLOBALISATION

1. **Believe passionately that there is only one way**

   There is only one god, one economic system that works, one way to live on this planet. Eventually there will be only one language. Do not tolerate diversity in these areas. Prevent people from being different. Discourage alternatives.

2. **Believe that nothing material is sacred**

   Everything is a resource. Treat everybody and everything as an opportunity for economic growth, development and progress.

3. **Disconnect people from nature**

   Work assiduously to disconnect people from their local natural environment. Indigenous people are connected to their immediate natural environment in two ways – through their indigenous spirituality and culture and through their subsistence lifestyle. All these ties must be cut.

4. **Create 'needs'**

   When indigenous people lose the possibility of living in a traditional way, they begin to have 'needs' which can then be fulfilled by global products and services.

5. **Remove the barriers to global business**

   Create a system of laws and financial incentives to discourage, wipe out and prevent small, locally-run, independent and culturally diverse businesses. Remove the barriers that protect local businesses.

6. **Create 'infrastructure'**

Build roads, railways, airports, harbours; instal electricity, gas and fossil-fuel supply lines; create high-speed telephone and digital communication systems. Transform the landscape and the lifestyle of the people so that there is no going back to old ways.

7. **Formally 'educate' all children**

Remove children from their parents and their home environment and institutionalise them in state-controlled schools. Get them accustomed to authoritarian control, to sitting still and to wearing a uniform. Make sure that the curriculum, the teaching methods and the methods of assessment are along global lines. Teach children to become producers and consumers, to compete against each other and to understand and believe in the principles of globalisation.

8. **Disempower people in relation to their health**

Make people dependent on the medical profession, the medical system and the drug companies.

9. **Promote uninterrupted growth, development and progress**

Convince people that to survive on this planet there must be continuous economic growth, continuous economic development and continuous progress.

10. **Ignore all warnings of collapse**

Convince people that it is possible to live sustainably on this planet without changing the present economic system, without seriously rethinking the concepts of development, progress and economic growth and without developing a new spirituality.

Dara Molloy

17

SPIRITUALITY
AND SUSTAINABILITY

Monotheism has been the mythological container for the process of globalisation. The monotheistic religions of the world have contributed to the development of a human way of living on earth which is ecologically unsustainable. Any new spirituality which attempts to contain and support a more sustainable way of living will need to detach itself from these organised religions and grow from the grass roots up. Spiritualities of sustainability in the future will be diverse, rooted in a settled community and a local place and will be independent of organised religion.

The process which, since World War II, we have called 'development' and even more recently we called 'globalisation' is in reality a process that began with Moses and the monotheistic vision. It has taken thousands of years to pull humankind out of ways of life that were rooted in diverse forms of polytheism and into a way of life that is rooted in monotheism. That process is now reaching its culmination, as an homogeneous, uniform and monochrome human way of life intrudes into and tries to dominate most corners of the globe.

The process has accelerated exponentially in the last hundred years. Change has become rapid and unstoppable. The rapidity of the changes has allowed us as humans to see the effects of these changes within our own lifetimes. On the negative side, we can see quite clearly the disastrous pollution we are causing, the rapid and irrecoverable destruction of biological diversity, the ever-growing consumption of non-renewable resources, the accelerating reduction of cultural diversity and the growing dominance of the English language.[1] We can see the effects on our climate and on our health.

Even though it is happening before our eyes and we are at this stage very conscious of it, we have, as yet, been unable to come fully to terms with its implications. The implications are more than our minds can imagine. This is because there is an almost universal belief in the world today that there is no alternative to the way we now live. Often written with capital letters and abbreviated to TINA (There Is No Alternative), the dominant view within Western economics and politics is that capitalism and globalisation are the only ways open to humankind. People find it almost impossible to imagine any alternative. As long as monotheism, in the form we know it today, remains in place, this will probably remain the case. Under monotheism, no alternative is possible.

The one-god project, initiated by Moses in the Arabian desert four thousand years ago, had a beginning and will have an end. That end may be very near. The signs are there, yet we are unable or unwilling to recognise them. It is clear that what we call 'progress' and 'development' are unsustainable. The modern economies of the world are healthy only if they are growing. Growth means more production and more consumption. This inevitably means more exploitation of the earth, more pollution, a continuing reduction of non-renewable resources and an accelerated disappearance of biodiversity. We cannot grow indefinitely on a planet of limited size and limited resources. If we cannot see ourselves stopping the growth, we are heading for inevitable destruction. No political leader of our time has yet said 'Stop the growth'.

Bioregionalism

The corollary of this argument is that, in a search for alternatives, it is not sufficient to look for economic alternatives. Some of those who oppose

---

1   English is the third most spoken language in the world (341 million speakers) and is the most widely distributed throughout the world (native speakers in 104 countries). It is matched in the number of speakers by the Spanish language (322 – 358 million) which is spoken on all 5 continents but less widely distributed (43 countries). Mandarin Chinese (874 million people in 16 countries) and Hindi (366 million people in 17 countries) have the greatest number of speakers but are not widely distributed. See: http://anthro.palomar.edu/language/language_1.htm.

globalisation have proposed in its place a structure called bioregionalism[2]. Bioregions are identified as natural ecosystems in which human habitation is an integral part. Bioregionalism would lead to the development of strong local economies. Within those economies, the basic needs of all living there would be met. It would be a type of regional permaculture.[3]

The thesis of this book is that this movement towards bioregionalism will not be strong enough on its own to achieve permanency unless it is given depth and breadth by an accompanying new mythology and spirituality. Most of the present world-view is underpinned by a spirituality that is locked into dogmatic monotheistic mythology in general and corporate Christianity in particular. A new sustainable human relationship with the earth is not reconcilable with that perspective. However, excluding all spirituality and becoming materialist is not the answer either. Humans have a spiritual as well as a material nature. Human spirituality must be catered for.

Below is a list of some of the essential elements that will be necessary in any bioregional spirituality that is to be relevant and sustainable:

- A bioregional spirituality will engage with the region and provide a framework of meaning for the way people live within that region.
- That spirituality will provide a reservoir of locally connected stories which attribute value, communicate wisdom and teach the young.
- It will establish right relationship between the local people and the local sources of their food, clothing and shelter.
- It will challenge the meaning of words like 'god' and 'religion', or other all-encompassing spiritual words, while at the same time drawing people into a greater consciousness and awareness of the spiritual aspects of life.
- It will remove words like 'development', 'needs' and 'resources' from the vocabulary, changing the way people see the world in which they live and providing a new vocabulary to match this new perspective.

---

2   Cf. Kirkpatrick Sale, *Dwellers in the Land: The Bioregional Vision*, Random House, 1985. University of Georgia Press, 2000. and Robert Thayer, *LifePlace: Bioregional Thought and Practice*, University of California Press, 2003.
3   A self-sustaining agricultural ecosystem using natural renewable resources.

- It will contain a store of spiritual practices for people to perform individually and communally. These practices will cement right relationships within the human community and within the wider natural community.
- It will offer an historical context for the people living in the region, giving them a sense of where they have come from and where they are going.
- It will be a tolerant, flexible, dynamic and open spirituality that will remain alive within the grass roots of the community and healthily resist dogmatism, authoritarianism and institutionalisation.

Right Relationship

The key to the way forward is for us as humans to find a right relationship between ourselves and the natural world of which we are a part. The present relationship is clearly dysfunctional. Right relationship cannot be achieved within the present worldview, because that view is part of the problem.

A right relationship between humans and the rest of nature is one that offers mutual sustenance in the long term, that is not abusive and that is based on deep respect. In particular, right relationship must be established with those other living things and those specific aspects of nature that provide humans with food, clothing and shelter.

The challenge to people today is to be in communion and in communication with the living beings of their area and with the spirit of the landscape in which they live. How they do this, what spiritual practices they develop, what mythological stories they spin and what vocabulary they use is completely up to them. But a community of humans that is at one with its broader community of non-human living beings and its natural environment will love all that surrounds it and will not allow any abuse or disrespect of it.

Human relationships are maintained through the exercise of love, respect, honesty, integrity, generosity and so on. These are not material realities. They are spiritual realities, in the broad sense of that word. Equally, right relationship with other life forms and with nature in general cannot be maintained without the practise of similar spiritual practices. Together these repeated life-giving and life-sustaining spiritual practices make up a spirituality.

Polytheism or Monotheism

I do not advocate a return to polytheism *per se*. This book has attempted to illustrate how polytheism, in its many forms, did constitute a completely other worldview from that of modern-day global monotheism. That alternative worldview led to a very different relationship with the earth from the one we have today. What polytheism illustrates, in all its diversity, is that it is possible to view one's world in many different ways.

However, a return to any particular form of polytheism present in earlier societies would be impossible for people today. Nonetheless, these earlier societies all have much to teach us. In particular, what we need to learn is how earlier societies acknowledged the presence of a spirit in other living beings and in the landscape. They communed with that spirit and showed it respect.

The challenge for people today is to move beyond both monotheism and polytheism. Philosophy has always had to deal with the problem of the one and the many. The one and the many are two aspects of the same reality. Therefore, to side with one or the other, in terms of polytheism or monotheism, is not the answer. At the same time, one cannot be both polytheist and monotheist. Unless one chooses to be atheist, one has to rise above this dichotomy. The challenge is to get to a higher point where there is room for both and perhaps for atheism also. It will be a point where one has moved beyond all three. This requires a higher level of consciousness than humans have heretofore had.

Reaching a higher level of consciousness requires humility. It is the realisation that the more we know, the more we know we don't know. The myriad versions of polytheism and the one dominant version of monotheism that we have had on this earth are all attempts made out of ignorance to understand the deeper aspects of our lives and this universe. It is still important to have our stories, our legends and our myths and even to craft new ones, but the way we relate to them has to be more conscious. Their value lies in their capacity to reflect back to us what rings true. The touchstone is that sense of deep truth we feel within us, not any external authority. In the spiritual world, what rings true is as far as we are ever going to get. The spiritual world does not deal in empirical truth.

The focus of humans, in the last hundred years in particular, has been on material reality. Humankind has made enormous strides in its understanding and use of the material world. The progress that has been made in this area has outgrown by far the spiritual containers that were there to support it. Spirituality has not kept pace with the changes that have occurred in our relationship to the material world. It is now time to divert our energies more towards the spiritual world. The amazing shifts in understanding and awareness that have taken place in relation to material things must now also take place in relation to spiritual realities. We must work towards achieving new levels of consciousness. This means mapping out more carefully and understanding more deeply the spiritual realities of our lives. It also means entering into what Freud and Jung called the unconscious, both personal and collective, so that more of what is unseen and mysterious to us becomes conscious and remains so.

Being Spiritual

It is important at this point to make a clear distinction between the terms spirituality, mythology, tradition and religion and to clarify what I mean when I use these words.

All of us have a spiritual side. It is that part of myself that can be distinguished from my physical body. It is my particular spirit or soul and it gives me a unique personality and orientation in the world. The distinction is clearest when a person dies. The body remains but the spirit or soul has gone.

My spiritual side is expressed through the way I relate to the world I live in – the values I practise, the goals I strive for, the relationships I maintain. Acts of love, of generosity, of kindness, of speaking the truth and so on are all spiritual acts. Acts of hate, of meanness, of cruelty or of deception are also spiritual acts on the negative side. Spiritual here is opposed to material. We can call these acts spiritual because they are not material. They do not directly concern matter.

Belief In Higher Beings

When people become conscious of their spiritual side and wish to develop it, they often describe themselves as spiritual. However, this description can also mean that they have a belief in a higher being or beings. It might be a god, or gods, or angels, or other spirit beings. Some people resist having a belief in higher beings. Such people might call themselves atheists or humanists. It does not necessarily mean that they are not consciously spiritual. One could say that their spirituality is horizontal but not vertical.

When one subscribes to a belief in higher beings, one is creating a container for one's spiritual values and practices. The mysterious side of life leaves many questions unanswered – questions like: who am I, why am I here, what happens when I die, what is the meaning of illness and so on. A belief in higher beings creates a framework in which one can believe one has found answers to these questions.

The existence of these higher beings can be neither empirically proven nor disproven. It is a matter of faith, not of science. If one is born into a belief system and grows up with it, one may never get to the stage of questioning it. For such a person, the possibility of not believing has never arisen. For others, who, as adults, have been searching for answers, subscribing to a particular belief is a conscious choice.

Myths

Myth is a word that is used by anthropologists to describe the beliefs of people in indigenous cultures and the stories that are woven around these beliefs. A myth, in anthropological terms, is usually a story based on a belief in one or more higher beings. Used in this context, the word myth is not a derogatory term but an accurate scientific way of describing the phenomenon. Such a story in a particular culture forms an essential part of a belief system for that culture. Mythological stories are woven together and intertwined by a culture to form a canopy of spirituality for the people's lives. For these people, the spiritual world created by their myths is as much their reality as the actual physical landscape around them.

Modern-day beliefs in higher beings and their stories are no different. They are myths, not in the derogatory sense, but in the sense that they are human beliefs of a world filled with the presence of a spiritual being or beings whose existence cannot be empirically proven. While Moses, Jesus and Muhammad were all historical figures, myths have been created about them that give each of them a unique relationship with 'God' and tell the story of that relationship. The stories of Jesus, of Muhammad and of Moses, as subscribed to by modern-day religions, are myths in the anthropological sense.

Humans in general prefer certainty to uncertainty. As a result, we often create certainty where there is no certainty. This applies very much in the spiritual realm but it can also apply in other areas such as economics or politics. Certainty is a dangerous phenomenon because it can make us blind to otherwise obvious realities. When we do not want to face those realities we often hide behind our certainties. When these certainties are wrapped in myths and involve belief in a god or gods, they are often even more resistant to questioning.

Nonetheless, our myths shape the way we relate to the world and to each other. If I am a monotheist and believe in a god who lives in the heavens, that shapes how I relate to people on this earth. If my monotheism is Christian, then I will have the Christian ethic to guide me in my relations with other human beings. This ethic teaches me to be kind, generous, forgiving and so on. In my relations to the rest of nature, my behaviour will be guided by a belief that this god has created all of nature for my use. I will also have a belief that individual living things, other than humans, do not possess a soul. This belief gives me latitude in my dealings with them and lessens the requirement for me to have respect towards them. Christian monotheism has contributed positively to the way humans relate to each other, but it has contributed negatively to the way humans relate to other species and to the material world.

If I am a pantheist (god is nature) or panentheist (god in nature) and believe that a god, or gods and goddesses, live around me in the natural environment, this belief will hold in check any inclinations I have to change or exploit that environment. Killing an animal or cutting down a tree may require consultations with these gods first. I may or may not get permission.

Our mythology shapes our world. It shapes the container in which we live out our lives. When we fully subscribe to that mythology, we have certainty in the truth of what we believe. It is as much a part of our reality as the trees and the water.

Myths are bubbles of belief inside which people live. Just as a scientific theory is an attempt to explain a material phenomenon, a myth is a culture's attempt to give meaning to the spiritual world. Both are approximations. In science, new theories supersede old ones. A paradigm shift takes place in the minds of scientists as they shed one theory and adopt another. Our myths are paradigms for how we understand the world we live in. Older myths have given way to newer ones. It is easy for us to see the bubbles of mythology in which previous cultures lived but it is very difficult for us to see our own. It is even more difficult for us to acknowledge that we may need to shed our old beliefs and take on new ones.

A Spiritual Practice

In today's Western world there are many people who have grown up in the spiritual bubble of an organised religion. As adults, a good proportion of these have managed to escape from this bubble. Many others have grown up without ever having participated in an organised religion. These non-religious people nonetheless often think of themselves as spiritual and maintain certain spiritual practices. Their spiritual practices are generally independent of organised religion and may or may not involve any belief in a higher being.

Many spiritual practices in existence today have been around for hundreds, if not thousands of years. Spiritual practices such as meditation, pilgrimage and fasting are as old as humanity itself. However, in today's world we find people practising new as well as old practices. In some cases, the modern practice is a combination of the old and the new, or is an adaptation of the old to a new situation.

A spiritual practice is any practice that relates primarily to the health of my spirit or soul rather than my body. Where it has a reference to the presence of a particular higher being, it has a narrow definition. In this case, the practice will be defined as prayer or worship or something connected with these. Outside the presence of a higher being, spiritual practice can have a much broader definition. It can include any practice that expresses, maintains or improves the state of my soul or spirit.

Many people today regard gardening, playing music, walking, dancing, singing, reading or listening to certain recorded material as spiritual practice. A wide variety of counselling and therapeutic treatments can also be included, as these also can be good for spiritual well-being. Widening the circle even more, one could include the practice of discipline in eating habits, staying physically fit or keeping a good work-life balance. There is no doubt that how we look after our physical well-being effects our spiritual well-being also.

Spiritual practice often involves the celebration of events. The event might be the birth of a child, a birthday, a marriage or another occasion in a person's or community's life. It could be a festive seasonal date such as Christmas that comes around every year. It could also be a ceremony to acknowledge or give support to someone with an illness or on the occasion of a death. Even though these ceremonies may, or may not, acknowledge higher spiritual beings they can still be termed spiritual practices. The simplest form of common spiritual practice found everywhere is a communal meal, where spiritual elements such as friendship or family values are acknowledged around the dining table.

The more spiritually aware a person is, the more that person is conscious of the experience of the spiritual in the material world. For that person, every action, every human encounter, every engagement with other living beings or with the material world becomes spiritual practice. The nature of that practice is shaped by the spiritual beliefs of that person. It can differ from person to person.

Spiritual Tradition

When spiritual practices become established in a culture over generations, they form part of a tradition. A spiritual tradition is a complex of spiritual beliefs and practices that has grown and developed over generations. It has usually grown and developed in combination with a broader cultural tradition, as is to be found in any indigenous nation.

To take an example, the Irish spiritual tradition is an integral part of the broader cultural tradition of Ireland. Ireland's cultural traditions are very much alive today. One can see their celebration, renewal and development in areas such as music, dancing, art, poetry, drama, literature and even language. The spiritual tradition is an integral part of this broader cultural spectrum.

Cultural traditions remain dynamic and alive when they are embedded in a people who continue to live by those traditions. People who take up the traditional practices of previous generations give these practices new life in their own situation. The practices may be adapted and changed to suit a new generation but they remain rooted. For this reason, a cultural tradition is a grassroots movement. It grows from the bottom up. It cannot be organised from the top down.

To illustrate – there are different styles of traditional fiddle-playing to be found in Ireland. Donegal, Sligo, Clare and other counties all have their own traditional style of fiddle-playing. When a young person from one of these places takes up the fiddle, he or she learns from the older generation. When that person comes of age and matures at playing the fiddle, he or she often adds something new to the playing. Young players may create new tunes or play traditional tunes in a new way, adding their own flair and style. A traditional musician who succeeds in adding new energy to old tunes, will create excitement and often become quite famous. This is an example of the tradition continuing to change and develop.

If someone were to claim authority over this tradition of fiddle-playing, perhaps through a representative organisation, it could spell the end. At present there is no such organisation setting standards or making rules for Irish fiddle-playing. The thought of having to submit one's new composition or playing style to an examining authority before it could be deemed authentically 'traditional' would be unthinkable for present-day traditional fiddle-players. The tradition has its own internal dynamic and control mechanisms. Those who listen to it judge its authenticity. Certification or registration is not required.

Living spiritual traditions operate in the same way. Spiritual traditions grow and develop within communities of people. People continue to practise and develop these traditions because they find them supportive, nourishing and relevant to their lives. The energy put into these practices and the direction they are given comes from the participants themselves. There is no need or cause for an outside agency to interfere or have any part to play in the administration or control of this tradition. Were an agency to interfere or take over, the chances are that the dynamism and creativity within the traditional practice would atrophy.

A clear example of a spiritual tradition staying alive among people over generations outside the control of organised religion is the Irish practice of visiting a holy well. On a visit to a well, the tradition has been to walk around the well seven times, travelling in a 'sunwise' or clockwise direction. This tradition originated many thousands of years ago when Irish people were polytheistic. For these early people, the well represented an entrance into the womb of the mother-earth goddess. Walking around was in imitation of the sun god Lugh circumambulating the earth. Nowadays, the practice has a more Christian veneer. That tradition has been kept alive solely through its continuing popularity as a spiritual practice.

Religion

When religion is spoken of today, it is usually in reference to a particular world religion. The word 'religion' is reserved these days for a set of beliefs and practices that is common and worldwide. Also, when religion is spoken of today, people are usually referring to 'organised' religion. They are implying that the religion has an institutional structure. 'Unorganised' religion is not a term that is used. Were one to speak of 'unorganised' religion, one would probably be talking about a spiritual tradition, that is a tradition that has not been institutionalised or universalised.

Particular local traditions of belief and practice are often referred to as 'spiritualities'. An indigenous native population sharing one culture is generally said to have a spirituality rather than a religion. It is only when people of various cultures practise a common spirituality worldwide that the term 'religion' is used. The major religions of the world such as Christianity or Islam are not confined to one place or one culture. Indigenous spiritualities usually are.

While spirituality is an essential element in all religions, not all spirituality is expressed through religion. Many Western people today think of themselves as being spiritual but not religious. What they generally mean by this is that they do not regularly attend a church, yet they do have spiritual beliefs, values and practices. While religion may not attract them, they are often attracted by a particular spirituality.

Spiritualities that are practised today can be broadly put into one of three categories. They are either New Age, indigenous or operate within an established religion.

New Age is a term used for a wide variety of spiritualities or spiritual practices that have been newly created or have become disconnected from their roots. It is a syncretic movement that takes spiritual practices from wherever it can find them, old and new and puts them together in any combination. One may find a mix that includes eastern traditions such as yoga and meditation, vegetarianism and belief in reincarnation and other practices such as astrology, angels and elements of holistic medicine. As its name suggests, it is a modern gather-all of spiritualities whose practices have grown and developed to suit people in the modern age.

Indigenous spiritualities may also be developed and adapted to suit the modern age but they cannot be classed New Age if they remain true to their origins. Indigenous spiritualities are more rooted in a particular culture and a particular place. Examples of indigenous spiritualities that are popular today are: Native American spirituality, Celtic spirituality, Australian aboriginal spirituality and Maori spirituality which is found in New Zealand. All these have a strong connection to nature and the natural world, to their particular place on this earth and to their own indigenous culture.

Within Christianity and particularly Roman Catholicism, there are many sub-spiritualities that exist alongside the mainstream traditions. These sub-spiritualities are often associated with the apparitions of Mary or with various saints and founders of religious orders. Lourdes, Fatima, Knock and Medjugorje are all places of pilgrimage where Mary is said to have appeared. These places attract large crowds of pilgrims. Roman Catholic saints or founders of religious orders such as Padre Pio, Mother Theresa, Francis of Assisi and Charles de Foucault have also spawned specific spiritualities. The practice of these spiritualities revolves around the values and the emphases of these saintly people. People who practise one of these spiritualities will usually practise it in tandem with regular attendance at more mainstream church services.

This book has shown how the Christian corporate church based in Rome succeeded in gaining control of the mainstream Christian traditions. What were initially diverse grass roots expressions of Christian belief, gradually became homogenised ritual ceremonies performed by professionals in standardised churches the world over. All the mainstream Christian churches today continue to have hierarchies of one form or another who keep control over these traditions. This creates a problem for many contemporary churchgoers who want spirituality or religion in their lives but who find the ceremonies in the churches partially or largely irrelevant.

A spiritual tradition that is organised and controlled from the top down has disconnected itself from the source of its own power, which is in the grass roots of the local community. The institutionalisation of the tradition prevents it from being dynamic and alive. The tradition cannot adapt, change and develop within a particular community because it is not allowed to do so.

The changes that are taking place in the world today are radical, as we adapt to an environmental crisis of our own making. For us to survive the crisis, a fundamental shift in our thinking has to take place. For many people in the Western world, the roots of their thinking are sunk deep in a religious belief. The religions to which they belong are not capable of changing or adapting quickly enough to respond to this crisis. These religions cannot provide a solution to the problem because they are part of the problem.

No modern-day monotheist religion can be expected to discard its belief in its god. Therefore people who care about the future have no choice but to walk away from these religions and participate in the creation of more relevant spiritualities that match our present and future realities.

Conclusion

Within Western society today there are growing attempts among people to get back in tune with nature. Many of us grow gardens with vegetables and flowers. We want our food to be locally produced, natural, organic and healthy. We want our houses to be built using sustainable, local materials, with a low energy requirement and blending with the landscape. We want the richness and diversity of our landscapes and ecosystems to be preserved and maintained. We want the land to be used in a sustainable way, preserving its fertility for future generations and protecting and supporting its wildlife. We want our energy to come from natural, renewable sources.

A spirituality to match a lifestyle of sustainability has to come from within a local setting. It has to engage in a positive way with the local landscape, the local wildlife, the local history and the local culture and traditions. It has to match and provide a container for the lifestyle of sustainability required of the humans resident in the area. Global spiritualities will not work; nor will the importation of indigenous spiritualities from other cultures. However, ideas and practices from anywhere can be used to help to build the local spirituality.

The challenge for the future, if we survive, is for each bioregion of the world to develop its own dynamic, relevant and nourishing spirituality for its own people. Each bioregion must have its own mythology, legends and stories that stitch the lives and culture of the people into the landscape, the climate and the history of the place where they live. This spirituality must be developed to give a framework, a context and a depth of meaning to a lifestyle that is sustainable in that region.

For this to work, the spirit has to be put back into the material world. That spirit must be recognised and respected in animals, in plants, in the natural landscape and seascape and in the cosmos. The words we use to name that spirit or those spirits are probably not important. Essentially, these new spiritualities of sustainability will be diverse expressions of a fundamental belief that matter in all its forms has a spiritual element, which must be regarded by humans as sacred and respected accordingly. What we have learned regarding how we should relate to each other as humans, we must now apply in our relations to the rest of nature.

The New Wine

There is a new wine
fermenting.
The bubbles
of the spirit
make their way to the surface
from the bottom up
and fill the air
with the fragrance
of ancient things.
For centuries the yeast
lay on the bottom
untouched, unstirred,
unnoticed.
But now there is a stirring.
Dana and Dagda are rising;
the stories are being told;
the music is being heard;
the fermentation has begun again.
Soon
the new wine
will be ready.
We must prepare
new containers
for it.

Dara Molloy

Appendix I

Dedication to Ivan Illich and John Seymour

I have been reading Ivan Illich since 1971. The first book of his that I read was *Deschooling Society*. I was in college at the time and the book made a deep and lasting impression on me.

Since that time, Ivan Illich has been the person who has most influenced my understanding and perception of the world we live in. His brilliant mind has put into words the most profound insights. In the process he has confirmed many of my intuitions. Many of the ideas he put forward, such as in his critique of development or in his views on modern education, underpin my life project.

Later in my life, I met Ivan Illich in person and he became a friend as well as a mentor. He came to Ireland and to Aran on a few occasions and I paid visits to him in Pennsylvania and in Bremen. I got to know his circle of friends and witnessed his heroism in the face of suffering.

The other great heroes of my life – John the Baptist, Jesus, Francis of Assisi, Mahatma Gandhi – have not been contemporaries of mine but Ivan has. It has been an immense privilege to have had the friendship and the mentoring of such a great human being.

*****

John Seymour is someone who came into my life in 1985, when I moved to live on the Aran Islands. His *Complete Book of Self-Sufficiency* became essential reading for those of us who were living close to nature and on a low income.

Since then, John's books have been in constant use in our house and his ideas have found expression in all sorts of ways throughout our project. Like Ivan Illich, he became a friend and mentor.

In 1990, I was delighted to be able to bring John Seymour and Ivan Illich together under the one roof. It was the first time they had met: Ivan the ultimate intellectual; John the ultimate practitioner, both of them gifted writers. They got on well together and later John collaborated with Ivan and others in producing a document called *A Statement on the Soil*[1].

❋❋❋❋❋

On 2 December 2002, Ivan Illich died in Bremen[2]. On 14 September 2004, John Seymour died in Wales[3]. Their passing brought into focus the major contributions they had both made towards fermenting ideas, critiquing the world we live in and showing a different way forward.

After their death, their work still lives on. Ivan used two Latin words to describe the nature of their work: *inspiratio* and *conspiratio*[4]. These words indeed sum up their lives – combinations of inspiration and conspiracy.

---

1   Ivan Illich, John Seymour and others, 'Statement on the Soil'. Published in *The AISLING Magazine*, Issue 4. Aisling Publications, 1991.
2   Cf.: Dara Molloy, 'Ivan Illich 1926-2002: Obituary'. Article in *The AISLING Magazine*, Issue 31. Aisling Publications, 2003. www.aislingpublications.com
3   Cf: Will Sutherland, 'John Seymour: Obituary'. Article in *The AISLING Magazine*, Issue 33. Aisling Publications 2005. www.aislingpublications.com
4   *Inspiratio* literally means 'breathing in' and *conspiratio* 'breathing together'. At the root of the English words 'inspiration' and 'conspiracy' is the idea of sharing the one breath or 'spirit'.

APPENDIX II

ABOUT THE AUTHOR

Since I was a young child, I felt drawn to spiritual things. To this day I remember a little book of gospel stories I had in primary school. It was my favourite book. From the time I began secondary school, I accompanied my father to Mass every morning.

One day, when I was about twelve years old, as our family sat around the table, my sister asked each of us to state a wish. When it came to my mother's turn, she wished that one of her sons would be a priest. I can remember the feeling I had as she said that. It was as if a knife went into my heart. I knew deep down that that was my calling. I would be that son. I said nothing at the time to anyone.

Of course, that was the Ireland of the time. I was born in 1949. Every Irish mother wanted a son a priest. Many an Irish son went into the priesthood with his mother's vocation. When I was ordained, I had to struggle with my mother's expectations of me. She not alone wanted me to be a priest, but to be a certain type of priest – one who wore the collar all the time and played the archetypal role of Irish clergyman. For my part, when I became a priest, I hated the collar, hated being called 'Father' and felt very uncomfortable when I was treated as somebody special or put on a pedestal.

While there is no doubt that my parents and Irish society in general influenced my decision to become a priest, I now know that my calling was deeper than that. I did have a genuine calling towards what I would now call a spiritually-centred way of life. Since that time, my father has passed away and my mother has changed and grown considerably. She has given up trying to influence the type of priesthood that I practise. She and I have both moved very far away from her original expectations.

Looking back, I would say that although I was drawn to spiritual things, there were many aspects of church and religion to which I was not drawn. This was clear from the fact that, in my youth, I had not become an altar boy or joined the Legion of Mary or St Vincent de Paul, although many of my friends had done so. When I finished school, I hesitated about going into the seminary immediately, as I felt I still had some growing up to do. I took a job for a year in an engineering firm, bought a car, dated a girl, began to smoke and drink and developed quite a foul tongue. Then I felt I was ready!

However, the thought of entering a seminary did not excite me. The all-male company and strict regime was something I was used to from school, but not something that I looked forward to. I approached seminary with the attitude that it was something I had to put up with, to achieve my goal of being a priest and living a religious life. I was drawn to the life of a priest and religious by some inner compulsion that left me no choice in the matter. The unattractiveness of the life before me in the seminary was of no importance.

The seminary was run by the Marist Fathers. These had been my teachers in secondary school. They are a religious order more formally known as the Society of Mary. What I found attractive about the Marists was that they were not dedicated to any one work, like teaching in schools, or working with the sick but were an order founded to respond to any spiritual need in the world. Intuitively I felt that my work as a priest would not be in any conventional area, so the Marists offered me this flexibility, at least in theory.

I found my studies in theology and philosophy to be, for the most part, uninteresting and uninspiring. I survived my ten years of seminary days, which included a science degree at University College Dublin, by immersing myself in community development work among the families and young people who lived in the neighbourhood of the seminary in Milltown, Dublin. To this day, many of these people are my friends.

Having put up with seminary to achieve my goal, I took perpetual vows of poverty, chastity and obedience and was ordained a priest at the age of 28. Theoretically life should then have begun. My first appointment was to a boys' secondary school in Dundalk as a science, maths and religion teacher. I had no particular interest in teaching these subjects but I saw working in a school as an opportunity to engage with young people at a spiritual level. I quickly found out that the institutional structure of school worked against this and I began to put most of my energy into working with young people outside of school. This led to exhaustion. I was doing a day's work in school, which I hated and then at 4.15 pm I was beginning another day's work, which I loved. The exhaustion led to a crisis. I knew that I had to get out of school and into work that was less structured and institutionalised.

Parallel to the developing crisis in my work was a developing crisis related to my living within a religious community of thirteen priests. Fundamentally, religious life is the rejection of the common values of the world in order to emphasise 'higher' values. The founders of religious orders were generally inspirational people who denied themselves material comforts and opportunities for status and power and lived a life in solidarity with those on the margins of society.

Historically, as institutional structures were built around the work of these charismatic leaders, the members of the subsequent religious orders were neither as inspirational nor as radical. When charismatic leadership gives way to democratic structures, the sharp edge of radicalism is severely blunted. Religious orders in Ireland in the latter half of the 20th century, while they often did attract young idealistic people, were places that offered a life of security and comfort, status and power.

Having chosen the inspirational road to what I believed would be 'living on the edge', I found myself living a comfortable lifestyle with no financial worries. Society, including some of my own family, put me on a pedestal because I was a priest. My role in society and in school gave me a position of considerable influence. In short, I had material comforts, high status and power – things that may be goals for many people in the world, but ones that I had wanted to reject in my search for something deeper or higher.

In reaction, I threw my bed and carpet out of my room. I became a vegetarian and would not drive a car, watch TV or drink alcohol. I ate my meals with the kitchen staff, wore shabby clothes and let my hair and beard grow long!

Of course, I could just have left the religious order and done something else with my life. Many others did exactly that. I refused to do that because I did not want to walk away from a visible spiritually-focussed life. In Irish society, the container offered for such a life was the religious community. There were few, if any, other options. Having committed myself to it, I now found myself blocked and frustrated. I was experiencing what Jesus identified when he said to the religious leaders of his time: 'You shut up the kingdom of heaven in men's faces, neither going in yourselves nor allowing others to go in who want to.'[1]

I spent six years in the school in Dundalk and another year giving school and parish retreats around the country, based in Dublin. During this period it became clear to me that the values that I was drawn to were: simplicity in lifestyle, hospitality, solidarity with people who were in poverty or suffering injustice, closeness to nature and an all-encompassing resistance to some of the major motivating forces in the world today. I wanted to live in a way that did not accommodate these forces and I wanted to show another way.

To my surprise I had begun to see that religious life did not allow me to do that. By their nature, institutions resist change because they are created to perpetuate something. Their structures are designed to outlive their members and to keep the institutional machine going, regardless of who the participants are. These structures therefore control and limit members' behaviour. Free-spirited, visionary people do not fit well into institutional living. Religious life was not going to allow me to live as I wanted.

I now have little respect for religious life as I knew it. As a friend of mine regularly quoted to me, 'the corruption of the best is the worst of all'[2].

At the heart of the religious life are the three vows – poverty, chastity and obedience. I took these vows when I was aged twenty-two. While at the time I accepted them, I now have some serious questions about them.

1   Mt.23:13
2   The friend in question was Ivan Illich, a man who himself had been a Roman Catholic priest and had resigned after he fell foul of the church authorities. His quote was an old Latin saying: "Corruptio optimi pessima". His own critique of the Roman church is contained in *The Rivers North of the Future: The Testament of Ivan Illich as told to David Cayley.* by David Cayley, Toronto: Anansi, 2005.

These vows are not what I was told they were in my seminary training – 'evangelical counsels' or gospel invitations – except in the case of poverty. The only idea among the three vows that finds a clear enunciation in the Christian gospels is poverty.

I had been taught during my training that poverty, chastity and obedience were at the core of the gospel that Jesus preached. Until I knew better, I believed this. It took a long time for my naïve idealism and trust in authority to give way, first to disillusionment and then to a sense of betrayal. I now know that the three vows, as practised during my time in religious life, had little to do with gospel values. They had a lot to do with keeping an organisation going.

In the case of poverty, religious life prevented me from living the sort of poverty I wanted to live, the sort of poverty that Jesus had lived and encouraged. Religious life required that I live a type of poverty – communal ownership – which was not really poverty at all. Communal ownership was not something that offered any solidarity to people who lived in financial hardship around me and bore no resemblance to poverty anywhere in the real world.

In the case of celibacy, there is only one line in one of the four gospels which may have some connection with celibacy, but in the context seems more to do with Jesus's views on divorce. This is the reference to: 'There are eunuchs who have made themselves that way for the sake of the kingdom of heaven.'[3] In my view, the vow of chastity was stressed in religious life because without it an exclusive community of men could not stay together very long. Celibacy is an invention of Roman Catholicism and is not a gospel value. The Roman church cloaked the invention in gospel language to hide its own agenda of patriarchal power, hierarchical control and the exclusion of women and children.[4]

---

3   *Mt.19:12*
4   In chapter 2 of this book, I illustrate how the creation of monotheism began a human journey towards disconnectedness. This journey removed people from a sense of belonging to the earth and of being an integral part of that earth. Monotheism achieved this by placing god away from the earth in the heavens and by forbidding any concept of a feminine deity. Christianity throughout its history has driven this agenda forward, building into human society the structures of disconnectedness. It's attitude to sexuality in general and its insistence on celibacy for its priests and religious in particular, is an integral part of this agenda. Within the monotheistic vision, power is achieved through disconnection from the earth and disconnection from the feminine. Both are really one and the same.

Jesus himself did not live in an exclusively male community, despite having apparently chosen twelve male apostles. According to the gospels, many of his apostles were married. Evidence in the gospels provides arguments for suggesting that Jesus was not celibate himself. He had a particular relationship with Mary Magdalene and he had a particular relationship with John, 'the disciple he loved'.[5] Whether these relationships were explicitly sexual we do not know. We have no evidence either way. Therefore in my view we cannot be definitive about it.

In the case of the vow of obedience, in my experience this vow was used by those in authority as a way of getting a vowed religious to do what he or she was told. The vow was understood to mean the denial or repression of one's own will. When I took my vows, the words I was required to use vowed my obedience to the Superior General of the religious order. It was put to me that obeying the Superior General or his subordinates was the same thing as obeying 'God'. This was undoubtedly very helpful for the smooth running of the organisation, but there is no evidence that Jesus ever practised this form of obedience.

On the contrary, it is quite clear in the gospels that Jesus regularly practised disobedience to the religious authorities of his time. He lost no opportunity to castigate these authorities for the way they imposed their wills on the people. Jesus's concept of obedience, as he announced even at the age of twelve[6], was to listen to and be obedient to the inner voice, the intimate personal voice that one hears in the most unexpected places and that rarely comes through human authority figures.

Religious life, as I knew it and experienced it, was a facade. We had all the externals – the dress, the titles, the roles – but internally, speaking for myself, I was all dried up and spiritually undernourished. What Jesus had identified, among the religious leaders of his own time, has resonances also now: 'You who are like whitewashed tombs that look handsome on the outside, but inside are full of dead men's bones and every kind of corruption.'[7] The major corruption that I saw was the corruption of gospel values. In relation to 'dead men's bones', I for one was spiritually dying. I would have become ossified spiritually had I not left that life.

---

5   Jn.19:26
6   Lk. 2:49
7   Mt.23:27-28

The crisis I experienced at this time in my life led me to look for a new way of manifesting my desire to live a spiritually-focussed life. In 1985, I moved to live on the Aran Islands. I was still a priest, still a member of the religious order, but I had negotiated for myself enough space to experiment with living as a Celtic monk and hermit. In moving to Aran, I was clear in my mind that I was not bringing the institution with me. On Aran I had no official role within Roman Catholicism nor within the religious order. My aim was to become de-institutionalised and de-professionalised.

In secular terms, I was taking unpaid leave. I still maintained a tie with the church and with my religious order, but I had plenty of rope. The rope could remain tied, but I needed it to be slack at all times.

Back in my teaching days, a friend who was deeply intuitive had given me a spiritual picture card. She knew intuitively that the card had an important message for me but was not able to interpret it herself. She was very nervous handing it over. In fact, she had attempted to give it to me twice and lost courage at the last minute. The picture card portrayed in the foreground a picturesque harbour with a few boats tied up at the pier. Outside the harbour there was a vast beautiful ocean. The card said: 'Boats are safe in a harbour, but that is not what boats are made for.' That card summed up what I was now choosing. I wanted to leave the institution that supported, protected and controlled me and I wanted to head for the open sea.

Having extracted myself from the structures of an institutional church, I began to create a new life for myself based on my own spiritual values. I drew inspiration from the Celtic spiritual tradition which I was excitedly discovering and claiming as my heritage. Despite having no official parish role, I regularly performed religious services in Roman Catholic churches on the Aran islands and elsewhere. This acted as an anchor, preventing me from drifting too far out to sea. The result was, however, that I found myself straddling a great divide, with one foot in the Roman camp and one foot in the Celtic camp. At first I thought these two positions were reconcilable. That reconciliation became the focus of my work. However, gradually the gap between the two began to widen. Eventually, I realised that Roman and Celtic were antithetical. They were irreconcilably opposed.

This realisation came when I began to see that the Roman Catholic church was a multinational, global church in contrast to Celtic spirituality, which was an indigenous and therefore intrinsically local tradition. Trying to reconcile the two was like attempting to reconcile the local grocer with a multinational grocery chain. When the two are side by side, inevitably the local grocer gets swallowed up.

What became clear to me was that Roman Catholicism and most other Christian churches are multinational corporations just like McDonald's or Coca Cola. They have products and services, albeit religious ones, that they distribute throughout the world, with the minimum of regard for culture or climate or history or particularity of place. Catholic churches throughout the world are recognisable, not just because of the style of building and layout, but because the ceremonies performed in them follow a distinctly recognisable pattern. It dawned on me that globalisation began with European Christianity. The Christian churches provided the model for the multinational corporations to follow suit.

Celtic spirituality, on the contrary, is a spiritual tradition that is an expression of a particular people with a particular history of living in a particular place. As an indigenous tradition, it existed in Ireland before the advent of Christianity. The Christian story was absorbed into it. Christianity was inculturated into this local tradition and became a new layer in that ancient spiritual history. The Celtic Christian tradition was an indigenous movement within a culture. Its spiritual practices, rituals and liturgies, while Christian, were specific to a place, to a people and to their history.

I discovered that, in the earlier centuries of its existence, this tradition was not controlled by Rome. It grew organically from among the people. Its monastic structure made it difficult for Roman Christianity to gain any control over it. Its abbots were locally appointed, it had no hierarchy of authority beyond the abbot and it had no central administration.

As I have illustrated in this book, it is in the nature of all multinational corporations, including global church institutions, to attempt to replace the indigenous self-reliant ways of living of particular peoples in particular places with their own multinational products and services. With their vision of global dominance and with the backing of powerful forces, the all-devouring aggression of multinational corporations leaves indigenous traditions with little or no chance of survival.

Once this realisation became clear to me, I had a choice to make. I could no longer stand with an institution that did such things. The rope that tied me to Roman Catholicism and my religious order had to be cut. Before any one else could do it to me, I excommunicated Roman Catholicism from my life.

Because I had chosen to leave the Roman Catholic institution, there was now a clear distinction in my mind between an institutional church and a spiritual tradition. The Irish spiritual tradition was never a church in the institutional sense, even in its Christian form.[8] It was the living expression of an indigenous people celebrating its spirituality. The form of that expression was influenced by its culture and history, as well as by its landscape, its climate and its way of living. To have institutionalised it would have been to have destroyed it.

While I now promote the Celtic spiritual tradition, I do not advocate its institutionalisation in a church structure. That tradition has a dynamic and a vitality of its own. It requires only that people celebrate it and continue to give it expression for it to stay alive and grow. There are many other examples of indigenous spiritual traditions around the world. Most of them are under threat or have already been wiped out by the globalising forces of world religions and world economics.

Once I had removed the anchor that held me tied to Catholicism, it did not take me long to distance myself from it. At first I found it daunting and overwhelming to be faced with a vista without boundaries or limitations. But, having been freed from such hindrances as dogma and orthodoxy, my inner compass quickly brought me to places of belief where I felt more at home. These were very different places from those I had left behind.

My feeling was that I had escaped from living within a bubble. That bubble was the monotheistic global Roman Christian church. It had been my whole life. I had believed that there was no life outside of it. But now, having escaped, I was surprised to find myself in an alternative world teeming with life. My imagination was liberated. I started to let go of

---

8   See Ed. Sellner, 'The Celtic Church as an Ecclesial Entity'. Article in *The AISLING Magazine*, issue 30. Aisling Publications 2002. www.aislingpublications.com

many of my old tenets. I began to question things I had never questioned – my own theology and Christology, Christian dogma in general and the role and content of rituals and ceremonies. I had to unlearn in order to start relearning.

The journey on Aran has had two clear stages. For the first 10 years, from 1985 to 1995, I experimented with living as a Celtic monk. Within the boundaries of Roman Catholicism, I practised some of the ancient Celtic spiritual traditions and immersed myself in their history. The second stage began in 1996 when I excommunicated Roman Catholicism from my life and promised myself that, while remaining a priest and monk within the Celtic tradition, I would not be a member of any institutional church. My work since then has been to promote the Celtic spiritual tradition, creating experimental elements of a new lifestyle that is true to that tradition and introducing new forms of ritual and celebration that are relevant and spiritually nourishing to the people I serve.

CHRONOLOGICAL TABLE

IRELAND	BRITAIN	EUROPE	THE EAST AND AFRICA
BCE			BCE
8000 End of Ice Age			2500 Egyptian pyramids
5000 First settlers in Ireland			2000 Arrival of Abraham in Canaan
Nemed			
Partholon			
Fir Bolg			
Tuatha de Danaan			1700 Patriarchs in Egypt
3000 Passage graves a Newgrange			1350 Pharaoh Akhnaton
			1250 Moses and Exodus
			1220 Invasion of Palestine
2000 Hill of Tara – spiritual and political centre of Ireland until 1169 CE			1000 Capture of Jerusalem by King David
			950 Building of Temple
		BCE	
		1000 Celtic tribes across Europe	
		900s Homer composes *Iliad* and *Odyssey*	
		850 Early versions of *Pentateuch* written perhaps about this time.	
		753 Founding of city of Rome	

IRELAND	BRITAIN	EUROPE	THE EAST AND AFRICA
BCE	BCE	BCE	
			740 Call of Isaiah
			622 Discovery of 'The Book of the Law'. Religious reform.
			598 Deportation of Jews to Babylon.
			538 Jews return from exile. Bible/Torah is compiled
			520 Building of Second Temple
500 Celtic people in Ireland	500 Celtic people in Britain	500 Greek civilisation	
			390 Celts invade Rome
			63 Pompey of Rome takes Jerusalem
		52 Celts defeated by Julius Caesar	
		Roman Empire dominates Europe for nearly 300 years	
CE	CE	CE	CE
			4 Birth of Jesus
			30 Death of Jesus
			36 Martyrdom of Stephen. Followers of Jesus disperse.
	43 Romans invade Britain Southern half of Britain occupied by Romans as far as Hadrian's Wall.		45 Paul's preaching begins
			Paul's letters
		64 Peter martyred in Rome Great fire in Rome. Christians blamed	64 Gospel of Mark

THE EAST AND AFRICA

65 Gospel of Matthew, Gospel of Luke, *Acts of the Apostles*

70 Jerusalem destroyed by Romans. Burning of Temple. Further dispersal of Christians.

95 Gospel of John Gospel of Thomas and other Gnostic writings Jerusalem, Alexandria, Antioch develop as major centres of Christianity.

100 Many variations in Christian doctrine. Sabellianism, Docetism, Monophysitism, Adoptionism, Apollinarianism, Arianism, Socianism, Donatism, Gnosticism and Pelagianism. A lot of controversy and so-called 'heresies'.

330 Founding of Constantinople

345 Paul of Thebes, anchorite, dies in Egyptian desert

354 Birth of Augustine of Hippo

EUROPE

67 Paul martyred in Rome.

200 St Irenaeus, bishop of Lugdunum, Gaul, now Lyons, France.

250 First major persecutions of Christians

313 Constantine becomes emperor.Edict of Milan. Christianity recognised.

325 Council of Nicea. Confronts Arian 'heresy'. First orthodox creed

BRITAIN

IRELAND

100 Maedhbh Queen of Connacht

IRELAND	BRITAIN	EUROPE	THE EAST AND AFRICA
			356 Anthony the hermit dies in Egypt
		360 Huns invade Europe St Jerome baptised in Rome. John Cassian born, d. 433.	
		371 Martin founds monastery at Tours	
300s Christianity develops in southern Ireland		380 Christianity declared official religion of Roman empire by emperor Theodosius. Pope declared *Pontifex Maximus.*	
Pre-Patrician monastic founders: Ibar of Wexford, Ciaran of Saighir, Ailbhe of Emly, Declan of Ardmore Pelagius becomes Celtic monk in Ireland or Wales	Roman Britain becomes Christian. Celtic Christianity develops in Wales. Pelagius becomes Celtic monk in Ireland or Wales	383 Priscillian, first Christian put to death by Christians.	
	397 Ninian founds Celtic monastery at Whithorn	400 Pelagius in Rome	
		406 Germanic invasion of empire	
400 Cashel capital of Munster			
405 Patrick slave in Mayo	410 Romans leave Britain Roman Christianity collapses	410 Alaric the Visigoth takes Rome	
411 Patrick escapes.			412 Synod of Carthage, Pelagius condemned.

IRELAND	BRITAIN	EUROPE	THE EAST AND AFRICA
			415 Council in Jerusalem, Pelagius exonerated. Synod of Diospolis acquits Pelagius
		416 Innocent I condemns Pelagius	416 2nd Synod of Carthage, Pelagius again condemned.
		417 Zosimus acquits Pelagius	
		418 Final condemnation of Pelagius by pope Zosimus.	
		418 Visigoths in Spain	
		419 St Jerome dies	
	420 Invasions of Angles and Saxons	422 Pope Celestine. Sends anti-Pelagian missions to Britain and Ireland.	
	425 Mission of Germanus	429 Hororatus of Lerins dies	430 Vandals take Hippo Augustine of Hippo dies
431 Mission of Palladius		435 Cassian dies	
432 Mission of Patrick	447 2nd mission of Germanus	447 Campaigns of Huns under Attila	
		448 Germanus of Auxerre dies	
		451 Council of Chalcedon	
450 St Brigid is born		455 Vandals sack Rome	

Year	IRELAND	BRITAIN	EUROPE	THE EAST AND AFRICA
461	Patrick dies			
476			Last Roman emperor deposed. Dark Ages – last until 1000	
480			Benedict of Nursia born.	
481			Clovis king of Franks until 511	
484	Brendan the Navigator born			
485	Enda founds monastery on Aran. St Caomhán and St Gobnait, Inis Oírr.			
495	Finnian of Moville born			
496			Clovis baptised	
500	Brigid founds Kildare			
503		Irish colony in Argyll		
507			Clovis takes Aquitane	
511			Clovis dies	
516	Ciaran of Clonmacnoise born			
521	Colmcille (Columba) born			
525	Brigid dies			
527	Enda dies			
529			Benedict founds Monte Cassino	
530	Finnian founds Clonard			
543	Columbanus born			
545	Kevin founds Glendalough			
548	Ciaran founds Clonmacnoise			
560		St David: monasteries Wales, Cornwall, Brittany		
561	Battle of Cúl Dreimhne			
565		Colmcille (Columba) founds Iona		
568			Lombards attack Italy Gregory builds monastery for Benedict's monks in Rome	
570				Muhammad born
574	Convention of Drum Ceat			

IRELAND	BRITAIN	EUROPE	THE EAST AND AFRICA
590 Columbanus leaves for Gaul		590 Columbanus in Burgundy Gregory I (The Great) pope	
		591 Goths converted to Roman Christianity from Arianism	
	597 Colmcille (Columba) dies		
	597 Augustine's mission to Britain Benedictine monasticism		
	601 Ethelbert of Kent converted		
	603 Meeting at 'Augustine's Oak'		
	604 Augustine of Canterbury dies Laurence takes over	604 Gregory the Great dies	
		612 Columbanus expelled from Burgundy. Founds monasteries throughout Europe St Gall founds San Gallen	
		615 Columbanus dies at Bobbio	
624 Adamnán of Iona born	626 Conversion of Northumbria to Celtic Christianity		622 Muhammadenism established at Medina
	634 Wilfrid born		632 Muhammad dies
	635 Aidan founds Lindisfarne		634 Arabs invade Palestine
	664 Synod of Whitby	650 St Fursey, abbot of Lagny near Paris, dies. St Cataldo (Cathal), bishop of Taranto, southern Italy.	
	665 Great Plague		

IRELAND	BRITAIN	EUROPE	THE EAST AND AFRICA
		670 St Fiachra dies. Patron saint of cab drivers in Paris. St Dymphna (Damhnait), Gheel, Belgium. Patron of mentally ill.	
	672 Boniface born in Devon		
	673 Bede born	689 St Killian (Cillian) martyred Wurzburg, Germany	
	678 Wilfrid dismissed as Bishop of York	700 Papal States established	
	709 Wilfrid dies. Pontifical of Egbert	714 Charles Martel, ruler of Franks. Dies 741	
		716 Boniface's first mission to Europe – Frisia.	
		718 Monastery of Monte Cassino re-established	
		742 Boniface and Martel call all-German council	
		747 Benedictine Rule forced on Irish monastery of San Gallen	
		749 St Fergal abbot of St Peter's, Salzburg. Clash with Boniface	
750 Céile Dé Reform movement (Culdees) until 900		754 Death of Boniface	
		754 Death of Boniface	

IRELAND	BRITAIN	EUROPE	THE EAST AND AFRICA
		766 St Fergal bishop of Salzburg	
774 Maelruan founded Tallaght, Féilire of Aongus. Stowe missal.			
795 First recorded Viking attack on Ireland at Lambay Island	793 First Viking attack – on Lindisfarne	800 Charlemagne crowned emperor of First Reich (Italian-German) by Pope Leo III. Lasted until 1806	
	807 Iona abandoned. Monks flee to Kells in Ireland	829 Irish monk St Donatus (Donagh) bishop of Fiesole, Italy.	
		830 Muslim attacks on Italy and Papal States	
840 Vikings settle in Waterford, Wexford, Limerick, Cork, Arklow and Dublin		845 John Scotus Eriugena arrives at court of Charles the Bald	
		855 Synod of Valence condemns Eriugena	
	875 Lindisfarne abandoned		
914 Vikings attack and settle with new intensity			
989 Columban federation united twice with Armagh federation for brief periods up to 1007.			

IRELAND	BRITAIN	EUROPE	THE EAST AND AFRICA
1002 Brian Boru declared himself high king of Ireland.			
1005 Brian Boru declared Armagh religious capital of Ireland.			
1014 Vikings defeated by Brian Boru at Battle of Clontarf			
		1049 Gregorian Reform begins with Pope Leo IX	
		1054 Schism in Church between East and West	
	1066 England conquered by Normans, William I. Final collapse of Celtic church in Britain.		
		1067 Marianus Scotus founds Abbey of St James in Ratisbon (Regensburg). *Schottenklösters.*	
		1073 Pope Gregory VII, main engine of reform. Dies 1085. Roman Curia. Canon Law. Celibacy	
	1093 Anselm, Italian archbishop of Canterbury til 1109		
1094 Malachy born. Muirchertach O Briain, king of Munster, on and off, until 1118			
		1095 Crusades until 1291	1095 Crusades until 1291

IRELAND	BRITAIN	EUROPE	THE EAST AND AFRICA
1096 Malchus, Benedictine monk, appointed bishop of Waterford by Anselm of Canterbury			
1101 Synod of Cashel			
1105 Cellach becomes abbot of Armagh			
1106 Gilbert, Benedictine monk, appointed bishop of Limerick by Anselm of Canterbury. Cellach ordained bishop of Armagh by Malchus and Gilbert.			
1111 Synod of Rath Brasil			
		1115 Bernard of Clairvaux founds Cistercians	
1111 Synod of Rath Brasil			
1119 Malachy sent by Cellach to train with Malchus			
1125 Malachy ordained bishop of Down and Connor			
1132 Malachy appointed bishop of Armagh and primate			
1137 Gilla Mac Liag appointed abbot of Armagh and takes primacy from Malachy. Malachy sets out for Rome.			

IRELAND	BRITAIN	EUROPE	THE EAST AND AFRICA
1142 First Cistercians arrive to set up Mellifont		1145 Pope Eugene III until 1153. Cistercian monk, disciple of St Bernard, pro-Norman	
1148 Malachy dies in arms of St Bernard. Canonised 1190			
1152 Synod of Kells. Ireland divided into 4 archbishoprics, directly subject to pope.		1152 Henry II marries Eleanor of Aquitane, extending Norman power in France	
1152 Monastery of Kells becomes Augustinian			
1154 Laurence O'Toole abbot of Glendalough	1154 Henry II king of England. Dies 1189	1154 Pope Adrian IV, Englishman. Dies 1159	
		1155 Papal bull 'Laudabiliter'. Claims Ireland as papal fiefdom, instructs Henry II to invade Ireland	
1157 Mellifont buildings completed			
1158 Synod of Bri Mac Thadhg in Meath establishes abbot of Derry as comharba of Colmcille			
1161 Synod of Derry exempts Derry monastery from secular tribute			
1161 Laurence O Toole bishop of Dublin			
1165 12 Cistercian abbeys in Ireland			

IRELAND	BRITAIN	EUROPE	THE EAST AND AFRICA
1167 First Anglo-Norman force sets foot in Ireland			
1169-70 Waterford, Wexford and Dublin taken by Normans			
1172 Henry II arrives in Ireland		1184 Inquisition. Papal and royal forces unite	
1200 39 Cistercian abbeys in Ireland		1215 Fourth Lateran Council.	
1216 Cistercians send 'visitors' to impose compliance		1216 Dominic founds Dominicans	
1217 No Irishman allowed as bishop of cathedral church			
1220-21 Further Cistercian attempts to impose compliance		1223 St Francis founds Franciscans	
		1225 Pope Honorius III condemns Eriugena	
1226 Mellifont 'Conspiracy'		1233 Fergal of Salzburg (and Ireland) canonised	
1228-30 Abbot Stephen			
1254 One third of episcopal sees occupied by foreign bishops			1294 Franciscan mission to China
1300 Most of Ireland under Norman control.			

THE EAST AND AFRICA	EUROPE	BRITAIN	IRELAND
1450 Franciscan mission to Cape Verde Islands			
1486 Dominican mission to West Africa			
1493 Priests sent with second mission of Columbus to New World	1492 Columbus discovers America		
1500s Franciscans and Dominicans begin missions in South America			
	1515 Pope Leo X 'restores' the *Schottenklösters* to Scotland		
	1517 Reformation. Martin Luther		
		1533 Henry VIII breaks with Rome	
		1536 -1541 Dissolution of monasteries in Britain and Ireland by Henry VIII.	1536 -1541 Dissolution of monasteries
1600s Jesuit missions to China and Mexico	1614 Publication of *Roman Ritual*		1649 Oliver Cromwell in Ireland.
			1681 Death of Oliver Plunkett
			1690 Battle of Boyne.
	1802 Monastery of Bobbio closed by Napolean. (Founded by Columbanus in 614)		1690 *Penal Laws* take on new intensity
1800s New wave of missions to New World			
	1847 Suppression of *Schottenklösters*		1829 Catholic Emancipation

IRELAND	BRITAIN	EUROPE	THE EAST AND AFRICA
1845-49 Irish 'Famine'		1856 Society of African Missions founded in France	
1849-78 Bishop Paul Cullen (Cardinal from 1867) leads devotional revolution		1870 Fifth Lateran Council papal primacy and infallibility	
		1871 Second Reich. Until 1918	1900s Consolidation of Christian churches presence throughout world
1916 Easter Rebellion		1934 Third Reich, until 1945	
1922 Irish Free State		1962-65 Second Vatican Council.	
1932 Eucharistic Congress			
1937 Irish Republic			
1973 Removal of 'special position' of Roman Catholic church from Irish constitution.			

BIBLIOGRAPHY

Abram, David, *The Spell of the Sensuous: Perception and Language in a More-than-Human World*. New York: Pantheon, 1996.

—, 'Returning To Our Senses'. Article in *The AISLING Magazine*, Issue 31. Aisling Publications, 2003.

—, 'On The Ecological Consequences of Alphabetic Literacy'. Article in *The AISLING Magazine*, Issue 32. Aisling Publications, 2005.

—, 'Language and the Ecology of Sensory Experience'. Article in *The AISLING Magazine*, Issue 33. Aisling Publications, 2005.

Adam, David, *The Edge of Glory: Prayers in the Celtic Tradition*. Triangle/ SPCK, London. 1985.

Alam, Niaz, 'Mc Theories and Mc Fallacies'. An article about McDonalds in *The AISLING Magazine*, issue 23. Aisling Publications, 1998.

Appignanesi, L. & Forrester, J. *Freud's Women*. London: Weidenfeld and Nicholson. 1992.

Armstrong, Karen, *A History of God: The 4000 Year Quest of Judaism, Christianity and Islam*. New York: Ballantine Books, 1993.

—, *The Battle for God*. New York: Alfred A. Knopf, 2000.

—, *The Great Transformation: The World in the time of Buddha, Socrates, Confucius and Jeremiah*. London: Atlantic Books, 2006.

Bahro, Rudolf, *Avoiding Social and Ecological Disaster: The Politics of World Transformation*. Gateway Books, 1994.

Bamford, Christopher, (translation, introduction, and reflections), *The Voice of the Eagle: Homily on the Prologue to the Gospel of St John, John Scotus Eriugena*. Lindisfarne Press, 1990.

Banks, Robert, *Paul's Idea of Community, The Early House Churches in their Historical Setting*. Exeter: Pater Noster Press, 1980.

Barnet, Richard J., and Cavanagh, John, 'Global Pop: The Sound of Money'. Article on Globalisation in *The AISLING Magazine*, Issue 25. Aisling Publications, 1999.

Bede (tr.Leo Sherley-Price). *History of the English Church and People*. Baltimore: Penguin, 1955.

Bender, Sue, *Plain and Simple: A Woman's Journey to the Amish*. HarperSanFrancisco, 1989.

Berry, Wendell, 'Out of Your Car, Off Your Horse'. Article in *The AISLING Magazine*, Issue 4, Aisling Publications, 1991.

—, *Sex, Economy, Freedom and Community*. Pantheon Books, 1992, 1993.

Bitel, Lisa M., *Isle of the Saints: Monastic Settlement and Christian Community in Early Ireland*. Cornell University Press, 1990.

—, *Land of Women: Tales of Sex and Gender from Early Ireland*. Cornell University Press, 1996.

Blamires, Steve, 'The Five Invasions of Ireland'. Article in *The AISLING Magazine*, Issue 24. Aisling Publications, 1998.

Bodo, Murray, *Francis: The Journey and The Dream*. Anthony Messenger Press. 1972.

Boff, Leonardo, *Saint Francis: A Model for Human Liberation*. SCM Press. 1982.

Bonwick, James, *Irish Druids and Old Irish Religions*. Dorset Press 1986. First published 1894.

Borg, Marcus J., *Jesus: Uncovering the Life, Teachings, and Relevance of a Religious Revolutionary*. HarperSanFrancisco, 2006.

Borysenko, Joan, *A Woman's Journey to God: Finding the Feminine Path*. New York: Riverhead Books, 1999.

Bradshaw, Brendan, and Dáire Keogh (Eds), *Christianity in Ireland, Revisiting the Story*, Dublin: Columba Press, 2002.

Brennan, J.H., *A Guide to Megalithic Ireland*. London: Aquarian/Thorsons, 1994.

Brenneman, Walter L. Jr., and Brenneman, Mary G., *Crossing the Circle at the Holy Wells of Ireland*. University Press of Virginia, 1995.

Buargque, Cristovam, *The End of Economics?: Ethics and the Disorder of Progress*. London: Zed Books, 1993.

Burgess, Yvonne, *The Myth of Progress*. Glasgow: Wild Goose Publications, 1996.

Butler, Gerry, 'Unmasking the Goddess'. Article in *The AISLING Magazine*, Issue 11. Aisling Publications, 1993.

—, 'Death and the Otherworld in Celtic Ireland'. Article in *The AISLING Magazine*, Issue 13. Aisling Publications, 1994.

Cahill, Susan (ed.), *Wise Women: Over 2000 Years of Spiritual Writing by Women*. New York: W.W. Norton, 1996.

Cahill, Thomas, *How The Irish Saved Civilisation, The Untold Story of Ireland's Heroic Role from the Fall of Rome to the Rise of Medieval Europe*. London: Hodder and Staughton, 1995.

Campbell, Joseph, *The Hero With A Thousand Faces*. New Jersey: Princeton University Press, 1968. First published 1949.

—, with Bill Moyers, *The Power of Myth*. Edited by Betty Sue Flowers, New York: Broadway Books, 1988.

Carey, Alex, *Taking the Risk out of Democracy: Corporate Propaganda Versus Freedom and Liberty*. Urbana: University of Illinois Press. 1997.

Carlson, Kathie, *In Her Image: The Unhealed Daughter's Search for Her Mother*. Shambhala, 1989.

Carmichael, Alexander, *The Celtic Gift of Nature: Selections from the Carmina Gadelica in Gaelic and English*. Edinburgh: Floris Books. 2004.

Carr-Gomm, Philip, *The Druid Tradition*. London: Element, 1991.

Carter (Fitzpatrick), Kate, 'Mother Goddess'. Article in *The AISLING Magazine*, Issue 7, Aisling Publications, 1992.

—, 'How We Lost Our Soul'. Article in *The AISLING Magazine*, Issue 10, Aisling Publications, 1993.

—, 'Healing The Split'. Article in *The AISLING Magazine*, Issue 11. Aisling Publications, 1993.

Cassian, John, *The Institutes*. Translated and annotated by Boniface Ramsey, O.P. New York: Newman Press, 2000.

Cayley, David, *Ivan Illich in Conversation*. Toronto: Anansi, 1992.

—, *The Rivers North of the Future: The Testament of Ivan Illich as told to David Cayley*. Toronto: Anansi, 2005.

Chadwick, Nora, *The Celts*. London: Penguin Books 1987. First published 1971.

Chomsky, Noam, *Deterring Democracy*. London: Vintage, 1991.

—, *Keeping the Rabble in Line: Interviews with David Barsamian*. London: AK Press, 1994.

Clancy, Padraigín (ed.), *Celtic Threads: Exploring the Wisdom of Our Heritage*. Dublin: Veritas, 1999.

Condren, Mary, *The Serpent and The Goddess: Women, Religion, and Power in Celtic Ireland*. New York: Harper and Row, 1989.

Corish, Patrick J. (ed.), *A History of Irish Catholicism*. Dublin: Gill and Macmillan. 26 fascicles, 1967 —.

Crossan, John Dominic, *The Birth of Christianity: Discovering What Happened in the Years Immediately after the Execution of Jesus*. HarperSanFrancisco, 1998.

—, *The Historical Jesus: The Life of a Mediterranean Jewish Peasant*. HarperSanFrancisco, 1991.

—, *Jesus: A Revolutionary Biography*. HarperSanFrancisco, 1994.

Curriculum Development Unit, *The Celtic Way of Life*. Dublin: The O'Brien Press, 1976.

Daly, Mary, *Beyond God the Father: Towards a Philosophy of Women's Liberation*. The Women's Press, 1991. First published 1986.

Dames, Michael, *Mythic Ireland*. London: Thames and Hudson, 1992.

D'Arcy, Mary Ryan, *The Saints of Ireland*. Minneapolis: Irish American Cultural Institute, 1974, 1985.

Dawkins, Richard, *The God Delusion*. London: Transworld Publishers, 2006.

Dawson, Jonathan, 'Regrowing Local Economies: A Tale of Two Ecovillages'. Article in *The AISLING Magazine*, Issue 33. Aisling Publications, 2005.

De Breffny, Brian, and Mott, George, *The Churches and Abbeys of Ireland*. London: Thames and Hudson, 1976.

De Chardin, Teilhard, *Hymn of the Universe*. London: Fontana Religious, 1970. First published 1965.

Dempsey, Rachel, 'The Guardians Speak Out'. Article about indigenous peoples in *The AISLING Magazine*, Issue 33. Aisling Publications, 2005.

De Waal, Esther, *The Celtic Vision: Prayers and Blessings from the Outer Hebrides. Selections from the Carmina Gadelica*. London: Darton, Longman and Todd, 1988.

—, *A World Made Whole: Rediscovering the Celtic Tradition*. Fount, New York: Harper Collins, 1991.

—, *The Celtic Way of Prayer: The Recovery of the Religious Imagination*. London: Hodder and Stoughten, 1996.

Doolin, Lelia, 'Institutions and Their Use of Power'. Article in *The AISLING Magazine*, Issue 32. Aisling Publications, 2005.

Dorgan, Carol, 'International Trading Relationships: A New Form of Colonialism'. Article in *The AISLING Magazine*, Issue 19. Aisling Publications, 1996.

Dorr, Donal, *Integral Spirituality: Resources for Community, Peace, Justice and the Earth*. Dublin: Gill and Macmillan, and New York: Orbis, 1990.

—, *The Social Justice Agenda: Justice, Ecology, Power and the Church*. Dublin: Gill and Macmillan, 1991.

—, *Divine Energy: God Beyond Us, Within Us, Among Us*. Dublin: Gill and Macmillan, 1996.

Douthwaite, Richard, *The Growth Illusion: How Economic Growth has Enriched the Few, Impoverished the Many, and Endangered the Planet*. Dublin: Lilliput Press, 1992.

—, 'The Amish Solution'. Article in *The AISLING Magazine*, Issue 7. Aisling Publications, 1992.

—, *Short Circuit: Strengthening Local Economics for Security in an Unstable World*. Dublin: Lilliput Press, 1996.

—, and Jopling, John (Eds.), *Feasta Review: The Foundation for the Economics of Sustainability*. Number 1. Dublin: Feasta, 2001.

—, 'Sustainable Territories'. Article in *The AISLING Magazine*, Issue 24. Aisling Publications, 1998.

—, 'Good Growth and Bad Growth'. Article in *The AISLING Magazine,* Issue 27. Aisling Publications, 2000.

Duchrow, Ulrich, *Global Economy: A Confessional Issue for the Churches.* Translated from German by David Lewis. Geneva: WCC Publications, 1987.

—, *Alternatives to Global Capitalism: Drawn from Biblical History, Designed for Political Action.* International Books with Kairos Europa, 1995.

—, and Hinkelammert, Franz J. *Property for People, not for Profit: Alternatives to the Global Tyranny of Capital.* London: Zed Books, 2004.

—, 'Biblical Perspectives on Empire'. Article in *The AISLING Magazine,* Issue 32. Aisling Publications, 2005.

—, 'Overcoming the Violence of Religion, Empire and Economy in the Inter-religious Spirituality of Gandhi'. *People's Reporter-A Forum for Current Affairs,* Vol 20, Issue 9, Mumbai/India, May 10-25, 2007, p. 3, under the title: 'Truth can never be achieved as goal'

Eason, Cassandra, *The Modern-Day Druidess: Discover Ancient Wisdom, Prophetic Power and Healing Arts.* Citadel Press, 2003.

Echlin, Edward P., *Earth Spirituality: Jesus at the Centre.* John Hunt Publishing, 1999.

—, 'From Development to Sufficiency'. Article in *The AISLING Magazine,* Issue 18. Aisling Publications, 1996.

Ekins, Paul (ed.), *The Living Economy: A New Economics in the Making.* London: Routledge, 1986.

Elder, Isabel Hill, *Celt, Druid and Culdee,* London: Covenant, 1986

Ellis, Peter Berresford, *Celtic Dawn: A History of Pan Celticism.* London: Constable, 1993.

Esteva, Gustavo, 'The Stench of Development'. Article in *The AISLING Magazine,* Issue 14. Aisling Publications, 1994.

Fooks, Matthew and Sydes, David, 'Sustainable Architecture and Culture'. Article in *The AISLING Magazine,* Issue 28. Aisling Publications, 2001.

Fox, Matthew, *Original Blessing: A Primer in Creation Spirituality,* Bear & Company, 1983.

—, *The Coming of the Cosmic Christ.* New York: Harper and Row, 1983.

Frazer, J.G., *The Golden Bough: A Study in Magic and Religion.* London: Papermac, 1995. First published by Macmillan Press in 1922.

Freeman, O.S.B., Laurence, (ed.), *Monastic Studies: Celtic Monasticism,* Number 14, Advent 1983. Benedictine Priory of Montreal.

Freeman, Mara, *Kindling the Celtic Spirit.* New York: Harper Collins, 2001.

—, 'Connecting Thread: Nature and the Celtic Tradition'. Article in *The AISLING Magazine,* Issue 31. Aisling Publications, 2003.

Furlong, Monica (ed.), *Women Pray: Voices through the Ages, from Many Faiths, Cultures and Traditions.* Skylight Paths Publishing, 2001.

Gandhi, Mahatma, *Autobiography: The Story of My Experiments with Truth.* Mahadev Haribhei Desai, 1993.

Geddes and Grosset, *Dictionary of the Celts*, Scotland, 1997.

—, *Celtic Mythology*, Scotland, 1999.

Geissel, Hermann, *A Road on the Long Ridge, In Search of the Ancient Highway on the Esker Riada.* CRS Publications, 2006.

George, Susan, and Sabelli, Fabrizio, *Faith and Credit: The World Bank's Secular Empire.* US: Westview Press, 1994.

George, Susan, 'Another World is Possible'. Article in *The AISLING Magazine*, Issue 31. Aisling Publications, 2003.

—, *Another World is Possible If...*, London: Verso, 2004.

—, *Religion and Technology in the 21st Century: Faith in the E-World.* Idea Group Inc., 2006.

Gibran, Kahlil, *Jesus The Son of Man.* London: Arkana, Penguin Books. 1997. First published 1928.

Goldsmith, Zac, 'Radical Relocalisation'. Article in *The AISLING Magazine*, Issue 32. Aisling Publications, 2005.

Goswami, Amit, *The Physicists' View of Nature: The Quantum Revolution.* Springer, 2002.

Gregory, Lady, *Lady Gregory's Complete Irish Mythology.* London: Bounty Books, 1994.

Guericke et al., Heinrich Ernst. *A Manual of Church History: Ancient Church History Comprising the First Six Centuries.* New York: Wiley and Halsted, 1857.

Gyorgy, Anna, *Ecological Economics: A Practical Programme for Global Reform.* London: Zed Books, 1992.

Hale, Reginald B., *The Magnificent Gael: Columba – Ireland's greatest son, Scotland's founding father.* Ottawa, Canada. 1976.

Hannon, Patrick, *Church, State, Morality & Law.* Dublin: Gill and Macmillan, 1992.

Hardinge, Leslie, *The Celtic Church in Britain*, New York: Teach Services, 1972. Reprinted 1995.

Harper, Tess, 'Birthing The Conscious Feminine'. Article in *The AISLING Magazine*, Issue 21. Aisling Publications, 1997.

Harvey, Ruth, (ed.), *Wrestling and Resting: Exploring Stories of Spirituality from Britain and Ireland.* London: CTBI, 1999.

Hayden, Tom, *The Lost Gospel of the Earth: A Call for Renewing Nature, Spirit, and Politics.* Dublin: Wolfhound Press, 1996.

Heaney, Marie, *Over Nine Waves: A Book of Irish Legends*. London: Faber and Faber, 1994.

Herbert, Máire, *Iona, Kells and Derry: The History and Hagiography of the Monastic Familia of Columba*. Dublin: Four Courts Press, 1996.

Higgins, Michael D., 'Drifting Towards a Homogenised Future'. Article in *The AISLING Magazine*, Issue 27. Aisling Publications, 2000.

Hinnells, John R. (ed.) *Dictionary of Religions*. London: Penguin Books, 1984.

Hirshfield, Jane (ed.), *Women in Praise of the Sacred: 43 Centuries of Spiritual Poetry by Women*. New York: Harper Collins, 1994.

Hoinacki, Lee and Mitcham, Carl (Eds.), *The Challenges of Ivan Illich: A Collective Reflection*. State University of New York Press 2002.

Holt, Bradley P., *A Brief History of Christian Spirituality*. London: Lion Publishing, 1993.

Hughes, Kathleen and Hamlin, Ann, *Celtic Monasticism: The Modern Traveller to the Early Irish Church*. New York: Seabury Press, 1981.

Guillaumont, A., et al., (translated), *The Gospel According to Thomas*. Leiden, E.J.Brill, 1976.

Illich, Ivan, *Celebration of Awareness*. London: Penguin. 1971.

—, *Deschooling Society*. London: Penguin. 1971.

—, *Tools for Conviviality*. New York: Harper and Row, 1973.

—, *Energy and Equity*. New York: Harper, 1974.

—, *Medical Nemesis*. London: Calder and Boyars, 1975. New York: Pantheon, 1976.

—, *Limits to Medicine: Medical Nemesis – The Appropriation of Health*. London: Penguin, 1976.

—, *Toward a History of Needs*. New York: Pantheon, 1978.

—, with others, *Disabling Professions*. London: Marion Boyars 1977.

—, *The Right to Useful Unemployment*. London: Marion Boyars, 1978.

—, *Shadow Work*, London: Marion Boyars, 1981.

—, *Gender*. New York: Pantheon, 1982.

—, and Sanders, Barry, *ABC: The Alphabetization of the Popular Mind*. London: Penguin, 1988.

—, *H2O and the Waters of Forgetfulness*. Berkeley: Heyday Books, 1985.

—, *In the Mirror of the Past: Lectures and Addresses 1978-1990*. London: Marion Boyars, 1992.

—, 'The Message of Gandhi's Hut'. Article in *The AISLING Magazine*, Issue 5, 1992.

—, *In the Vineyard of the Text: Commentary to Hugh's "Didascalion"*, University of Chicago Press, 1996.

Ivan Illich, John Seymour, and others, 'Statement on the Soil'. Published in *The AISLING Magazine*, Issue 4. Aisling Publications, 1991.

Johanisova, Nadia, *Living in the Cracks: A Look at Rural Social Enterprises in Britain and the Czech Republic*. Dublin: Feasta – The Foundation for the Economics of Sustainability. 2005.

Joyce, Timothy J., *Celtic Quest: A Healing Journey for Irish Catholics*. New York: Orbis Books, 2000

Jung, C.G., *Psychology and Religion: West and East*. Volume 11 of the Collected Works. Princeton: Bollengen Series, 1989. First published 1969.

Kairos Europa, 'The European Monetary Union and the Globalisation of Money'. Article in *The AISLING Magazine*, Issue 20. Aisling Publications, 1996.

Keaney, Marian. *Irish Missionaries: from the Golden Age to the 20th Century*. Dublin: Veritas, 1985.

Kelly, J.N.D. *Early Christian Doctrines*. London: Continuum International, 2000.

Kelly, Joseph F.T., 'Irish Monks and the Papacy'. Article in *Monastic Studies: Celtic Monasticism*, no. 14, Advent. Montreal: Benedictine Priory, 1983.

Kendrick, T.D., *The Druids*. London: Senate, 1994. First published 1927.

Kennedy RSC, Stanislaus, (ed.), *Spiritual Journeys: An Anthology of Writings by People Living and Working with those on the Margins*. Dublin: Veritas, 1997.

Kenny, Austin, 'God, Allah and the Tsunami Disaster'. Article in *The AISLING Magazine*, Issue 33. Aisling Publications, 2005.

Kingsolver, Barbara, with Hopp, Stephen L., and Kingsolver, Camille. *Animal, Vegetable, Miracle: Our year of seasonal eating*. London: Faber and Faber, 2007.

Klein, Naomi, *No Logo*. London: Flamingo, 2000.

Kohr, Leopold, *The Breakdown of Nations*. London: Routledge and Kegan Paul, 1986.

Kondratiev, Alexei, *Celtic Rituals: An Authentic Guide to Ancient Celtic Spirituality*. Cork: Collins Press 1998, New Celtic Publishing 1999.

Korten, David, *When Corporations Rule the World*. Kumarian Press and Berrett-Koehler Publishers. 1995.

Kroll, Jerome and Bachrach, Bernard, *The Mystic Mind: The Psychology of Medieval Mystics and Ascetics*. London: Routledge, 2005.

Küng, Hans, *The Catholic Church: A Short History*. Modern Library, 2003.

—, *Tracing the Way: Spiritual Dimensions of the World Religions*. London: Continuum. 2006.

Lannigan, Paul.R., 'Women and the Celts'. Article in *The AISLING Magazine*, Issue 32. Aisling Publications, 2005.

Lehane, Brendan, *Early Celtic Christianity*, New York: Barnes and Noble, 1968.

Lévi-Strauss, Claude. *Structural Anthropology*. (trans. Claire Jacobson). New York: Basic Books, 1963.

Low, Mary, *Celtic Christianity and Nature: Early Irish and Hebridean Traditions*, Belfast: Blackstaff Press, 1996.

Macbain, Alexander, *Celtic Mythology and Religion*. London: Oracle, 1996. First published 1917.

Macbain, Gillies, 'Moonlight on Newgrange'. Article in *The AISLING Magazine*, Issue 10. Aisling Publications, 1993.

—, 'Pilgrimage to the Moon'. Article in *The AISLING Magazine*, Issue 17. Aisling Publications, 1995.

—, 'Newgrange, Knowth and Dowth'. Article in *The AISLING Magazine*, Issue 28. Aisling Publications, 2001.

Mac Ginty OSB, Gerard, *The Rule of Benedict: Themes, Texts, Thoughts*. Dublin: Dominican Publications, 1980.

Mackey (ed.), James P., *An Introduction to Celtic Christianity*. Edinburgh: T & T Clark, 1995.

Malone, Mary T., *Women and Christianity, Volume I: The First Thousand Years*. Dublin: Columba Press, 2000.

—, *Women and Christianity, Vol. 2: The Medieval Period AD 1000-1500*. Dublin: Columba Press, 2001.

—, *Women and Christianity, Vol. 3: From the Reformation to the 21st Century*. New York: Orbis Books, 2003

Manning, Conleth, *Early Irish Monasteries*. Dublin: Townhouse and Country House, 1995.

Martin, Calvin Luther, *In The Spirit of the Earth: Rethinking History and Time*. Baltimore: John Hopkins University Press, 1992.

Matthews, Caitlín, *Sophia: Goddess of Wisdom: The Divine Feminine from Black Goddess to World Soul*. London: Aquarian/Thorsons, 1991.

—, Caitlín and John, *The Encyclopaedia of Celtic Wisdom: The Celtic Shaman's Sourcebook*. Dorset: Element Books, 1994.

Max-Neef, Manfred A., *From The Outside Looking In: Experiences in 'Barefoot Economics'*. London: Zed Books, 1992. First published 1982.

McCone, Kim, *Pagan Past and Christian Present in Early Irish Literature*. An Sagart, Maynooth Monographs. 1991.

McDonagh, Sean, *To Care for the Earth: A Call to a New Theology*. London: Geoffrey Chapman, 1986.

McGrath rsm, Catherine, 'Origins of the Celtic-Roman Tussle'. *The AISLING Magazine*, Issue 4, Aisling Publications, 1991.

McIntosh, Alastair, *Soil and Soul: People versus Corporate Power*. London: Aurum Press, 2001.

—, 'Theology Rocks Superquarry Project'. Article in *The AISLING Magazine*, Issue 19. Aisling Publications, 1996.

—, 'Deep Ecology and the Last Wolf'. Article in *The AISLING Magazine*, Issue 23. Aisling Publications, 1998.

McKeown, Kieran and Arthurs, Hugh, *Soul Searching: Personal Stories of the Search for Meaning in Modern Ireland*. Dublin: Columba Press, 1997.

McKnight, John, *The Careless Society: Community and its Counterfeits*. New York: Basic Books, HarperCollins, 1995.

McMahon, Sean, *The Island of Saints and Scholars*. Cork: Mercier Press, 2001.

Mead, G.R.S., *Pistis Sophia: The Gnostic Tradition of Mary Magdalene, Jesus, and his Disciples*. New York: Dover Publications, 2005.

Minahane, John, *The Christian Druids: on the 'filid' or philosopher-poets of Ireland*. Dublin: Sanas Press, 1993.

Mitchell, Frank, and Ryan, Michael, *Reading the Irish Landscape*. Dublin: Townhouse, 1986, revised 1997, 2001, 2003.

Mokhiber, Russel and Weissman, Robert, 'Corporate Predators: Hijacking Science'. Article in *The AISLING Magazine*, Issue 27. Aisling Publications, 2000.

Molloy, Dara, 'Sacred and Profane: A View of the Earth'. Article in *The AISLING Magazine*, Issue 6. Aisling Publications, 1992.

—, 'The Cuckoo In The Nest: The Religion of Development'. Article in *The AISLING Magazine*, Issue 12. Aisling Publications, 1993.

—, 'Commodification Gone Cuckoo'. Article in *The AISLING Magazine*, Issue 14. Aisling Publications, 1994.

—, 'Refounding The Celtic Church'. Article in *The AISLING Magazine*, Issue 18. Aisling Publications, 1996

—, 'Ecclesiastical Empire and the Feminine'. Article in *The AISLING Magazine*, Issue 20. Aisling Publications, 1996.

—, 'Spirituality and Sustainability'. Article in *The AISLING Magazine*, Issue 25. Aisling Publications, 1999.

—, 'Celtic Spirituality and Church Decline'. Article in *The AISLING Magazine*, Issue 29. Aisling Publications, 2001.

—, 'Gay Marriage and God'. Article in *The AISLING Magazine*, Issue 33. Aisling Publications, 2005.

—, see also Ó Maoildhia, Dara.

Molloy, Dara (ed.), *Kairos Europa 1990-2002: Action, Solidarity, Resistance*. Co. Galway: Aisling Publications, 2003.

Monk Kidd, Sue, *Dance of the Dissident Daughter: A Woman's Journey from the Christian Tradition to the Sacred Feminine*. HarperSanFrancisco, 1992,1995.

Moody, T.W., and Martin, F.X., *The Course of Irish History*. Revised and Enlarged Edition. Cork: Mercier Press, 1984. First published 1967.

Mooney, Brian, 'The Druid'. Article in *The AISLING Magazine*, Issue 8, Aisling Publications, 1992.

Moorhouse, Geoffrey, *Sun Dancing: A Vision of Medieval Ireland*. New York: Harcourt Brace, 1997.

Morgan, Marlo, *Mutant Message Down Under: A Woman's Journey into Dreamtime Australia*. New York: Thorsons, Harper Collins, 1991, 1994.

Morris, John Meirion, *The Celtic Vision*, Wales: Y Lolfa Cyf, 2003.

Neumann, Erich, *The Origins and History of Consciousness*. New Jersey: Princeton University Press 1995. First published in English 1954.

Newton, Michael, 'Tribal Totems and Clan Trees'. Article in *The AISLING Magazine*, Issue 23. Aisling Publications, 1998.

Newell, Philip, *Listening for the Heartbeat of God: A Celtic Spirituality*. London: SPCK. 1997.

Ní Chatháin, Bláithín, 'Early Irish Monasteries: Monastic Routine and Organisation on Iona'. *The AISLING Magazine*, Issue 13. Aisling Publications, 1993.

Ní Mheara, Róisín, *In Search of Irish Saints*. Dublin: Four Courts Press, 1994.

Noble, David F., *A World Without Women: The Christian Clerical Culture of Western Science*. Oxford University Press, 1992.

O'Brien CSSp, John, *Seeds of a New Church*. Dublin: Columba Press, 1994.

Ó Cróinín, Dáibhí, *Early Medieval Ireland 400-1200*. London: Longman, Pearson Education. 1995.

O'Donohue, John, *Anam Chara: Spiritual Wisdom from the Celtic World*. London: Bantam Press, 1997.

Ó Duinn OSB, Seán, *Where Three Streams Meet: Celtic Spirituality*. Dublin: Columba Press, 2000.

O'Dwyer, Barry W., *The Conspiracy of Mellifont, 1216-1231*. Medieval Irish History Series, No. 2, Dublin Historical Society, 1970.

O'Dwyer O.Carm, Peter, *Céilí Dé – Spiritual Reform in Ireland 750-900*. Dublin: Carmelite Publications, 1981

—, *Towards a History of Irish Spirituality*. Dublin: Columba Press, 1995.

Ó Fiaich, Tomás, *Gaelscrínte San Eoraip*, Baile Átha Cliath, Foilseachán Ábhair Spioradálta, 1986.

—, *Columbanus: in his own Words*. Dublin: Veritas, 1974, 1990.

Ó Fiannachta, Pádraig, 'Colm Cille 597-1997'. Article in *The AISLING Magazine*, Issue 22. Aisling Publications, 1998.

O hOgain, Daithi, *Myth, Legend & Romance: An Encyclopaedia of the Irish Folk Tradition.* New Jersey: Prentice Hall Press, 1991.

Ó Laoghaire, Diarmuid, *Ár bpaidreacha dúchais: cnuasach de phaidreacha agus de bheannachtaí ár sinsear.* Baile Átha Cliath, Foilseacháin Ábhair Spioradálta. 1990. First published 1975.

Ó Maoildhia, Dara, *Legends In The Landscape: Pocket Guide to Árainn.* Co. Galway: Aisling Publications, 1998, 2002.

Ó Riordáin C.Ss.R, John J., *The Music of What Happens: Celtic Spirituality: A View from the Inside.* Dublin: Columba Press, 1996.

Palmer, Martin, *Living Christianity,* USA and Australia: Element Books, 1993.

Paterson, Jacqueline Memory, *Tree Wisdom: The definitive guidebook to the myth, folklore and healing power of Trees.* New York: Thorson, HarperCollins, 1996.

Pennick, Nigel, *Celtic Sacred Landscapes.* London: Thames and Hudson, 1996.

Potter, Philip, 'Haiti: A Mirror and Microcosm of 500 Years of Colonialism'. Article in *The AISLING Magazine,* Issue 5, Aisling Publications, 1992.

Power, Patrick C., *Sex and Marriage in Ancient Ireland.* Cork: Mercier Press, 1976.

Poynder, Michael, *Pi In The Sky: A Revelation of the Ancient Wisdom Tradition.* Rider, Random Century. 1992. Republished in 1997 by Collins Press, Cork as *Pi In the Sky: A Revelation of the Ancient Celtic Wisdom Tradition.*

—, *The Lost Magic of Christianity: Celtic Essene Connections.* Cork: The Collins Press, 1997.

Primavesi, Anne, *Gaia's Gift: Earth, Ourselves and God after Copernicus.* New York: Routledge, 2003.

Reeves, Rev. Donald, 'Christianity: Time to Rethink'. Article in *The AISLING Magazine,* Issue 24. Aisling Publications, 1998.

Reeves, William (ed.). *Adamnan, Life of Saint Columba: Founder of Hy (Iona).* Facsimile reprint 1988 from Historians of Scotland, Edmonston and Douglas, 1874

Reilly, Patricia Lynn, *A God Who Looks Like Me: Discovering a Woman-Affirming Spirituality.* New York: Ballantine Books, 1995.

Richter, Michael, *Medieval Ireland: The Enduring Tradition.* Dublin: Gill and Macmillan. 1998.

Rigoglioso, Marguerite, 'Awakening to the Goddess'. Article in *The AISLING Magazine,* Issue 25. Aisling Publications, 1999.

Robinson, John M., *Christianity and Mythology.* Second edition, revised and expanded. London: Watts and Co., 1910.

Robinson, Mary, 'In The Footsteps of Columba'. Article in *The AISLING Magazine*, Issue 21. Aisling Publications, 1997.

—, 'Ethical Globalisation in our Times'. Article in *The AISLING Magazine*, Issue 32. Aisling Publications 2005.

Rolleston, T.W., *Myths and Legends of the Celtic Race.* London: Constable, 1985.

Ross, Hugh McGregor, *Thirty Essays on the Gospel of Thomas.* London: Element Books, 1990.

Rutherford, Ward, *The Druids: Magicians of the West.* Dartford: Aquarian Press, 1978,1983.

Ryan S.J., John, *Irish Monasticism: Origins and Early Development.* Dublin: Four Courts Press, 1992.

Sachs, Wolfgang, 'On The Archaeology of the Development Idea'. Published in 6 parts in *The AISLING Magazine*, Issues 1 - 6. Aisling Publications, 1991-92.

—, 'The Shadow of Development'. Published in 3 parts in *The AISLING Magazine*, Issues 20 - 22. Aisling Publications 1996/97.

—, with Loske, Reinhard; Linz, Manfred et al. *Greening The North: A Post-Industrial Blueprint for Ecology and Equity.* London: Zed Books, 1998.

Sachs, Wolfgang (ed.), *The Development Dictionary: A Guide to Knowledge as Power.* London: Zed Books, 1992.

Sale, Kirkpatrick, *Dwellers in the Land: The Bioregional Vision*, New York: Random House, 1985. University of Georgia Press, 2000.

Sams, Jamie, *Earth Medicine: Ancestors' Ways of Harmony for Many Moons.* HarperSanFrancisco, 1994.

—, *Dancing The Dream: The Seven Sacred Paths of Human Transformation.* HarperSanFrancisco, 1999.

Schneider, Pat, *Wake Up Laughing: A Spiritual Autobiography.* Negative Capability Press. 1997.

Scott, Michael, *Irish Myths and Legends.* Time Warner, 1992.

Sellner, Edward C., *Wisdom of the Celtic Saints.* Ave Maria Press, 1993.

—, *The Celtic Soul Friend: A Trusted Guide for Today.* Notre Dame: Ave Maria Press, 1995.

—, 'Druids and Druidesses: Spiritual Leaders of the Celts'. Article in *The AISLING Magazine*, Issue 18. Aisling Publications, 1996.

—, 'Heavenly Fire: Celtic Spirituality and Intimations of the Future'. Article in *The AISLING Magazine*, Issue 22. Aisling Publications, 1998.

—, 'The Celtic Church as an Ecclesial Entity'. Article in *The AISLING Magazine*, Issue 30. Aisling Publications 2002.

—, *Finding the Monk Within.* Hidden Spring Books, 2008.

Seymour, John, *The Fat of the Land,* New York: Taplinger Publishing and Wexford: Metanoia Press, 1962.

—, *The New Complete Book of Self-Sufficiency: The Classic Guide for Realists and Dreamers.* London: Dorling Kindersley, 2002. First published in 1976.

—, *Blessed Isle: One Man's Ireland.* California: Collins and Brown, 1992.

—, *Fat Cats: More Subversive Verses.* Wexford: Metanoia Press, 1998.

Sheldrake, Philip, *Living Between Worlds: Place and Journey in Celtic Spirituality.* London: Darton, Longman and Todd. 1995.

Shinoda Bolen, Jean, *Goddesses in Every Woman: A New Psychology of Women.* New York: Harper Colophon Books, 1985. First published 1984.

Shlain, Leonard, *The Alphabet Versus The Goddess: The Conflict Between Word and Image.* London: Penguin Compass. 1998.

Shiva, Vandana, and Mies, Maria, *Ecofeminism.* London: Zed Books, 1993.

—, 'The Masculinisation of Agriculture'. Article in *The AISLING Magazine,* Issue 24. Aisling Publications, 1998.

Simpson, Ray, *Celtic Worship Through the Year.* London: Hodder and Stoughten. 1997.

Sims, Bennett J., *Servanthood: Leadership for the Third Millennium.* Boston: Cowley Publications, 1997.

—, 'Old Heresies Never Die, and One of Them Shouldn't'. An article on Pelagianism in *The AISLING Magazine,* Issue 23. Aisling Publications, 1998.

Smyth, Daragh, *A Guide to Irish Mythology.* Guernsey Press, 1988.

Sjöö, Monica and Mor, Barbara, *The Great Cosmic Mother: Rediscovering the Religion of the Earth.* HarperSanFrancisco, 1987. First published 1977.

Sölle, Dorothy, 'The Spirituality of Globalization and the Spirit of Resistance'. Article in *The AISLING Magazine,* Issue 32. Aisling Publications, 2005.

Spong, John Shelby, *The Bishop's Voice: Selected Essays 1979-1999.* New York: Crossroad, 1999.

—, *Why Christianity Must Change or Die: A Bishop Speaks to Believers in Exile.* HarperSanFrancisco, 1999.

Stalker, Peter, *Workers without Frontiers: The Impact of Globalisation on International Migration.* Geneva: International Labour Office (ILO), and Lynne Rienner Publishers, 2000.

Staniforth, Maxwell (trans.), *Early Christian Writings: The Apostolic Fathers.* London: Penguin Books. 1968.

Starhawk, *The Fifth Sacred Thing.* London: Bantam Books, 1994.

Stewart, R.J. *Celtic Gods and Goddesses.* London: Blandford, 1990.

—, and Williamson, Robin, *Celtic Bards, Celtic Druids*. London: Blandford, 1996.

Stiglitz, Joseph E., *Globalization and its Discontents*. New York: W.W.Norton, 2003.

Streit, Jakob, *Sun and Cross, From Megalithic Culture to Early Christianity in Ireland*. Edinburgh: Floris Books. First published 1977. Republished 2004.

Sutherland, Will, 'John Seymour - Obituary'. Article in *The AISLING Magazine*, Issue 33. Aisling Publications, 2005.

Teasdale, Wayne and Cairns, George, *The Community of Religions: Voices and Images of the Parliament of the World's Religions*. New York: Continuum, 1999.

The AISLING Magazine, Aisling Publications, Inis Mór, Aran Islands, County Galway, Ireland. www.aislingpublications.com.

Thayer, Robert, *LifePlace: Bioregional Thought and Practice*, University of California Press, 2003

Thom, Catherine, *Early Irish Monasticism, An Understanding of its Cultural Roots*. T&T Clark, 2006 .

Tobias, Michael and Cowan, Georgianne (Eds), *The Soul of Nature: Celebrating the Spirit of the Earth. A book of essays*. London: Plume/Penguin, 1996.

Tobin, Brendan, 'The Protection of Traditional Knowledge'. Article in *The AISLING Magazine*, Issue 29. Aisling Publications, 2001.

Toulson, Shirley, *The Celtic Alternative: A reminder of the Christianity we lost*. London: Century Paperbacks, 1987.

Thoreau, Henry David, *Walden*. New York: Barnes and Noble, 1993. First published 1854.

—, *Walden* and *On the Duty of Civil Disobedience*, New York: Perennial Library, Harper and Row, 1965.

Vallance, Peter, 'The Irish Celtic Magical Tradition'. Article in *The AISLING Magazine*, Issue 26. Aisling Publications, 2000.

Vallés, Jaume Botey, 'Bush and His God'. Article in *The AISLING Magazine*, Issue 33. Aisling Publications, 2005.

Vardey, Lucinda (ed.), *God In All Worlds: An Anthology of Contemporary Spiritual Writing*. New York: Pantheon Books, 1995.

Walsh, John R., and Bradley, Thomas, *A History of the Irish Church 400-700 AD*. Dublin: Columba Press, 1991, 2003.

Whelan, Dolores, *Ever Ancient Ever New: Celtic Spirituality in the 21st Century*. Dublin: Columba Press, 2006.

Whitmont, Edward C., *Return of the Goddess: Femininity, Aggression and the Modern Grail Quest*, London: Routledge and Kegan Paul, 1983.

Wilcox, Joan Parisi, *Keepers of the Ancient Knowledge: The Mystical World of the Q'ero Indians of Peru*. Shaftesbury, Dorset: Element Books, 1999.

Woklski Conn, Joann (ed.), *Women's Spirituality: Resources for Christian Development*. Paulist Press, 1986.

Workman, Herbert B., *Persecution in the Early Church*. Oxford: Oxford University Press, 1980.

Yeats, William Butler, and Gregory, Lady Isabella Augusta, *A Treasury of Irish Myth, Legend, and Folklore*. New York, Gramercy Books, 1986.

Websites

www.daramolloy.com

www.aislingpublications.com

INDEX

Printed in the United States
By Bookmasters